Praise for Jody Wallace

"A delightful, fast-moving story
with an imaginative and interesting take."
—*RT Book Reviews*

"I'm going to stalk this author,
at knifepoint if necessary, because I need more!"
—*The Demon Librarian*

"It's obvious I loved this book.
The whole novel was just hilarious and interesting
and amazing and funny. Overall Rating: B+."
—*Romance Books Forum*

Also available from Jody Wallace and Carina Press

PACK AND COVEN

Witch Interrupted

JODY WALLACE

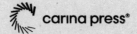

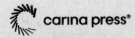 carina press®

ISBN-13: 978-0-373-00250-4

WITCH INTERRUPTED

Recycling programs
for this product may
not exist in your area.

www.CarinaPress.com

Printed in U.S.A.

Dear Reader,

My first foray into the secret world of wolf shifters and witches was such an enjoyable writing experience (*Pack and Coven*), I felt compelled to visit again in *Witch Interrupted*. Since wolves in my stories heal themselves when they shift, I wondered...would a wolf ever want a tattoo? If so, why?

That's how a former assassin and powerful witch hiding out as a tattoo artist met a lone wolf with a penchant for disappearing tattoos...and a lot of secrets.

For *Witch Interrupted*, I researched new settings—Northern Alabama, Western Kentucky, Ohio. I had a lot of fun with Google Street View as well as various nonfiction books as I expanded the magical world of my witches.

Two volumes I referenced extensively were *Culpeper's Complete Herbal*—reprinted in 1975, I believe, from a volume published three hundred years ago—and *Cunningham's Encyclopedia of Magical Herbs*.

The more I delved into the mysteries of my witch and wolf network, the more I realized how huge it was. And the more I realized how much I'd love to visit it myself. Which is why I had to write *Witch Interrupted* and why I have many ideas for further books in the witch and wolf universe.

Thank you for reading this story! I hope you enjoy it with a nice cup of herbal tea and a slice of pie. Or cake. If you're like me, you're not picky, as long as it's dessert.

Jody Wallace

Author, Cat Person, Amigurumist of the Apocalypse

www.jodywallace.com

www.meankitty.com

Witch Interrupted

For Charles

ONE

THE SHOP DOOR chimes bonged, rattling the test tubes and Katherine Zhang's teeth. Her hands jerked, and she scattered the point thirty-three ounces of granular ginseng she'd painstakingly measured.

By the Lady, she hated that damn doorbell.

"Ba," she yelled into the next room, where she could see her father snoozing in the recliner in front of the giant flat-screen television. "Wake up."

He lurched, shaking his head. "I'm not asleep. Huh? What?"

"The chimes gotta go, Ba. I mean it." She swiped the ginseng into a pile for later and walked to the door of the den. What she wouldn't give for a real stillroom instead of a converted dining room—but it was better than the bathroom she'd used in their last safe house.

He raised two gray, bushy eyebrows. "I didn't hear anything."

"That's because you're half deaf." She glanced around for the remote and spotted it beside Dad's coffee mug. "Somebody came into the shop. Switch it over to the store cam."

He waved a gnarled hand. "Just go tend to it. I'm watching my program."

"You can miss ten seconds and let me see who's in the shop before I go downstairs." Depending on the customer, she, Dad and Tonya, who was technically the shop owner, donned magical disguises to put clients at ease. And make them more likely to shell out for a tattoo. Walk-ins weren't their staple income, but money was money.

"Don't waste juice on a whole mask," Dad advised. "I finished ten tats this week. Tonya did eight. With the money from the permabrand you cast on that Brazilian witch, we're flush for two months." Her father might be half deaf and arthritic, but he was an ink and accounting whiz.

"Fine." Katie whipped off her lab gear, found her regular glasses and clomped down the stairs to the shop below. With her everyday mask that concealed her genetics but not appearance, she looked like herself. The only people likely to want to be tattooed by an inconspicuous, half-Asian nobody were middle-aged women, and they didn't get a lot of middle-aged women in this neighborhood. Their block boasted a lot of empty lots, empty buildings and For Lease signs in windows.

She paused at the Employees Only door and checked herself in the mirror. No smudges of spell components, or lunch, marred her face, her hibiscus tunic or her blue jeggings. Jean leggings. So comfy and clever only a witch could have invented them.

She unlocked the dead bolt, slipped through the protective barrier around their living area and stepped into the shop. The customer wasn't in the back room, so she called out, "Welcome to Ink Inc. Be right with you."

She grabbed the phone receiver in case Dad called, trotted to the bead separator and peeked through.

Her friendly smile dissolved.

That damn wolf again.

She knew she should have slipped some be-gone powder into the last tat he'd gotten! She'd done a shit job on the design in hopes he wouldn't come back.

So much for hindsight.

Marcus—his name was Marcus—lifted his chin as he sniffed instead of looked. Sampling her scent. He was the one with hackles, but hers rose anyway.

"Good evening," he said in a rich, cultured voice, either oblivious to or not caring about her leap of anxiety.

"Sorry you had to wait," she managed. Why had he come back? What kind of idiot didn't care that the cash he kept sinking into tattoos disappeared every time he changed form?

Granted, she was assuming he'd lost the tats. He'd had different limbs done all four times—three times by Dad and once by her, when she'd been fully masked as a pink-haired biker chick—but there were only so many parts of the body she was willing to work on.

Even a body as fine as his.

"I'm in no hurry," he told her, his attention on the flash wall.

She edged into the room, bead strands clacking. It was all she could do not to grab the gun under the counter. Marcus hadn't displayed criminal tendencies on previous visits, but one could never be too safe with wolves. She, Tonya and Dad had chosen this area to set up shop because it was a hundred miles from the closest pack compound and almost as far from the closest coven headquarters. They didn't want witch or werewolf traffic if they could help it, and the only thing they had to juggle were the weekly pack patrols.

Yet here the blasted wolf was. Back for more.

Instead of acknowledging he'd been here before, she decided—after putting the counter between them—to play dumb.

"First time in an ink studio?" She used her perky voice and hoped he didn't notice it was forced. Her fingers tightened on the phone. If she held down the 3 it would dial Dad, 4 would dial Tonya. Which one would be more help?

Not Tonya. She was away at a festival and not especially inclined to warn Katie away from wolves who looked like Marcus.

Come to think of it, Dad might not be any help either. He was the one who'd convinced her not to use be-gone on Marcus last month, despite the obvious hazards in having a wolf hanging around. Said he felt sorry for the poor bastard. Wolves without pack affiliations in this part of the country lived lonely lives.

"No, ma'am. Not my first time." One hand in the pocket of his trousers, disrupting the elegant lines of his suit, he strolled along the wall, inspecting the art. A silver metal briefcase was in his other hand. "I've become somewhat of a connoisseur."

When he ambled closer to the counter, Katie tensed. Some wolves had a certain effect on her. It was a weakness she'd grown to expect, a weakness she could handle. Wolves didn't intimidate her—when she could prepare for them.

She wasn't sure she could ever prepare for Marcus. With his suits and his calm demeanor, he wasn't like any wolf she'd ever known. No leather, no leering, no hassling, no aggression. Combined with innate sexiness, at least as far as Katie was concerned, it was a lethal combination. "Let me know if you have any questions." She set down the phone and reached under the counter to stroke the pistol's cool handle with one finger. She'd never had to use it here, but she sure as hell knew how.

He nodded as if reaching a decision. He turned to face her, finally.

His brown eyes widened, then narrowed.

Damn, she'd forgotten how good-looking he was.

Which was a lie. She'd found it next to impossible to put him out of her mind. And out of her fantasies. For an entire month, she'd been plagued by memories of his chiseled cheekbones, tight black curls, sensual lips, broad shoulders, slim hips, well-tailored clothing—the works.

Despite what she knew about his DNA, or because of it, her stomach fluttered as they locked gazes.

"You aren't Betty."

She debated lying, but a few shifters could smell dishonesty. Most could sense panic and other strong emotions—like attraction. Reluctant, deep-rooted, morbidly fascinated attraction.

God, she hated dealing with wolves. "I'm Katie."

"You smell…" He paused and frowned. "What I mean is, your voice sounds like Betty's. Sisters?"

"Close enough." Her Betty mask must have sucked if he could connect the two of them. "But, uh, she was fired."

He raised an eyebrow. "You fired your own sister?"

"Her art lacked permanence," Katie improvised. "She didn't get the pigment deep enough. Is that why you're here? If you have your receipt, we'll refund the money."

He rubbed his right forearm, where she'd inked him as Betty. "I'm not here for a refund."

"You still have the dragon?" she asked dubiously. It had been two inches high and ugly as crap. She'd cursed to herself with every *zizz* of the needle into his smooth, brown skin.

Tattooing a wolf.

What. A. Waste. Of. Time.

He studied her for a minute. "How did you know it was a dragon?"

Shit. "You look like a dragon kind of guy." Which is why she'd given him a mutant cow.

His chin dropped an inch. "Not a wolf kind of guy?"

Shit more. Did he know something? Smell something? After the shake-up between the coven and pack in Millington, West Virginia, a few years back, when the coven had allowed a wolf to learn the truth about them, witches across the globe had been tense.

She understood that reaction. The thought of a coven not wiping the guy's memories was sacrilegious and stupid. They might have fooled themselves into thinking not all wolves were bestial, but she knew better than anyone how a wolf's veneer of modernity could disappear at the drop of a hat. Or a blouse. Or a gun.

"Your chi says dragon," she told Marcus as artlessly as possible. "Or Chinese characters. Wolf chi is more hairy." His veneer of modernity was the thickest she'd ever encountered. What would he do if she took off her blouse?

"Chi? What do you mean by chi?"

"It's like your inner being. Your personality." Katie pushed her glasses up her nose to read his expression better. To many witches, *chi* was a term for the magic inside them, which could be visualized through a spell known as the true eye. But to humans—and to wolves who didn't know about witches—it wasn't as literal. "Some customers get into that. I'm guessing you don't?"

Wearing a slight smile, he shook his head.

It wasn't like her to let a wolf unnerve her, but there was something about this guy. Something beyond him being dead sexy, beyond her being out of practice. "I confess. We keep a database of all our work and customers."

"I see." The man's gaze was infernally steady. He was doing that wolf thing where he stared and stared without blinking. "Then you know I'm not here for the first time."

She shrugged, her emotions reined tight. She refused to be curious about why he kept blowing money on dis-

appearing ink. She refused to be curious about him, period. "Do you still have the dragon?"

"I do, although some of my other tats faded."

Katie stiffened with surprise. "You do have the
dragon?"

"Oh, yes." He rubbed his left forearm. "I don't need
a refund for ones that disappeared, though. There were
extenuating circumstances."

If he'd kept a tattoo, that was cause for concern. Wolves
who maintained ink, brands, scars or piercings through
shifts were few and far between. They were either really
strong or really weak, both of which presented their own
set of problems.

"I'm sorry about your other tattoos." Her everyday
mask could hide some of her inner turmoil from his keen
senses, but not all of it. "How can I help you?"

"I'm here for another tattoo." The corner of his mouth
curled up. "Would you like to read my chi and choose
for me?"

The wolf had a sense of humor? Since when? Last
month he'd been quiet. Courteous and gorgeous, but quiet.

She popped open a canister of disinfecting wipes and
buffed the counter, giving herself an excuse to walk the
length of it. She trailed her other hand along the cluttered
shelf underneath, feeling for the small plastic tub that
held the be-gone. "You trust me to pick your artwork?"

He sniffed again but didn't growl at her. "You aren't
planning on saddling me with a teddy bear, are you?"

"I… No." More humor. Maybe someone had given him
a nice hunk of raw meat for lunch.

"I liked the idea of Chinese characters." He slipped
off his suit coat and set it on the counter. His muscular,
lean build filled out his dress shirt oh so nicely. "What
would you suggest?"

That he leave. Soon. Her reaction to this wolf was unmanageable. She couldn't use it to her advantage as she had in the far-off past. He had to go.

"Lots of people get symbols for luck or prosperity." She continued groping for the be-gone dust under the counter. When he unbuttoned his collar and the button that came next, revealing a slice of flawless brown chest, her hunt came to a screeching halt.

"Are you taking off your clothes?"

"My shirt. I'm interested in a larger tattoo this time. One that covers a greater expanse of skin. Simple lines, preferably straight ones, but multiple colors. I've blocked out the afternoon and evening in my schedule. If you need to do the artwork in stages, I could return Sunday or Monday."

He was proposing they spend the rest of the day together. And perhaps other days as well. When Katie gaped at him, he said, "Do you happen to know the Chinese character for moon?"

She wrenched her gaze away from those long agile fingers slipping buttons through buttonholes. "What?"

"Moon," he repeated with a small smile. "Other astronomical terms would also be acceptable."

He unbuttoned another button. Her mouth dried out.

It suddenly felt urgent that she convince him to leave before his shirt came off. Goddess, she'd lost her nerve. "I don't, ah, know Mandarin. Or any other Chinese dialect."

"I didn't assume you did, Katie." Many people did assume it when she wore her true face, but her family had been in this country for two generations. In witch lifespans, that was a long, long time. "Do you have somewhere we could look them up? A series of Chinese characters would suit my purposes."

He made the tattoo sound more like an experiment than a form of self-expression. "Let me check an art book."

She ducked behind the counter and spotted the be-gone in the far corner. *Gotcha.*

Now how could she get the powder from her hands to him without being obvious? The be-gone was premixed, a staple Tonya ordered from a coven in West Virginia. All Katie had to do was infuse it with magic and sprinkle it on him.

Her most potent option would be to rub the powder directly on his skin. Some shifters required more than a flick of spell components. Some were stubborn. Intractable. Suspicious.

She heard him inhale. What was he sniffing now, her nervousness?

Or something else?

She pulled the lid off the powder too hastily, jolting the container. The greenish-brown dust scattered all over the shelf.

Into her face.

Katie sneezed, hard. She lurched up, thonked her head on the underside of the counter and went down like a sack of beans.

In a flash, Marcus was around the counter, crouching, hands all over her.

"Katie?" He checked her pulse. His fingers were hot on her wrist. Her throat. His shirt, unbuttoned halfway to the waist, gapped open like a model in a Hunk of the Month calendar. "Are you all right?"

"Fine," she croaked, hissing when he threaded his other hand into her short hair, probing for wounds. And found one. "Ouch."

He pulled his hand back, fingers red with her blood. "You're hurt."

Oh, hell. He couldn't be touching her, and now he had her blood on him. *He had her blood.*

"It's n-nothing." The knot on her skull throbbed like a bass drum. *Boom, boom, boom,* as rapid as her pulse. Her vision swam. She wasn't sure if it was because she was woozy, because her glasses were crooked, or because he was so close to her, his hands at her neck, his strength five times hers. "Let me go."

"Not so fast." He caught her arms when she resisted. Unsurprisingly, he had no trouble holding her still, and that panicked…aroused…her more.

So did his nearly inaudible growl when she batted at him.

"I'm okay."

Effortlessly, he trapped her wrists. His fingers were manacles. "Take it easy. You're bleeding."

Reacting on instinct—instinct and training—Katie swept a leg under his feet, knocking him on his ass. She leaped to her own feet, where she quickly confirmed that her blurry vision had been due to wooziness.

Marcus caught her when her knees gave out. Wolf reflexes trumped witch reflexes any day. He scooped her against his chest. Blood speckled his white shirt.

Even with the dizzies, she could see his smile. "I did warn you."

"Don't be smug." She adjusted her skewed glasses. He smelled like aftershave, starch and…rooibos tea. It shouldn't be so exciting. The urge to taste him dried her mouth. "I'm in pain."

"I can imagine. That was a nasty hit."

What the hell was she going to do? Ignoring her personal reaction, she had bigger problems. Her blood was all over him, and her everyday mask couldn't conceal that.

Not from a wolf. What if he sensed the aspect of her blood that witches had to conceal from wolves, no matter what?

Wolves and witches were the same species. The same, except witches never shifted, not once, else they'd lose their magic forever in exchange for four legs and a tail.

A terrible bargain, if you asked her. She had to free herself, restrain Marcus, warn Dad. Tonya. They'd have to wipe him.

Hell, did they have the strength for a full wipe? That ceremony took a coven, and it was just the three of them. No coven would have a witch like Katie.

Who could blame them?

"Where is your restroom?" He rose, lifting her with zero difficulty. Goddess, he was strong. "We need to get you cleaned up and see how bad the damage is."

"Not we. Me. Alone." She risked a glance at his eyes, surprised to find his baby browns wolfish. Literally. They'd turned pale, which meant one of two things. Either he was struggling with his inner beast, or he was an alpha trying to assert his dominance over her.

She didn't feel like cooperating. Much. That meant it was the first thing.

"Put me down," she ordered. Why the hell was a man his age having trouble with his wolf? Shifters mastered that in their late teens, one way or another. Shifter age could be tricky to guess, but Marcus had to be about thirty.

He raised an eyebrow. "And have you fall again? I can't do that."

"Try," she suggested. His outward demeanor was placid, but she could feel the wolf rippling near the surface. This one didn't like being told what to do.

"Don't think so." His arms tightened. "You could have a concussion."

"I don't have a concussion." She had an emergency. Dad was upstairs, ignoring the store cam. Tonya was off at some Gaia festival in Tennessee.

"How do you know..." he began, but then he sniffed. Sniffed again. Before she could protest, he brushed his nose across her cheek. "What's that smell?"

"What the hell do you think you're doing?" Her skin prickled with embarrassment. She grabbed his ear, twisted and yanked his face away from hers. "Are you trying to kiss me?"

Or sort her DNA?

Both were a bad idea.

He raised his eyebrows, and Katie licked her lips. *Kiss me, wolf. Ignore the blood and kiss me.*

"Until you mentioned it, it hadn't crossed my mind." His gaze dropped to her mouth, and his fingers bit into her flesh. "Had it crossed your mind?"

He might know if she lied. She lied anyway. "That would be unprofessional."

"If you say so." He smiled again, despite her pincher-grip on his ear. It was on his mind now, all right. "Did you know you have dirt all over your face?"

"I do?" She let go of his ear and touched her jaw. Gritty residue coated her.

"It smells odd." He lowered his head again. Her cheek tingled. When he spoke, his lips brushed her skin. "What perfume are you wearing?"

"None." Katie pushed his chest. Sexual awareness flooded her. He probably knew that smell too. They all did. "I think you need to leave."

He needed to leave.

That was it! She was covered in be-gone dust, and so was he. One jolt of magic, and he'd be out of here like a cat fleeing a bath.

Before she could muster her power, he growled, low and deep.

She froze.

"I know that smell," he said in a dangerous voice.

Suddenly Katie found herself on her feet, pressed against the wall, Marcus in her face.

"Cumin. Black tea. Lemongrass. Clove. Chalk. That's be-gone dust." His hands clamped on her shoulders. His eyes blazed. "You're a witch."

TWO

THE WOMAN, KATIE, turned even paler. Tiny freckles stood out on her nose like cinnamon. Her eyebrows rose briefly. "I don't know what you're talking about."

Marcus didn't have to smell it to know she was lying. "If I feel like I suddenly want to leave, I'm taking you with me." He realized with some surprise he'd enjoy that. Taking her with him. Tossing her over his shoulder and toting her out of here like a Neanderthal.

She shook her head, denial all over her. "You can't do that."

"You know I can." Without spells or backup, she didn't have a chance.

"What I know is…" She blew a flake of herb off her full lips, her dark, nearly black eyes furious. Shouldn't she be frightened? For all she knew, he could be as brutal as many other wolves, willing to terrorize anyone who got in the way. "If you don't let me go right now, you're going to regret it."

In the year he'd been in hiding, this was his first unplanned encounter with another of their kind, witch or wolf. This had to be trap.

Except…why would she be covered in be-gone mix instead of hops or valerian to knock him unconscious until she and her cohorts could deal with him?

He smelled her again. She failed to conceal a shiver. Definitely be-gone. Threaded through it, desire, which he tried to ignore. It wasn't easy. "Why were you trying to make me leave instead of immobilizing me?"

"If I could make you leave, I would." Spell components dusted her short, shiny black hair. "I have the right to refuse service to patrons for objectionable behavior. That includes threatening me in my place of employment, Marcus."

She remembered his name, as well as his tattoo. He was willing to bet she remembered all sorts of things about him. The question was, what had she done with that knowledge?

"You know what I am. Admit it."

"Someone who's about to get arrested."

"By your coven?" He eased off her shoulders, conscious of his strength and her fragility, but remained alert. She'd knocked him on his ass once, something she shouldn't have been able to do. She was agile, and stronger than she looked.

"Coven? What the hell are you talking about? Arrested by the cops." Her small breasts rose and fell quickly under the gauzy tunic she wore over skin-tight denims. She wasn't unaffected by him, which was affecting him too.

He sniffed her a final time, something he appreciated about being a wolf. The lemongrass meant the be-gone was Millington coven's blend. If she had access to coven products, she had to be part of the system.

"You wouldn't drag the human cops into this."

Her expression didn't change. "Are you on drugs?"

"No." How had he been here multiple times and not realized the shop was witch-run? Though it did explain why she sounded like Betty.

She *was* Betty.

"Christ. You drew that shitty dragon on me," he accused. The tattoo he'd hated had been the one he'd finally managed to keep. While the breakthrough in his research had pleased him, the so-called dragon didn't.

"My sister drew it." With one finger, she pushed lightly at his bare chest, trying to back him up. "Told you we were right to fire her."

Should he allow the contact? Skin to skin would give her more power if she charged the be-gone dust. Would she risk finding out if he really would drag her with him?

He almost wished she'd try.

She was pretty, but it wasn't only that. She exuded confidence. She wouldn't go easily. His wolf had honed the part of him that liked a challenge to a sharp, toothy point.

"Betty was the disguise." He lowered his head to see what she'd do. She stiffened. He smiled. "The pink hair and piercings were chicanery. This is you."

"You're crazy." She said it matter-of-factly, but he could hear the tension in her voice. Her palm joined her fingers on his chest as she pushed. "And maybe high."

He peered closer, inspecting her bone structure, her coloring, and realized why else she seemed familiar beyond her genetics. "Is the man who tattooed me on my other visits your father?"

Her jaw clenched. He'd guessed correctly. "I'm going to ask you one more time to let me go. In my nice voice."

If he did as requested, she could pull the gun he smelled behind the counter or cast a spell he couldn't counteract. Any witch-run business worth its salt stocked a number of safety measures. At the same time, he didn't want to scare her. Much. He just needed to find out what she and her father knew about him—and whom they might tell.

"I'm not going to hurt you, Katie." He'd revealed too much, but there was no backing down now. He'd been shocked into it, his wolf reacting to the danger she posed. "I'm not pack, and I've no plans to be."

Katie sighed and her slender body deflated. Her touch softened. He could sense her acquiescence as clearly as if she'd admitted it.

Satisfaction surged inside him.

"I guess that's one point in your favor."

Now that she'd quit denying the obvious, they could make headway. A witch here was probably an extension agent of Birmingham, the largest group in the Southern region. "Are you coven?"

"Of course," she answered quickly.

His senses weren't honed enough to smell lies, but it seemed like another one. Could she be independent, like he was? His short list of registered independent witches didn't include a tattooist in Alabama.

"What about your father?" Zhang Li had been elderly and more talented artistry-wise.

Her gaze flicked to a corner of the ceiling, paused there and returned to him. It seemed calculated. "What about him?"

"Does he know what I am?" Surely if they'd figured out who he was, not just what he was, they wouldn't have continued to tattoo him without a fuss.

"He's watching us right now." Her fingertips tapped his chest. "We have video cameras everywhere."

A year ago, when he'd begun this process, the first witch he'd approached hadn't been amenable to helping him. In fact, she'd indirectly sicced the keeper council on him. As if those bastards needed any help nipping his heels. After that, he'd lost access to the witches he'd hoped to consult and had had to relocate to dangerous territory. Worst of all, he'd had to reformat his study to exclude witch participation.

It had thwarted his models like baking soda on a grease fire.

But stumbling across Katie woke new hope in him. Was she likely to report a cognizant wolf, one who knew about witches, when she was outside the system herself? She was attracted to him; he could smell it. If he could interest her in his research, he could turn this blunder into a windfall.

And finally his sister's death could have served a purpose. Finally he would have justice.

As he watched Katie for signs of…anything, blood from her head wound dribbled onto her neck. Guilt pinged at him.

"If I let you go so we can spray heal-all on your cut," he said, "are you going to try to get rid of me?"

She answered with a question of her own. "How do you know about covens and magic?"

"Does that matter?" Most witches would want to defuse any wolf who knew about them. But his research could revolutionize their society in a way that would mean more power and security for them all.

It would also mean his life could go back to normal. *He* could go back to normal. Normal and safe. He could quit worrying that tomorrow would be the day he died like Elisa had.

"Of course," Katie said again, in a different timbre than the lie. "There are limited explanations for how a wolf could know about magic. Outside of Millington, I haven't heard of any coven pets, but—"

"I'm no one's pet." He barely restrained a snarl. Though hers was a sentiment he might have echoed at one point, now it was offensive.

"Then who are you?"

His luck, at last, had changed. She didn't know who he was.

"Marcus Delgado," he told her, the name he'd picked when he'd gone underground. "Who are you?"

She flashed her teeth in a grin worthy of any wolf. "Katie."

"This is getting us nowhere, and you're bleeding." How should he play this? His first witch had been perfect and, he'd thought, progressive. But she'd reported him. He had to convince Katie not to do the same. "Can we declare a truce?"

"I'll make you a deal." Underneath the scent of her blood, he detected the delicious flux of aversion and attraction that had made no sense until he'd realized what she was. Aversion because he was a wolf. Attraction because—the same reason he found her attractive, he supposed. Because. "If you leave and never come back, that will be the end of this. We'll wipe the slate. I'm sure neither of us want trouble."

"I don't care for your use of the word *wipe*."

Her jaw clenched. "We'll pretend this never happened. I won't tell, and you won't tell. Nobody will ever know. Is that better?"

He should take her up on the offer. Disappear before she could report the renegade wolf to the region elders, who would inform the keepers he'd been spotted in Alabama. It wouldn't be a stretch to connect Marcus Delgado with the man they sought. But he found himself reluctant to go.

This was the closest he'd come to another of his kind in months, someone who could help him. His thirst for knowledge, as it had in the past, was overriding caution.

Danger signs flashed. He shrugged them off. Would she help him? As someone so far outside the system she didn't show on the list of registered independents, she was an unknown quantity. She didn't act like a sympathizer, but the strides he could make if he had a cooperative witch on his side would be incredible.

Even if she wasn't open to certain tests, her magic could enrich his work tenfold. His desire to work with her had nothing to do with his desire for her.

"I'd prefer to discuss a few professional matters with you before I leave," he said. "First, heal-all. There's no reason for you to be in pain. Then we can talk."

"Fine. Quit mauling me and I'll go—"

"I'm coming with you. You could fall again." Or chase him off. Or get a gun. He kept one hand on her neck, ready to toss her over his shoulder. "Lead the way."

After casting him a mistrustful glance over the top of her glasses, she stalked through the hanging beads that separated the front room from the more private back one, where clients received tattoos. It was as clean as a witch's stillroom or his laboratory. Paintings by local artists and photos of intricate ink adorned the walls, with a television mounted in one corner. During his second tattoo, he and her father had watched an old black-and-white movie, one he remembered first seeing in a theater for thirty cents.

The restroom was small. He shut the door behind them, blocked it and released her.

"Let me see." He motioned at her head. "I have first aid training."

"Like that matters. I'm going to spell it away." She grabbed a wad of paper towels and wet them. When she pressed them to the scalp wound, her lips pinched.

"Don't get be-gone into the cut," he observed, as she dabbed herself gingerly. "It's in your hair, and the interaction of the cloves and lemongrass with water will—"

She inhaled audibly. "Holy mothering hell, that smarts."

"—make it sting," he finished. She didn't hide pain as

well as her other emotions. "You'll have to flush it before the heal-all will work."

"I'm not a baby in my first pass-through," she snapped. "I know these things." She shoved the paper towels back under the faucet. It rinsed the blood, turning the water pink.

He couldn't help himself. Nearly a hundred years of conditioning, five dealing with ferals and keepers, couldn't be discarded in three hundred and eighty-three days. "You shouldn't be using a simple mask in an occupation that involves blood and the public. You never know who might walk in. Blood is a neon sign to wolves."

"*My* blood isn't involved in tattoos." She set her glasses on the counter, bent over the sink and applied the saturated towels to her head. Pinkish water dribbled down her cheeks. "As for who might walk in, other wolves don't get ink, Marcus. You're the only one we've had in here longer than a minute or two." Water dampened her collar as she awkwardly cleansed the wound. "Are you into pain or something, getting tattoos for kicks?"

He'd been celibate since his initial phase of experimentation. The transformation had roughened his sexual preferences, but it hadn't reversed them. "Not exactly. How about you?"

He'd meant it to be a throwaway quip but was reminded, with his next inhale, of her attraction to him, lurking beneath the hostility.

Escalating beyond the hostility.

Was she into pain? Or into him?

He found himself twice as curious as he had been moments ago. Curiosity didn't stop at killing cats.

She turned to look at him. Her pupils were dilated, her expression haunted. "That is also none of your business."

A clichéd line about making it his business crossed

his mind. He didn't say it. His senses gave him an unfair advantage, and she probably knew what he was reading off her. "I was kidding. I don't care what you're into."

When she humphed and twisted her shoulders, it knocked be-gone from her hair. She hissed again. "That fucking hurts. Lemongrass. Whose bright idea was that?"

He was surprised she didn't know. "Vernon Harrower."

She squinted at him. "Vern? You know that old goat?"

Most witches did. Vernon Harrower was a region elder rumored, in certain circles, to be involved with the keepers. Marcus knew the rumor to be true. "Does that surprise you?"

"You're not…are you Harry Travis? The wolf from Millington?"

"No." Harry Smith Travis, a "coven alpha" in Millington, was a fascinating case study of how witches could run ethical tests on cognizant wolves when the wolves were volunteers. Not prisoners who'd rather bite off the witch's hand. Harry had been the one to explain to Marcus how wolves carried tattoos and clothing through shifts. Harry and his wife, an alpha witch, had also elaborated on certain aspects of witch and wolf relations.

The line between witch and wolf, Marcus had come to believe, was less strict than witches assured themselves. While most witches weren't as fanatical as the purists, most regarded their hairy kindred as dangerous—as shifters who'd failed to find the strength of will to become witches.

But were they? Wolf magic could heal in a way no spell could simulate. It strengthened, it heightened the senses, it increased athleticism and agility. As long as one controlled the aggression, how was that a failure? How was that not worth pursuing, when the power of a wolf could save a witch's life?

When he found that link, the keepers wouldn't be able to touch him. Perhaps the keepers wouldn't be able to touch anyone, ever again.

Katie straightened. Water dripped down her face, plastering some of her hair to her head. Her thin shirt clung to her small breasts in a way that shifted his attention to sex. The dampened shirt was half-transparent, and she wore no bra. Her scent swirled around him, spicy and arousing as her emotions rose.

Her shapely, soft lips parted. They would taste of her and blood and cloves and lemongrass. Marcus found himself stepping forward, away from the door, inches from grabbing her.

She didn't so much as flinch. When she spoke, it belied her sexy appearance, so Marcus was able to contain himself. "Did Vern send you here? Hell, it would be just like him to break covenant and use a wolf. Well, you can tell him I don't care what bribe he's offering this time. I'm never coming back, and—"

"I'm not allied with Vernon." Nor was he connected to Vernon any more than he was the other elders and keepers after him. Katie, on the other hand, seemed to know the old witch well. "What do you mean about going back? Were you Millington?"

Coven affiliations were looser than wolf pack bonds, and the benefits of membership outweighed the negatives. Access to elders, trade shares, coven energy, knowledge, fellowship and the safety of numbers were among the advantages. Even though he'd planned for it, he often found himself floundering in their absence.

"You enjoy asking questions that are none of your business, don't you?" She turned sideways and thrust out her elbows as she twisted the faucets. The knobby joint caught him in the ribs. "Oops."

"Excuse me," he said dryly. "And yes, I do enjoy asking questions. What is it you're not returning to with Vernon?"

A horrible thought crossed his mind. He could think of a reason outside Millington coven why she'd know Vernon and why he might want her back.

"I didn't date him, if that's what you're asking." Anger tipped the corners of her mouth down and flattened her ears, ever so slightly. Like a wolf. Or a witch. She tousled the dry patches in her hair carefully, sending be-gone components into the sink.

"That's not what I was asking." The reason that had popped into his head had been a lot more lethal.

A witch wouldn't have to like her employer to be a keeper. Unlike most witches, the keepers were convex. Spells that inflicted harm on others neither harmed nor backfired on them. In fact, their contorted magic returned the spell with interest, for twice the effect it would have had otherwise. They could kill with a spell, and it didn't hurt them one bit.

While convex witches weren't unheard of, the keepers they became weren't common knowledge to rank-and-file witches. Region elders across the North American continent employed keepers to deal with precarious situations. Wolves too cunning for local covens to outwit. Wolves on killing sprees. Wolves in positions of human power and influence. Wolves who knew too much.

Wolves like Marcus. And his sister.

This petite, lovely woman… He couldn't imagine Katie as a killer. He knew keepers. If Katie had been one, he'd already be in custody. Or dead. Yet here he was, locked in a bathroom with her and her very wet shirt.

In profile, the tunic clung to her breasts, outlining them

perfectly. Should he tell her about the see-through fabric or just enjoy the view?

He needed to prove he was a gentleman, someone she could work with. He unbuttoned his blood-speckled shirt the rest of the way and shrugged out of it.

She snatched her paper towels from under the faucet. "Put that back on."

He offered her the garment. "You need this more than I do."

She blinked at his chest for a moment and exhaled. The gush of water from the faucet filled his ears. Then she glanced at her own chest. "Do tits bother you?"

Since she was looking, he looked too. Her nipples were faintly visible. Her scent heated further. But he didn't think she was coming onto him, exactly. It was more like a challenge.

He felt the growl and swallowed it. He disliked this aspect of being a wolf intensely, the reduced control of primal responses. To challenges, to danger, to hunger. And to sex.

Challenges and sex together? Nearly irresistible.

"Don't do that," he warned.

She inhaled. Her nipples poked the fabric, their darker color playing peek-a-boo through the floral pattern. Then she jutted out her chin. "Do what?"

"Don't push me."

"What good would it do me to push you?" She ran her hands up his chest, splaying her fingers on his pectorals. "You're so much bigger than I am. I couldn't..." She glanced up through her lashes, coy. "I couldn't fight you off."

"That's factual." He suppressed the urge to demonstrate. "It's also irrelevant. What makes you think I want to fight you?"

"You're a wolf. Not a natural alpha, I don't think, but assertive." Her cheeks flushed, a primal response she couldn't control either. And still she taunted him. Tip-toed along the thin ice of witch and wolf relations. "It's your nature."

Wolves did have a reputation for sexual ferocity. It lured some witches to stray and lose themselves to the wolf. But Katie wasn't, as she'd told him herself, a young-ling. If she were likely to be seduced by the call of the wild, it would have happened long ago. What was she trying to accomplish, goading him?

And why did she smell so deliciously of desire?

She couldn't be any more perfect for his experiments.

"I'm not particularly combative, as wolves go." He avoided situations that would provoke him. His dimin-ished willpower threatened to spiral him off course. "I'm more of a…"

"A what?"

He could say he was a lover, not a fighter, but it was an-other cliché and didn't describe him anyway. "A scientist."

"A wolf scientist," she said disbelievingly.

"That's what the résumé says." He enjoyed surprising her almost as much as he suspected he'd enjoy taking her against the wall and…proving a hypothesis. "How about that heal-all?"

"I'm not quite ready for it." She raised her arms, slowly, to apply the sodden paper towels to her head. The wet fabric of her shirt tugged her breasts. He couldn't help it. He looked again.

Her nipples hardened. His probably had too. Other parts of him definitely had.

She squeezed water on herself, rivulets trickling down her head, her neck, her shirt, dripping to the floor.

"Think I'm clean enough now? Or should I get wetter?"

Her dare was so calculated, he found it easier to block. With concise movements, he hung his shirt on the door hook behind him. She raised an eyebrow. His wingtips slid on the wet floor as he reached past her to turn off the faucet.

He wouldn't play—wouldn't let his wolf play—dominance games when he didn't know what the prize was. "You're wasting water. Where's the heal-all?"

Instead of pouting or teasing, she shrugged. Her breasts jiggled. He had no idea why she would deliberately tempt a wolf. Sure, part of him liked it, but he needed to analyze this. As long as she didn't notice his erection, she ought not know how much she'd affected him.

"It's behind the mirror, in the medicine cabinet," she said. "The can marked Feminine Hygiene Spray."

He laughed, jolting her into a beautiful smile. Their gazes locked with shared amusement, but she quickly terminated the moment of connection with a neutral expression. Hopefully she was done prick-teasing. They had a lot to talk about.

"I guess you don't run much of a risk a human will use it inadvertently." His stock of heal-all was in oven cleaner bottles. He dispensed most of his stash gingerly since once it was gone, it would be exceedingly difficult to procure more now that he was a wolf.

"That's the idea." She opened the cabinet, swinging the mirror toward him.

He was disappointed to see how pale his eyes had turned. How wild he looked. Damned wolf. It should take more than a provocative woman to rouse him like this.

He couldn't let the wolf take over. At the same time, he

couldn't let his conscience inhibit him. He had to exploit the opportunity that had fallen into his lap.

His opportunity closed the mirror and held out a pink, flowery can. He took it, their fingers brushing.

She turned her back. "Since you seem to know what you're doing around magic, if you don't mind?"

Perhaps she'd wanted to see how trustworthy he was before accepting his help. Perhaps he'd passed the test when he hadn't pounced on her.

He'd always been excellent at tests.

Gently, he touched her vulnerable nape and the fine, damp hair clinging to it. For a moment, he let his fingers wrap around her neck, holding her in place.

She sighed so softly, he suspected he wasn't supposed to notice. In the mirror, he caught a glimpse of her profile, her eyes closed and her lips parted. She'd caught her opposite elbows in her hands, her forearms tight to her stomach.

He parted the wet strands on her scalp. The shallow wound oozed blood. He sniffed and didn't notice any remaining be-gone components. All he could smell was her clean skin, her shampoo and a faint swirl of need. "Here goes."

He depressed the button. Spray misted. His ears filled with pressure before popping, a sign magic was in use. The cut knit itself before his eyes.

"That's better." She started patting her front with dry paper towels and no monkey business. "I'll, ah, borrow your shirt, if you don't mind."

She had just started to button it when the door flew open, banging Marcus in the ass.

Zhang Li aimed a gun at his head, his arm steady. "I

let you come here, dog, because I felt sorry for you. But you've hurt my daughter. Get on your knees and put your hands behind your head."

THREE

Katie leaped sideways as Marcus backed away from her father. She didn't want Marcus to use her as a hostage. "Ba, he knows about us."

"Figured that out." Dad kicked the door when it swung back, never losing his line of sight. A bullet wouldn't stop a wolf Marcus's size unless it was right between the eyes.

Her father, canny as always, remained out of Marcus's reach and waved for Katie to exit the bathroom. She hastened to comply. Dad's aim was shit.

"I told you to get on your knees," he repeated.

She squinted over Dad's shoulder. Marcus knelt as if he had all the time in the world, though his eyes were as pale as the moon. His nostrils flared. In the same leisurely manner, he stretched his hands up and behind his head.

She didn't need glasses to tell his torso was magnificent. Muscles, dark nipples and, Goddess, his shoulders and biceps. He was the most hairless wolf she'd ever seen, and she'd seen a lot of them in her old profession.

She wished she'd touched him more when she'd had the chance. Pushed him, like he'd told her not to. He hadn't rattled as easily as other wolves she'd neutralized. She'd used her own weakness against them and had loathed every minute of it.

She couldn't say that she loathed her interactions with Marcus, which was a surprise. Was it because he was so reserved?

"Why didn't you get the cayenne spray instead of the gun? Works better on wolves," she hissed at Dad. Flustering Marcus with sexiness hadn't been effective. Maybe he didn't make passes at girls with glasses.

"Gun's more obvious," Dad said. "Besides, I like my gun."

"We should place an anonymous call to the region elders." She didn't want other witches poking around here, but if it had to happen, they'd handle it like they did the weekly wolf patrols.

"I'd prefer you didn't." Marcus's face angled toward her, even though Dad was the one with the gun. "I've gone to some trouble to avoid the elders."

"Bet you have," Dad said. "You're a mongrel, aren't you?"

Marcus sighed.

"Aw, hell." Katie felt like slapping herself. Molasses brain. How had she not guessed? He knew about witches because he'd been one—before succumbing. This told her two things about him.

One, he'd slept with a wolf. Two, he wasn't alpha. Millington coven had discovered that witches who were natural alphas didn't change after sex with a wolf. However, the only way to tell for sure whether a witch was alpha—resistant—was to sleep with a wolf.

"The term mongrel is outdated and offensive." Marcus hadn't made a single move to retaliate, though he didn't seem concerned. "I'm a shifter, as are you both. We're the same inside. We simply focus our magic down different paths."

"Shut it. Mongrel." Dad, who hadn't taken up this generation's banner of political correctness, shifted his grip on the gun and smiled, dentures gleaming. "You don't get to speak."

"You knew what he was all along?" Katie asked her father. Now that she knew part of Marcus's story, it explained why he was the opposite of what she expected from wolves. A scientist. She wished his story explained why she was unusually attracted to him, but that was just her weakness rearing its humiliating head. Wasn't it?

"I had my suspicions when you went into a tizzy after you tattooed him."

"A tizzy?" Marcus asked.

"I may have questioned the wisdom of a wolf hanging around here, but I'd hardly call it a tizzy." She'd argued with Dad about giving Marcus a be-gone permabrand— adding spell components to the tattoo ink and infusing them with her magic, the effects of which lingered for years. But Dad had insisted the wolf was toothless and to let him waste his money however he wished.

She'd only mentioned Marcus a few times. Seven or eight. That was nothing compared to how often she'd thought about him.

A tizzy. Groan. Her father was more astute than she'd given him credit for.

"You weren't yourself," Dad said. "I did a little digging."

Instantly suspicious, Katie asked, "What kind of digging?"

Nobody outside Vern and Tonya, her handler, was supposed to know where they were. Katie and her father had been listed as deceased, while Tonya maintained a tenuous link to the coven network. It allowed them to maintain a cover for Katie's lucrative permabrand work.

If Dad had contacted any of the elders, any of his old friends...

He made a disgusted noise at her. "Nothing like that. Don't go all wet hen on me."

Tizzy or no tizzy, she had every right to be mad if he'd blown their safe house again. "Ba, what did you do?"

"I found out he's a mongrel. A threat."

"How dangerous am I, if you didn't turn me in a month ago?" Marcus dropped his hands, and Dad didn't say anything. "You didn't even tell your daughter about me."

Marcus didn't realize they couldn't have reported him without jeopardizing themselves. They didn't want any witches, especially keepers, sniffing around any more than Marcus did. However, no one had come, so it was possible Dad had been more discreet this time.

That didn't excuse Dad for not telling *her* about Marcus.

"I didn't need to tell Katie." Dad shrugged, the gun bobbing. "She knows how to handle animals like you."

She did know. It had been her job to know. But Dad had kept Marcus's origins to himself, so she'd leaped feet-first into this mess.

"I'm not a threat to either of you," Marcus said.

"Any wolf who knows about witches is a threat," Katie stated, not caring when Marcus growled. "How is it you're still cognizant?"

No witch could have transformed without his coven knowing it…and coming after him. Or sending the keepers after him.

Dad answered for him. "Incompetence. Pansy-ass covens today aren't like—"

"Like they were in your second pass-through." Katie wasn't in the mood to hear it. "I really need to know, Marcus. Is anyone hunting you?"

"It's nothing I can't handle. Unless you plan to turn me in."

"You hurt my Katie," Dad said. "Of course we're gonna turn you in."

"Actually, he didn't hurt me." Marcus had visited several times without incident. Today would have been without incident if she hadn't bonked her head. If anyone was trailing him, he hadn't led them here. Yet. "Anyway, it's partly your fault. Hell, if you'd have told me a month ago, I'd have chased Marcus away before he so much as…"

Stared at her with bedroom eyes. Held her against him. Took her by the nape. Sniffed a lot more than her perfume. "Before he said hello."

"I don't like the way he's looking at you. I twice don't like the way you're looking at him."

"Zhang Li, my father, you mean well," Katie warned, "but let it go." Her weakness wasn't something Marcus needed to know, any more than he needed to know her past. "What are we going to do?"

"I haven't decided." Dad waggled the gun. "Think we should involve Tonya?"

"Judiciously. She might…overreact." A cognizant, arguably cooperative wolf in their safe house—Tonya would want to make a pet of him. Katie would never hear the end of it, and not because her handler was worried about safety.

More like she was worried about Katie's love life.

"With you going full-out, the three of us might have enough juice to wipe him," Dad mused. "Got fresh poppy and whatever the crap goes in the spell?"

She poked him. "Seriously, Ba. Stop feeding him intel."

"Are you alpha, Katie?" Marcus smiled, as if that pleased him. "A resistant witch. I couldn't have planned this better if I'd tried. Your being alpha is wonderful."

They were only ninety-nine percent sure she was alpha. She'd never given it the ultimate test, and didn't plan to.

"Nothing about this is wonderful," Dad said, annoyed. "Now we're going to have to poppy you."

"Even if Katie's alpha, you can't erase long-term memories without a full coven," Marcus said. A full coven was at least thirteen adult witches, the more the merrier. Not three—one sexually frustrated, probably alpha; one cranky old man; and one soft-hearted wolf sympathizer. "Do you have a coven handy?"

"We have Katie," Dad blustered. "Is that why you're here? Are you after my Katie?"

"How could I be? I didn't officially meet her until today," Marcus said. "I won't jeopardize witch secrecy, if that's what you're afraid of."

"You're wrong." Katie had heard all the excuses. Seen all the tears. "Every second you exist, you put us in danger. If—no, when—you join a wolf pack, the pack bond will kick in and you'll tell them everything. Then, after they find out about witches? All hell breaks loose."

"I've taken precautions against pack impressment."

"You've taken the opposite of precautions." She wanted to remain cool, impartial, but her voice rose. "This isn't a Gaia festival where they kumbaya about tolerance and love and all of us being one big, happy family. This is the Bible Belt. The packs here eat indies for breakfast."

"I chose this area because of its reputation." Her impassioned speech hadn't fazed him. No doubt he'd heard it before. All witches had. "What indie with half a brain would set foot in Alabama? Since my pursuers know I'm not stupid, my being here throws them off my scent."

"Clever," she conceded. None of her targets in the past had tried that, but the world had been different then.

"I'm not dangerous either. My methods have kept me safe for a year with few issues."

She scoffed. "I'd call us finding out about you an issue, wouldn't you?"

He rubbed his forehead briefly before speaking again. "My surprise got the better of me. You don't understand what I'm trying to do, but if you let me explain, you'll change your mind."

He thought she didn't understand, but she did. She'd processed countless mongrels in her time. Most were worse than born wolves, angry at what had happened, resentful of what had to happen. Tricky bitches, cunning bastards, vicious and half-mad and too well versed in magic to let witches get close. Willing to kill to keep the memories and life they considered theirs. Except they'd lost that privilege when they'd fucked up—literally—by sleeping with a wolf.

You didn't sleep with wolves. Ever.

You could imagine it. You could discuss it. You could read about it—the wolf fic websites Tonya had shown her were astounding in their variety and inventiveness. You could even brush it with your fingertips. Rubbing it, taunting yourself, until you ached somewhere deep.

But if you happened to be aroused by certain wolves' virility, ferocity and dominant nature—and you also happened to be an unholy strong convex witch—you could become a secret weapon who terrified even the other keepers.

"Give me a chance," Marcus urged. "What I'm trying to accomplish could revolutionize everything."

"I don't like revolutions." Dad's gun barrel dipped. "You using alpha on us?"

"I'm not alpha. Recessive, possibly."

"Definitely," Katie corrected, trying not to wonder what he'd been like as a witch.

"But not alpha, or I wouldn't have these." His eyes had

bled pale blue. "Katie, you wouldn't have these, would you? No matter what you did."

It was probably true. She wouldn't change into a wolf if she had sex with one. Marcus was trying to tempt her. Thanks to his nose, he knew she desired him. He might not know how much, but he knew. He wanted her to imagine sex, with him, free of consequences. Free of discovery.

An experiment. An experiment a scientist might want to conduct.

"I wouldn't have them because I wouldn't fuck a wolf, and that's all you need to know." Her hands balled into fists. "Call Tonya. Let's poppy his butt."

Marcus looked as if he might resist. Then he nodded. "Trust has to start somewhere. Tie me up. You don't need to, but I'll let you. Will that make you feel safe?"

"Hell, yes." Dad prodded Marcus up the stairs, into their apartment, and instructed Katie to chain him to her wrought-iron headboard. They had several sets of handcuffs, provided by Tonya. You never knew what you might need when you were supposed to be dead.

Marcus cooperated. He allowed them to trap him without uttering one word of complaint. He couldn't be too uneasy about pursuit.

Katie tried not to touch him as she secured the cuffs. Tried not to admire how stunning he was. So difficult not to stroke his bare chest, his biceps, his delicious-looking lips. Marcus's steady gaze never left her face.

"It's going to be all right." His voice was like liquid chocolate, deep and satisfying, seeping into her pores. "I understand why you're scared. I just want to talk. Let me tell you what I've been researching. It's fascinating, Katie. I think I've discovered—"

That's when Dad had hit him with the sleep spell, nearly catching her in the cross fire.

FOUR

THREE HOURS LATER Marcus was still asleep, sprawled on her bed, shirtless and sexy. Katie didn't want to cast eyebright to offset the sleep spell; that particular herb would interact poorly with the memory magic to come.

"I just figured he was a kinky little puppy with a tattoo fetish. I never expected him to be a scientist. How interesting." Tonya, her handler, friend and the main reason Katie had security in her life, often joked about screwing a wolf so she could lose weight without cutting calories. She often joked about screwing wolves, period. She tried to get Katie to joke about it, telling her the levity would make her problem easier to bear. As would actually screwing some wolves, but Tonya was dead wrong about that. However, the minute Katie told Tonya what— who—was chained to the bed, her friend dropped onto the couch and into professional mode.

Shrewd blue eyes narrowed as Tonya studied the closed bedroom door. "What are the chances he's led anyone here?"

"He thinks he's outsmarted everyone, but it's worth noting he didn't outsmart us." Nervous about Marcus, about everything, Katie had double-checked their go bags and packed extra belongings. Sudden relocations weren't high on her list of favorite things, but they'd done it enough that they'd learned not to wander too deep into possessions and paperwork.

Tonya opened her massive handbag and started sorting through it. "You're sure he's a transformed wolf and not a coven pet? I wouldn't put it past the California covens to try it just because someone else did. They're always jumping on fads."

"He was definitely one of us."

"Is he one of mine?" Before going into hiding with Katie and Zhang Li, Tonya had been a sympathizer, part of the underground railroad for transformed wolves. Tonya and Katie had been on the exact opposite sides of the fence and had had to learn to laugh about it, or at least not discuss philosophy. "That could explain why he's still cognizant. Of course, mine aren't supposed to remain in the continental United States."

"I don't think so." Katie scrubbed the hair that had dried into an awkward cowlick on the back of her neck. "He mentioned a recent transformation, and you haven't been in that line of work for, what, twenty years?"

"Something like that."

Tonya had had to let that vocation go, and unlike Katie, she'd loved her work. Katie often wondered how isolated her friend had remained from her former collaborators. But the sympathizers were the best at disappearing people from witch radar, which is why Vernon Harrower, the then-director of the keepers, had cut a deal with Tonya to save Katie. He would step down if Tonya would hide his protégée and her father.

It has been better for Katie to disappear than face the results of the inquest—and the wrath of the new council director, Hiram Lars, who'd intended to execute her.

Twenty years wasn't long enough for Katie to be comfortable with a cognizant wolf, no matter how polite and handsome. "We're going to alter his memories. Play it safe. I have everything ready. All we need to do is link up and cast the spell."

"A life wipe, if we manage it, will suck us as dry as a drought. Tomorrow is patrol day," Tonya said. "We can't be power-drained on patrol day. Let's wait."

"And give you time to talk me out of it? No way. We'll avoid the patrol old-style." Without reserves, they'd use the primed disguises in their go bags to cover their DNA and travel in the opposite direction of the wolves. The Birmingham sentries were predictable, and their duty was to seek indies and claim jumpers, not witches. They didn't know witches existed.

"He may have family. Children. A wife. What if he's married to the wolf who loved him?"

"The wolf who loved him. He's not James Bond, he's just some guy." Katie's cheeks heated. "Anyway, he said he was single when I gave him the tat last month."

"You asked if he was single?" Her handler smirked, the skin beside her eyes crinkling with amusement. "Why would you want to know that, Katie-kins?"

"No reason." Katie ducked her head until her glasses slid down her nose, blurring her view. "He didn't mention dependents or pets or anything time-sensitive when he let us handcuff him. That says alone to me. We're wiping him."

Depending on how old Marcus was, fine-tuning memories wasn't simple. It required steady magic and surgical precision to coax and nudge the brain into accepting that it had always belonged to a wolf, that witches didn't exist.

Katie was good at it. One of the best. She'd participated in countless wipes on the keeper council. But there had, indeed, been a full coven, thirteen per team. Eleven or twelve when they'd had a member down, but usually thirteen.

No one had ever suggested they manage a wipe with fewer, whether Katie was involved or not. She'd be testing the limits of her strength soon. It would have to suffice. The only other witch she could trust was Vern, but she'd rather stab herself with a fork than ask him for help. The cost would be too dear. Moreover, Tonya and Vern hated each other so much their animosity would negate the benefits.

Tonya crunched up a mint from her handbag before answering. "What if we just tweak the part where Marcus found out about us and let him go? That wouldn't drain us."

"Insufficient." Short-term memories weren't tough to mold, but a transformed wolf required a life wipe. "He could get ambushed by the Birmingham pack any day, and then what would happen?"

"Sounds like he's got that under control. It's not unheard of."

"People brag." Though Marcus hadn't seemed like a braggart. "He's not that clever, Tonya. He flubbed up in front of me."

"I had to try." Tonya shook her tin of mints like a maraca. "Tell you what. I'll help modify his memories, as long as you agree we're not turning him in to the elders or your old friends."

"The keepers were never my friends." They'd gotten their hooks into Katie as soon as she'd mastered the wolf and come out of it with convex magic. Over the next thirty years, they'd chewed her up and spit her out. Some days her soul still felt like a piece of old gum.

"That's because you were on the wrong side. You're a sympathizer at heart."

"You know better than that." Whichever way she might have leaned as a youth, after thirty years as a keeper, she'd

seen and learned too much about wolves to be a sympathizer. Before the digital age and advances in forensics,
wolves hadn't been as inhibited. "But let's not talk about
me. Let's talk about Marcus."

"Have you thought about what we'll do if we don't
have enough energy for the spell? I'm flush right now,
but there are only three of us."

"I'm flush too, and Ba's always full of it."

Tonya grinned. "Full of something."

"Too true." Her father's confidence and magical muscle often made up for his lack of precision. "Anyway, I
strengthened the memory mixture with cayenne." Cayenne pepper stored magic but had no effect itself, beyond
skin irritation. Katie liked to supercharge her cayenne far
beyond the standard, a habit developed during her keeper
days. Difficult to work with, but a little went a long way.
"It should increase the impact when I do Marcus."

Tonya's eyes widened dramatically. "Do him? Oh,
Katie, I'm so proud. I thought you'd never wise up."

"Come on, Tonya." Katie sighed. "Not now."

"Would you prefer I be serious?" Tonya crossed her
legs and leaned against the back of the couch, a sure sign
she was digging in for an argument. The woman could
nag the head off a horse. "Would you prefer I compare a
memory wipe to rape?"

Katie gritted her teeth. "Don't go there. It's not the
same."

Tonya launched into her case, and Katie regretted fuss-
ing at her. "Marcus doesn't want this done to him, and
we're going to do it anyway."

"We're not going to hurt him." Marcus didn't ooze the
hostility Katie associated with the wolves she'd neutralized as a keeper. Yet that, in and of itself, made him more
dangerous to her personally. He was pure temptation. "He

just doesn't get to keep any memories a wolf pack could use against witches."

"It's cruel. Inside, we're all the same," Tonya said, echoing Marcus.

"Agree to disagree. It won't change what has to be done."

"I know. But I don't have to like it." Tonya, to Katie's surprise, acquiesced. They'd argued many times to impasse, but they'd never been faced with a situation where push had come to shove.

Katie risked some deeper honesty. "I don't like it either. Thank you for helping."

"I'm helping all of us. We're in this together, we three." Tonya held out the tin of candies. "Want a sweetie?"

Katie shook her head and checked her watch. "I'm worried about Marcus. I don't know why he's not awake yet. Hey, Ba? What did you put in that sleep spell?"

"It was your blend, not mine." Dad clumped out of the stillroom with a mason jar so full of Katie's simples it looked like sand art. She didn't even *want* to know. "I can't help it if I'm strong as an ox."

"I didn't know I had any sedative left." Most of the time she used pure valerian out of laziness, but when she mixed a batch, it contained valerian, lavender and cinquefoil to instill good dreams—as well as cucumber to ensure they weren't naughty ones.

No wonder Marcus was out cold; wolves were highly susceptible to lavender.

"I kept some for emergencies," Dad said. "Good idea, huh?"

"We shouldn't poppy him until he's alert." On one hand, she wanted to postpone the spell because it was fraught with peril. On the other hand, since Marcus couldn't truly be *in* her bed, she wanted him out of it ASAP.

"Then we should definitely wait," Tonya said. When Katie glared at her, she waggled a finger. "Waiting would give us a chance to find out more about him."

"I'm not sure we need to know more." Katie hadn't told her about Dad's snooping yet. Tonya wasn't going to be happy he'd gone digging. "Let me just peek in the bedroom." She headed for the door and turned the knob quietly.

Marcus, sound asleep, sprawled on her bed like a deep, dark fantasy of a man, his wrists handcuffed above his head and his face relaxed.

Supine. Harmless. Nothing stopping her from…

Shutting the door and vowing not to check on him again for ten whole minutes.

Katie turned and found Tonya right behind her. For a large, not-exactly-youthful woman, Tonya moved like a cat.

She winked. "What's he look like? Is he hot?"

"Tall."

"Everyone's tall to you, honey." Tonya bumped Katie out of the way and opened the door. Almost immediately, she whistled. "Good Goddess in heaven, do you suppose he looked like that when he was a witch?"

"Put your tongue back in your mouth," Dad said.

Katie didn't want to consider Marcus as a witch or it would make him too relatable. A dangerous path to tread. "I doubt it."

Wolves, along with cracking good health, had two things going for them—high metabolism and the magic of the shift. Witches believed wolves subconsciously altered their forms when they changed. It was simplest way to explain why many were at the top end of the physically attractive scale while witches were not—or no more so than humans.

The last time Katie had skimmed a region newsletter, Millington coven had been putting Harry through his paces. Answers about wolfish mysteries might come out of Harry eventually. Tonya stayed abreast of goings-on in the coven network, but Katie was content to live quietly and try to forget her first pass-through had ever happened.

She counted herself lucky she'd escaped alive. Most keepers didn't.

"He looks familiar." Tonya, in addition to being big-hearted and cheery, had a mind like a steel trap—not a politically correct simile around wolves, but the only wolf here was unconscious. "What pass-through was he on?"

"He looks about thirty. Second, tops." Their kind aged at the same rate as humans until they mastered the magic in their late teens, when the ageing process slowed down. Way down. For wolves, it slowed too, though not as markedly.

Tonya clucked her tongue. "I say we interrogate him."

"He doesn't get to talk," Dad said.

"I suppose we could ask a few questions," Katie agreed. "He wasn't, ah, disobliging." There had been a moment or four that she'd wished he'd drop the polite-ness and grab her. He hadn't.

Damn, she should date more. It had been too long since she'd had sex. Was that why Marcus affected her twice as strongly as she remembered other wolves doing?

"I bet he wasn't disobliging." Tonya waggled her eye-brows at Katie and slipped the mints into a pants pocket. "How obliging were you?"

Dad held the pint jar up to the light. "I held a gun to his head. How obliging do you think we were?"

Katie wasn't going to take Tonya's bait…in front of

Dad. "Marcus didn't seem upset. He wanted to discuss his research."

"Research he's been doing since he changed or before he changed? Depending on what he studied, we could find out who he was. I swear he looks familiar."

Katie fiddled with the hem of her T-shirt. Her tunic and Marcus's shirt were soaking in cold water to remove the bloodstains. "Have you heard of any scientist witches going missing?"

"I can have Nathaniel ask around," Tonya assured her. "The covens don't always publicize their transformations, but we know who to ask."

"Don't bother. I already found out who he is." Dad tightened the lid on the jar and started shaking it. "I think I put too much shit in here."

"Zhang Li, you did not," Tonya exclaimed.

"Definitely did," Dad said. "I need a bigger jar. Maybe that pickle jar. Is it empty yet, Katie?"

"I recycled it, Ba. You can't use just any container for simples. Your spell components can become tainted." Recipe spells were tetchier than single-ingredient spells. Not many witches could work around impurities. That was why some spell-grade components were often so doggone expensive and hard to come by.

Tonya interrupted. "What I meant was, you'd better not have gone poking around. Hellfire, old man. That's why we had to relocate last time. You and your big mouth."

"I hadn't decided how to tell you that part," Katie said with a sigh. "I wanted to deal with the immediate situation first."

"Who did you call, mister?" Tonya pointed at Dad, and he quit shaking the jar. "If it was Shirl, I'm going to break your TV."

"I called nobody." He smiled. "I dug around in the elders' forums. I'm a hacker now."

"Gaia bless it." Tonya returned to the couch and buried her face in her hands. "I was just starting to like it here."

"He did it a month ago." Katie sat beside Tonya and nudged her friend's leg with her knee. "I don't think he broke our cover."

"Quit bellyaching. Of course I didn't," Dad put in.

"And it's possible they've been biding their time." Tonya had her own reasons for participating in Vern's witchy witness protection program. She didn't want to be reintroduced to the network either. "Lying in wait like snakes in the weeds."

Katie rubbed her temples. Tonya was their front. Ostensibly, Tonya was the one with the handler——Nathaniel Oman, another sympathizer. Oman knew nothing about Katie and her father. This had been the deal they'd worked with Vernon after Katie's inquest...and after the keepers had tried to wipe her.

They'd failed. A convex, alpha witch, Katie wasn't wipeable. No one had known that was possible prior to her. The memory magic had ricocheted off her the same as destructive spells. Her final sentence, the only way to eliminate a wild card like her, had been death.

Hiram Lars had spearheaded that sentence. If the keepers——if Lars——found out she was still alive, they'd never be safe.

"I don't believe they'd bide their time," Katie said. "If anyone knew about us, we'd already be dead. However, I did update our go bags."

Tonya nodded, growing more solemn. "I could have Nathaniel look into a new site."

"I'm not going anywhere," Dad said. "I'm tired of moving. I was dodging coven schemes, human eyeballs and

wolf packs a century before you two were even born."
Her father had been a West Coast region elder. "I'm at
the tail end of my third pass-through."

Tonya shot him an evil glance. "Code for senile."

"Speak for yourself. I'm sharp as a gorram tack. I know
who wolf boy is, and you can't remember somebody you
met ten years ago."

"What do you mean I met him?" Tonya asked. "I don't
forget a face, and I don't forget someone's chi." One of
Tonya's abilities was viewing the chi of witches and
wolves, like Katie had joked about with Marcus.

"Dummy," Dad said. "His face now wouldn't be the
face you saw. You're not the only one good at camouflage."

"I'll look at him with the true eye. It doesn't take much
energy. If we have a history, it's best we know everything.
It will also tell us what kind of man he is."

"A man who can't resist dipping his wick." Dad shook
the jar. "That's what kind of loser he is."

"Don't be ugly. Love is an unstoppable force."

The change had taken Marcus, but Katie couldn't
imagine him, even as little as she knew about him, becoming foolish over a lover. His wolf seemed close to the
surface, but he hadn't hurt her—or done anything else to
her—when he could have. His manners were impeccable.

What would it be like to break through that restraint?
Katie mentally kicked herself for even wondering.

Dad cleared his throat. "His name's Luis Del Macario
Rodríguez. Formerly New York West coven, or what's left
of it." Coven membership in some urban areas had been
struggling against wolf incursion for years. More wolves
in an area meant more witches interacting with wolves
and more witches who failed to just say no.

Tonya frowned. "Rodríguez. That's sounding more familiar, but it's a common name." She dove back into her purse and located the chi capsules. "Very handsome man, Mr. Luis Del Macario Rodríguez. Better verify his chi."

"My, my," Katie said dryly. "Why would Tonya have met someone from a New York coven ten years ago? We were off the grid."

Tonya twisted the cap of the amber pill bottle. "A festival? I always wear my best disguises there. Nothing to worry about." Tonya's best disguises were impenetrable to…anyone. Some days, Katie wondered if she really was a roly-poly, matronly blonde with large breasts and equally large hair.

Dad snorted. "Perhaps you met him when you and your sympathizer buddies were carting some mongrel off to Mexico."

"Impossible. I haven't been involved in the freedom program in—"

He cackled. "Now it's my turn to tell you to stuff it. Told you. I hacked the elder forums…Lady Pimpernel."

If true, this confirmed what Katie suspected about Tonya's festival visits. "Are you still involved with your group?"

"*Involved* is a strong term." Tonya tucked the pill bottle in her purse and rolled a capsule between her fingers. "I made a deal with the Evil One that I wouldn't participate in the freedom program as long as he quit the keeper council."

"Are you saying Vern hasn't quit?" Katie asked. "He couldn't go back with Lars as director." The person Lars had hated most in the world, next to all wolves and to Katie, who'd been ahead of him in status, had been Vern. During a change of leadership, Vern had been sent in to manage the council by the elders, who'd wanted more control. Vern had lasted ten years before the incident with Katie.

"I'm saying I honor my deals," Tonya answered evasively.

"Then who's Lady Pimpernel?" Dad asked. "Sounds like someone with your aptitude for fake faces."

"As you pointed out, I'm not the only witch blessed in the art of disguise." Witches, like physicians, often specialized. While Katie's convex power had written her fate for her, Tonya's training had taken other paths. Like the true eye…and espionage. Tonya could fool anyone about anything. Her masks had saved their butts on several occasions.

"You know what? It doesn't matter," Katie decided. If Tonya had been breaking her deal with Vern, she hadn't caused Katie any trouble. "All that matters is we poppy Marcus and double up on security. People might come looking for him."

"If you don't have the heart to cruelly obliterate him," Tonya said sweetly, "I could see if he's on Nathaniel's refugee list." The sympathizers tried to monitor transformed wolves who might be in need of their services. The region elders hadn't spread the existence of the freedom program around any more than they had the keepers. Some witches knew about the sympathizers, but not all.

"No." To the sympathizers, one former witch's memories were worth risking everyone's safety. "It's not just that he's cognizant. He knows too much about me and Ba."

Tonya sighed as she stood back up. "I give up, Katiekins. Let's do this. First, though, I'd like you to link into the true eye with me. That way you can witness his chi and won't have to take my word for it."

"I'll hop in," Dad said. "Katie needs to stay as far away from the mongrel as possible."

Tonya paused, her hand on the doorknob. "Oh?"

"She's got a thing for him." He held up the jar. "He's nice enough, as wolves go, but they're both moony. This is a super-duper love killer. I'm going to cast it on her."

"So that's what you've been doing." Katie would never let her father cast a spell as tricky as a libido dampener on her.

"That's a lot of dampener," Tonya observed. "Are you expecting Marcus to be chained in Katie's bed for a while?"

"Dirty-minded woman," Dad said. "You should take some too."

It would do no good to change the subject. The weakness was part of who Katie was. There was no denying it, no escaping it, not with a wolf in the house. A wolf she may have been attracted to regardless of his species.

His manners, his self-confidence, his looks and his flashes of humor appealed to her. His wolf was icing on the cake.

"I appreciate your effort, Ba, but I'm covered." Or she would be, when she dug out her libido dampener recipes and…shit, she'd need fresh cucumber and that meant a trip to the organic grocer and…ugh.

Marcus needed to be gone. Her stillroom was a wreck, thanks to Ba. They needed to pack, just in case. The life wipe was going to drain her magic. The patrol was tomorrow. She didn't even want to *do* this…

Everything was coming to a very frustrating head.

"Nobody's libido is going to cause trouble. We're all adults here." Tonya opened the bedroom door and waved Katie through. "Your spell casting, my dear Zhang Li, is too unmodulated for the delicate art of the true eye. Save it for the poppy."

"As long as his chi's all you look at," Dad warned.

Tonya shot Katie a sly glance and said, "Anything you say, old man," before shutting the door in his face.

Katie remained by the door as Tonya prepared. With Marcus out of commission, her nerves had settled. Kind of. No need to take it personally that he'd tried to use her lust to manipulate her. Why wouldn't he? He was in danger of losing whatever life he'd created for himself.

Wolves in traps weren't known for good behavior. She and Dad were lucky he hadn't hurt them, and it spoke highly of his character. *Dammit.*

He couldn't be the standard macho asshole. Oh, no. He couldn't swagger and treat her like a stupid female, her desires his due. He was rational, curious and calm, making the wolf in him, that whisper of wildness, all that much more enticing.

Tonya ducked into Katie's bathroom and scrubbed up, talking over the running water. "Any signs of him waking?"

Katie pushed her glasses up and checked his eyes— closed. His face—relaxed. His arms—limp against the pillows under his head. His chest—rising and falling evenly. His abdomen—ripped.

She thought about shaking him and decided against it. "No."

Drying her hands on a disposable towel, Tonya reentered the bedroom. She'd left the true eye pill on the dresser and plucked it up now, replacing it with a wet washcloth. "Let's form a circuit over his beautiful, beautiful body."

With some reluctance, Katie crawled across the wide bed and sat beside Marcus. Her knee bumped his hip.

Tonya took her hand in a firm grip. With her other hand she popped the spell capsule. Katie smelled a pungent whiff of kava before she felt Tonya pull a little energy from her, sending it into the mixture. The magic inside witches took shape when they funneled it through the proper organic substances.

"Touch his skin," Tonya ordered.

Both of them—Tonya with the hand holding the herbs and Katie with her free hand—placed their fingertips on Marcus's chest. Because Tonya had linked her into her spell, Katie saw the glow of Marcus's chi waver around him, a blue-streaked gray with sharply defined edges. The blue streaks were brighter next to his skin, almost glowing.

Tonya spread the herbs on Marcus's chest. "Oh, yes. That Rodríguez."

Katie leaned forward, her hand flattening on Marcus's smooth skin. "You know him?"

"He's a clever son of a gun." Tonya tapped him with her fingertips, one at a time, as if she were impatient. A tiny frown line formed between her brows. "I never thought I'd see him like this."

"What else?"

"He's conflicted."

Anyone could have guessed that—he was a witch who'd lost his power and transformed into an animal, a lesser version of himself.

"Strong. Smart. He's endured a lot." Tonya continued to tug magic out of Katie, a gentle thread that didn't tire either of them.

The outlay softened her mood and her spine. The urge to cuddle up to Marcus hit her. The warmth of his skin under her palm tempted her to caress him, to let her fingertips explore his dark nipples. Or down, tracing his muscles, finding that lean hollow near his hip.

Kissing it. Licking it.

Katie bit her lip and concentrated on the aura around Marcus instead of the body behind it. A faint purple tinged the edges of the blue in his chi.

Tonya looked up, meeting Katie's questioning gaze. "He's honest. Other people may not agree with my reading due to certain events in his past, but I think we can trust him."

"I thought honesty was brown?" Would Tonya tell the truth about Marcus's chi if it meant she could sway Katie and Zhang Li to her way of thinking?

"Brown. Or brownish gray. Or gray."

"What's purple?"

Tonya grinned. "Let's just say I bet your chi's purple too, when you think about him."

"Ah. That." Lust. Marcus could have been horny before coming here. Oversexed. Chi wasn't like mind reading, so Tonya had no way of knowing whether Marcus's purple had anything to do with Katie…did she?

She didn't have a chance to ask. The luminous shimmer around Marcus rippled as the man in question opened his eyes.

He glanced at their clasped hands and then at his chest. Katie was tempted to snatch her hand back, but it would interrupt the power circuit. After a long, silent moment, he turned his gaze on Tonya.

"Hello, Ms. Applebaum," he said in a calm voice. "I can't say I'm pleased to see you here, still reading people's chi without permission."

Tonya let the aura dissipate and dropped Katie's hand. "You'd think after what happened to your sister, you wouldn't have done the same thing?"

Marcus frowned, deepening the groove between his brows. "I don't care to discuss my sister."

"You're a great deal younger than you were the last time I saw you. That was a remarkable age mask. I wouldn't have guessed. It seems we have more than the true eye in common."

"He had the true eye?" Katie returned her hands to her lap, her fingers tingling with magic residue—and contact with Marcus's skin.

"All good scientists do. He can probably read a lattice with it. I only read character." Tonya dabbed his chest with the washrag from the dresser, cleaning off the spell components. "So what have you been up to the past ten years? Aside from dating a wolf, I mean."

"I don't care to discuss that with you either." Anger Katie had never seen from Marcus in her admittedly short time of knowing him tightened his expression. "Not after you and your sympathizers bungled your promise to help my sister and got her killed."

"You what?" Katie shot Tonya a shocked glance, but Tonya was concentrating on Marcus.

"Yes, you would think that. And then you went with *them,* so we couldn't stay in touch with you."

"I went with no one. I was taken," Marcus spat.

"Oh, dear. Were you? You know, I always wondered. You seemed so earnest. I guess this is a good time to tell you that your sister…"

Marcus lunged. Tonya leaped back with a squeak. The metal of his handcuffs clanked against the headboard, followed by a crack.

One of his arms swung free. The handcuff on that side twirled loose on his wrist.

Katie started to scramble off the bed, but Marcus grabbed her. Jerked her toward him, hard. She fell across him awkwardly. Her glasses flew off, landing somewhere on the floor. Before she took another breath, he had his hand around her neck.

Tonya froze and held up both hands. "Don't hurt her because you hate me."

"I don't hate you. I was there. I know your errors weren't malicious." Marcus firmed his hold on Katie, and she felt the edge of his control slip. The tips of claws poked her throat. "I simply regard you as inept. You may as well have killed her yourself. She was the only family I had left."

Their species—witches with their covens, wolves with their packs—weren't solitary beings. Losing one's family would tear any of them apart. Katie's sympathies went out to the man, but then she remembered he was two centimeters from strangling her. Tonya tried to placate the angry wolf. "Honey, listen to me. Your sister—"

"Not another word about my sister." He raised Katie's chin to demonstrate the risk. "Do I make myself clear?"

Tonya's voice thinned when she answered. "Clear as crystal."

Katie's heart pounded. Her mouth dried. Her upper body was squashed against Marcus's muscular torso, and it felt…good. He felt good.

She reacted how she ought to, instead of how she wanted to.

With a vicious twist, she went for his groin. He caught her legs between his. She struggled, pushed him with all her strength. Bit him, kneed him, gouged him. Nearly freed herself, but he caught her again.

This time, he wasn't as careful. Katie yelped when fingers dug into her throat.

"I'm getting Zhang Li," Tonya warned.

"Stay where you are." Marcus's claws stung Katie.

He'd broken the skin. She, who used to be the bane of
transformed wolves, had been defeated in forty-five seconds. "And you. Hold still before you puncture an artery."

She smelled blood. Hers again. Shimmering behind
her panic and anger, she felt desire. He could yank his
other arm free, pin her down, do whatever he wanted.
They both knew it.

Her question was, were they both fantasizing about it
or was that just her?

"I asked you not to hurt her." Katie had rarely heard
Tonya upset. She hardly recognized her friend's voice.
"Now we're going to have trouble."

"We don't want that." To her shock, Marcus bent and
inhaled near her throat. "What do we want, Katie?"

"I want you to let me go."

"Is that so?" The corner of his mouth curled, and his
gaze locked with hers. His eyes were pale with the wolf.
Against her hip, where he'd restrained her legs between
his, his cock hardened. "Pain isn't what she's feeling right
now. Is it, Katie?"

"Shit," Tonya muttered. "You're right. Let's leave
Zhang Li out of this. Perhaps *I* should take myself out
of this."

"Tonya, don't go." Katie closed her eyes, humiliated.
Dammit. Hell, dammit again.

She'd hated being a keeper so much, she'd discarded
everything about it she could. She'd tried to become the
person she'd always wanted to be, and it had left her so
out of practice.

Marcus adjusted their position until he was sitting
against the headboard. He curled her against him, her
face to his chest. He smelled like kava and man. Her
breasts rubbed him. His fingers around her throat eased,
but she made no move to escape. She'd allow this. Yes,

allow it. If she allowed it, it meant she was in charge of the situation.

But then he shifted his grip, and his hand fisted in her short hair, holding her head immobile.

Her nipples tightened. Her pussy woke with an ache she hadn't felt in a long time. As a male, his physical response was easier to read. She parted her lips and pretended to be helpless. Just for a minute, she pretended she was in his arms voluntarily.

"Ms. Applebaum," Marcus said calmly, "now that we've agreed there's no need to call Katie's father, perhaps we can solve the quandary I find myself in."

Katie heard Tonya's footsteps as she came closer to the bed. "I'd like nothing better, my friend."

"Not your friend." He jiggled Katie's head until she opened her eyes. His fierce expression deepened, and his eyes glinted with anger. "Nor yours, keeper."

"I'm not a keeper," she said, hoarse. "Not anymore."

"Obviously." He let his gaze travel down her body and back to her face. "I don't think this was in your combat training, was it?"

He had no idea.

"You were faking sleep," she guessed. He tugged her hair as though she was a doll he could reposition. Her hands were trapped between them. "You heard us talking. Could you have gotten loose anytime?"

He pulled his other arm. His muscles bunched. The handcuffs gave with a metallic snap, the lock popping.

He wrapped that arm around Katie too. There was no chance she could get away without magical intervention.

There was no chance she'd *want* to get away without magical intervention.

Katie groaned and rested her cheek against him in defeat.

"I knew I shouldn't have ordered those from that sex catalog," Tonya said, disgusted. "They promised to hold like the real thing."

"Perhaps they did," Marcus said. "Now, as much as it pains me to ask you two for anything, I stayed here on purpose. Would you hear me out?"

Katie, an inch from agreeing with whatever he wanted, stopped herself. The fact he knew about keepers meant he knew what they did to wolves who threatened the covenants.

Goddess, if he brought the keepers down on them…

"We'll be happy to listen," Tonya answered. "First let her go. I'll make us tea and cookies."

"I don't want to let her go," he said thoughtfully, addressing them as if conveying a scholarly thesis. "It would relinquish my advantage over you. What's more, I find restraining Katie like this, considering who and what she is, to be…invigorating."

"Is that what you kids are calling it these days?" Tonya quipped.

Marcus smiled, and it was so very difficult not to smile back at him. "It's been an educational year. Now that I'm a wolf, it's harder to stop myself from doing what I want."

"You just need time," Tonya said, hands on her hips. "You'll get the hang of it. You could start by letting Katie go."

"You're assuming I don't have the hang of it." Marcus pulled Katie's hair until her head tilted and her throat arched. Her skin smarted where his claws had marked her. She didn't moan. It was there, wanting out, and she swallowed it. "You're assuming I'm not in control."

"Your eyes are blued out," Katie said. And his cock was hard. It was looking likely that he did make passes at girls with glasses.

"Occupational hazard. I don't want to lose control, therefore I don't. That want, so far, has surpassed my need for…" He paused and glanced down Katie's body again. "My need for other things. But restraint isn't as easy as I'd like."

She inspected his jaw, the whiskers starting to darken his skin, the handsome arch of his nose, his heavy eyebrows and long lashes. His sensuous lips. He watched her as she watched him, and she wondered what he was thinking. Was he resenting the fact her body and scent gave him an erection? Was he thinking he'd like to break her neck?

"Start talking," she said. "I'm getting a crick."

"Drop your mask first." He stared at her. "The everyday one."

She swallowed, the bow of her neck making it difficult. "My mask?"

"I want to know who I'm dealing with. What are you doing in Alabama, keeper, running a tattoo parlor with an incompetent sympathizer and, if I'm not mistaken, a dead region elder formerly known as Bob Chang?" While Katie hadn't been in the system since she was part of the council, her father had been deeply imbedded. His death, in a falsified boating accident, had been mourned.

"She hasn't been on the council for years," Tonya said. "Don't hold it against her too much."

"Keepers don't quit. Lose the mask," he insisted.

"No." Witches didn't drop their everyday masks around strangers. Certainly they didn't drop them around wolves. That tiny barrier was the only thing between her and total meltdown.

"Take it off."

She could release it. Marcus had already scented her blood. Except…he hadn't scented everything.

"I don't want to." He'd learn the full extent of her weakness, and that was none of his business. Let him think she had a crush on him because he was good-looking. "If you're so concerned about appearances, why don't you tell us what you looked like before the change?"

"I looked a lot like this," he said. "Softer around the middle though. Don't miss that. Your turn."

"This is my true face."

"Pretty. But you're not showing all of it." He ran a finger down her throat, smearing blood from the feel of it. "I don't have a mask, Katie. Play fair."

"Like you're playing fair?" How could her body jitter and melt at the same time? He was already using her attraction against her. She didn't want to hand him the larger weapon.

He touched her lip, his finger sticky with her blood. "I want to see you…naked."

"Fine. Fuck. Whatever. I don't care." Katie accessed her magical core, the flame burning inside her, and torched the mask spell. Her skin heated. The hairs on her arms prickled with static.

Then her only protection was gone. She was completely exposed. Her weakness. Her want. Her intense need.

Marcus inhaled. Blinked. Exhaled long and slow, his eyes silver.

Katie didn't require a wolf's nose to realize he was stirred by her scent and what it meant. No wolves since her final mission, the one where she'd nearly died, had been exposed to her without any trace of a mask.

Would he react like they had?

And why wasn't she sickened by the thought?

He trapped her head in one hand while the other gripped her shirt. Did he tremble? He shifted his hips, his erection a hot bar of steel in his slacks. Confusion wrinkled his brow. "I didn't expect... I don't understand how you could have been a keeper. Unless..."

"You got what you asked for. Let her go." Tonya flew at Marcus, tugging him with frantic hands. Katie smelled peppermint and hairspray. "Don't make me hurt you."

"It's you," Marcus breathed. "Chang Cai. The Black Widow."

FIVE

MARCUS PUSHED KATIE off the bed and himself to the far side so fast, he was up before Tonya finished casting her spell.

It missed. The air popped harmlessly, and minty freshness filled the room.

Tonya cursed. Katie rustled on the ground, unseen. The bedside table rattled. "Dammit. Where are my glasses?"

"Here, Velma." Tonya kicked them across the hardwood.

Katie's hands trembled as she slid on her ugly black spectacles and adjusted her clothing. Marcus tensed to spring again.

"Chang Cai is dead." She shoved her hands into the pockets of her skintight jeans as if holding herself in check. "Did nobody tell you? She was killed in a plane crash."

Tonya, some kind of candy in her hand, drew back to throw at him again. "Are you going to behave?"

Marcus had never been wonderful at thinking on his feet. For most of his life, he hadn't needed to. Being a wolf on the lam required it of him, and he hated it. "What are you going to do with peppermint and sugar? Cure my headache?"

"Hold still and you can find out." Katie eyed Tonya in surprise, and the woman shrugged. "It was all I had."

Not since Marcus had lost his sister—and then five

years of his life to the blackmailing keepers—had he been this stunned.

Not by Tonya this time, but by Katie. She wasn't just a keeper. She was the Black Widow.

The best, or worst, of all keepers in recorded history. More captures and wipes than anyone outside Hiram Lars, whose record spoke more of longevity and malice than anything else.

And this small woman, this vulnerable, mortified woman, whose smile was like a star, who smelled like sex and shampoo, was the amoral Chang Cai?

"You shouldn't have put a name to my first pass-through." Her eyes glistened behind her lenses. She fingered the cuts on her throat gingerly. "You shouldn't have told us you knew about witches. Do you realize what we have to do now?"

"Kill me?" If anyone could commit murder with magic, it was a convex witch like Chang Cai. The rumors all over the keeper stronghold had left no doubt on one topic— Chang Cai had been powerful and remorseless.

The gun he'd seen took on an additional significance. What had he gotten himself into?

"I don't want to," Katie said, reminding him how she hadn't wanted to drop her mask, either. With good reason. The full force of her longing had dazed him, and his wolf had leaped to meet it. He'd barely held out.

If he would have kissed her, no doubt she'd have bitten off his tongue.

"How will you kill me?" he asked, rubbing his wrist where the dangling handcuffs scraped him. "Gun? Poison? Death spell? How much magic do you have to use, Chang Cai, to kill someone?"

Her expression crumpled. "I can't let you leave here with this knowledge."

"My chi says I'm trustworthy." He laughed. "Change your mind?"

"I'm not sure," Tonya said. "You could have hurt her, and you didn't."

"I could still hurt her. I could hurt you both." He stalked around the foot of the bed. Both ladies stood their ground when they should be scared. But he supposed the Black Widow feared no shifter, and Tonya Applebaum thought wolves were harmless.

She was wrong.

"You won't hurt anyone." Without further ado, Tonya threw the mint.

He dodged easily. The spell puffed open, brushing past him with a tingle. She fumbled at her pocket for another.

Ignoring Tonya and her pathetic candy, he faced the real threat. He halted almost within arm's reach of her. Black Widow. Whoever she was. "What are you going to do, Chang Cai?"

"Katie," she corrected, lifting her chin. How could she be a heartless assassin? Why did he still want to kiss her? "Call me Katie or Katherine. It's my name now…Marcus."

"Will it be painless, or will I suffer?"

"I don't know how you heard of the keepers. I don't know why you recognize Tonya. All I know is I'm not Chang Cai anymore, and I don't want to do this."

"But you can," he said softly. "You're convex, and by your father's admission, alpha. You warp our gift, our magic, in a way it's not meant to be used. With power like that, how can I not believe everything I've heard about you?"

And even as he said it, he wanted to know. How did a convex alpha use magic? Would she transform if she slept with a wolf?

If she slept with him?

"Believe what you want about me. I don't have to prove anything to you." Blinking fast, she nudged her glasses up her nose. The woman all keepers had feared quivered with nerves, had terrible eyesight and oozed so much desire for him—a wolf—that he couldn't wish away his hard-on.

It didn't add up.

Damned curiosity. Why couldn't he just run? Jump through the window behind him, hit the empty street and go. Why did he have to know everything about everything?

That's when it occurred to him he *could* run.

And he could take her with him.

He'd wanted to convince Katherine Zhang to assist willingly. Did he owe Chang Cai the same consideration? She'd wipe him, kill him, to protect herself. She'd admitted it.

Giving in to the impulse, he pounced on Katie and tossed her slender body over his shoulder. She pounded his back, her fists more like a massage than a defense mechanism.

Marcus laughed. After a year of living as a wolf, rarely had his id ruled. He'd fought it and hated it and fought it some more.

This felt magnificent.

Tonya screamed. Katie cursed. Zhang Li thumped through the living room, shouting questions. The noise faded to a low buzz as Marcus's adrenaline surged. He leaped beyond the bed, kicked down the bedroom door and dodged the old man brandishing a glass jar.

He was out of their apartment, down the stairs and in the darkened street before Katie had taken a third breath.

His truck, parked outside, wasn't locked. The crappy streetlight blinked off, as if eager to conceal his escape. He swung open the door and tossed Katie into the cab.

She hit the seat, bounced and scrambled toward the opposite door.

Her reaction time was impressive. He'd expect no less of an assassin. But he was faster. Marcus latched on to her ankle and slid her back to the passenger's side, clapping a hand over her mouth.

She bit him. He winced but didn't let go. He needed to hurry; he could hear movement inside the shop as Tonya and Zhang Li marshaled whatever weapons they had handy.

"I'm acting in self-defense." Using his thumb, he popped open the metal cuff around his wrist. Katie hit him and kicked at his legs. Landed a solid blow. It would bruise and heal within an hour, like his hand. "You threatened to kill me, Chang Cai. Did you expect me to bend my neck?"

She quit biting long enough to snarl something as furious as a wet cat.

The night air whooshed his bare torso, a crisp October breeze. Marcus wanted to laugh again, he felt so galvanized, so completely alive. Instead he flopped his prisoner over on her stomach. As soon as he released her mouth, she screamed, the sound piercing enough that it hurt his ears worse than her teeth had hurt his hand. He handcuffed her more roughly than necessary and let his gaze rest on the curves of her ass.

He wanted to bite it. And more. The cuffed wrists, the struggling woman... He was enjoying this too much.

"If you don't quiet down," he growled, "I'll make you quiet down."

As threats went, it wasn't particularly menacing. His prisoner responded in kind, inhaling deeply and loosing another shriek.

He slanted across her body, his hips pushing against

her, knowing she'd feel his erection. She bucked, and not in a sensual way. Her heels whipped up to drum him wherever she could land a kick. The tense situation wasn't having the diminishing effect on his libido one might expect.

She might smell aroused, but she wasn't going the Stockholm route anytime soon. Marcus stuffed his pocket handkerchief into her mouth.

She hurled curses at him, distinguishable though the hankie. He crawled over her, slammed and locked her door, and started the truck with the key still happily in his trouser pocket. He was losing his tie, his shirt, his briefcase, his travel pill pack and his suit coat, but he was gaining a test subject.

Good trade.

Just as Zhang Li limped through the shop door, Marcus peeled out, grateful this run-down neighborhood was mostly vacant and little trafficked.

He quickly realized Katie wasn't going to make his first ever abduction easy on him. She scooched to the passenger door and tried to open the lock with her chin. He grabbed the back of her stretchy pants and yanked her to his side.

She rammed his shoulder with her skull. He looped his right arm around her until he could grip her throat.

"Are you crazy? You can't jump out of a moving vehicle. I'm doing almost fifty." Not used to driving with one hand, he took a turn too fast. Braked. Thank Goddess for automatic transmission. The truck fishtailed onto another side street. He braced his knee against the wheel and flicked on the headlights with his steering hand. While his night vision was superior, human drivers didn't have that advantage.

Marcus knew the roads through this town and everywhere on the Birmingham border patrol's path like the screen of his smartphone. When you were a fugitive, it paid to know the escape routes.

As he held her, Katie's breathing whistled with anger. She crooked her left leg and started kicking him, throwing her small weight into the blows.

He let the claws of his right hand jab into her soft neck. Again.

She froze.

"Calm down," he advised.

She worked her jaw furiously until the soggy hankie plopped out of her mouth. "I wasn't going to kill you, but you're changing my mind really fast."

"If you scream, I'll duct tape your mouth. I've got a roll in back. In fact, if you keep kicking me like little mule, I'm going to duct tape your legs." An image of her restrained on the Murphy bed in the Airstream flashed before his eyes. Was turnabout fair play?

"Why don't I get to excuse my actions with self-defense? For all I know you're going to kill me."

"I'm not going to kill you."

"You manhandled me."

"I'm a man. I have man hands."

She choked out something so enraged it wasn't even words. The truck whizzed beneath a broad overpass. Marcus kept his eyes on the road ahead, the area around them, for signs of pursuit. Witch or human. He wasn't exactly obeying the posted speed limit. A light mist had risen as the chill of the night met the warmth of the humid Alabama day.

"That's the dumbest thing I've ever heard," Katie said abruptly.

"It may be the dumbest thing I've ever said," he concurred, slowing as they neared a four-way crossroad. He hadn't planned an abduction, so he was glad as hell he'd docked the Airstream in the state park instead of the motor home village.

Nobody to hear her scream but him.

He felt guilty, suddenly, that he was doing this to her. Soon he'd be wanting to take her home—but he couldn't give in. He needed her.

"What exactly are you trying to achieve by kidnapping me?"

Her tone had gone from furious to curious. He didn't trust it. Chang Cai would be a master manipulator. "This was the best way for us to have an uninterrupted conversation."

"We were having a conversation in the apartment."

"About how you were going to kill me."

"I told you, I wasn't going to kill you. Just wipe you." She squirmed in his grasp, arching her neck away from his claws.

"I tell you what. Let's assume neither of us wants the other dead," he said. "There are only so many times we can say, 'I'm not going to kill you,' before it becomes meaningless."

That silenced her for a moment. A short moment. "Tell me how you know about the keepers."

"I suppose this is a story your sympathizer friend wouldn't have shared." The truck whizzed out of the city limits, and Marcus felt safe enough to slow to the fifty-five-miles-per-hour speed limit. An ounce of worry dissolved. "Eleven years ago, I made the mistake of contacting the sympathizers after my sister Elisa transformed into a wolf. A colleague told me about them, and I took a chance."

"That's how you know Tonya? She wasn't even supposed to be… Never mind. Go on."

"Tonya and her team failed." Katie didn't need to know the other circumstances of Elisa's life—like the fact she'd been pregnant at the time and desperate to find a cure for the cancer that threatened to kill her before the baby was born. "The keepers hit, and hit hard. There wasn't much the sympathizers could do against your people, and Elisa died in the chaos."

"Goddess. I'm sorry about your sister, Marcus."

He had no idea what route his life would have taken if Elisa hadn't gotten cancer, but it wouldn't have been here. He would have been an uncle, a brother, not a lone wolf with a dangerous mission. "Why? You probably did the same thing to a hundred wolves."

"I tagged," she said. "I didn't bag. Unless it was self-defense. That wasn't my...function."

"Sure." That wasn't what he'd heard. However, he'd heard so many things about the Black Widow, they couldn't all be true. "Hiram Lars blackmailed me because of my part in the fiasco. I lost five years running experiments for him to pay for my treason."

"Experiments?"

"On wolves."

Not sounding as disturbed as she ought to, she said, "I thought the experiments were pure speculation on Tonya's part."

"I wasn't sure Chang Cai was entirely real, yet here you are." What had he expected—that the Black Widow would be horrified by what other keepers considered animal testing?

In the corner of his eye, he saw Katie frown. "Are you going to use me to cut a deal? It won't work."

He'd been thinking more along the lines of using her in his research. Running tests on her like Lars had forced him to test wolves. What he'd do to convince her—bribe, bargain or coerce—he hadn't decided. "What do you mean?"

"Giving me to Lars won't get him off your back. He'll kill us both and anyone connected to us."

"Don't be so sure." It was, ironically, the perfect inducement. That kind of strong-arming might not have occurred to him. "He often expressed regret you were dead because he didn't kill you himself. Surely he'd reward anyone who gave him that chance." Chang Cai had become a legend among the keepers, reviled and revered. Whenever Lars had spoken of her, he'd frothed at the mouth with loathing.

"You can't believe everything you heard about me—especially if you heard it from Lars. I honestly didn't know experiments were being conducted on wolves. Then again, Lars only took charge after I…left." Her voice turned bitter. Since she was no longer struggling, he eased his claws back into his fingertips.

"I don't know how the keepers functioned when you were there. Lars kept me sequestered. I interacted with him and his subordinates. But I can confirm the experiments are real and not especially humane."

Most witches believed wolves to be their inferiors, shifters not strong enough to resist. Marcus had assumed it himself in his first pass-through. He'd since learned otherwise. It wasn't a question of worth. It was a question of magic. Magic and focus. Unfortunately, Lars, a purist who advocated the eradication of wolves to keep the bloodline untainted, hadn't allowed the research Marcus wanted to pursue. Marcus had no intention of letting Lars catch him again.

"That figures," she said. "I don't like wolves, present company included, but that's crossing the line."

"I'm deeply wounded, Katie." Her preferred name

slipped out of his mouth. Was it because he didn't like to see her flinch? Or because she'd stopped flinching?

"Am I to assume the keepers are after you as well as the elders?"

Marcus shrugged. If he got mired here, he wouldn't be able follow normal evasive techniques. It would hinder him with Birmingham's patrol. The sentries could sense other wolves within a certain radius. As far as the keepers, he wasn't sure where they were, but he had no desire to be a sitting duck.

"The keepers *are* after you, aren't they?" Her head thumped against his arm. "Did you lead them right to us? Perfect. A passel of homicidal maniacs to go with the rest of this crap."

"If they knew where I was, I wouldn't be at liberty." He'd sent the keepers on a wild goose chase to West Virginia after his close call in California. He'd propositioned a witch in Sacramento, and she'd reported him to the elders. Luckily Marcus had contingency plans for his contingency plans.

Katie exhaled a very exasperated sigh. "How did you manage to escape them in the first place? Were you an elder?"

As if that would have protected him from Lars. The man had constantly chafed against the restrictions placed on the keepers by the region elders. "Do I look like an elder?"

"Dumb question, I guess. You're not that old." Elders came in all shapes and sizes, but one consistency was age. Second pass-through minimum, usually third. "If you'd been an elder, I would have heard of you."

"Correct. The relationship between keepers and region elders was less strained when Vernon was in charge of the council." Not that he'd known about keepers during his first pass-through, as an unglamorous magical lattice researcher. It hadn't been until his sister had gotten sick that he'd learned the truth. And the true meaning of loss. "Lars described Vernon as weak."

"Weak, humane, non-purist—all the same thing to Lars."

"You aren't a purist?"

She made a disgusted noise. "Do you see any froth around my mouth?"

"Yet you were able to leave the council with your memories intact too." It was one thing for a scientist to leave the keeper stronghold intact and another for Chang Cai to manage it. Now that he'd met her, he couldn't help but wonder how much of what he'd heard was factual.

"They tried to poppy me. It didn't take."

"Because you're alpha?" There was no call for them to be at total odds when they had a common enemy. The thought of having someone on his side again pleased Marcus more than he cared to admit.

Except that this was Chang Cai.

"The theory at the time was because I'm just that perverse." She laughed half-heartedly. "Shortly after that, they thought I was dead, so they didn't have a chance to try again. Your turn. How'd you get out?"

He slowed the truck as they neared the entrance to the state park. Current magical theory taught that wipes weren't damaging, since covens that performed them experienced no backlash. Katie's experience with the wipe failure suggested wipes weren't benevolent after all, but it took a convex alpha's strength to refract a coven-led spell.

"I wasn't wiped because I was put on retainer. Not many witches have PhDs in biology and chemistry." Their lifespans allowed for as much education as desired, but most found human systems to be constraining. "I convinced Lars wiping me, not to mention killing me, would destroy my ability to consult for the council."

"I can't believe he listened. To anybody. I can't believe he let you go. He's not a man you can reason with." Bitterness crept back into her voice. Since she was talking about Lars, he guessed he could understand.

He felt a lot of bitterness toward the murdering bastard himself. While he'd told Tonya she might as well have killed Elisa, Marcus knew who was truly responsible.

Hiram Lars.

"My experiments weren't producing the results Lars wanted," he explained. "I made sure I was...expensive to keep around." He'd requisitioned exorbitant laboratory equipment, created numerous chemical incidents and nearly exposed the keeper stronghold on a regular basis while acting the part of an absent-minded genius. He'd given them enough to keep them from killing him but not enough to employ him.

"And since you've been free? Did he threaten you?"

"Oh, yes. Being out was like being on parole. My activities were constrained. I wasn't allowed to communicate with elders or sympathizers."

"No, Lars wouldn't have wanted that." They passed a park sign. "What are we doing here? This is Nashville pack territory."

"So?"

"Everyone knows Nashville wolves are lazy. The keepers might look here for you."

"The location serves its purpose." When that purpose might involve making a woman scream.

"You're still running experiments." Katie twisted to look at him, and he fixed his eyes on the road. The headlights flickered against tall walls of trees. "On yourself. Is that why you got tattoos? To see if you could keep them?"

"I preferred them to scars. Less painful. Well…" His arm bumped her shoulder as he adjusted his fingers around her neck. She twitched when he encountered one of the small scratches he'd made. "The dragon is painful in a different way."

"Sorry." Actual embarrassment tinged Katie's voice and scent. "Ba wouldn't let me use the be-gone, and I hoped you wouldn't come back if we gave you bad service."

He laughed at her crestfallen expression. "You didn't want to see me again?" He didn't reiterate that her pheromones told a different story, because they both knew it.

Why did she want him? Sure, it was convenient for his purposes, flattering and undeniably arousing, but it wasn't convenient for her. Her desire increased whenever he felt as if he might lose control, whenever he dominated her. He disliked that aspect of his new self and did everything he could to subsume it, but it seemed to excite her. Was her reaction specific to him, or was this why she'd had such a bad reputation with the keepers?

He couldn't imagine having wolf lust when she'd spent thirty years opposing feral and transformed wolves.

She stared at the floorboard and said in a low voice, "Let me see if I have everything straight. The keepers blackmailed you, kept you on retainer and are now hunting for you. Why would you let us handcuff you for a minute? We could have trapped you. If you have any sense, there's no one on earth you'll want to avoid more than Hiram Lars. I know I do."

"I would not love to see him again."

"Are they close behind you or not?"

"They don't know where I am." Not at present. "Like with pack patrols, I have precautions against the keepers too."

"Like what?" Her hair tickled his arm as she turned to watch him.

"Magical defenses." His primed mixtures, stockpiled while he'd planned his transformation, bolstered him every morning. "Sleep spells, pack bonding spells and their ilk aren't going to work on me as expected."

"The true eye worked."

"The true eye is harmless," he countered. "I concentrated on spells that would kill me or hinder my freedom. Not all, mind you, but the standards."

Katie, blinking owlishly, inspected him as if he were a puzzle to be solved. "Did you protect against being wiped?"

"First thing," he lied. Despite having years to plan, he hadn't been able to design a shield for memory erasure or the berserker spell that forced wolves to go temporarily feral. The keepers had been developing it when he'd left, unfortunately based on some of his research.

As for wipes, if he was ever in a position to have his memory erased, it was too late for him.

It wasn't too late yet, was it? Katie said she didn't want him dead, and the next step would be convincing her she wanted to help him. His cause was vital—and essential if he wanted to honor his sister's name. It sounded like Katie wouldn't mind some vengeance on Hiram Lars herself.

If he had to underscore the fact she wanted him to get her help, he wasn't above using any means necessary.

He'd prove his theories faster if he had witch participation. If he had Katie's participation.

Normally he tried to stifle the wolf, the wildness in himself, as if remaining the person he'd been before would ease his return path. The struggle taxed him, and today he'd struggled more than usual. Technically, he'd lost the fight when he'd threatened Katie with sexual as-

sault and kidnapped her—but his loss was looking like
a gigantic win.

Should he give in to the urge to stop the truck, shove
her back on the seat and bury his face in her…

No. He was a scientist, governed by reason and logic.
He was not a beast.

"I don't know. You were pretty worried about us al-
tering your memories," Katie finally concluded. "I think
you're bluffing."

"Think what you want." The truck bumped along the
pitted gravel road to the site where he'd parked the Airstream. "I didn't want you to know what you were up
against."

"I know what I'm up against."

She was up against him. Her softness rested against
him, and her breathing quickened. He parked the truck
and stared down at her. Neither of them exited the vehicle. Not that she could, since he was restraining her.

Marcus slid his thumb along her jaw. His gaze dropped
to her lips. His id chanted something nonsensical about
plunder and sweetness and taking advantage.

His defenses against lust? Well, he didn't seem to have
any.

Reluctance and fascination warred on Katie's pretty
face as she examined his. "You didn't fake everything.
Some things can't be faked, Marcus. Some things happen whether you want them to or not."

He smiled. "No. I didn't fake everything."

"I didn't think so." Her pupils dilated with interest.

It was working. Somehow. She was playing into his
hands. If their discussion led to intimacy, how would
she react when he asked her to relay her experiences as
clinically as possible during the different phases of lovemaking?

He'd best broach his business proposal before seducing her, despite the fact her scent and body were seducing him.

"Let's go inside where it's more comfortable," he suggested, before he mauled her in the truck. "I'll show you my research."

One corner of her mouth curled in a reluctant smile. "Is that like your etchings?"

He smiled back. She had a quick wit, and he enjoyed the banter. "No, but there are a considerable number of photographs."

She allowed him to help her out of the vehicle. Her body slid against his.

Yeah, he wasn't faking everything.

Biting her lip, she scooted sideways, cheeks pink. She rolled her shoulders, which probably ached from having her wrists cuffed behind her. "What would it take for you to share your defensive recipes with us? We'd like more protections against the keepers too."

He took her by the arm and led her to the trailer. "Look at it from my point of view. Why would I freely give you anything when you'd like to take everything from me?"

"We could pay you," she offered, not mentioning whether her intent to wipe him was still a factor.

"I don't need money." As he followed her into the Airstream, he prepared to haggle. The longer he kept her curious, the better chance he had of persuading her. "I need my memories. My freedom. And I need help. Don't you want to defy Lars?"

From the far side of the room, she stared at him as he shut the door. They should be safe here until he and Katie reached an agreement; Tonya and Zhang Li would hardly be in league with any wolves or human policemen who could track them. Katie's lips, where she'd bitten them, were reddened and plush. The desire in her scent ramped up again, and her gaze kept dropping—below his chest and lower.

Did she like what she saw? What parts of his body did she favor? It wasn't easy to remain analytical in a small space with a beautiful woman. One who wanted him carnally, even though she shouldn't.

"What kind of help do you need?" she asked.

"I need you." When her eyes widened, he swallowed a grin. He could get used to being ogled. "It has to be you. You're alpha. You have so much power. I have a theory that transformed wolves can be recovered and that witches can access wolf magic. You can help me prove it. Imagine what that would do to the council."

"Your sister." Her shoulders relaxed. "This is about her."

"This is about science." But Katie was right. "And my sister. What happened to her haunts me. I freely admit that."

If she cooperated, he could have these answers and more. He'd never had to exploit his sexuality and wasn't sure how to go about it. Should he pose with his hand against the cabinet? Stick a thumb in his waistband? How long before she wondered why he hadn't put on a shirt?

Silently, he urged her closer. Close enough to touch, so he could prove he wasn't dangerous. Granted, he wasn't positive it was true, considering the thoughts in his head, but she didn't need to know everything.

"Do you think you can figure out what thousands of years of witchery hasn't?"

"You'll never know if you poppy me," Marcus pointed out.

"No, we wouldn't, would we?" she mused. "What about the fact I was a keeper? You hate keepers."

"If you wanted to be a keeper, you'd still be with them," he told her, mostly believing it. He couldn't reconcile the two parts of the woman before him, the one who'd nearly cried at the thought she might have to kill him, and Chang Cai's reputation or the way he knew keepers to be. She seemed to be Lars's polar opposite. When things didn't add up, it was because he was missing several factors in the equation.

There wasn't a scientific calculator in the world that would multiply Chang Cai times the keepers and get Katherine Zhang as the product.

"I brought you here to tell you about my research." He tapped his temple. "Let me prove to you why you don't want me to lose anything up top."

"You'll share the spell recipes?" She seemed unaware of the fact she'd crossed the room, drawn to him like a magnet. She had no interest in the diagrams on the walls, the lab equipment, the computers, the charts. She was completely mesmerized by him.

He liked it.

"I'll share…if you agree to research with me instead of wipe me."

She licked her lips, glanced up at him and jangled her handcuffs. "If we're going to work together, we should shake on it. Which I can't do like this."

Her scent spiked. His wolf did too. A flicker in her throat indicated her racing pulse. Was she excited to touch him? Or excited by the sexual tension sizzling in the air, so obvious even a clueless scientist like himself could taste it?

"If I take the handcuffs off, are you going to behave?"

She smiled at him then, a bright, unexpected beam that lit up her otherwise serious face. "Define behave."

She was…flirting.

"Have I convinced you to listen? We're safe here. No keepers, no Birmingham packers, no covens, nobody but us." He felt like an idiot, but he rubbed his hand across his chest, attracting her attention to it. "This place is fully warded. I'll show you everything. Hypotheses. Recipes. Secrets."

"I want to see," she breathed.

It would have been practical to remove the handcuffs from behind her. Instead, Marcus reached around her and caressed her arms. His palms grazed her skin until he encountered metal.

He clasped her wrists long enough that she glanced up at him. "Marcus?"

"Good thing I don't need keys." He popped one ring, careful not to let the metal bite into her. The handcuffs clinked as her wrist came free.

She brought her arms in front of her, between their bodies where there wasn't much space, and awkwardly shoved one hand into a front pocket while offering him the other. "Shake?"

He took her hand, rubbing the back of it with his thumb. Her skin was silky, but her fingertips had faint calluses. It was an agile hand. A witch's hand.

He wanted her. Wanted that hand touching him everywhere. It took most of his willpower not to act on it.

"Do we have a deal, Katie?"

Her other hand joined the clasp. "I'm sorry, Marcus," she whispered.

"Why?" He smiled down at her, feeling oddly possessive, and then smelled valerian.

Reacting faster than thought, he leaped back, landing on the other side of the trailer. Lab equipment rattled. A stack of charts hit the floor, scattering papers everywhere. His ears popped.

"Shit," she exclaimed, a wad of valerian root in one hand. She'd obviously secreted it in her pocket at some point. She held it out like a weapon. "You're really fast."

"Too slow to realize you didn't mean a word of our conversation," he growled.

She advanced. He avoided. He didn't want to hurt her, but an alpha witch could knock him out long enough to do a lot of damage. All it would take would be that valerian, or her, contacting his skin. Luckily she didn't have it in projectile form, like keepers used for combat situations.

By the Goddess, he would not let the Black Widow chase him out of his own secret hideout.

SIX

"COME ON, MARCUS." Katie swung the herb, and the blasted wolf dodged again. "I might be the most despised person in both of our worlds, but I know my duty."

"Your duty?"

"My duty to protect shifters from discovery. The sheer chaos that would erupt if wolves found out about witches. It would be the end of all secrecy."

She considered breaking for the door, but he'd be on her before she got two steps past the threshold. She had to knock him out if she had any chance of escape. She'd worry about neutralizing him later. Without other resources, dealing with Marcus might mean accepting Vern's latest bribe—some new location spell that used family DNA. Vern hadn't badgered her in months, which was unusual for him, but he'd jump at the chance to buy her services.

Marcus, eyes glittering, grabbed a blanket off the back of a chair and shook it. "You're about to be very sorry."

"I'm already sorry." She snapped off a thread of valerian and flipped it at him, but it didn't have enough heft to reach his skin. "You're the biggest threat to my existence since Lars decided to kill me after the memory wipe. That was what they were going to do, you know. Vern just let them think they succeeded."

"You've spent too much of your life being a traitor to

be able to trust anyone else," Marcus snarled. "That's your problem."

It hit Katie deep, somewhere she tried to hide from Tonya and Dad. Was she broken? Was she unforgivable? "That's not—"

Marcus sprang at her, blanket first, as if he was capturing an angry cat that didn't want to go to the vet. He'd wrapped half her body before she'd finished registering his attack. Her valerian hand stuck out at one end of the blanket.

Katie writhed in her fuzzy prison. All she needed was a whisk of his skin. A tap. Damned cognizant wolves. Always a trial, and Marcus wasn't as fooled by her tactics as others had been. He'd covered her exposed areas with the blanket, including her head.

She could hear him bitching and growling, but she couldn't see him.

She kicked and yelled. One moment he was friendly and thought-provoking, the next hot under the collar—and in other places. The constant U-turns were getting old. She suspected he shared her sentiment, but what else could she do? Go along with a wolf who was obviously imbalanced, just because she liked him?

Wolves couldn't turn back into witches. Becoming a wolf was a banishment from which there was no escape. If he preferred magic to fur, he should have kept it in his pants.

And whoever he'd slept with to become a wolf, she was one lucky bitch.

Katie tried to curl into a defensive ball. Marcus's strong arms held her upright. A stinging blow smacked her extended hand, numbing it. She yelped and dropped the small tangle of valerian.

He scooped her up, yet again, bundling her through

his trailer. Her head swam as she fought. The blanket smothered her. He jostled her, slinging her forward. She landed on a relatively soft surface. Fabric tangled her arms, her face, part of her legs. His fingers grabbed her handcuffed wrist and dragged her arm up until she heard an ominous, metallic click.

She tugged, hard, confirming she was now cuffed… to something.

Uh-oh.

Her nightmare. And her something else, something sordid and forbidden. She was almost entirely at his mercy, except for the lavender stashed in her bra and shoe and the mint in her pocket.

Katie yanked anyway, to see if the handcuffs would hold. His abuse of the lock should have weakened it, but it wasn't weak enough for her to break. She'd have to pick it.

She'd never done this without backup. Keepers didn't work alone. There was no way Tonya and Dad could find her in time to prevent…what?

What was Marcus planning? If his primary goal was to keep her from wiping him and stopping his all-important research, wouldn't running have been his best choice?

He unfurled the blanket from around her. She was on a pull-down bed.

Katie gasped for air. "Are you trying to smother me?"

When he tossed the blanket, her glasses clattered to the floor somewhere. *Dammit.* The needle concealed in the temple had been her best bet for the handcuffs. The specs were pricey for more than just the prescription.

He loomed over her with an annoyed frown. His muscles rippled under his smooth brown skin, and she tried to suppress lascivious thoughts.

"No, I need you breathing." He opened a drawer under the bed, and she scuttled into a sitting position. The cabinets above her had inset lights. Her wrist was cuffed to a fabric loop she presumed had something to do with the pull-down construction. Surely he hadn't had it custom-installed for handcuffs.

Censoring that part of her imagination, she assessed the area for makeshift weapons, lock picks, anything she could use.

He shrugged into a long-sleeved gray T-shirt and opened another drawer. "You understand, of course, I'm going to have to make sure there are no more herbs." He snapped on surgical gloves.

Surgical gloves?

If she went for the hidden lavender, he'd see. To put him off guard, she turned out her pockets with her free hand. The mint fell out of one, and a scrap of valerian fell out of the other. "This is all I've got."

"I'll take that, if you please." He watched her expectantly. "No magic."

She infused the herb anyway.

He wriggled a gloved finger in his ear. "I said no magic."

"You say a lot of things." She flipped the dried roots at him, gave him her meanest look and ate the mint. It wouldn't do anything to either of them—there wasn't enough of it—but she wanted to be defiant.

"Is that all?" He slipped a green capsule into his pocket.

He had to know he couldn't harm her with magic. "What's the pill for?"

"Monkshood remedy."

"I don't have any monkshood." For starters, spell-grade monkshood was hard to come by. And if she had any, she wouldn't have used it. She'd always—*always*—avoided killing when she could, and Marcus wasn't a feral trying to rip her to pieces.

"I'll be the judge of that." He lowered his hands to his belt and started unbuckling it.

"What exactly are you doing?" As much as she'd like to see him naked, did he truly mean to...

Marcus smiled and tucked his shirt into his pants. Despite her best efforts, she kept watching his hands. She imagined them on her body, without the latex coating... Hot and hard and demanding. She was handcuffed, trapped, unable to stop him. Her body reacted with a surge of lust.

When he rebuckled his belt, she returned her gaze to his smirk.

He knew what she was feeling. Of course. Goddess, he must think she was insane. He was right. She had to be insane to be turned on by this particular state of affairs.

He reached across the thin mattress and drew her ankles down, trying to uncurl her defensive posture. Trying to position her for whatever he had in mind.

"Are you ready?" His eyes, brown and unruffled, bored into her.

Yes!

But...no.

She crooked her legs, knees toward her chest. He wasn't expecting it. The movement knocked him off balance, and he stumbled against the edge of the bed. As soon as she had the right angle, she let him have it.

He took the kick against his torso with an *oof*. Grimacing, he snagged her ankles again and hauled her body toward him until she was stretched flat. "We can do this the easy way or the hard way."

"Neither." She scissored her legs, twisted, threw pillows at him with her free arm. She jogged and swam to maintain her strength and dexterity, but she was no match for a wolf.

Marcus, a neutral expression on his handsome face, let her kick and curse at him. She used every nasty insult thirty years of living around nasty people had taught her before she realized he was waiting for her to wear herself out. Like a child having a tantrum.

Well, if that was what he expected… She pretended to be winded and settled down, breathing hard. Nodding, he slid off her tennis shoes one at a time, tossing them to the floor.

"You're right about one thing," he said. "I am going to undress you. But not for the reason you're fantasizing about."

"I'm fantasizing about kicking you in the head." Her desires wouldn't, never had, beaten her. Dammit, she was so out of practice. And so attracted.

Marcus was harder to resist than any wolf or man she'd ever met.

"Be that as it may, you might as well cooperate," he continued. "I won't stop until I'm satisfied you don't have any more surprises on you. I will search you quickly, and I won't violate your person in any way, shape or form."

The impact of his announcement slammed into her. He was about to remove her clothing, all of it, and inspect her. Everywhere.

Goddess. An ache woke in her pussy that was impossible to ignore. "If I don't cooperate, are you going to violate my person?"

She was *so* not cooperating.

"Absolutely not." He peeled off her pink sock, shook it and smirked when lavender fell out. He inserted it into a small medical waste bin before his gloved hands tightened on her bare ankles. "I'm not a keeper. I don't violate people."

Without further ado, he grasped her jeggings at the knees and yanked.

They slid off her as if she was oiled. Katie squeaked and tugged her T-shirt to hide her underwear. Marcus examined the seams of her pants before giving them a vigorous shake.

Then he looked at her. Her cheeks burned as his gaze traveled up her legs, lingering at her hips. She pressed her thighs together.

"You're in good physical condition," he observed. It didn't feel like a compliment—merely an observation. "That's not always the case with a witch."

She glared at him. "I never know when I might need to kick someone's ass."

He didn't look the least bit intimidated by her declaration and eased himself onto the mattress. When he reached for her free hand, she flailed at him. "Do you see any lavender? No. You found it. Back off."

Instead, he sprang. In a fraction of a second, he had her spread on her back. His hands grasped her shirt at each shoulder. Their eyes met right before he ripped her T-shirt in half, laying her nearly bare.

But...he'd promised not to!

He was just like the wolves she'd dealt with. Violent and crude. She hated him—she had to hate him for this. He fell on her, his weight pinning her down. Her traitorous body responded with a joyful pulse of desire.

Her thrashing wedged his hips between her thighs, increasing their intimacy tenfold. She tried to pull his hair, claw his eyes, but he grasped her wrist and held her away from his skin.

"I'm going to check your undergarments for spell components. That's all I'm going to do." He stared down at her, his irises fading to pale blue. She watched the brown disappear until only the wolf was left. "In case you were wondering, casting my antidote capsule would increase my vitality."

She considered cursing some more, but something in his expression silenced her. Especially when his gaze dropped to her lips...and his cock hardened against her pussy.

Katie barely withheld a groan. His shirt, she noticed distractedly, smelled like her favorite fabric softener.

Marcus adjusted his fingers around her wrist. When she struggled, the rubber of his gloves tweaked the tiny hairs on her arm. His other hand patted her shoulder.

"This isn't personal," he said, though his arousal told a different story. His gloved hand cleaned the shreds of her shirt away and slipped between their bodies.

The lavender hidden in her bra prickled her skin. Could she use it like that? She'd never cast a spell with her boob before, but there was always a first time. She just needed him to touch her. She licked her lips hopefully. She'd get him to kiss her a few times before she infused the lavender. Of course, then she'd have a big, sexy wolf passed out atop her and still no way to escape him.

But he didn't kiss her. He adjusted his torso and ran a finger under the strap of her satin demi-bra. He was going to find the lavender if he continued downward.

He swept his fingers under the material, her breast in his rubber-coated hand. Her nipple hardened. The stimulation tumbled through her helpless body, landing right between her legs.

She bit her lip to keep from whimpering. Goddess, she wished he'd drop the pretense of searching her and...

He brought the lavender out and twirled its silvery stem between them. "Look what I found."

"Oops."

He pitched it behind him without taking his gaze off her. "Did I miss any leaves?"

He folded the lightly padded cup inside out, checking with his fingers instead of his eyes. Satisfied, he shifted to check her other breast. This time it was almost a caress. The bra strap slid off her shoulder. His palm, the glove, dragged across her tight nipple. She tried to control her breathing, but it rushed out of her as if they were already having sex.

His eyelashes fluttered down as he gave in to the urge to look at her chest. This was her opening. She could whip her knee into his groin and wound him long enough to...

What? She was handcuffed to his bed, and he'd stolen her lavender.

And she was enjoying his strip search so much more than she should.

"Are you happy now? There's nowhere else I could hide anything."

Rising to his hands and knees, he slid his hand down her body and hovered over her hips.

"No," she said, when what she really meant was, *Please.*

Staring into her eyes, Marcus palmed her between the legs. And she let him. She just let him. With gloves on, he hopefully wouldn't notice the dampness, but his nostrils flared all the same.

His fingers pressed but didn't probe.

Or pleasure.

"You'll regret this," Katie said in a surprisingly relaxed tone, considering how crazed she felt inside.

"Oh, I really doubt that." His huskiness was the first

sign this was affecting him more than he let on. It went beyond his body's obvious reaction, beyond his wolfish irises. He slid his hand farther, curving around to her ass. Her thighs separated of their own volition.

He paused for a moment, and his dominance of her sank in. Katie swallowed hard. She knew what she smelled like to him, what it meant that she wasn't lifting a finger to fight.

He suddenly released her wrist and slid his fingers between hers. Their hands twined and clasped, but his expression didn't change.

Her breasts felt swollen, her nipples sensitive. The bra cups he'd searched barely covered her. The heel of his hand chafed her clit through the damp satin as he checked for lavender. Or whatever he was doing, because it was feeling more and more like foreplay.

The contradiction of one hand twined around hers like a lover and the other searching her for weapons only made it worse. His touch roused her so much she began to ache.

Katie needed to squirm. Spread her legs. She'd never been this conflicted about a man, a wolf. Wolves were forbidden for witches. All witches. It was wrong to feel this way, to want him to force this on her, to exert his power over her.

She wanted him wild, wanted to be driven wild. The wolf was supposed to be her deepest fear, only the truth was, it was her deepest fantasy.

"What are you thinking?" he murmured. "Your face is so expressive when you aren't being Chang Cai. Tell me what you're feeling."

"Anger," she lied. Both their voices were hushed.

"You don't smell angry." He lowered his chin, staring down her body, at her breasts, at the way his hand wrapped between her legs.

"And you don't feel impersonal," she retorted. He felt wonderful. Darkly seductive. She throbbed with need. "Your eyes are wolfed out. Are you losing control?"

"The wolf isn't simple to manage. It's not my favorite part of the transformation."

"What did you expect? That you'd be unchanged, except stronger? The wolf takes over, Marcus." She'd seen it too many times, a witch turned feral after transformation. Born wolves spent years learning control; they didn't leap into the wolf-state overnight.

"You're wrong." His lips tightened. "A good scientist verifies every hypothesis."

"You have a hypothesis?"

"I have several." He stretched the elastic of her panties, checked the inside of the fabric and snapped them back into place without touching her. "One down."

A devil possessed her. An aching, infatuated, needy devil that knew Marcus was close to the edge and wanted to send him over. "No cavity search?"

He smiled down at her slowly, triumphantly. "Do you want one, Katie?"

Lord, yes.

"No." She clutched his hand convulsively, as if she could send him the message that way. "But I thought you didn't trust me."

"I don't." His fingers brushed her thigh. "I also don't think you're hiding any more herbs."

"Then you don't need the gloves," she said, hating herself for it.

Not taking his eyes off hers, he raised his hand to his mouth. He caught the bottom of the glove between his teeth and peeled it off his long fingers. The latex fell onto her chest. His gaze scorching, he let his hand drift down, not quite touching her breasts, her stomach, her hip. Not quite touching between her legs.

He traced the edge of her panties. Katie, unable to bear the tension boiling inside her anymore, closed her eyes and gave herself up to sensation.

Marcus lowered himself half on, half off her, his body a cage. She parted her lips eagerly. Instead his cheek brushed hers, whiskers rasping, and he whispered in her ear, "On a scale of one to ten, how aroused would you say you are right now?"

"Wh...what?"

He drew hypnotic circles on her hip, widening them, coming closer and closer to her pussy without giving her what she craved. "Can you feel the wolf inside you? Like when you were young and learning to control it?"

No. Yes. She didn't know what she felt. Desperate. It wasn't like this with humans or witches. And she'd not let it get like this with any of her...victims. "I don't know."

"It's a powerful sensation. Impossible to resist." His lips tickled her ear. Tingles poured through her. His fingers teased. "Have you ever had sex with a wolf, Katie?"

"No." She tilted her hips, trying to angle herself closer to his touch.

One sly, seductive finger brushed her mound. She shivered. "Your pheromones are off the charts. Do you know how difficult it is for me to concentrate right now?"

"I have an idea." Lust swirled inside her like a cyclone.

"I don't appreciate these impulses." She could feel the heat from his hand. She was so sensitized it made her squirm. "I don't want to feel like I might...do things to you against your will."

"If you don't like it, let me go." Common sense was disappearing fast. How much of this was actually against her will?

"I can't seem to stop," he said, raspy-voiced. He nipped her neck, and she grew that much closer to begging. "This exhilarates me. Is this normal for you?"

She licked her lips. Focusing on the conversation, his breath on her neck and his touch at her hips was almost too much for her. "You mean, do I often get kidnapped by mad scientists? No."

"Your desire." His fingers strayed to her other thigh. "It seems out of character for a keeper. For any witch. I've never smelled a woman as hot as you."

"I told you already, I'm not..." She hissed when he tapped her between the legs. "I'm not discussing that."

"I need to know all the variables. I want to study you."

"Study?"

"I want to form a new hypothesis." He rubbed the wet satin over her pussy, his fingers sliding, sliding. "I want you. I want to run tests on you. I want to perform experiments on your body. Your magic. Your abilities. Your reactions to stimuli." He drew his fingernail across her clit, and she gasped. "I want to dissect you."

"Sounds painful." Painful and hedonistic. When could they start?

"I won't use a knife." A claw grazed her, applying sharp pressure to her inner thigh. Her legs parted to escape it. He scratched with all four fingers, right across her pussy, the underwear not enough barrier, and too much of one. "But I'll need to take samples."

He licked beneath her ear then, a long, slow stroke. The softness of his tongue contrasted with the claws between her legs. One razor-tipped finger located her clit. Katie jerked as electricity shot through her. "Undo my handcuffs."

"No." He nibbled her earlobe, her neck, her jawline. Whiskers and teeth. Soft lips and wet tongue. Claws teasing her, tickling her. "That variable isn't part of today's experiment."

"I'm a lab rat now?" She'd be anything he wanted at this point.

"Test subject. Do you consent?" His belt buckle dug into her hip as he maneuvered his leg across her. Claws pricked her lower belly. Slid down. Beneath her panties.

Oh, Goddess. She couldn't breathe, so she whimpered.

"I'll take that as a yes," he said, his voice deeper, more growly.

He was right, of course. But she wasn't going to say it.

"Describe the sensations when I do this." He laced his claws through her curls. The tips pricked her flesh, outside her slit. "Could you use magic right now? Or are you too agitated?"

"Give me my—" her boast was interrupted when he slipped a claw oh so carefully into her folds, parting her "—lavender and find out."

He smiled against her neck, arrogantly secure in his command. She was his, and he knew it.

"What about when I do this?" The pad of one finger located her clitoris. Skin to skin. She moaned. "Your heart rate jumped. I should have put you on a monitor. My systolic pressure reached approximately one hundred seventy when I transformed, and my oxygen levels increased measurably."

He'd been measuring himself when he'd had sex with his wolf girlfriend? Who was this guy? "Shut up."

He inhaled, his breath hot on her neck. "You smell so good. I could almost…" His teeth latched on to her, a burst of pain, while he continued to touch her clit, barely moving, taunting her.

Then he flicked her.

Katie's hips jerked instinctively. She tugged her arms, struggling enough for him to notice.

He laughed. Claws raked her outer labia. His fingertip began to stroke the slick bud of her clitoris the way she needed. She pressed her cheek to his forehead, her lips on his skin. She said his name. At her response, her compliance, his movements became rougher.

"Marcus. You should stop." He should stop before she was reduced to begging him to keep going.

His rumble of displeasure burrowed into her. He didn't like her to tell him what to do. "No."

"Don't…" Goddess, how could she say this? He licked her pulse point, and she shuddered. "Don't stab anything important."

His touch disappeared.

Was he actually stopping? She was such a hypocrite. Saying no, meaning yes. Giving women and witches everywhere a bad name.

She opened her mouth to thank him anyway. His blunt fingers returned to her before she said a word. He parted her, finding the opening of her vagina and sweeping a groan from her.

No claws.

"So wet." His voice was barely human. "Katie, I'm weak. I can't wait. I want to make you come. Say yes."

He rubbed moisture up to her clit, catching the erect bud so perfectly she flinched. His intentions had firmed like the rest of him. He was forging ahead.

Scientist. Kidnapper. Wolf. To hell with common sense. To hell with the risks. Katie wanted Marcus.

She angled her face toward his, seeking his lips. "Yes."

That was when he froze. His head came up and he growled, low and deep.

"Someone's here."

Not even a wolf's reaction time was enough to defend against the witch who kicked open the Airstream's door, hosing him down with cayenne pepper spray.

SEVEN

Marcus howled, rubbing his eyes, which would only make the cayenne spray worse. He shook his head like the wolf he was before crashing to the floor.

Katie sat up and squinted at the fracas. "What are you doing here?"

"I'm the cavalry." Tonya, about to advance on Marcus and lay the second of the one-two punch on him, raised her eyebrows at Katie. "Oh. My. Should I not have come to rescue you?"

"No, no." Katie, thoroughly embarrassed but thankful for Tonya's appearance, tried to make herself decent without her clothes. "Knock him out."

Marcus, huddled on the floor, whined. Her cayenne spray was not a delicate defense, and he would be in great discomfort.

"Faster. He's in pain," Katie demanded.

"Working on it." Tonya patted his hand, jerking back when his claws got her. "Down, fella. Let me take the hurt away."

Magic built and popped through the trailer, knocking Marcus out. Finishing the spell would not only put him to sleep but would defuse the cayenne. When he woke, the agony would be just a memory.

Or, if Katie had her way, he wouldn't remember any of this. Her cayenne blend didn't interfere with the poppy mix—they'd been formulated to be compatible.

Blood dripped from a shallow claw mark on Tonya's hand. She shook the spray bottle. "Never thought I'd have to use your wolf-pel."

Katie pulled the sheet up to her neck. "Where's Ba?"

"Keeping the car running so we can make our getaway."

They wouldn't be making an immediate getaway. They'd be wiping Marcus first. This was their best shot. She didn't think they could keep him restrained long enough for the situation to improve—and she didn't trust herself not to be seduced again.

"I need my glasses." The spray, a weapon from her keeper days, might not work against Marcus much longer than her original sedative. "We can't dawdle. I have no idea how long he'll be asleep."

Tonya handed her the frames. "Days, poor guy."

"He's done something to himself so sleep spells don't take." The spray, a mix of cayenne, poppy and other herbs, could knock out a whole pack of fractious beasts. It had a wider range than spell pods, which required aim instead of simply depressing a button.

"Not surprised. He's smart as hell," Tonya said.

Katie used the needle in her glasses to ping the simple lock of the handcuffs. She scuttled out of the bed. Pants… there. Her shirt was ruined. From Marcus's drawer, she liberated a top that hung on her like a sack dress.

Tonya watched her with amusement and concern.

"We, um." Katie's cheeks burned. "He was trying to convince me to, um…"

"Umm," Tonya said salaciously. "Are you sure about this? You should consider the benefits of getting this sex thing out of your system. Marcus is ideal, and it's obvious he has the hots for you."

"He kidnapped me and threatened to slit my throat."

"You knew he wouldn't hurt you. You loved every minute of it."

Katie rubbed her forehead. "There are more important things at stake than my love life. How did you find me?"

"Had to call a guy about a dog," Tonya said gruffly. Her lips pinched with annoyance. "We'll pay for it soon enough."

Katie would get the details of that, she was sure, but right now they had a duty. "Did you bring the poppy memory blend?"

Her friend sighed. "You're a wet blanket to end all wet blankets." But she'd already agreed with the wisdom of wiping Marcus once. "Zhang Li brought it. Stubborn old man. If you insist on doing this, I suppose I have to fetch him."

"Scrub your hands," Katie barked at her father and Tonya as soon as they returned to the trailer. "Give me the poppy mix. We don't have much time."

Katie heard the water in the sink gush. She dropped to her knees at Marcus's side. His face didn't have that peaceful, relaxed expression like when he'd been faking sleep. His floors—his whole trailer—were neat as a pin, but Marcus himself was a mess.

She wrestled his pepper-sprayed shirt over his head and ran a wet washcloth over his face. Mixes that weren't oil-based washed away easier. She wiped his neck and hair too, then each finger on his elegant hands, trying not to think how recently one of them had been between her legs. She traded the cloth for another and touched up his arms. The cayenne mix wouldn't skew the wipe, but it might complicate it.

She didn't want to do this spell. Didn't want to risk a life wipe with three witches. But they had to try. Marcus's discovery of them could get them all killed. Lars would never rest until she was dead—until they were all dead.

Marcus might have honest chi and captivating fingers, but he couldn't control the future. The longer Katie let him coax her, the more she'd want to believe in his cause.

She couldn't afford causes. She had a family to protect.

"Come on, come on." She motioned for the other two to join her. Not even Dad argued, though he muttered under his breath about arthritis as he knelt beside the prone man. "Don't stop me if it feels like I'm pulling out your fingernails. The power drain's going to hurt." It wouldn't be easy struggling through the next couple days on empty, but they were out of options.

Marcus hadn't left them any—not any reasonable ones. Avoiding tomorrow's patrol was one thing. Avoiding the keepers was another. Marcus had been deliberately vague, but how close on his muscular, well-shaped tail was their mutual enemy?

"You make it sound lovely," Tonya said. Neither she nor Dad hesitated to give Katie full access to their reserves. She could sense them opening up to her.

She'd be the focal, the spell wielded by her. She'd be the one doing this to Marcus, who seemed to be a wolf who didn't deserve it.

He was different. She wished she could trust him. Keep him. And other things. To him, she'd said yes and would say it again given half the chance.

No. She couldn't think like that. Not safe, not safe at all.

Katie unceremoniously dumped the baggie's contents on Marcus's bare chest. They all stuck their hands in the mixture, fingertips touching. Dad grumbled. The cayenne was a hot burn on her skin.

"Here goes." No time for delicacy. Katie opened up and poured all the energy inside her into Marcus.

The considerable torrent she mustered ripped the magic out of her father and Tonya like a tornado splintering a barn. Tonya squawked. Dad cussed some more. The three of them had never joined in a spell this urgent. Katie hoped they wouldn't pass out, but she'd need everything they possessed for a chance of making this work.

She centered on the poppy mixture, forcing magic through the organic particles and crowbarring open Marcus's spirit. The world blanked out, and she was inside him.

He didn't want her here. She knew that. But they never did.

His sense of self and his memories leaped into being around her, an endless, many-dimensioned jigsaw of experiences and sensations, thoughts and impressions. As far as she could see, his life lay before her, hazed by a faint layer of poppy. She didn't like going in with him asleep, but she'd have to compensate.

Katie took threads of power and dove. She soon remembered the routine, searching out the pieces of Marcus's life that needed to be tweaked. She couldn't interpret them like pictures or videos. She had to sense them. Find the parts of him that were witch and erase them.

Take his life away from him.

There. And there. Those parts. Katie nudged him, rearranging his substance. Changing his memories to keep witches hidden. It had never before seemed so unethical. Every slice of his essence she manipulated felt like a hook in her stomach, gutting her with wrongness. Her ears rang as she drained herself too quickly.

The skeins of power thinned…wisps in her grasp. This

shouldn't be happening so soon! She should have added more cayenne. She had to have more magic. But where?

Could she get it from him? Desperate, she probed his essence, seeking the magic he claimed was no different than hers. The force that allowed him to change from wolf to man.

There it was, the lattice. Instead of a soft wellspring and thousands of connections like a witch had, it was a bright heart with a single channel. As if he could only work one spell.

Why had she never noticed this inside a wolf before?

Because she'd never looked for a wolf's lattice. Because she'd never cared.

Katie wavered. Pieces of Marcus began to snap back into their original positions. She reached desperately for his power, only to be smacked viciously out of the lattice, rubber whips stinging every inch of her skin. She was buffeted to one side, then the other, losing more and more of the spell. She tried desperately to control the magic, Marcus's memories, but she simply didn't have enough of a foundation to do this.

Three people and a pile of cayenne couldn't do this.

She delved inside herself further than she ever had before and came up short.

Story of her life.

Her inadequate push rebounded off him as if he were convex. It smashed into Katie…and ricocheted off her in turn.

Harmful magic couldn't affect a convex witch. But it had to go somewhere. It was going somewhere.

That was Katie's last, terrified realization before she blacked out.

"Wake up." A hand patted her cheek. "Katie."

Pain shot from temple to temple like a shish kebab.

Katie whimpered as she became conscious. She had a magic hangover the size of a tractor-trailer, and she'd rather sleep this shit off. "Owwwww."

"What's wrong with the girl, Doc?" her father asked. "Is she sick?"

"Are you okay, Ba?" The last thing she remembered was the unfinished wipe bouncing off her. "How's Tonya?"

"Out here," Tonya called happily. Why couldn't Katie open her eyes? "That's me, right?"

An ominous suspicion joined the skewer of pain in her head. She grasped the hand near her face and levered herself to her side, gritting her teeth. She appeared to be on a bed instead of the floor. Her body ached like elephants had used her as a trampoline. Her magical reserves were completely nonexistent. She was amazed she was conscious.

Regretting it as soon as she did it, Katie let Dad help her sit up and opened her eyes.

Surprise. Dad wasn't holding her. It was Marcus, and he looked really fucking pissed.

"She's not dead." Dad, at the foot of Marcus's bed, nodded with satisfaction. "Good. What happened to you, girl? Were you in the accident?"

"What do you mean?" Katie, who was still, thankfully, wearing her glasses, stared past Marcus's grim expression to her father. "You don't remember?"

"Should I?" Dad asked warily.

"You experienced a significant misfire when you attempted your ill-advised stunt," Marcus informed her pleasantly. He'd donned a blue dress shirt at some point.

She pressed a hand to her roiling stomach. "What happened?"

An attractive, fortyish blonde woman reentered the

trailer, tying a knot in her oversized shirt. It was Tonya...
minus her pants, one hundred pounds and a decade.

"Hi there," she said cheerfully, pausing for a big yawn.
"Is this your motor home? I wanted to thank you for the
use of it. I seem to have, ah, forgotten what I'm doing
here." She lifted her hands in resignation. "Your wonderful boyfriend is going to take us to the hospital as soon
as we get you mobile."

Katie exchanged a horrified glance with Marcus. She
was horrified; he was furious. It had nothing to do with
Tonya's assumption of their involvement. "What about
my father? How's he?"

"The same," Marcus answered in a low voice.

"I'm not your dad, kid." Her father's appearance,
while haggard, hadn't changed like Tonya's had. Obviously Katie had been right that Tonya had been masked
the whole time they'd known her.

"How much of them is missing?" she asked.

If it took a coven to poppy someone, it took two covens
to restore memories...when they could be restored. The
keeper council rarely had reason to revert wipes. Since
this hadn't been intentional, were the losses temporary?

"You took their witch. You took their lives." Marcus's
smile wasn't kind. "You won't fool me again. You're a
devil, like the keepers said."

Katie wanted to close her eyes, roll over and pretend
this was a bad dream. Wake up without the pain and
nausea and relive today, minus...Marcus. She was dev-
astated. Completely empty. She had no defenses, no of-
fenses, no answers, no ideas, no anything. "You'd have
done the same thing in my position."

"You're wrong. I've never been foolhardy enough to
try that with three practitioners and some cayenne. You
brought this on yourself, Chang Cai."

"Thought her name was Katie," Dad said. "Is Chang Cai her Chinese name?"

Tonya looked at Dad. "You're Chinese."

"I am not," he argued, thumping his cane. His nature seemed intact, which wasn't going to help anyone during this crisis.

"You lost your memories too, Li," Tonya said sympathetically. "Dr. Marcus says we were in some kind of accident that affected us nemo…nero…"

"Neurologically," Marcus offered. "That's my professional opinion. I believe it was a gas leak. You're in no further danger."

"Whatever it was, it plumb wore me out." Whatever Marcus had told Tonya and Dad, it wasn't freaking them out like most people would be upon being stricken with amnesia. "Anyway, Li, you might want to check the mirror."

Dad hobbled into the tiny bathroom and cursed. "Oh, hell. I'm old."

"The one thing I don't understand is why my clothes don't fit." Tonya's nature seemed intact as well as Dad's. She eyed Marcus's backside appreciatively as he bent over Katie. "My pants wouldn't stay up. Chang Cai, hon, do you mind if I borrow some clothes? I don't want to go to the hospital in nothing but this shirt."

"It's Katie. And it's not my trailer. I don't have any clothes here." She shut her eyes and flopped down, unwilling to face Marcus's censure or Tonya's and her father's blankness.

"I guess my shirt covers everything important. Lord, am I tired. I need coffee."

A hot lump blocked Katie's throat. Marcus's silent, condemning presence only drove it home. They were in deep shit, and it was all her fault.

What was she going to do? She had no magic. As empty as she was, it wouldn't be restored for days. She couldn't call on a single coven to help with the memory loss, much less two. What witches would ever help Chang Cai, supposedly deceased former keeper and convex alpha?

None of them.

They'd just want her gone. Dead or otherwise out of the picture. There was a reason convex witches across the world devoted their lives to the keeper council, and it wasn't simply that the council forced the issue.

If the memory loss was permanent, how could she explain to Tonya and Dad what and who they were? They'd have to stopper their magic or who knew what would happen? Witches without knowledge were witches without control—not a direct equivalent to a feral shifter but hazardous nonetheless.

Moreover, any wolf who came near the three of them without masks would peg them as shifters who hadn't yet undergone the change. Juveniles. In theory, that's what witches were. But born wolves never went longer than their early twenties without turning.

Katie, barely old enough to start her second passthrough, could pass without a huge stretch, but Tonya looked forty. And Dad, well, there was no way his existence as a juvenile wolf was going unremarked.

She only had two days of Tonya's primed disguises in the go bag at the shop, and her stillroom was trashed. Tonya was the one who contacted Nathaniel when they needed anything, not Katie. He didn't know about her and Dad, and loyalty was everything to the sympathizers. He'd be furious to discover Tonya had tricked him into aiding and abetting Chang Cai for twenty years. He'd cast them all to the wolves. Literally.

How could Katie, without magic, without assistance, without anyone on her side, keep them safe?

Safe from wolves. Safe from witches. Safe from keepers. Safe from humans. Safe from…

Marcus.

"What are you going to do, Marcus?" she finally asked around the lump in her throat. Luckily the nausea had subsided. Why was he still here? He could have dumped them in the park and taken off the second he'd regained consciousness.

Revenge. It had to be revenge.

Marcus touched her cheek, stroking it in a way that would appear loving to an observer. His eyes paled, and Katie gulped. "If you want my help to clean up this mess, you're going to have to give me something in return, Katie. What I want is your cooperation in my research. All of my research."

EIGHT

Katie, Chang Cai, Black Widow, whoever she was, stared at Marcus for a long moment before resignation settled across her tired features. "We can draw up a standard consulting contract."

"For this? No." Marcus let himself stroke her warm cheek another few seconds, tipping her face up. Shadows of exhaustion darkened the skin beneath her eyes. The only reason he still desired her had to be her scent—luscious, leery and longing, all at the same time. "You owe me, and you need me. You're not in a position to bargain."

The time for negotiation had passed. Considering her biases, blackmail seemed like his best chance of success.

"Fine, fine. Just watch what you say." She rubbed the bridge of her nose. She probably had a monster headache. "You can't mention certain things around…the others."

"I worked for your council. I know." Newly wiped individuals had to be handled with kid gloves until their memory gaps adjusted. Katie's backfired spell seemed to have erased all supernatural knowledge from Tonya's and Zhang Li's heads. Upsetting them with information could have unintended consequences. It would also make it harder to restrict their movements.

He might be infuriated with them—mostly with Katie—but he wasn't stupid. If Birmingham wolves ran across people who smelled like juvenile witches but were this old, they'd investigate. Keepers would flock to this area like migrating swallows.

War between the packs, covens and keepers would be a negative for everyone.

"I know I screwed up," Katie said. "I just want to take care of our guests." She frowned at her father, who was watching them curiously. "We had to have been asleep for a couple hours. You did something to them, didn't you? Something I won't be able to do until I'm strong again."

"Correct." When they'd woken, he'd dosed a panicky Tonya and Zhang Li with a calming mix. It was the common form of another blend keepers used to force the truth out of someone when torture failed. He'd also told Tonya and Zhang Li he was a doctor, which was true—he just wasn't a medical doctor. "I estimate I'll need to do it again in six hours."

"Nobody did anything to me," Zhang Li said. "I just can't remember today or who you people are. And I'm tired as a sloth."

"I remember who I am," Tonya said. "I'm a makeup and tattoo artist." She peeked down her voluminous shirt. "I don't seem to have tattoos, though."

"I do ink too." Zhang Li had a Chinese dragon on his forearm that actually looked like a dragon. Presumably Katie hadn't created it. "See here."

While Tonya and Zhang Li discussed tattoos and Katie watched them with a very un-Chang Cai-like expression of misery, Marcus considered their situation.

"If you two would give us a minute?" he asked Katie's father and Tonya. Marcus had confiscated their keys. On foot, they couldn't wander anywhere he couldn't find them.

Katie glanced at Marcus fearfully when the Airstream's door snicked shut behind them. "What do they remember?"

"Nothing that would confuse them. They think they're human." He hadn't delved into their recollections. There was too much to secure before he could worry about more of Chang Cai's victims.

"Do you think it's permanent?"

"Your intentions were permanent when you cast the spell on me. What do you think?"

"I don't know." Her chin trembled, and her lashes clumped as tears filled her eyes. "I've never heard of a witch undergoing an accidental life wipe. I guess nobody besides me has ever been dumb enough to try it with three people."

Who would have thought the Black Widow was a weeper? He hated the fact he wanted to comfort her. She didn't deserve comfort. She was manipulative and dishonest. If he could read her chi, no doubt it would be as black as her heart. He touched the bay capsule in his pocket to remind himself what she was capable of.

"Your father and Tonya chose to participate," he conceded after a tear trickled down her cheek. "Your being convex undoubtedly made it worse on your accomplices."

Vulnerable, almost pitiful, she drew her knees to her chest. Her short, glossy hair cowlicked in all directions, and she hugged her legs. "I agree. This is my fault. What's our next move?"

"I told you. I'm going to conduct experiments. You're going to facilitate them."

"What, right now?" she asked, startled. "With the patrol tomorrow, and whoever else is after you, don't we have other things to worry about?" Katie's lips pursed obstinately even as her gaze skittered away from his. "I guess we can get it over with."

She might want to sleep with him, but she seemed unhappy to do so on his terms. Perhaps he should have dosed her with the calming mix as well.

Except, did he want her pliant? It would be satisfying to boss her around when she was fighting him. That was his wolf talking—and for a change, he didn't care. He was done being respectful, done battling his urges. She'd had her chance to treat him as an equal and blown it.

"The fact is, most of the experiments will involve your magic, not your body."

"Oh." She pleated the hem of his T-shirt between her fingers. "Well...good."

He wondered if she realized how disappointed she sounded. This woman confused him more than anyone he'd ever met. "Can you read chi?"

"I know the basics from Tonya."

With someone as powerful as Katie, innate skill mattered less than it did for other witches. "Should be enough. I can access chi and the lattice from that." Comparing her chi and lattice graphs to the ones from his and his lady friend's coitus should be informative.

She dropped her gaze to the pale coverlet. "For what it's worth, I'm sorry I tried to poppy you. I wanted to be done with that type of work. Done with the keepers."

She smelled sincere, but he didn't budge. How many of her responses was she able to fake? Her lust—was it real? Her regret? Was this one of the reasons she'd been such a deadly opponent? Wolves had no reason to disbelieve what their noses told them.

He couldn't trust her words or her scent. He couldn't trust the way she'd clung to him, the way she'd parted her thighs for him. He couldn't trust the slippery, hot memory of her pussy beneath his fingers and the sweetness of her skin between his teeth.

He might not be able to trust himself.

"I need to set some rules." He crossed his arms. "When I make decisions, they aren't suggestions. They're orders. It's unproductive to argue all the time." It made it harder for him to concentrate on the science, when his wolf rose to her constant challenges.

Her countenance switched from vulnerable to stony in an instant. Ah, there was the Chang Cai of legend. Back again, like the split personality from hell. "I agreed to cooperate with your experiments. I didn't agree to be treated like I have no rights."

"Do you want my help with your father and Tonya?" She twitched. He continued. "Or do you want me to leave you to stew in your own mess?"

"I could avoid the patrol."

"But can you safeguard your father and Tonya alone?"

"You think you've got me, don't you?" she said, eyes glittering. "Keep in mind, Marcus, that sooner or later, I'm not going to need your help anymore."

"Sooner or later isn't now." He required her presence after her full strength returned if some of his theories were going to be tested. Could he handle her then? Monkshood antidote or no monkshood antidote, he couldn't protect against everything. He wouldn't have the advantage when she had power…unless he found a sterile environment to keep her in.

Or another hold over her.

"You can't life wipe me alone," he told her. "And just like you could make one phone call to ruin me, I could make that phone call too. I could ruin you and your family."

"Fuck you."

"Soon enough," he said, unable to keep from stooping to her level. "I'm looking forward to it. Are you?"

She sighed, her spine bending, and rested her chin on her knees. Vulnerable again. Which Chang Cai was the true face? "I'm not going to answer that."

"It doesn't have to be unpleasant. I'll just require detailed reports." Even now, her scent was faintly layered by interest. He wished there was a test to discover whether that, at least, was authentic.

"What do you want me to say? That I find you attractive?" She slipped off the bed and picked up the pieces of her ripped T-shirt. "Is that in question after what happened?"

"Your responses were genuine?" Damn, that sounded insecure. "Authenticity is critical. Data fabrication will only hinder research that could benefit all of us."

She huffed. "Data fabrication. Wow. I can't fake certain things any more than you can."

Spells could create lust, but she wouldn't have had the opportunity to doctor herself. Granted, she was Chang Cai. Would it be wise to put anything past her or reveal anything about himself she could manipulate?

Such as how close he'd come to pleasuring her before setting his environmental protocols, his charts and the digital recording device to log responses. He'd almost taken her because he wanted to, to hell with research. He couldn't be led by the wolf with science on the line.

When the memory of his sister was on the line. He'd never missed Elisa more than he had in the long, lonely year since he'd turned wolf. With a cure for cancer, a way to deactivate the need for keepers, what had happened to her would never happen to any witch again.

"I'll accept your physical reaction for now," he said, "but I'll need to investigate it later. Step by step."

"I already said yes."

He remembered her halting gasp when he'd stroked

her and the feel of her lips against his face. He remembered her fingers squeezing his. How many times would he need to melt her to believe it was real? "But you didn't say please."

She reddened again. "I realize you're enjoying this, but it serves no purpose."

"I disagree. It all factors in to my computations." One had to understand how and why witches succumbed to the wolf before one could reverse the process. Witches beat the wolf in their teens. Why did they fail to beat the wolf later? Why was sex the trigger? Why did alphas remain witches? He had theories but had only partly confirmed them. Marcus had wondered whether he could withstand the wolf using knowledge as his guide, but clearly he hadn't.

Witch magic and wolf magic were practically identical. Only the lattice—the metaphysical reservoir—changed. Logic said the transformation should go both ways. Witch could become wolf. Wolf could become witch. It should only be a matter of expertise and focus. He needed a test subject.

He needed Katie.

"Right now we both want the same thing." After rubbing her eyes, she used the T-shirt scraps to sweep the herbal residue on the floor into a pile. "To stay hidden. Let's worry about the rest later."

"I want more than that," he said softly. "But we'll postpone phase one until I calculate the experiment variables." Or he could try. The sight of her on the floor, at his feet, his shirt gaping around her neck…

He hadn't been this stupidly horny since he was a teenager. Visualizing the periodic table wasn't righting him like it should, so he turned away to fetch a dustpan.

"You're the expert." She gathered the last of the dust in a pile and rested on her knees.

"Technically, I've only engaged in witch and wolf intercourse once."

She licked her lips. "What is it you *do* hope to prove?"

"That wolves and witches are interchangeable." He waved his dustpan. "I want my magic back, my longevity, my discipline. But I want the wolf too. I want the strength and these senses, to be able to heal from wounds and diseases. I want protection from ever being at the keepers' beck and call again. Protection for everyone from the keepers and their methods. We've no need of them if we can shift between forms at will, Katie. And I want…"

He wanted to go back in time and stop his sister. She'd been so desperate to stay alive for her baby she'd done the unthinkable. Then he'd done it himself. If it couldn't be undone, it was possible he'd wasted his life and hers. "I want to know everything."

"Lofty, but there's no animal inside me." She patted her chest, swallowed up by his T-shirt. "It's gone. One hundred percent witch, no wolf."

"She's there. As much a part of you as your magic. Why wouldn't you want access to that power? You're only half of yourself as a witch."

"That's ridiculous. Did you feel like an animal before you screwed up, Marcus?"

"I didn't screw up," he said, disappointed in her. Why would she understand what it meant to lose one's family? Her father was still alive. "And I'm not an animal. I dated a nice young lady for several weeks before I accepted her offer to stay overnight. At that time I carefully analyzed the process by which—"

"You did it on purpose." She shook her head, bemused. "I knew you were unique, but now I know you're nuts.

Maybe there was a wolf inside you, but there's not one inside me."

Marcus smiled at her, feeling predatory. She was so confident, so certain that she was better than him, yet they were the same.

He couldn't wait to prove it.

He was going to make her lose control. Maybe that would help him recapture his.

"Let's go back to your shop after I…" *Tie you to the bed. Taste every inch of your body. Take you until your wolf makes you howl.* "…pack as many supplies as I can." Many spell-grade components were available from limited sources, expensive or perishable. They should load up on what Katie already had on hand. "I assume you have standard protection wards on your building?"

"Yes." Standard protections would keep their essences, masks or no masks, concealed from wolves or witches outside the apartment.

Marcus positioned the dustpan near the pile she'd collected and handed her a whisk broom. "What time does the patrol usually hit your street?"

"Midmorning. Not much around for them to check." She guided the residue into the dustpan. "I won't be able to renew the protections. I have enough primed disguise spells to get us through two days, but that's it. Will you need a disguise?"

He preferred to stay out of the patrol's sensing range, not rely on his masks. It was tricky, as a wolf, to get his hands on more. "Yes and no. We should avoid the patrol."

"We can do that."

"When do you predict you'll be restored?" And when would he have to start keeping her away from organic substances that could be used to incapacitate or kill him?

As sly as she'd been with the lavender, it was conceivable daily strip searches might be required.

Such hardship.

"Don't know. Four days? Five? I don't mend fast when I'm out of practice."

Most witches didn't bounce back quickly from a comprehensive drain, and if Katie were alpha, she'd have that much further to go. Her combat bonus, where a convex witch's refill rate accelerated in a crisis, wouldn't kick in immediately. And a witch who didn't have enough power to cast a spell in the first place couldn't access cayenne for a boost. "What about for less costly spells, like the true eye?"

"A day." She finally looked at him, squatted on the floor beside her. "If I waste my energy on small magic, it will be that much longer before I top off. Unless...I could drain myself repeatedly. Might be smart to trigger my combat bonus."

"Don't worry about it." She'd be easier to manage with limited magic. Monkshood took a lot of energy. "I'll hide you...as long as you keep me happy."

THEY SPENT A restless night in Katie's apartment, he and Katie in her bedroom, Zhang Li in his and Tonya in hers. Marcus had to redose Zhang Li at the six-hour mark, though Tonya showed no signs of becoming a problem. As for Katie, she'd cooperated with a watchful stillness that did nothing to hide the fact she was probably plotting, every second, how she was going to escape him.

He'd gotten tired of the staring and popped her with a sleep spell. Neither of them was going to rest otherwise. Her bed was big enough that they didn't have to come into physical contact. To his wolf, that didn't matter. He could smell her and feel every wiggle of her body on the mattress. It was enough to keep him, and his cock, alert.

Luckily wolves didn't need as much sleep as witches who'd been drained.

The sun barely peeked through the window in Katie's bedroom. He turned to look at her. In sleep, she lost her frown, her wariness, her flashes of guilt and doom. They resonated with him, so similar to the guilt he felt over his failure to protect his sister and the doom he felt whenever he considered his mad experiment might come to naught.

He'd lost his family. She didn't want to lose hers. They had that in common, but it hadn't been enough for her to overlook her prejudice against wolves.

Katie's cheek pillowed on her fist. He hadn't secured her to the headboard since the sleep spell would last the night if he didn't wake her.

This was probably the only time he'd get away with that. With every sleep, every moment of rest, her power would build, along with her poise. He'd do what he could to keep her from getting her hands on any spell components, but he'd keep a bay capsule on him at all times.

Marcus had planned his exile for years, plotting wolf territories and patrol schedules, setting up safe houses with labs, memorizing everything he could about keeper operations.

The near miss in California had driven him to the southern United States. Some packs' border patrols were harder to predict, but Birmingham's alpha was former military and prided himself on discipline. The keepers' and elders' efforts centered in West Virginia under the belief Marcus would turn to the Travises.

He'd cultivated the Travises prior to his transformation but had only pretended to go to them afterward. On one hand, it meant they weren't a resource. On the other, de-

spite having to redirect his study, he'd made some progress, mastering various aspects of the shift. Retaining
tattoos and clothing was the first step in changing what
he wanted, how he wanted. It was the first step toward
regaining his witch...and his security.

With Katie, he was about to take giant leaps. He
couldn't deny his excitement. He was mentally stimulated. Physically stimulated. He had a hard-on right now,
in brain and body, due to the woman beside him.

He smoothed a piece of black hair off Katie's forehead.
Should he exclude her from decision-making or attempt
to win her over? If his experiments succeeded, it could
solve both their problems. The covens would embrace
the ability to rescue the transformed and heal cancer and
would presumably protect him and Katie from Lars and
the council.

Ultimately, Marcus believed they'd disband the council or redirect it to beneficial tasks instead of death and
destruction.

It would be better to have Katie as a partner, but he'd
only known her a day. Better that he keep her dependent.
Vulnerable. He couldn't lose sight of who she really was.

Today he'd have to protect three people who couldn't
be trusted. Zhang Li and Tonya weren't trustworthy because they knew nothing. They could wander into trouble easily. Katie wasn't trustworthy because she knew
almost everything.

Today would be complicated.

Tonight would be his reward.

NINE

"YOU DON'T GET one." Marcus plucked the pill out of Katie's hand before she could use it to turn herself into a person no wolf would look twice at. Marcus had woken her an hour ago, at eight, and Katie estimated that the house protections were now gone.

Was he an idiot? She needed that mask.

"Give me that." Katie lunged for it, but he let her bounce off his shoulder. He dropped the pill into the bottle and the bottle into an overnight bag.

He caught her chin and tilted her face toward him.

Patronizer. She slapped his hand. "No touchie, no feelie."

"Hold still. That's an order." He'd given her several orders this morning, out of her father's and Tonya's hearing, and had reminded her what would happen if she didn't obey.

So she stood, fists clenched, as he softly drew a fingertip from her forehead to her temple to her chin. He'd been touching her all morning, which he claimed was to convince Tonya and her father of their relationship.

Her father and Tonya were downstairs right now.

"No wrinkles," he said. "You're young enough to pass. Save the spell."

Katie wanted to kiss him. He probably knew it too. But more than that, she wanted to kick him. Thank goodness she hadn't lost her brain entirely. The Birmingham patrol was due in two hours or less, and Marcus had spent the morning side-eyeing her while joking with Dad and Tonya as if they were his friends. Granted, one had to treat the recently wiped with care, but did he have to treat her like pond scum?

If he'd just smile at her, she might…

Throw herself at him.

She hated him. She needed him. She couldn't quit thinking about sex with him. Partly because he kept touching her and partly because, well, she wasn't blind.

The man was gorgeous.

Would it be tonight? Would he…would he enjoy it? Or would it be a demeaning, mechanized experience?

The kitchen clock ticked loudly, emphasizing what was at stake. Katie should be eradicating all evidence witches had ever been here. She knew the process. It shouldn't take long. She, Dad and Tonya lived in a way that allowed them to mount a quick escape. Yet she'd put off shredding papers, burying simples and pushing Marcus to go, go, go. Instead she'd made everyone eggs and bacon for breakfast.

Without being ordered to.

She trailed Marcus into the living room. He hadn't ordered her to stay in the kitchen, and he hadn't ordered her to drop the subject.

"What if we can't avoid the patrol? I need that mask. We're talking a twenty-foot radius. At least, that's how far wolves could sense an unmasked witch when I was a…" *Keeper honeypot.* "In my prior occupation."

He shrugged. "You're of age." Juvenile wolves weren't all minors. "I'll say you belong to me."

"Like that will matter," she scoffed. Tonya and Dad were downstairs filling a tattoo kit, per Marcus's instructions. He kept glancing at the store camera, as did she, so she knew he wasn't a hundred percent comfortable with the separation. "They'll force us all to join the pack. Me, you, Ba, Tonya. You're withholding my mask to bully me, and it puts us all at risk."

He adjusted the volume on the television. "How long will the mask last?"

"Thirty-six hours." Tonya was a master of disguises. Most spells lasted twenty-four hours, tops.

"No can do. I don't want you to have a mask on. I'm not using one either, so it's not bullying. It's procedure."

"You're not masked?" she yelled, stiffening. "Jesus. They can sense you a lot farther than twenty feet away."

Calmly, he rubbed his chin as if reconsidering. "I don't want either of us to have anything on tonight, Katie. At all."

She tried so very hard not to blush and failed. "Oh. Right."

"While we're on the subject, are you ovulating?" Marcus's expression didn't change, but his stare unnerved her. "I'll need to procure condoms."

Why was she insulted by the fact he didn't seem enthused by the idea of sex with her? She shouldn't care. But she did.

He raised his eyebrows. "Your heart rate just increased."

"I'm stressed."

"Finish packing."

She stomped into the bedroom, grabbed the go bag from the closet floor and tossed it on the unmade bed. "I finished fifteen minutes ago. Tonya's and Dad's bags are complete too."

"I know. I put them next to the door. I just assumed since yours was in your closet, you weren't done." Coming up behind her, he reached for it. "Does it have more space? I'd like to pack extra simples."

She didn't want him touching her luggage, so she tapped his watch. "We should go. If we're not going to mask, we don't have a huge safety radius."

"Large enough."

"Don't be so sure. Have you considered that the two of us together might be more…noticeable?"

"Tonya did say we make an attractive couple." His hands settled on her shoulders, and he set her aside as if moving a piece of furniture.

"Marcus," she said, hoping to divert him from her duffel, "it's a legitimate question."

"You mistrust my self-preservation instincts?"

He was too close to the bed for her to wedge herself between him and her luggage without being obvious. "It seems like you're being careless."

"I'm never careless. I've avoided Birmingham for six months. I know my radius well." He unzipped her bag, the corner of his mouth curling up when she growled at him in irritation. He sorted through her possessions until he located the items she'd secreted with the more innocuous things. He pulled out the spell baggies and a small bottle labeled Shampoo. "Aren't these supposed to be in the case with your organics?"

"I was in a hurry."

He set the baggies aside and sniffed the bottle. "Tut, tut. What do you need with a strong emetic?"

Dammit. It had been like pulling teeth to stow those things while he'd been staring a hole through her every move. If he found what was inside her tampons, she was really going to hear about it. "I figure at some point in the next five days I might want to puke."

"It's harmful. It wouldn't affect you. What could you

mean to do with it? Are you old enough to remember when *Arsenic and Old Lace* was first in theaters?"

"Are you?" she shot back.

"Born in 1908." Witches didn't reveal their ages easily, and it surprised her that he'd just...shared. As if they were friendly. "You?"

It shouldn't hurt to share back. "1941."

"Not quite juvenile," he said generously.

"I was twenty-one when the council..." Took over her entire life and twisted her into a secret weapon he had good reason to hate. He didn't want to know anything about her except what she could do for his research. "Never mind."

"I gather they don't give convex witches much choice." He refolded her clothing more neatly than she'd packed it. "Could your father not protect you?"

Those were not the days of her life she cared to remember. "Why would he? Convex witches are unnatural and wrong. We warp the precious gift." She fluttered her fingers at him. "Ooooh, evil. That's what normal witches think."

Her father, in the past twenty years, had come around, but they'd not had a healthy relationship while she'd been with the keepers. She hadn't had anything healthy or good while she'd been with the keepers.

Marcus frowned. She wondered if he realized she was throwing his own words back at him. "Evil's a strong word."

"I'm a strong witch."

"I could formulate a side study of convex versus regular magic."

She crossed her arms. "Why?"

"The unknown causes fear. Fear makes people assume the wrong thing." He cleared his throat. "Also, such a study could be fascinating. The keepers wouldn't let me see their materials, but with you on staff, I could eliminate a lot of…unknowns."

"So I'm staff?" She let out an amazed laugh. "Will I be getting a salary? Perhaps a glowing letter of recommendation when we're through?"

He just smiled, that awful, awful smile that made her want to jump him in a sexual way. Setting her clothes aside, he returned to her bag. With a sniff, he located a packet of herbs in a pair of socks. Then, to her dismay, he opened her zippered pouch of feminine articles. "Sachets?"

"Tampons," she said. "You were curious about my menstrual cycle. Put those in your database."

He smelled the pouch anyway. "Interesting hiding place." He withdrew the fake tampon, ripped off the carefully glued paper and held up the finger-sized tube of herbs. "But I assure you, you don't need to give me the gift of extra libido."

He slid it into his trouser pocket while Katie did her best to maintain a poker face. If she'd sprinkled any of that delightful medley into his food, he'd have become as distracted as she was, and—maybe—she could have overcome her wolf lust long enough to neutralize a rapacious beast intent on having sex with her.

A dangerous ploy if she didn't want to be forcibly seduced. Lust spells and wolves were…combustible. But technically, Marcus was already planning to have sex with her. And she'd agreed. And she damn well wanted it, so she'd been willing to risk his combustion.

"I forgot that was there," she deadpanned.

Marcus fiddled with the herbs in his pocket, studying her with narrow eyes. "Tonight you can fight me if that's what you enjoy in bed, but can't it wait? I have to ensure everyone's safety."

Even her ears grew hot at the images now in her mind. "That's hardly the reassurance I want." Goddess. She needed to nix the fantasizing and behave like an adult.

"What do you want?"

Him. She forced her mouth to speak other truths, though.

"I don't want you to underestimate the situation. Out of negligence, out of a desire to scare me, I don't know. I don't care." She took a deep breath and exhaled to calm the butterflies. "I've agreed to work with you and I understand your motivation, but I don't want your choices to endanger my father and Tonya. And me, of course. I sure as hell don't want the keepers to find out I'm alive."

"You've fooled Lars into thinking you were dead for twenty years," Marcus said, repacking her bag. "I'm sure you have plenty of ideas for avoiding him."

"With magic," she insisted. "That's how we managed. My advice is, find a witch who can hide us until my magic comes back. That's what works, Marcus. We can't be shitting around with our lives. But I guess that's out of the question because you think you...know everything."

He zipped her duffel. "Yep."

"Are you not going to tell me any of your plans?" Katie paced across the room. She raked her fingers through her hair. Finally, finally, as thoughts of actually being found by Lars intruded, her sex obsession ebbed. "You must have nothing to tell. We need to make some calls. We might get lucky and dodge the patrol—but it's less likely the longer we hang around here." When he didn't immediately leap into action, she continued. "That doesn't help Ba and Tonya get their memories back. Our situation is desperate. I could telephone Vern."

She was babbling. Her mood had escalated into the panic she should have been feeling this whole time, and she was paying for the delay with a vengeance.

Zero to sixty in under ten seconds. She buzzed with a harsh panic she hadn't felt for years. They were going to get caught. Marcus was being a dumbass. Why were they lingering? They needed to mobilize hours ago to avoid the Birmingham patrol.

"I got the impression you don't want to rely on Vernon. What about Tonya's sympathizer friends?"

"They won't be her friends when they find out what she's been up to the past twenty years. They'll cut her off without question for helping me," Katie explained. "They aren't very forgiving."

Many sympathizers considered wolves to be their better aspects. Their attrition rate, however, wasn't as high as one would expect for witches who seemingly worshipped the wolf.

Purists, on the other hand, wanted all wolves dead. Lars had been rabid about it. Purism had been a calling for him, barely kept in check by region elders and various directors of the keepers. There were other purists on the council, but none as zealous as Lars.

Katie would have expected a council led by Lars to try to take over the world, but oddly enough it had become less effective once he had become director, according to Tonya.

"The sympathizers wouldn't help me either. They think I'm on the keepers' side," Marcus said.

"That leaves Vern. He'd hide us all." She might need to tell Vern a few lies to get him here, but once he arrived, the old donkey would do the right thing.

He always did.

"Vernon Harrower might be Harry Travis's friend, but

he won't hesitate to notify his fellow elders about me," Marcus said. "That's assuming he could reach us unnoticed. The Travises and Vernon are both being watched by the council."

"Lars hates him. Of course they spy on him. But Vern knows how to duck spies." Staying in touch with Katie had been child's play for the former director of the keepers.

"I realize you have great faith in Vernon's abilities, but it's not safe to contact him." He checked his watch and sighed. "Five minutes. Come here."

"What for?"

He just crooked his finger at her. She kicked a pillow on the floor, walked over to him and glared. "Is that an order?"

Marcus, completely unexpectedly, caught her in a strong embrace. He held her against him, no claws, no innuendoes, no comments about monkshood, and scuffed one big hand across her hair. "It's all right, Katie."

She hadn't cried today, but her throat lumped with a sudden threat of tears. "It's not all right. Third worst day ever."

"Not first?" he asked, stroking her neck and back. "I like to be first."

Damned competitive wolf. "The day they came to get me for the council and the day Lars tried to kill me were worse. You're number three on my list of suck. You'll have to try harder."

He laughed, a rumble that started deep in his chest. "If I told anyone Chang Cai, the dreaded Black Widow, could be funny, they wouldn't believe it."

"I didn't use to be," she said, relaxing against him. The life of a keeper hardly lent itself to comic relief. "I changed."

"I didn't use to be either."

She drew back and looked at him. "You're not funny."

"You're kidding, right? I got off some great one-liners yesterday when I was trying to impress the pretty tattooist."

"You were flirting with me before you knew I was a witch?" Was he flirting now? He didn't have to. This was a blackmail slash business relationship, and he'd garnered her cooperation by other means.

"You're clever, you're attractive and you smell really, really good." She didn't think he realized his eyes had flashed blue. "Of course I was flirting."

"Marcus," she said, licking her lips, "I want to get through today alive. If I know your plan, I can help with Ba and Tonya. I can help if anything goes wrong. I would do anything to save them the way they saved me twenty years ago. I would never put them at risk."

"Until yesterday."

"You and I both sucked yesterday. And now we can't be egoists fighting over who's giving orders and who's tricking whom."

He rested his cheek against her hair. "You're right."

"What is going to happen until my magic comes back? Tell me your strategy to keep us hidden. I don't give two shits about your research right now. The one thing you can definitely trust about me is that I don't want Lars to find out we're alive. That includes you."

"I don't need magic to take care of you and your family. I have a route planned that avoids the patrol. My Airstream is warded, and there's another location we'll go after that. I can't let you relay the address to anyone, but I won't let anyone hurt you."

Katie tried not to let the panic overwhelm her at the not knowing, at the helplessness. Marcus's arms around her comforted, as did the fact he was willing to hold her, but he was one man. Too much was at stake. "If the keepers find us together, they'll kill us."

"The benefits of our partnership outweigh the risks." One of his hands settled at the small of her back, while the other curved around her neck, steady and powerful. Her awareness of his body heightened. "Aren't you curious, Katie?"

"About what?"

His gaze lowered to her mouth. "So many years tracking witches seduced to the other side. Did you wonder how they could be so foolish?"

"No." She already knew why. Temptation in the form of a large, masculine hand was spreading across her back until his fingertips brushed the top of her ass. If she'd been sent against Marcus twenty years ago, would she have been able to resist him?

She sure as hell couldn't now.

"Did you wonder what it was like?"

"No."

He lowered his head. "Are you wondering right now?"

"No."

His lips grazed her brow and her cheekbone, lingering. "Are you going to fight me?"

"No. I mean yes. What?"

Teeth nipped her jaw. Breath feathered across her lips. Katie closed her eyes and willed him to stop. And to keep going. She couldn't even answer herself properly. He licked the corner of her mouth, and her fingertips dug into his chest.

"I haven't been with a woman since a week after I transformed." He drew his cheek across hers, his face smooth-shaven, his lips hot. "I'm extremely curious. I can already sense differences."

She found herself rising on tiptoes to get closer to him, bending her neck to allow him better access. Her hands slipped up, past his shoulder, to caress his nape.

Was it the first time she'd touched him without it being a ploy? His hair curled around her fingers. His scent, a heady mix of her sheets and his skin, enveloped her. His hand dropped several inches until he blatantly cupped her ass.

Katie exhaled as his cock stiffened against her. He nuzzled her, nipped her, everything but kissed her. Need rose in her precipitously.

"I smell your desire and lose focus. I can't say I'm fond of my reaction, yet I keep seeking it out. I've had more erections in the past twenty-four hours than—"

The television crackled into loud static.

Marcus tensed, growing as still as a brick wall. "Someone's here."

"Not again."

Beneath them, a gun fired. Tonya screamed.

TEN

MARCUS BURST INTO the tattoo parlor to find a middle-aged Caucasian man he didn't recognize confronting Tonya and Zhang Li. Both men were scowling.

"What the hell is wrong with you?" The unknown man gestured at the bullet hole in the shop window. "Why did you shoot at me?"

"My goodness, Li." Tonya hastened to the newcomer's side and held out her arms as if protecting him from assault. "I know he ran in here like his tail was on fire, but is that any reason to gun him down?"

Zhang Li studied the pistol in his hand as though he'd never seen it before. Dammit, how had the old weasel found it? Marcus had shut it in his briefcase. Zhang Li set the gun on the counter. "Hell if I know. Been jumpy lately. Too much caffeine."

"You could have killed me." The newcomer swung a backpack off his shoulder, dangling it by his side.

More complications. Would anyone nearby report gunfire to the police? How was Marcus going to keep this stranger quiet? Not with a hug, that was for sure.

"I wouldn't, and I didn't," Zhang Li snapped. "So quit your bitching."

Tonya shook her head. "You can't go around assaulting our customers. I'm so sorry, sir. What can we do to make it up to you?"

Marcus sniffed. Over the scent of gunfire, he realized it wasn't a customer.

It was Vernon Harrower.

Vernon appeared to be as confused as Tonya and Zhang Li. "I'm not a damn customer. I'm…" His bright blue gaze fell on Marcus. "Rodríguez? I can't believe you're not dead."

Katie's footsteps pounded up behind Marcus, but he barred the doorway so she couldn't enter the front room. She must have called the bastard—and told him she was going to kill Marcus.

His stomach pitted. His disappointment was naive. He'd known what kind of person she was from the beginning. A keeper. He had to quit trying to convince himself she wasn't like the other keepers simply because he was too fastidious to lust after a killer.

"What do you want, Vernon?" Had he not found all Katie's monkshood? She hadn't had as much as he'd expected to find. He shoved a hand in his pocket to tap the bay capsule. Still there.

"Vernon, is it? And you know Dr. Marcus?" Tonya batted her eyelashes at the stunned region elder. Marcus sniffed, but couldn't tell if the weathered, handsome face Vernon wore was a disguise. Considering he looked like he could be on television, Marcus was betting on disguise. "The doctor is our hero."

"Hero?" Vernon gaped at Tonya. "What is going on?"

Tonya tossed her curly blond hair over her shoulder and smiled. "We're a little tense after the accident. Don't worry about it, honey. My hands are steady as rocks. Are you sure you're not a customer?"

Marcus blocked Katie, who was trying to wriggle under his arm.

"Marcus, let me go," she hissed. "I have to explain."

Surely she'd explained everything to Vernon when she'd slipped in that phone call. He'd told her it wasn't safe to contact the elder, and she'd done it anyway.

She didn't trust anything he said any more than he ought to trust her. But if she hadn't spelled him or killed him when she could have...

"Vern, it's a code six," Katie yelled over Marcus's shoulder.

Code six was shorthand for recently wiped individuals in delicate condition. The keepers must not have changed their system since Katie had been Chang Cai.

Vernon frowned. "How could you have a six when the wolf knows who I am?"

"Who's a wolf?" Zhang Li asked. "Is that a gang sign? Better not come around my shop flashing colors. I'll shoot you."

Vernon ran a hand over his dark blond hair, streaked a distinguished gray at the temples. "Hell, it doesn't matter. I've got keepers on my ass. We need to split."

Katie cursed, but Marcus could tell she was more frightened than angry. He strode to the window to inspect the street, and she trotted after him.

"You led them here?" he said to Vernon. "Way to go."

"I had no clue Hiram could tap my fricking phone. The moron was still checking into Foursquare to announce he was the mayor of McDonald's this time last year."

"Then you haven't been paying attention." The keepers weren't cutting edge technologically, but they weren't bumbling fools.

"It's not like I got myself into this fix on purpose, Rodríguez. You can't exactly get high and mighty on me, considering the condition you're in."

"His name is Dr. Marcus Delgado," Tonya corrected.

"Not Rodríguez. And there's nothing wrong with his condition."

"When did Katie call you?" Marcus snapped at Vernon. "Why do you think I should be dead?"

"She didn't call me. Applebaum did. And I figured you were dead because nobody could find you for a year."

Marcus turned to Katie, who was watching him anxiously instead of the street. "You didn't contact him?"

"You thought I…" She huffed. "No, I did not. You convinced me it was a bad idea."

"Huh." He kept it to one sound so his relief wouldn't be obvious. Marcus was hardly a teenager, but this speeding from one emotion to another was going to break him out in acne if he wasn't careful. Nevertheless, the consequences of anyone calling Vernon were the same.

The keepers could be here any minute. If they kept arguing, his cushion for the pack patrol would disappear as well.

"Applebaum said she needed a special way to find something that had been stolen. Apparently, since Katie's here, it worked?"

"It was functional." That explained how Tonya and Zhang Li had stumbled across his Airstream. They'd conned some kind of location spell out of Vernon, though Marcus had never heard of such magic working over a distance.

Or cutting through protective wards.

Damn, Vernon was talented.

Was he so talented Katie would prefer to entrust her safety to Vernon instead of Marcus?

"Poor Vernon. Have you got amnesia too? I didn't call you about stolen goods," Tonya said. "I've never met you before today. Unless I forgot, I suppose."

"Somehow I don't think I'm getting paid what you

owe me," he grumbled to her. Vernon wasn't an elder and the former director of the keepers because he was slow on the uptake. He speared Marcus and Katie with an evil glare. "I see what's going on here, and I have an idea why. You shouldn't have done it, Katie. You should have cut and run."

Katie's lips tightened. "I know."

Marcus felt a distinct urge to defend her, even though Vernon was right. He stared out the window instead.

Nobody suspicious on the street, no vehicles except for a tiny Smart car, his truck, Zhang Li's sedan and a hatchback missing a tire, which had been here last night. Nobody darted through the early morning shadows. Nobody crept through the empty lots and buildings. But with Vernon's announcement, he could feel the keeper's presence like a looming thunderhead.

Tension rising, he addressed Vernon. "How close are they?"

"I don't know."

"Any signs of the scheduled patrol?"

"Don't know that either. Let's make tracks. Sorry, Dr. Delgado, no room for you in the car I borrowed. Count yourself lucky I'm letting you go free."

Katie and Marcus locked gazes for a moment. Vernon's arrival, his power and preparedness, changed the scoreboard. Marcus had dosed himself with his preventative medley as usual, excluding the mask, but he couldn't prevent Vernon from wresting Katie, Tonya and Zhang Li from him.

Katie would know this. And realize she no longer needed him.

Unacceptable. She wasn't leaving him until he chose to release her. She was…his.

In a soft voice, she said, "Vern, take Tonya and Zhang

Li. Help them. I'm with Marcus. He and I have an agreement."

Stunned, Marcus wasn't sure how to react to that or to the fact he felt as possessive of her as a toddler with a new toy. He blinked twice.

"Don't be stupid." Vernon, bristling with annoyance, pinched herbs out of a side pocket of the backpack. "Since Katie doesn't look hurt, I'll give you once chance to get lost. You'd best take it."

It was one thing to deal with three witches who had no power or didn't remember they were witches. It was another to deal with a live, loaded Vernon Harrower. Marcus sniffed, trying to determine what spell Vernon was considering. Could he counteract it?

Tonya stuck her hands on her hips. "Don't be nasty to the doctor. He helped us after a gas leak affected our memories."

"Bet he did." Vernon crushed the herbs on his palm, creating a dust. He'd have to get close to smear it on Marcus, so all Marcus had to do was avoid him. "Everyone but Delgado, get your things. Let's go."

"I don't think I want to go anywhere with you," Tonya said.

"I'm damn sure I don't," Zhang Li added. "You look like a shithead."

"Look, this isn't a request. I'm the ranking… Oh, hell." Several blue-silver minivans with dark-tinted windows approached from the east. Vernon smacked the herbs off his palm and gestured at everyone to duck. "Get down."

While the keepers hadn't favored minivans when Marcus had been there, he and Katie responded instantly to the warning, dropping below the level of the shop window.

"Upstairs, through the kitchen," she murmured. "Exit

behind the china cabinet." Witches always had a secret door or two. "You get Tonya, I'll get Ba. He'll trust me whether he realizes why or not."

Tonya regarded a crouching Vernon with skepticism. "I don't know who you think you are, Mr. Hot Britches, but I don't get on my knees because some guy told me to."

"Tonya, hide," Katie urged. Marcus hadn't heard anyone behind the shop, which didn't mean no one was there. Who was driving the minivans?

Vernon cursed at the standing woman. "Idiot woman, they will shoot you. They have better aim than Zhang Li."

"Who is they?" Tonya gestured toward the street. "The soccer moms?"

"Whoever they are, I'll shoot 'em back." Zhang Li picked up the gun. "I hate soccer moms."

"You hate everybody," Vernon snapped. "Get your wrinkled ass behind the counter."

Outraged, Zhang Li disappeared. Marcus risked a glance above the sill. The minivans slowed near their parking lot. A window rolled down. A rifle barrel poked out.

"God, I hate being awesome." Vernon sprang off the floor and tackled Tonya right before buckshot sprayed the window.

Zhang Li released a warbling war cry and began shooting back. Glass flew everywhere. Marcus dragged Katie half beneath him, safeguarding her from the worst cuts. He'd mend in an hour; she'd need heal-all. He could hear Vernon and Tonya bickering on the other side of the door but stayed alert for footsteps outside, out back, any signs that the keepers were charging into the building.

Had to be them. The border patrol drove trucks and didn't shoot first.

Instead he heard the roar of diesel engines and the

screech of tires. The gunfire ceased. Zhang Li cursed about not having a spare clip. Marcus then heard him dial the cordless phone.

"Don't call the cops," Vernon shouted. "That's all we need. Ouch, woman, that's my family jewels."

"Your family's not very rich, then," Tonya retorted. "Of course he needs to call the police. Soccer moms can't go around shooting up tattoo parlors."

"Hello, 9-1-1?" Zhang Li said. "We're under attack. No, I don't know where I am. A tattoo store. On some crappy road full of potholes. Can't you trace the damn call? I'm an American citizen…I think. No, this isn't a prank. Get me some help. A SWAT team. I'm out of bullets."

"Stay down," Marcus told Katie. Since Zhang Li was out of ammunition and the keepers weren't shooting, he risked another glance outside.

Several pickup trucks skidded to a halt near the mini-vans, blocking the street in either direction. Masculine voices, loud and aggravated, cut through the arguing and shushing inside the tattoo parlor. Burly armed men began pouring out of the minivans and pickup trucks.

Well, shit. The Birmingham patrol, ahead of schedule. And the keepers. Were the region elders next?

A fat, smoking bundle lobbed through the shattered window and bounced on the glass-covered floor.

"Gaia bless it," Vernon complained. "I thought we could get out faster than this."

Marcus had too. His ears popped. Magic. He shook himself as heaviness descended. His herbal cocktail buoyed him above the creeping exhaustion.

No so for the others. Beneath him, Katie sighed. Her dark brown eyes, lids drooping, stared into his. She touched his cheek, her hand sprinkled by droplets of blood. "I'm too drained to resist. Goddess, I'm out of practice."

"Fight it." Marcus breathed deeply, oxygenating himself. Escaping the spell's radius wouldn't help because it had already been cast. The keepers used industrial strength sleep magic, thyme along with some combination of hops, lavender or valerian, and the massive size of the herbal bomb meant physical proximity wasn't required.

"They won't move in immediately. They're used to wolves. If you wake up first," she said, her voice fading, "please save my father."

Marcus's ears, however, popped a second time, from a closer source. Vernon released Tonya, who had the sense to stay down. He slithered nimbly through the glass to the smoking bundle and sprinkled herbs all over it.

Katie's eyes sprang open, and she blew out a breath. "That's a relief. Guess I'll save Ba myself."

"I can't do that many times," Vernon said. "The spearmint crop got leaf blight this year, and the good stuff is scarce."

Marcus met the other man's gaze, recognized in him the determination to save everyone here—even if he didn't particularly like them—and nodded.

"They're distracted. Everyone upstairs. Stay low."

Vernon scowled when Tonya, Katie and Zhang Li did as Marcus requested. Once they passed through the beaded curtain between the front and back rooms, they rose from their crouches and ran.

Katie, stumbling up the stairs in front of Marcus, wiped her wounded arm on her shirt. His nose told him the cuts weren't deep. "My blood was on the floor," she warned him and Vernon, "and the pack patrol probably knows someone interesting was in here."

Vern followed them into the apartment. "We need to increase the distance until they lose track of you."

Marcus's scent would draw the pack wolves like rain on a hot summer day, but they weren't the main threat anymore. The keepers were. On the bright side, the keepers would likely subdue the patrol and wouldn't be able to track their group as easily as wolves. Marcus could never have dodged the packers from this close.

In the apartment, Marcus scooped up Katie's duffel and his supplies. When he hoisted the large briefcase, the latch Zhang Li had apparently picked to get the gun sprang open, dumping half the contents.

"Shit." Katie dropped to her knees, shoveling Marcus's gloves, swabs, books, test strips, granola bars, and odds and ends into the hard-sided case. "Your stuff."

"Leave it." He caught her arm, dragged her up. "Get us through that back door."

"We're parked out front." Katie took the gun from her father. "We have to scare them off if we want the cars. Tonya's car is parked in a long-term lot a mile away. The panic room won't do us any good since I can't cast the—" She broke off and looked at Vernon.

"Panic room?" Vernon said. "I can set the boundaries. Where is it?"

"I understand why we'd need a panic room in this violent neighborhood," Tonya added.

"I had to get creative since we couldn't afford two leases. It's in a Dumpster." Katie retrieved ammunition clips from a vase on the mantel and stuffed some into her pockets and one into the gun. Her efficient movements let Marcus know she'd done this, or trained for this, hundreds of times. "Just in case, rendezvous at location G-160, forty-eight hours."

"To hell with a rendezvous." Vern glowered. "You're

staying with me, Katie. If your dog stays too, he's officially your problem."

From downstairs, a small explosion shook the building. Glass crashed in Katie's bedroom. Shouts echoed outside as a battle of fists and howls erupted between the keepers and the Birmingham pack patrol.

Tonya clutched Vernon's arm. "What in the world are they doing, shooting bazookas? Lord, are we Mafia or something, and I forgot?"

An odd expression crossed the elder's face as he regarded his companion. "I wouldn't say that."

"Hey, this china cabinet's on wheels," Zhang Li called from the kitchen. "There's a door behind it."

"I'm going first," Marcus said. "I can smell and hear anyone outside."

Vernon tried to beat him to the doorway. "I'm first. You can smell, but I can stun." He pulled out another wad of herbs. It was Tonya's turn to cast Vernon an odd look.

Vernon wouldn't knock him out since he needed Marcus's help. "The keepers followed you here, Vernon. They'll be expecting your skills, and they'll know how to counteract them."

"It's you they're here for. I'm a side dish."

"Doubt that," Marcus said, remembering the way Lars used to talk about Vernon. "They're as anxious to catch you committing treason as they are me. Overly anxious, I'd say."

The keepers seemed to be operating free of the witch covenants, confronting wolves in the street, openly bombing places of business. They weren't permitted to be this blatant. If standards had become this lax under Lars, it was all the more reason why the council's teeth needed to be pulled.

Marcus's experiments were the way to do it.

"Treason my ass," Vern said. "Get out of my way."

"I don't know what you two are talking about," Tonya said, "but I vote we call the police. They need to know there's a gang war in our street."

While they argued, Katie slipped past them.

"My gun is going first," she called over her shoulder before disappearing into the kitchen.

She wasn't in any shape to take on keepers or packers. No magic, no mask, bleeding. They might know he and Vern were here, but she didn't have to expose herself. Marcus wheeled after her, growling.

Vernon hustled a reluctant Tonya along. Marcus couldn't wait for them. He hurried Zhang Li down the narrow, dark stairwell, arriving at the bottom in time to see Katie duck through a short door. While he didn't want to imagine what would happen if he wolfed out in front of Zhang Li and Tonya, he might have to, so he released a little of his hard-won restraint.

With the boost of speed, he zipped past Zhang Li and bent nearly double to jet through the exit. Whatever was out there, Katie and a pistol couldn't handle it alone.

The sun and sense of openness in the alley fazed him momentarily, but he regained his bearings in a second. No people but Katie. No cars.

The weedy, rutted track was lined by deserted buildings, a few empty lots and several Dumpsters on the near side. The other side was a field overgrown with tall weeds and a low-income residential area in the distance.

Behind him, Zhang Li emerged, followed by Tonya and Vernon. Marcus caught a whiff of calming mix and noticed Tonya was content to let Vernon guide her. She smiled at Marcus when she saw him.

Katie cleared the immediate area and gave them an OK sign. He didn't snap at her, though he felt like it.

"Which Dumpster?" Vernon whispered, looking extremely dubious. There were four within sight. He patted Zhang Li on the shoulder, and Marcus smelled the calming mix again.

"The stenchy one. Don't worry—it's not real carrion. It's a ward," Katie explained. While house boundaries had to be renewed daily, subtle aversion wards could linger for weeks if the witch who cast them was strong enough. "Vern, the packet's center front, inside. Chalk-based, amaranth, chicory, heliotrope."

Katie pointed across the open space toward the next structure and gestured for everyone to go.

"Run," Vernon said.

As the packers and keepers clashed on the street, they sprinted through the gap, skidding to a halt where a half-rusted Dumpster waited. Zhang Li was spritely as hell for a man his age. Marcus stiffened his upper lip as a noxious odor smacked him like a fish's tail.

Vernon lifted the lid of the Dumpster and began helping Tonya into it. Zhang Li muttered about the smell. Calming balm didn't seem to work that well on Katie's father—big surprise. Marcus turned to lift Katie in.

She hadn't followed.

No, she crept like a shadow along the back wall of the first building, closer and closer to the side the keepers and pack could see. Her opposite arm braced her gun hand as she scooted around the corner.

Was she trying to tick him off or get herself killed? That would put her in plain view. Even if the keepers didn't notice, the packers might. And the keepers, well, if they caught sight of Katie, she was as good as dead.

The question was, who was winning? Pack or keepers?

"Getting Katie," he told Vernon. He dropped their bags and took off.

Marcus poured on the speed. The weeds were tall and
he was fast. Even if someone glanced between the buildings, they might not see him. He snagged Katie's shoulder
before she'd taken many steps toward the confrontation.

Angry, he flattened her against the wall behind a concrete ramp where trucks could make deliveries. A decrepit wooden frame around the huge sliding door hid
them from sight.

"No." He didn't bother making it an order, just snarled
at her until she stilled.

"Need to see if they have tranqs or guns. Need to know
what and who we're up against," she whispered.

"I'll do it. Get your ass to the Dumpster."

"I'm with you," she said stubbornly. "Remember?"

Marcus breathed fast and deep. The wolf wanted to
haul her ass away. Careful, careful. Stealth was required,
and deliberate cunning. The situation was too crucial to
waste time on a clash of wills and his unstable id.

He heard the yelp of a wolf, a muffled gunshot, curses
and shouts. His wolf growled. No, he growled. The keepers and pack weren't being discreet, even though the pack
would have no idea it wasn't facing humans. Did none
of them care about the people who populated this area?

"What do you hear?" Katie mouthed the words. Her
pupils had dilated so much her eyes were black.

The keepers and elders could clean this mess up if
they had to, but Marcus didn't intend for the five of them
to be part of the crackdown. He leaned back, his hands
trapping Katie against the wall, and peered around the
wooden frame. She strained to see as well, angling her
line of vision through a broken slat.

The pack wolves weren't winning. Two shaggy four-
legs were crumpled in the middle of the street. Dead or
asleep, he had no idea. Several denim-and-flannel-clad

bodies were also strewn on the ground. One in black, a keeper. More keepers, in dark military gear and bullet-proof vests, were arrayed throughout the tangle of mini-vans and trucks, pistols up and ready.

Most looked like tranq pistols. One tiny favor. They wouldn't die immediately if shot.

Several keepers broke from cover and darted to a truck. A naked two-leg, perhaps a wolf unable to shift fast enough, hurled out of the bed and took two of them down.

But not for long.

Almost casually, a tall, lean man stepped out from behind a minivan. Though he was dressed like the other keepers, Marcus instantly recognized him. Recognized the arrogance in the posture, the thinning gray hair, the icy profile.

Hiram Lars.

Katie clutched Marcus's shirt with trembling hands. "Fucking hell."

He let her lean on him. Her heartbeat pounded against his chest. They watched as Lars raised a weapon, a hand-held pneumatic launcher with a fat, short barrel. Held it straight up, like a Roman candle. Pumped it.

Something shot out the opening.

Marcus's ears popped, and Katie grabbed his head, yanking him toward her.

She caught him in a desperate hug. Her fingers jerked his hair. She spoke in his ear, her words urgent. "Spell bomb. We should be safe here."

Magic buzzed him like a swarm of bees. The urge to shift assaulted him in a thousand stings of need.

What the hell? A berserker spell, here?

With the council, he'd studied what compelled wolves to go feral—to shift in passion and commit mayhem. He'd wanted to know what might transform a wolf back into a witch, while Lars had only wanted weapons.

Marcus had given him one.

Savagery knifed through him, and he fought. Fought hard. Katie's grip on him tightened.

"What the hell is going on? They're all shifting. In the middle of a populated town."

Marcus's skin twitched. Redness like fire misted his vision. This woman, restraining him. She couldn't stop him if he wanted to shift. He was wolf. She was nothing. Two-legs. He grew dizzy, struggling against it.

On the street, wolves howled. Many wolves. He bared his teeth. They sharpened. Claws sprouted. *Yes.*

"Not you too." Unafraid, the woman pushed her face into his, their noses an inch apart. She had black eyes. Bottomless. "Come on, Marcus. Stay with me. Stay up here. Look at me, Doc. Focus."

Marcus's lungs heaved out like bellows. He needed to be free! Katie hauled back and slapped a hand over his mouth. Hard. The sound cracked through the air. He tasted gunmetal, blood and skin.

Katie's skin. The magic passed. As one, they turned to look at Lars.

He was staring right at them.

And he started running first.

ELEVEN

KATIE DIDN'T WASTE a second. She sprinted for the back of the building, Marcus on her heels. Hiram Lars. After all this time. She could feel him, like a dragon's hot flames scorching her neck.

He'd know what she could do. He'd know how she could hide, what escape routes she might have planned, where she might run. They'd been trained by the same council, except he'd taken it over and she'd played dead to escape it.

The Dumpster wasn't safe anymore. She had to get her family out of that trap.

She wheeled around the corner, intending to do that, but Marcus clutched her arm and spun her into the field.

"Lead him away from the panic room." Half dragging her, he bolted through the tall weeds. She caught the tempo quickly, met him stride for stride. Briars whipped her exposed arms.

Her father. Tonya. Vernon would have to take care of them. Could he?

The field blurred on either side as they fled. Katie settled into a ground-eating pace so Marcus wouldn't have to lug her. Weeds smacked her. She didn't slow, praying to the Goddess her feet wouldn't stumble on rocks or holes. Though fit, she couldn't maintain top speed forever.

Would it be long enough?

Lars wasn't as young as she was. He was in his third

pass-through. He wasn't a wolf, with wolf senses to track her essence. But his underlings would be faster and hardier, maybe faster and hardier than Katie. And it was possible, if Lars had grown cannier, he could enlist—force—the Birmingham wolves to help.

If he did, there was nowhere she and Marcus could go on foot that a wolf couldn't find them. Not without magic, without the primed masks they'd left with Vernon and the others.

She risked a glance back. Lars was nowhere to be seen. Slower than expected. Had he been distracted? She couldn't forsake her family. She and Marcus could drop behind this tree and wait, then circle around…

Lars tore around the corner, a group of keepers at his heels. Even at this distance, Katie could see the hate and rage twisting his face. "Chang Cai!"

Katie stumbled. Her blood chilled.

Hiram Lars had resented her position as Vern's protégée. He'd hindered her work with the council, whispering in ears, ensuring she had the worst jobs, the worst backup. As Lars's influence had grown, he'd opposed Katie at every turn. He'd almost killed her once, and she'd always wondered if it had just been the once. Not that she'd liked her job, but he'd been most of the reason she'd had to resort to desperate measures to escape the keepers.

Now he knew the truth, and he'd never stop coming after her and her family.

One keeper halted, raised a rifle, but Lars cawed out an order like a bird of prey and smacked him in the head.

Guess he didn't want her dead by anyone else's hands.

Marcus grabbed her arm and shoved her forward. "Don't look, just run. I'll let you know if they're close."

They were already closer than Katie liked. Three states away was closer than she liked.

"Describe this neighborhood. Streams? Public places?" Loping beside her, Marcus didn't seem winded. From the blue of his eyes, his wolf was up. But he was sticking beside her when he could outdistance her and save himself. She knew monkshood scared him, despite his bragging about an antidote.

"Residential." Her feet sped through the dead grass and scrub. She kept her elbows tight, her fear focused. "Then farms."

"River would be good. You swim?"

"Yes, but no river." Katie envisioned an area map. They were headed north. Beyond this neighborhood was another residential one, then farmlands, then an unincorporated bump in the road with a gas station and dentist's office. That was…four miles. Marcus's Airstream in the state park—not that they could escape in it without a tow—was much farther north.

They needed supplies. Masks. Heal-all. Her blood from the broken glass would make it easier for any trackers.

If they were going to outsmart Lars, they had to have a better plan than *run away, run away.*

"All-Guard Parking," she panted, glad she'd worn her running shoes along with a dark-colored T-shirt, light jacket around her waist and loose pants. Standard getaway couture. "Left on Crosby. Downtown." The streets they'd need to take led through a warehouse district and past a school.

"Key?" He wasn't wasting his breath on words. She shouldn't either, but if she wanted him to follow her, he ought to be told why.

"Hidden there." She hoped Tonya, Dad and Vern wouldn't need the car, because she was going to appropriate it. They'd have to find another way to the rendezvous point.

Cries of pursuit mounted behind them. No lupine howls. She and Marcus neared a line of saplings and pines. A barbed wire fence marked the end of the large field. Cuts from the glass, now from thorns, stung her arms. Terror and guilt stung her heart.

The worst that could happen. Right here, right now.

She'd brought it on herself.

If she hadn't tried to wipe Marcus... If she'd been smarter. If she hadn't fought him, driven him to kidnap her... If, if, if.

If Lars caught her, the torture he'd inflict would put all her past terrors to shame.

She couldn't dwell. She couldn't fall to pieces. She could only run.

They slowed at the barbed wire. It stretched from the road to the other side of the field. As short as she was, she'd have to climb it.

Or not. Marcus hauled her off her feet and leaped, thudding onto the shorter grass on the other side with a *whomp*. Without a word, he set her down and they resumed running.

Now they were among houses. Buildings. People. Humans who might not appreciate two strangers bolting across their properties. Humans who might call the cops. In three seconds, once they passed the first house, Lars would lose sight of them, giving them a small advantage.

As if realizing it, Lars roared behind them.

Gunfire.

Something whizzed past Katie's ear. *Way to be discreet, assholes.* If no one had called the cops yet, they would now.

Grimly, she dodged left, then right. It would slow her progress, but a gunshot wound or a tranq would put a much bigger crimp in her escape plans than zigzagging.

"Dammit," Marcus cursed.

More gunfire. Just in time, they reached the other side of the backyard and banked a hard right behind an outbuilding.

"Follow me." Katie, decelerating enough to avoid a parked car, guided him on an evasive course through backyards, side yards, gravel driveways and outbuildings. The sounds of pursuit split apart. A horn honked as a van zoomed past. Since it didn't stop, she assumed it wasn't a keeper vehicle.

Now would come the crucial test. Would Lars release the hounds? Or the wolves?

She plotted a route, an alternate route and a third route. Did Lars have wolf noses on his team? If he did, raising a ruckus and hoping the human cops showed soon would be the smartest ploy.

For her. Not for the humans.

But should she die to keep this confrontation hidden from a few cops and locals whom the elders or keepers would memory-wipe anyway?

Marcus was breathing heavier now, though she could barely hear him over her own huffing. Then she realized he wasn't panting so much as sniffing.

"No wolves with Lars," he assured her. "Unless they're masked."

She had no air left for words and managed a nod. It had been twenty years since her life had been in this much danger. They skidded to a halt at the edge of a house, peering into the side street they intended to cross. Another car cruised past, driving at normal speed. Nobody right or left. Her hearing distorted as her pulse thundered in her ears. Her lungs and muscles hating her, she charged across the space.

Marcus's forearm bumped her as he nudged her off her trajectory. "That house—there. Children in the backyard."

No good. No kids. She veered into another yard. Even as a keeper, her job hadn't usually required running flat-out for long distances. Tall fence around the fifth house on this street, but they could fit behind it. Next they'd reach an intersection where they needed to head west.

There wouldn't be cover for several hundred yards on that street. It would be busier, a highway leading downtown. It couldn't be avoided if they wanted to reach the parking garage.

"Traffic. Bridge," she managed. She pointed in the direction she wanted Marcus to go as he took the lead.

They pounded toward the overpass. No shouts behind them, but they were in the open now, arrowing for the road.

Could they make it?

The whine of an overtaxed motor blasted her surge of hope to smithereens. Tires squealed on pavement. A mini-van roared past them, fishtailing into their path.

Marcus whirled around and cursed. Katie froze, like a rabbit with a hawk circling above.

She hadn't lied when she'd told Marcus Chang Cai was dead. That hated life and dismal person were gone. She was Katie Zhang now, tattooist, daughter, friend, lover of jeggings and organic produce. Katie hid from danger instead of confronting it, because it was the easiest way to keep herself and her family alive.

She'd failed.

Marcus tried to goad her back in the direction they'd come from, but her legs wouldn't cooperate. A harsh command stopped him from tossing her over his shoulder.

"Halt or you're dead," Lars ordered. A car door

slammed. "Turn around slowly with your hands in the air."

Katie didn't. Marcus didn't. She looked at him, and his eyes were completely wolfed out.

Not even when she'd threatened to wipe him had she seen him look so fierce. But no wolf could outrun a bullet at this distance.

"Now!" Lars barked, sounding as much like a wolf as any shifter Katie had heard.

Slowly, Katie did as requested.

"I don't believe it. It's really you." He squinted at her, as if his eyesight was poor. Perhaps it was.

The years had not been kind to Hiram Lars. His tall form was gaunt, his skin tinged by yellow. Sweat beaded his brow and his gun barrel shook in his hands, like palsy. Witch remedies couldn't cure some diseases—like old age—and she hoped whatever he obviously had was miserable.

Katie didn't say anything. Marcus hadn't turned around, but Lars didn't seem to care. The keeper who'd been driving the minivan slid out from behind the wheel, a rifle in his hands. Two more men stepped out of the backseat.

Four men and their large guns against Katie and Marcus and their small gun. She had great aim, but drawing her pistol would not improve this situation.

"How?" Lars demanded.

If she pretended to be someone else, it would just annoy him. Then again, if she annoyed him, would he lose his temper and kill her quickly? Would he focus his rage so acutely on her that her family could escape?

"Magic," she answered, proud her voice didn't shake. Maybe she had a little Chang Cai left. "You look like hell,

Hiram. You sick? Or have years of bad living caught up with you? Sucks to be two-seventy."

"Tiresome bitch." Lars had lost none of his elegant way with words. And none of the madness in his smile. The skin tightened across his haggard face. "You'll be telling me soon enough. You'll be telling me everything."

"Thanks for asking how I've been." Katie's false bravado probably wasn't fooling anybody. "Pretty fantastic, really. I'm rich and successful and have a good laugh every day at how easy you were to trick."

"You can't provoke me, Chang Cai," Lars said, but his teeth snapped on the words. He was provoked, all right. "This might be the best day of my life."

"I get that a lot." Katie didn't want to take her eyes off Lars, but she glanced at Marcus. His head turned slightly to one side, and his nostrils flared. So far, no humans had taken notice of the confrontation. A car cruised past the turn to the bridge and didn't slow down to rubberneck.

She knew this neighborhood was rough, but a van full of dudes waving guns around should have attracted a few onlookers, at the least.

Or maybe the onlookers were as scared as she was.

"Get her gun," Lars told one of the men. "She might use it on herself. She was always a coward."

"A coward? Really, Lars?" A man Katie didn't recognize from her keeper days strode confidently forward. "I went after the worst of the ferals, the ones that killed people, the ones you were too chicken shit to handle." Granted, she'd been sent in as a distraction most of the time, a sweet-smelling juvenile female with a bad case of wolf lust. But she was no coward.

Or she hadn't been then.

Right now, she was terrified in a way that facing down a pack of rapacious shifters couldn't equal. Now, not only was she about to die, but Marcus would too. Marcus, who simply wanted justice for his sister. Then Lars would find her father, Tonya and Vern.

They'd all die because of Katie.

"Who's your friend?" Lars asked. "Best apologize to him now for the pain he'll be suffering."

He didn't recognize Marcus? Could she use that?

"Human," she said. "A customer who got spooked when you guys started shooting in the street like a bunch of idiots. Involving or harming him is against the covenants. Not to mention harming the cops on their way."

Surely there were cops on the way.

Lars laughed, a raspy chuckle like a serrated knife on wood. "The covenants have no jurisdiction over me. I do as I wish. The elders are so busy chasing mongrels we pretended we couldn't find that they have no idea how powerful we're becoming."

Tonya had mentioned the council had been less competent since Vern and Katie's departure and the sympathizers more successful.

Except in the case of Marcus's sister.

"However, we do capture a few mongrels and primitives. Enough to hone our skills. Test our weapons. I confess, we prefer females for that. I like the way they cry. I'm excited to show you the advances we've made in your absence, Chang Cai."

Beside her, Marcus growled low and deep. He had to be thinking of his sister and the way she'd died.

Goddess, Katie hoped Elisa had died and not been one of Lars's torture victims.

The keeper who intended to take Katie's gun had nearly reached them. Marcus stiffened and cocked his head to the side.

"This is the dreaded Chang Cai?" the man asked, staring at her. "This tiny thing?"

"You know nothing," Lars spat. "Take her gun and tie them both up."

"Get ready," Marcus whispered.

Get ready for what? To die? Or did he have a plan?

"You there." The keeper kicked Marcus in the back of the knee, but he kept his balance. "Put your hands behind your back. Don't give me any trouble or I'll shoot you."

Marcus's shoulders flexed as he moved slowly to comply.

No, Marcus. Don't give up.

His surrender jolted something loose inside her. Something that had been frozen in horror and now burned hot with the will to survive.

The keeper, satisfied by Marcus's obedience, sneered at Katie and grabbed for her.

After that, everything happened at once.

A line of traffic crossed the bridge from downtown, headed right for them. She chopped the keeper's forearm with a bone-breaking blow. Hopefully not her bone, because her hand stung like shit. Lars shouted orders, his voice a shriek of rage.

Marcus launched into action as if released from springs.

He hurled the closest man across the gravel shoulder. The guy howled in shock until his body slammed into a guardrail with a sickening crunch.

The vehicles approaching from downtown slowed at a stoplight. A car horn blasted. Someone shouted at the combatants about 9-1-1.

Katie had one chance. She dashed for the humans in the cars, screaming her head off. She was a small, defenseless-looking woman and she wasn't afraid to use that.

"Help us! Please help us!"

She could hear scuffling, fighting. Cursing. Bodies hitting the ground. Gunfire echoed behind her several times.

Agony chiseled her upper arm. She'd been shot. *Shit. Shit!* How bad?

Arm. Just arm. Fiery pain stole her breath but her legs still churned. Her vision fuzzed in and out.

Didn't matter. She called for Marcus to come.

He did. Thank the Goddess he was upright. Fate finally shifted in her favor. The light turned green and several vehicles began to reverse, trying to escape the crazies with the guns.

Several, however, remained to watch. She could see people with their cell phones, calling the cops or filming it for the internet. Either way, this would be harder for Lars to handle.

She approached the truck in the lead, driven by a bearded guy she recognized from the neighborhood they'd just exited.

He was kind of a dirt bag. And alone in the vehicle. He'd do.

"Truck," she wheezed to Marcus. She zagged as gunfire erupted behind them. The windshield of a car burst. A woman screamed.

Katie crossed the road and slammed into the far side of the truck. Using it as a shield wasn't enough.

Marcus, guessing her intent, yanked open the door and hauled the driver out. "Sorry," he growled. "You'll get it back."

"Hey, you can't jack my ride!" The guy tried to jump Marcus. The sedan behind them honked. Maybe to applaud the show, maybe to scare them.

She knocked the guy out of the way with a few well-placed kicks. He was so surprised, he lost his footing, landing on his ass at the side of the road. He ducked and rolled as the keepers fired a few more shots, warier now that multiple humans were included.

Katie didn't have a black belt, but smelling lustful and being convex weren't her only talents. She was quick, wiry and fought dirty. And she had a high pain tolerance.

Marcus leaped into the truck. Slid to the passenger's side. She followed, glad he didn't argue over the wheel. Wolves with their dander up weren't easy to manage. She smacked the truck into gear and shredded in a half-circle, tires squealing.

She gunned it toward downtown. In the rearview mirror, the bearded guy chased after them, shaking a meaty fist. Lars, the only keeper standing, scrambled for his minivan. Another group of keepers emerged from the neighborhood, on foot and running. She hoped Lars's people wouldn't hurt the witnesses, but she and Marcus couldn't stick around to find out.

She floored the truck. It zoomed across the overpass, jouncing into the air where the pavement buckled upward. They landed with a crunch, and Marcus grabbed the dashboard.

"Don't wreck," he said in a tight voice.

Adrenaline fizzed in her veins like carbonation. The gunshot wound faded to background annoyance. She gripped the wheel tight, perching on the edge of the seat.

When they reached a queue of cars at a red light, she slammed on the brakes. Tires screeched. People in front of them pivoted to see. The light turned green, and she swerved around cars like a slalom racer. She chose a side street that should have less traffic.

The direction shift concealed them from pursuers. The

fact that no cars had rammed the back of the truck was a good sign the keepers hadn't caught up.

Yet.

Marcus turned his attention to their rear view. "I don't see Lars's minivan."

She followed a twisty route to the parking garage. Marcus rifled through the car, its glove box and behind the seat. He tucked things into his pockets and put a dirty ball cap on his head. He also found a camouflage jacket that was too warm for the weather but would alter his appearance.

Soon, they reached downtown, where Katie pulled into a parking garage a block from the one she wanted. She was relatively sure this one had exit cameras, not internal ones.

She parked the truck in a slot on a crowded level. Before she could get out, Marcus stopped her with a hand on her arm. "Let me see where the bullet struck you."

"It's nothing." They'd faced Lars. They were alive. A gunshot wound was a small price to pay.

His grip tightened. "Shut up and cooperate. I'm having enough trouble containing myself without you egging the wolf on."

"Sorry." She tried for docile as he inspected the wound.

He dabbed the cut with a handkerchief. Her blood seeped into the white cotton, stark and copper-scented. "It's shallow. Hurt much?"

"Feels great." She pulled the keys out of the ignition and folded them into the driver's side visor. "I love getting shot. Makes me giddy as a schoolgirl."

"Giddy or woozy?" He wound the hankie into a strip and tied it around her arm. "You got lucky."

"I'm not lucky, I'm good." Happily the keeper shooters weren't. "It looks worse than it is."

"I should have hung on to my briefcase so we could purify the truck."

"It's okay." Her fingerprints and DNA weren't in human databases and wouldn't show as unusual if tested. The people who'd witnessed the shooting, including the guy whose truck they'd stolen, would report the incident and the theft. She didn't know how high priority the case would be. It depended on what else the keepers did besides shoot guns and wolves and vandalize a tattoo parlor and terrorize a neighborhood.

Yeah, it would be high priority, until the keepers wiped everyone. No matter how powerful Lars thought he'd become, no matter how desperately he wanted to kill her, he wouldn't ignore the human witness portion of the covenants, and he'd activate his media specialists to handle any internet issues.

That being said, she'd rather be caught by human cops than Lars any day. She still couldn't believe they'd gotten away.

Marcus tightened the handkerchief. Katie hissed in pain. "You're going to cut off my circulation." When he released her, she hopped out of the truck.

He slid out her side and straightened her T-shirt over the makeshift bandage. "The wound is visible. Put your jacket on."

She bit back the urge to snark—with relief—and donned the windbreaker. He still looked wolfish. As he watched, she zipped it to hide the blood spatter on her shirt. He frowned down at her, licked his thumb and wiped a few spots on her face.

This time she batted him away. "Seriously?"

Ignoring her, her plucked leaves and twigs out of her hair and then finger-combed it. He tucked strands behind her ears. Katie shivered.

"I can't do much with the cowlicks," he said.

"You and me both." Self-consciously, she palmed her crown where her hair tended to rooster up. "Am I presentable for someone who recently escaped certain death?"

Joking about it helped. Her insides jittered with amazement. She felt as though she was going to rattle apart.

Marcus's big, warm hand lingered on her neck a moment, rubbing the delicate skin over her pulse. "I owe you an apology."

Not what she'd expected. "Just one?"

The cap's brim shadowed his face, making him hard to read. "We should have used masks this morning."

Why the masks mattered this late in the game, she had no idea, but it couldn't be changed. If she obsessed over that particular what-if, she'd spin around and around the vicious cycle of all the what-ifs pertaining to her own behavior and how she'd gotten them into this situation. Forward momentum would be history.

She pulled away from his touch before she went weak in the knees, and headed for the stairs. Her legs were uncertain enough after the mad dash away from Lars. She didn't need her crush on Marcus interfering. "Lars almost had us. Now he doesn't. I can't obsess over what we did wrong, only what we're going to do next. I never thought I'd face Lars and survive, but together we did."

His eyes, dark again, met hers as he opened the metal stairwell door for her. Two hours ago, this man had planned to tie her up and have sex with her. Now he was fixing her hair, fretting over her wound, opening her doors. "You're the last person I expected to find a bright lining in our predicament."

"Keep in mind you don't actually know me that well." The stairs reeked of urine and fast food. She hung on to the peeling industrial paint of the railing. Her leg muscles bitched at her. Her body wanted to collapse. "You look at me and see a keeper, a convex alpha, a guinea pig." She could have added lecher, since he'd observed that aspect of her too.

"Multifaceted, yes. Optimist, no."

"I'm not an optimist. I'm a realist. A survivor."

"You've done this before—gone on the run." They reached street level. He opened the door for her again.

"Not for a long time," she admitted. "And not without my family. This is the closest call I've had in twenty years."

"You handled yourself well."

"I have substantial motivation." And shaky legs. She didn't think Marcus would mock her for it, but if she vocalized it, it might overwhelm her. "Since we survived Lars, this means we have a chance to help my family. We need to sneak back to the shop. Make sure he didn't find the others."

"Not safe." He skirted past her to the street side and slid an arm around her shoulders.

To shove him away would be conspicuous, so Katie allowed it. The protectiveness of his gesture, placing himself between the traffic and her, flustered her. She stumbled a little until their strides began to mesh.

"He knows Vern came to Alabama. Now he knows why. He might not know about Tonya or Ba, but he'll turn the shop upside down. Panic rooms don't work that great when other witches know what to look for."

Witches rarely warred with other witches. Their kind tended to be pacifists, the elders shuttling awkward jobs off to the keeper council so their hands stayed clean. The keepers had little cause to go after witches, unless those witches were aiding and abetting a transformed wolf.

How much of Lars's boasting could she believe? Had

he been going after witches too? If they survived this, Vern needed to alert the elders to the fact Lars was pulling some massive shit behind their backs.

"Vernon wasn't drained. He can defend them. He had all of our supplies." Marcus's arm tightened around her when they neared a mass of people waiting at a crosswalk. He kept his face tipped down, toward her, as if he couldn't take his eyes off her. She tried not to give any cameras a full view of her features either. She stayed tucked under his arm, letting him block as much of her as possible.

"Vern isn't convex," she said in a low voice. "Tonya and Ba won't be any help at all. They have no memories and no magic. And Ba, well, he's difficult in the best of times. I can't wait forty-eight hours to find out if they're going to make the rendezvous point. It'll drive me insane."

"With us out of the picture, it may be easier for Vernon to get aid from the coven network. Your father and Tonya aren't former keepers."

Katie had excised her ego a long time ago. It shouldn't matter that Marcus was right. Dad and Tonya were safer without her. Then again, Lars would be doubly furious because she'd slipped through his grasp.

Pedestrians milled around them as cars whizzed past. Katie's gaze skipped from driver to driver and scanned the sidewalks. Marcus, tension oozing off him, checked her as much as he did their environment.

Did he think she was going to bolt? Her course was set. She'd given her word and wasn't going to—okay, probably wouldn't—double-cross him again. She'd try to convince him to let her dial Vern's cell, but she wouldn't ditch him. She'd be stupid to ditch him. He was the only person who could help her now. Maybe he'd come to understand that, and maybe not.

Maybe she'd come to understand it too.

Trying not to let his agitation crank her higher, Katie kept an eye out for men in black military gear or police uniforms. She assumed the keepers had quashed the human onlookers at the bridge, any cops and the Birmingham border patrol. For now. The patrol would have notified their superior as soon as they'd picked up Marcus's essence and possibly phoned in a warning about the attack by unknown operatives in minivans.

The keepers could more easily erase their activities from the human's system than the pack's system. Though Lars was the bigger threat, she couldn't ignore the threat posed by any packers who might stumble across them. She stepped toward Marcus as they waited at the crosswalk. "Notice anything out of the ordinary? Sirens in the distance? The musical sounds of Lars venting his rage at our daring escape?"

He kind of smiled at her and shook his head slightly. "I see the garage. Make and model?"

In case they got separated? "Tan Ford station wagon, ninety-eight, looks like it's been in a wreck." It had. Dad had shit aim behind a gun and behind a wheel.

When the light changed, a tall man in a business suit, intent on his cell phone, barged into Katie. She lurched into Marcus, glad he was close or she might have eaten some pavement.

Marcus's whole body stiffened. "Watch what you're doing."

"Maybe you and your girlfriend shouldn't stand in the way when the rest of us are busy making a living, redneck," the guy said with an insulting sneer.

Quicker than the guy could ask Siri to find him a wine bar, Marcus clapped a hand on his shoulder and whirled him out of the crowd. The fancy phone clattered to the pavement. "A simple apology would suffice."

"I'm fine." Katie raised her hands. "It's not a big deal." If she'd wanted the guy flattened, she'd have flattened him herself.

But the guy's jaw dropped when Marcus's eyes flash pale blue.

Dammit. They'd almost made it to the garage. What the heck was up with Marcus? Was it residue from that weird spell Lars had cast that made all the packers shift, or just residue from the tension?

"Wh…what are you on, buddy?" the guy asked loudly. Several people halted and stared.

When one flipped out a cell phone, Katie sidled over to him and placed a well-mannered hand on the young man's wrist. She hoped he recognized how quickly it could become an ill-mannered hand.

What she wouldn't give for a sachet of lemongrass right now, to chase away snakes and annoying humans.

"No camera," she told him.

"Don't touch me, lady." The kid jerked away from her but replaced the phone in his pocket. She smiled politely. A witch couldn't always rely on magic.

Now to separate Marcus and the business suit guy.

The guy shoved Marcus. "I'm not apologizing for shit. You don't know who you're messing with."

Marcus's eyes narrowed. Good. It hid their color. "I don't need to know."

"Get out of my space, druggie." The guy swung a punch at Marcus's jaw.

Crap. Katie dashed toward them. Before she got there, Marcus caught the guy's fist and held it. Simply held it.

The guy wrenched back, but Marcus's wolf-inspired strength would put any human to shame. They stood there, snarling at each other, like the front pair in a square dance of hate. More people stopped to watch, whispering, and Katie couldn't convince them all to put away their stupid phones.

She had to end this.

Business suit guy lurched, jumped and pushed, but Marcus didn't budge. A fierce grin lit his handsome face.

"You're on meth." Sweat beaded the human's brow. "Crazy redneck."

"It's a fight," someone said excitedly. "You getting this?"

Hell, hell, hell. There was nobody around to wipe the memories of these humans. Let the redirection commence.

Katie inserted herself between them, flung her arms around Marcus and kissed him.

TWELVE

MARCUS FORGOT ALL about the dolt who needed to be taught a lesson and caught Katie before she could get away. Her lithe body plastered against him. Her cheek bumped his chin. She raised herself onto her toes, and her lips found his.

Her mouth was warm. Anxious. This wasn't desire. She meant to distract him. In his peripheral hearing, the dolt yelled some nasty things and strutted off, as if he'd won the argument.

Marcus didn't care. He'd been a testosterone-addled idiot to fight a human in public, and Katie's ambush was the reminder he needed.

That didn't mean he wasn't going to turn it around on her. He wouldn't be manipulated anymore. They'd escaped Lars together, barely, but that didn't mean he could trust her. What they did, whether they kissed—that was his call, not hers.

When he tolerated the embrace but didn't respond, she opened her eyes.

"My hero," she said, her expression apprehensive. "You saved me. Can we go?"

Marcus hadn't been certain he should kiss her. Kissing was personal, an exchange for lovers. She was his to test, not his to love. He'd been aware that she'd wanted him to kiss her before and had denied her several times.

But since she'd started it…

He captured her lips, parting them roughly. The sweetness of her mouth lured his tongue, and he licked inside her, tasting and retreating. When her tongue answered his, his fingers dug into her back.

He explored her lips until her scent edged from worry to passion. She needed to remember who was in charge, and why, and how quickly she would lose herself if he willed it. Her hips pressed him. Her hand caressed his neck, his shoulders. When he bit her lip, she let out a breathy little moan only he could hear. She curled her tongue against his upper lip, inviting him to continue.

"Get a room," someone yelled.

If they'd had a modicum of privacy, he'd have wound her up until she was aching and wet before stopping. He couldn't let that part of himself rule.

Despite his best, most mature intentions, his cock hardened.

Abruptly he set her away from him.

"Your reminder was well-timed." He forced his voice to come out measured and unaffected.

"You're welcome," she said gruffly, her cheeks flushed and her lips reddened. "I thought that might be less conspicuous than kicking your ass."

As if she could. He'd known he was stronger and faster after the transformation, but he'd just taken out three trained keepers and had zero injuries to show for it.

It was one of the first times he'd truly appreciated what it meant to be a wolf.

"Adrenaline is tricky. I haven't been in many confrontations in the past year." He took her hand and led her across the street toward the garage, trying to walk as if he didn't have an erection. Yet again.

"This wasn't because of the spell Lars cast?"

"The berserker spell? I don't think so. That forces a shift and temporary...ah, rage."

"Feral." She shook her head. "Like wolves need encouragement to freak out."

He raised his chin as the faint wail of police sirens tweaked his consciousness. It might have nothing to do with them. But it might be cops responding to the fracas at the tattoo parlor and the bridge. He increased his speed as much as he could without making Katie trot.

"Do you hear something?" she asked.

"Sirens." They reached the garage and ducked their heads, hiding their faces from cameras. Since Lars had been unable to mobilize his troops in time, their pursuers would have no way of knowing they'd gone into this building unless wolves, magic or technology told them.

Tonya's station wagon was parked on the fourth level. They snagged the hidden key, got into the battered car—with him behind the wheel—and exited the garage. While Katie hadn't wrecked the stolen truck, he didn't trust her driving.

Perhaps she'd been affected by panic and blood loss. And perhaps she'd been the one to inflict the damage on the station wagon.

Katie buckled up. "Find a...I mean, could we find a public phone and call Vern?"

"No." Vernon had known the keepers were in the vicinity. The old fox would have plans and more plans. "He can handle it."

"I just want reassurance they're okay, and I want to tell them I'm okay. We rendezvous in forty-eight, but anything could happen in two days." She pulled antibacterial wipes and a spray can of heal-all out of the glove box to tend her wounds. The small magic popped Marcus's ears. "We took Tonya's car. What if they need it?"

"I suspect Vernon can procure another vehicle," he said dryly. "Wasn't he the one who taught you everything you know? Like, say, carjacking?"

"A witch can't rely on magic alone." Gunshot healed, Katie plucked briar stickers and flower fuzz off her pants from their flight through the pasture. "Where are we going? The tattoo shop isn't far, and if we drive by it fast enough—"

"No. Birmingham could have shown up in force or Lars may get a wolf to track us." It wouldn't matter to Lars if the wolf were willing; he would be all too happy to use pain to enforce cooperation.

"If he had wolves, they'd have been able to catch us."

"They almost did. And now, I daresay he's more motivated." Lars had had no interest in treating wolves as anything but beasts when Marcus had worked for the council. Would Lars let his purism and hatred for wolves get in the way of opportunism? "He has several packers to choose from."

"That did occur to me," she admitted. "You have an answer for everything, don't you?"

"I'm a scientist. That's the idea."

She grumbled one last time, more sound than words. He hoped it was an acknowledgement the tattoo parlor was unsafe. Katie herself had said she was a realist and a survivor.

He hit the highway that led to the state park. Every minute or so, Katie stared behind them, expression pinched. He didn't think her uneasiness was because of what lay ahead but what she was leaving behind. No matter what he thought of her character, her loyalty to her family was formidable.

He wished she'd throw her loyalty—and magic—into his corner.

He accepted that Katie wasn't evil. Perhaps she never had been. He was driven by family loyalty himself, and he'd done questionable things. Like kidnap a woman, tie her up and grope her in the name of science.

Did she mean it when she'd told Vernon she had an agreement that bound her to Marcus? Or had she been placating him until a more auspicious time to escape?

He'd have to make sure she didn't get one.

He tested the power of the station wagon's motor, satisfied it would pull the Airstream. No suspicious rattles, good response to the gas pedal. He'd noted a trailer hookup.

Marcus glanced at Katie, who was, of course, watching the road behind them. Her lips tightened and pursed as she...well, he didn't know what she was doing, moving her mouth like that. Her freckled nose scrunched next. Perhaps it was a reflexive gesture.

"Are you hungry?" he asked.

She wrinkled her nose one last time and faced the windshield again. Sunlight reflected briefly off her glasses. "I could eat."

"I have food at the trailer. I thought we'd go there first. Lars would expect us to disappear immediately." He wasn't asking for her thoughts, he was telling her. "So we won't."

"At least not until after the rendezvous," she said, as if it were her choice. "Birmingham won't sense us in rival pack territory, and the Nashville pack doesn't patrol frequently. I don't think they bother with this border. They have more trouble with Louisville."

"They last patrolled in September." The farther they traveled unhindered, the more Marcus unwound. The more he let himself think beyond escape. His bastard of a wolf subsided, thankfully, and he regained…himself. Goals beyond survival returned to the top of his list.

Even if anyone linked him and Katie to the hijacked truck or the parking garage, they'd have no idea where the station wagon had gone. There were no traffic cameras on the quiet, wooded road to the state park. If Lars co-opted wolves, it was too wide a search radius, and Nashville territory to boot. Without a spell like Vernon's location magic that Tonya had apparently used to find Katie the first time, there was no way Lars could trace Marcus and Katie. As long as the two of them played it safe.

Once they reached the Airstream, Marcus could renew the perimeter spell and get back to his original quest—the experiments that would render the keepers irrelevant and hopefully liable for some of their past actions. It would take him part of the afternoon to replot his variables. After he sanitized his workspace, he could run his first test on Katie.

Phase one. He was getting excited imagining his newest avenue of research. Could he be a witch again this time tomorrow?

He thought of that with great satisfaction, thought of beating that son of a bitch Hiram Lars, thought of how proud Elisa would be—but then other thoughts took over.

Tonight he'd have Katie in his bed again. His to do whatever he wanted to.

Dammit, he had to be structured about this. His wolf had to behave.

Scientist Marcus. He needed scientist Marcus to be ascendant tonight.

"After you eat, do you think you can fall asleep or will you be too tense?" he asked as they approached the cutoff for the park. He'd prefer she sleep naturally. His sleep spells were weapons-grade, like the keepers'. Hit a woman her size with one of those, and she might be out for days. The delay would be bothersome.

"Why?"

"To rebuild your magic. We're going to need it." At least enough to read chi during the experiment. Once in the beginning to set the baseline, once near the peak—preferably during, but he'd understand if she was unable to concentrate—and once afterward. Alas, no combination of technology and magic had enabled him to film an aura or lattice. They had to be seen live.

"I could use a nap," she admitted. "Full drain yesterday, late night, joke around with Lars, narrow escape from death… Hell, I'd sleep for two days if nobody woke me."

He directed the station wagon off the main park road and onto the gravel lane that led to the campsites. He didn't always stay here when he made this loop—no trailer hookups—but he kept the Airstream stocked. Yes, it was definitely looking like tonight would be the night. For scientific advancement, and that was what mattered. As long as…

"Will a nap allow you to cast minor spells by, say, 10:00 p.m.?"

"10:00 p.m. How specific."

"I like specifics."

"Specifically, can I call Vern's phone at 10:00 p.m.?"

"We already vetoed that. If they do get caught…" He held up a finger when she shot him a dirty look. "Lars could have Vernon's phone. It could be the phone they traced in the first place when they chased him to the tattoo parlor. You want to take that chance, even from a public location?"

She sighed. "You're right, you're right. Can't call Vern."

Hopefully that would be the end of that. "So, your magic renewal rate?"

She wasn't sulking, exactly, though her expression wrinkled. "I should be able to cast minor spells by ten if I get a nap."

One hurdle down. The true eye mix was innocuous enough that she couldn't subvert it into a weapon. "Can you link someone else into the true eye spell?"

If she couldn't, it would require a mirror and additional Q&A during the act as she described what she saw. He'd use a digital voice recorder so he wouldn't need to pause for note-taking, but still. It would be easier if he could see her chi for himself.

The more he considered proper procedure, the calmer he grew.

"I've never been the focal of a true eye link." She crooked a knee onto the seat as she turned toward him. The station wagon bumped to a stop. "Here we are again. Home sweet home."

He went around the nose of the car to open her door. Or he tried to. She was already half out when he got there. She gave him an odd look.

"This way." They reentered the trailer, securing all the locks. If he'd done so last night, Tonya couldn't have busted in on them, and the rest of the day might have gone very differently.

Katie watched him set the protection spells using his primed components. No wolf or witch would realize the people in the trailer weren't human for twenty-four hours unless they barged through the door. That gave him ample time to enact phase one and begin programming phase two.

"I actually need to tell you something," she said. "Before we—do anything."

He dusted the chalk from the perimeter spell off his hands. "What's that?"

She leaned against the kitchen-cum-laboratory counter. "When I attempted to wipe your memories, I sensed something unanticipated. I assume it was your lattice."

"Interesting." Marcus booted up the laptop so he could start crunching numbers after lunch. She'd observed, all on her own, one of the essential similarities between witches and wolves. The magic. Tonight, she'd realize they had even more similarities. "Did it surprise you?"

"Does it not surprise you?"

"I already knew. I suppose as a keeper who merely wiped your victims, you wouldn't have viewed a wolf's lattice, but my work for the council included it." How much more should he share with her? How much did she care to know? She was participating in his research out of obligation. Well, obligation and sexual prurience, but mainly obligation.

If prurience were enough to drive her, he wouldn't be her first wolf.

He did like that—being her first. It made his wolf—all right, it made him—impatient. Possessive. The reaction had nothing to do with research.

But it was within acceptable parameters. Even a scientist attempting to cure cancer and take down a corrupt military organization while running for his life needed the occasional frivolity.

"I never denied wolves have magic. That's common sense. Biology and science, as far as I know, don't allow a person to change into an animal."

He smiled, but hid it behind the refrigerator door as he assembled the ingredients for sandwiches. Despite the semi-popular belief science would one day account for shifters in Earth's genome—or prove them to be aliens—

he hadn't seen anything in his studies to suggest their powers were anything but mystical, even if certain aspects of magic could be studied with scientific methodology. And, of course, wolf shifters didn't realize witches existed, which might reverse their outlook about magic entirely.

"But your essence, your magic...there was only one path for it, Marcus."

He'd observed that during his time with the keepers too, but disagreed it was permanent. He sniffed the bread to make sure it hadn't molded and laid four slices on two paper plates. "Witches form new outlets for their power every time they master a spell. Mustard or mayo?"

"Mustard."

"Me too." He spread the yellow condiment with a knife. "As I was saying, witches can add to their magical repertoire limitlessly. I don't see why it shouldn't be the same for wolves."

Each spell a witch used, each ingredient or recipe, forged a unique path, creating a lattice of connections and power. It wasn't difficult for witches to work new spells if they had the capacity, so he ought to be able to regain the magical paths he'd lost.

He knew how to cast the spells. He knew the magic was there, simmering inside him. But the wolf had driven a channel so deeply into his soul that the magic had nowhere else to go.

"It isn't the same for wolves. That's what being a wolf means." Though she'd watched him make the sandwiches, Katie peeled back the top slice of bread in the sandwich he'd given her to inspect the cheese, meat and lettuce. "You have one way to use your magic. One all-consuming way. It's a tradeoff."

"Pack bonding ceremonies and other wolf rituals involve component-related magic use," he pointed out. "Is something wrong with the sandwich?"

She stuck the bread back together. "Habit."

"I'm not trying to drug you, if that's what you're worried about."

"I just like to see what I'm getting," she said around a bite. After she swallowed, she returned to their topic of discussion. "Pack spells aren't the same as witch magic. Wolves can't cast them at will. Do pack wolves' lattices show signs of the rituals?"

Marcus didn't like to eat standing. It was bad for digestion. After he wiped all traces of bread crumbs from the countertop, he seated himself at the tiny table. "No, but I'll be able to remove my constraints. I just need a... backhoe."

"A backhoe," she repeated dubiously. She sat across from him.

"Magical TNT. That's where you come in. But first we need to become accustomed to linking."

"Is that a euphemism?"

"Magical linking." He wouldn't mind becoming accustomed to fucking, but outside the scope of the experiment, it wouldn't be strictly necessary. "There are waters in the bottom drawer of the fridge if you like."

She got up, opened the door. "In the crisper? No veggies?"

"I've sort of lost my taste for them," he admitted. "I'd appreciate a water too, please."

"Just because you have magic doesn't mean we can link. I couldn't, well..." As she opened the water bottles, her back to him, her voice grew formal and concise. "I may have tried to use your magic to augment the spell I was working at that particular time."

"You tried to use my own essence to life wipe me?" It was so ballsy, he almost admired her.

"I failed." She handed him a drink but didn't return to the table. Holding her plate in one hand, she paced to the Airstream's door to stare through a crack in the blinds. "I don't know if I can bring you into the true eye."

"You can."

"How can you be so sure?"

"Not all the experiments I did for the keepers were unsuccessful." With the right herbal inducements, a witch could link with a wolf and absorb wolf magic to bolster a spell. That discovery, which he'd made under the keepers, was part of the foundation of his entire hypothesis.

Witches and wolves. The same.

She glanced his way, her expression blank. "Did you hurt any wolves in your time with the keepers?"

"Did *you* hurt any wolves in your time with the keepers?" He raised an eyebrow.

"Yes," she said simply. "Though not as many as rumor would have it. I neutralized a much higher proportion than I had to...put down."

Though their acquaintance was short, he believed her. If she was being honest, he could be honest as well.

"I didn't see the point in hurting anyone for the trials I did." It had taken fancy footwork to avoid cruelty while making himself valuable enough not to be killed. Lars had wanted weapons. Marcus had given him theories. And, apparently, the foundation for a large-scale berserker spell. "Are you concerned I'll hurt you?"

"Hurt *me?*" She crumpled her empty paper plate. "Honestly, I hadn't thought that far ahead."

"Do you like being hurt?" He had wondered. That was another variable he hadn't calculated and wasn't sure it would lend itself to his thesis anyway.

She crossed her arms. "What kind of question is that?"

"It's not complicated. Do you like pain?" He pictured her on her hands and knees, her ass pink from a spanking. Her slit wet and shining because of it. Perhaps that was something he could incorporate, if required. The sexual urges he felt toward Katie were more forceful than he'd ever experienced. He hadn't been around enticing females since his transformation, and wasn't sure if it was him—or her.

He hoped it was her, because he didn't appreciate his wolf changing him in yet another intrinsic fashion.

"When I said the bullet wound made me giddy, I was kidding." Her fingers tapped her elbows. "Is there some reason you need to know my pain tolerance?"

So he wasn't the only one who enjoyed asking questions. "Your, ah, completion is necessary in phase one."

"Well, that's good news." Red tinged her cheeks. "And here I thought you wanted to see how tough I was."

"Is there anything else I should know about your preferences?" One thing he'd verified—non-orgasmic sex acts didn't push a witch over the edge. He'd had several encounters with his test female before spending the night with her and transforming himself.

"I like chocolate, gift cards to the organic grocer and long walks on the beach."

"You require romance?" he asked, secretly intrigued. Romance meant pursuit and seduction, and pursuing Katie appealed to him. "Last night you were ready to—"

She cut him off. "That was another joke, courtesy of that hilarious comedienne Chang Cai. I agreed to your terms. Trying to woo me would be ridiculous at this point." She lowered her gaze. "I know this is business to you."

He'd do his best to make it business, but pleasure

snagged his imagination. Carnal images that had little to do with professional inquiry flashed before him. The idea of removing Katie's clothing was giving him his three hundred and seventh hard-on of the past twenty-four hours.

"You'll benefit from my success," he told her, uncrossing his legs for comfort. "If we can recover transformed wolves, keepers won't be as necessary. Lars will be demoted. He won't be able to attack us. You'll be safe. One assumes the community will be grateful to you for your part in the discovery."

"Is that your locker room speech?" She raised a fist. "Go team. We got spirit."

What did she expect? As much as he'd like to coax her, seduce her or chase her, she'd nixed wooing. "We don't have to be antagonistic. We just have to follow procedure."

She sighed and sat on the bed, which he hadn't put up last night. She toed off her shoes. "Do you have the whole thing diagrammed?"

"Not yet. I'll work on it this afternoon while you nap."

"Mmm, titillating. Have at it, Dr. Ruth. I'm going to sleep." She crawled onto the mattress and curled on the far side of it, her back to him.

Katie wouldn't transform tonight—but he had to make damn sure she felt as if she was going to. She needed to understand the wolf inside her in order to help lead him back to his magic.

The niggling discomfort he felt with regard to their bargain meant nothing. He'd had sex for science five point five times, and the ladies hadn't considered themselves mistreated. Sure, they hadn't known, but Katie being in the loop should enhance productivity.

Moreover, she desired him. They both knew it. If he

could approach this from a research angle, he should be able to remain objective. He'd get his analysis and she'd get her sex. Why was this transaction in any way a bad thing?

THIRTEEN

KATIE HANDED THE sex charts back to Marcus and shot him a sour look. She'd managed to sleep, despite her guilt over deserting her family in a Dumpster, her unease about Lars and her qualms about the night ahead. A small, fresh pocket of magic simmered inside her. She was loathe to use it for Marcus's bullshit experiment.

Yes, she wanted to sleep with him. Oh, hell yes. But why did they have to jump into this? They had larger concerns. His crazy theories weren't going anywhere, and Tonya, Dad and Vern might be. His rationale that recovering transformed wolves would protect her from Lars wasn't that compelling.

Lars wouldn't let anything stop him from finding her now that he knew she was alive.

They should check the rendezvous point. They should don masks and sneak back to the shop. They should drive to a public phone several counties away and call Vern's cell. They should go see a human she knew about buying a lot of guns.

But no. They were going to screw. In a very stupid way.

She suspected this was more about Marcus's personal goals than outside factors. The sooner she did this, the sooner she could be free of him. Which was what she wanted—right?

"Did you read the charts?" Her handsome scientist, her sexy wolf, wore a lab coat, latex gloves, goggles and a frown. He'd mutated into another person while tucked away in his Airstream, his safe space, crunching numbers and diagramming the missionary position. "You can't possibly have read the whole thing."

"It won't work." Her desire had been squelched by the dispassionate way he planned to go about this. She hadn't had sex in four years, and she'd been fantasizing about Marcus for a month.

This was what she got?

Where was the man who'd kissed her in the middle of a crowd of humans? Where was, good Goddess, the man from last night? The one who'd strip searched her and made her so wet she'd been ready to toss their hostilities aside and beg?

If she had to fuck someone for science, she wanted that guy.

Only that guy could make her forget what she should be doing right now—finding her family.

"Why won't it work?" Marcus shuffled the papers, returning them to chronological order. "This is a non-strenuous series of movements that should lead to the desired conclusion within an economical time frame."

At least he hadn't illustrated his diagrams with stick people. "So you want me to lie on my back…"

"That would be simplest."

"When the clock chimes once, I cast true eye and link you in."

"I need to read your chi. At that juncture I will rise until I'm perpendicular to your body."

"Perpendicular. Perpen…dicular." She felt like a twelve-year-old, giggling because she'd met someone named "Peter."

"That means our bodies form a ninety-degree angle."

"I know what it means." She had to bite her lip. The

entire situation was becoming so farcical she wanted to laugh.

Better than crying. She could either think about Marcus's boffing blueprint or about the torture Lars could be inflicting on Dad, Tonya and Vern. While she hadn't had a brainstorm for rescuing them yet, hiding here, prepping for sex like a horny little coward, sat poorly with Katie's conscience.

"What about when the clock chimes twice?" Marcus asked patiently.

"That's when I'm supposed to narrate into the digital recorder whether I'm feeling anything magical."

"We'll place the recorder in a handy location," he offered. "By stage eight you should be quite conscious of the wolf inside you."

"Stage eight. Is that the one with the…" Was she really going to say this? "Once-per-second thrusts?"

He inserted the papers into a manila folder. "So you did read it."

She pressed her hand to her forehead. "This is not happening."

"You agreed," he reminded her. "And need I remind you, I know you're interested?"

"Am I right now?" she asked bluntly. "Smell me."

His lips tightened. "I'm sure it's nerves. Those should disappear once we're underway."

When, in stage one? That's where he'd committed himself to two minutes per breast. That was his first move. Nowhere in the chart had he mentioned kisses. He hadn't even graphed in a handshake.

"It's important we don't amend any variables." He stripped off his lab coat, placing it in a hamper. "Think of it as a spell recipe. You create the mixture the same way each time if you want the magic to be the same."

Her lust was gone. She had nothing left inside but worry. "No two women are the same."

"I allowed for a five percent margin of error." Marcus removed his shoes and stashed them in a drawer under the bed. Next he stripped off his socks.

"Are you undressing?"

He paused, socks hovering over the hamper. "Nudity is standard during sex, Katie. Is that an issue?"

"I…" Good Goddess. Did he expect her to strip like it meant nothing? Nervous and flustered—but not in an eager way—Katie stalled. "So we're doing this now."

"It's 10:15 p.m., and you have enough magic for three chi readings." He unbuttoned his shirt. Because she was so flummoxed by the situation, the sight of his chest didn't intrigue her. "We're fifteen minutes behind schedule, and we took the dittany. Can you sense its effect?"

The honey-based mix had given her a sweet taste in the back of her mouth and a tingly tongue. He claimed it would enable her to link with him as she did with witches.

"I can tell the spell is ready to be activated." She'd used wild dittany in healing concoctions, but not for this. "Whether or not it will behave as promised remains to be seen."

"Then we can proceed."

Reluctantly she rose from the bed and walked to him like a child dreading punishment. "Can I get some privacy?"

"To undress?" He switched on the light in the bathroom, a harsh, white glare. "I've seen most of you already. And I am a doctor."

"Not that kind of doctor." She couldn't tell if he was ribbing her. Surely, if he was in the mood to rib her, he'd be flirting. Offering her libido enhancer, complimenting her figure, double entendre-ing about completion.

From the minute he'd walked into the tattoo parlor yesterday, everything between them had felt like foreplay. Now that the time had come, he was as enthused as a fence post.

Marcus folded his shirt into a neat packet. Then he tucked the ever-present bay capsule into a bottle and slid his pants down his long, powerful legs. His entire body, everything about his physique, was perfection. His build was neither too bulky nor too lean. His white briefs, as geeky as the day was long on most men, did his hips all the favors in the world.

To her disappointment, not even the sight of his manly radiance motivated her.

Marcus calmly folded his pants, set them atop his shirt and raised an eyebrow at her. "I would like to document phase one before midnight, Katie. The intercourse stage will take twenty minutes. Then I'll need to input the data."

Twenty minutes. Nine stages of one to three minutes apiece. And he thought this would complete her?

Katie licked her dry lips. He'd find out, she supposed, when she did as the charts bade—and lay there. "You're serious about this."

"Very." According to the fit of his white briefs, this wasn't arousing him any more than it was her.

She stripped off her dark T-shirt, throwing it onto the floor. He frowned, of course. Next she unsnapped her pants, watching for a reaction. Any reaction.

Nope.

She slid the pants beside the crumpled shirt. She'd stashed some flower fuzz in her cuffs. The dried agrimony could turn out to be useful, and she'd noted some cedar outside the Airstream. Marcus had put his other, more interesting simples in lockboxes, as well as the gun and ammunition.

Her brassiere was a sports bra, her preference during situations that might include running and jumping. Marcus blinked twice. *Dammit. Here goes.* She stripped it over her head and shoved her panties off without ceremony.

Here she was. Birthday suited up. About to have sex.

He placed a big, warm hand on her chilled shoulder. "Place yourself on the left side of the bed so you can reach our materials."

In stage one, she was supposed to be flat on her back. Actually, he'd written her as flat on her back the entire time, with minimal input into the proceedings, but he had allowed for her to arrange her legs as needed.

With an eyeroll, she flopped onto the bed. If Marcus remained in his scientist persona, this wouldn't be as orgasmic an experience as he was assuming. She had a lot on her mind. Life and death, mistakes and regrets, pain and suffering, and another man. A man named Hiram Lars who wanted to kill them all.

If it turned out she wasn't alpha and lost her magic after this, it would serve him right.

But in her heart, she knew that wasn't the case. She was alpha. It explained too much.

Marcus fetched the kava powder he'd prepared, the digital voice recorder, a clean cloth and the small clock. She was surprised he hadn't included a bay capsule. "Are you ready?"

"Are you?"

"Of course." He set the clock as if readying himself for a night of sleep. "True eye first. We need a baseline."

He'd stored the herbal mix in a shaker, which he extended to her. "Hold out your hand." She did. He sprinkled the powder into it and clasped her hand with his own. "Link us."

If only he meant that in a sexy way. Katie closed her eyes and spooled out her magic, stingy and cross. Sent it through the kava, waking the true eye. She sank further into Marcus's psyche in search of his essence.

As he'd said, it wasn't hard to connect him to the chi spell. In fact, she realized, with a poke or two, she could scoop up his magical essence from the lattice and...

Katie felt her probe snap back with a stinging blow. The true eye flared around her body, and her vision misted with the hazy dark blue of her chi.

"That's got it," Marcus said, satisfied. His handclasp was strong but not particularly ardent. "I should have warned you not to try and filch any power. I incorporated some defenses against that. You probably noticed the first time too."

"I wouldn't have taken much." The possibilities intrigued her. Witches could borrow from wolves. If Marcus had discovered this in his time with the keepers, why hadn't it been acknowledged by the rest of the coven network?

But then something occurred to her. "Marcus, I've been drained since last night. We've been in danger. If you could have shared your magic with me to protect Tonya and Ba, and they end up getting hurt, I will personally—"

"Your assumption is off-base." Marcus hovered over her, his free hand outlining her aura as if caressing it. "When you're drained, you can't precipitate a link to absorb the magic in the first place."

She opened her mouth to ask more questions, but he started talking into the digital recorder. "Mostly dark blue, turquoise highlights, elements of forest green, white core, of course, approximately ten percent illumination. Moving deeper, a vigorous lattice, impressive range, all directions, some that aren't familiar. Many threads seem doubled. I'm wondering if that's the portion of the test subject that's convex. She's the first keeper I... Never mind, take that out. Where was I?"

"Blue, turquoise, green?" Tonya had read Katie's chi any number of times, if not her lattice. She said it told her Katie was quick-tempered, untrusting, passionate, practical and—most stupidly of all—easily hurt. She wasn't so sure Marcus categorizing her as easily hurt worked in her favor.

"Not as much purple frill as I'd have expected." His gaze cut through the aura and trained on her face. "I thought you said you were ready, Katie?"

"What, for my visit to Doctor Marcus's Good Time Sex Clinic?" she asked. "It's super. I'm all kinds of turned on." As perturbed as she was, it surprised her that she continued to speak to Marcus as if they'd known each other years. Her father, Vern and Tonya were the only people she'd ever been informal with. The intensity of her and Marcus's time together had breached her normal barriers.

Or maybe at this point she had nothing to lose.

"Ah. Well." He wiped their palms with a damp towel as the effects of the true eye faded. "This did seem to go differently when my subjects weren't aware it was an experiment."

"I'm sure your Casanova act had them aflutter." Marcus could be charismatic and sexy—she'd witnessed it herself. Apparently she didn't merit the effort.

He climbed over her as if she was an obstacle and stretched out at her side. "Can you reach the chi mix and the digital recorder?"

She should be feeling anticipatory. Instead, she found herself wondering where Vern would have taken Dad and Tonya to hide.

"I asked you a question," Marcus reminded her.

Right. She stretched an arm. "I can reach the table."

"Make sure the clock is positioned where I can see it. The stages are timed. Please release the stopwatch button and place your hands above your head."

Katie stifled a sigh. But she complied, stretching up, wondering if she could pretend this was last night and he had her handcuffed. Last night, he'd been into this. He'd been wrestling her, desiring her, and she him. It had been the hottest thing she'd ever experienced.

He cupped one of her breasts softly. His thumb skated across the nipple. His attention was laser-focused on her chest. "Are you sensitive here?"

"Normally." Right now he could have been giving her a breast exam for all the feelings he was rousing in her. He dutifully palmed her, alternating sides, until he glanced at the clock.

"Huh."

She clasped her hands, wondering whether it would offend him if she dozed off briefly. "What's huh?"

He met her gaze, his eyes a deep, dark brown. "It's been four minutes."

"Already?" she asked in mock surprise. Time sure flew when you weren't having fun.

He gruffed at her, "I'm going to move to the second stage."

He rested his hand on her stomach. Katie tried to conjure up some eagerness and failed.

"There's no stage where I get to touch you, is there?" Despite her fantasies about wolves and about Marcus— about fighting, forced seduction and handcuffs—in practice Katie had never been passive in bed. She trusted no man enough to surrender control. She chose her partners, what they did and when. What would he do if she flipped him onto his back and went down on him? Would he deny himself a blow job because he hadn't calculated it as part of the trial?

"That's not a variable in phase one." What she was doing with Marcus wasn't surrender. There was no taking, no giving, no excitement. There was no passion. He traced circles on her abdomen. Then he caught her opposite hip firmly, leaned over her and checked the clock again.

"Not bad," he said. "I only went thirty seconds over."

A cool breeze from the ceiling fan swept her, and she goose bumped from head to toe. Marcus regarded her face for a moment. "You aren't saying much."

"What is there to say?"

"It's not unusual for one partner to encourage the other by this point."

She had to admit, she was beginning to feel insulted. "It doesn't matter if I encourage you or not. You've got your mind made up how this should go."

He touched the hair between her legs gently. "I would think a woman who lives in a witness protection program would appreciate knowing what to expect."

"In life, I do. Surprises can mean danger when people want to kill you. But some surprises can be inspirational." She was philosophizing in bed with a naked wolf while his hand plopped on her as if she wasn't even attractive.

"All right." He applied pressure between her legs, massaging the entire area. "Next time I won't show you the chart."

Katie stared at the plastic lights in the ceiling. She tried not to worry about her family, tried to relax, tried to recapture the thrill. The only spark of life in the room was the near-silent ticking of the little clock and the *shush* of the generator.

"I need you to narrate stage four."

Irritation flashed in her, the prickliness Tonya and

now Marcus had read in her chi. She grabbed the digital recorder and clicked it on. "Dear diary. I'm at stage four of the sex experiment Marcus blackmailed me into. I'm thinking about sleeping until the end of it. If I were asleep, I could quit wondering whether Lars is torturing my family while I'm laying here like a corpse, having the worst sex of my life."

His hand stilled. "The worst? That's not what I had in mind for narration."

"This isn't what I had in mind for sex." She pressed pause. "Is that enough for now? I hate the way my voice sounds on tape."

"So you aren't…"

Katie stared at him through her lashes. If she'd had her glasses on, the stare—over the top of the frames—would have been more effective. "Why would I be?"

He leaned forward, closer than he'd been all evening, and sniffed her neck. "I don't understand. We've wanted to sleep together since we officially met."

"Two whole days. We're practically engaged." Tired of this, she reached down and grabbed his penis, surprised to find it erect. "I *did* want to sleep with you. And I'll be the first one cheering you on if you cure cancer. But I'm too worried about my father and Tonya to concentrate. You'll have to work harder to make me forget I'm being a selfish shithead right now."

"You're not being selfish." When she looked at his face again, his eyes were beginning to lighten. So she was affecting him.

She decided to hassle him. She fondled his shaft, checking proportions. His eyes continued to lighten. His heavy cock grew under her touch. "True. I'm not exactly getting anything out of this, am I? Though you do seem to have a decent-sized dick."

"I set procedures for a reason." He grasped her hand and removed it from himself, firmly but decisively. "If I botch the variables, the experiment will be negated. We only get one shot at a first encounter."

"I'm not fighting you." She raised her hand above her head again, proving it. "I even complimented your penis."

He shook his head. "You're not responding."

She huffed. "I told you. I'm worried, and this is dull. How can *you* be responding when I'm practically a bystander?"

"It's not dull to me," he said, perturbed. "There's a beautiful, naked woman in my bed. A woman who's agreed to help me with something that's as important to me as your family is to you. Something I've been trying to achieve for years, rather...desperately."

She'd heard of people being single-minded and wasn't sure she was flattered. "The science has given you a boner?"

"You knock me off course." He openly admired her body, his eyes silver now. He cupped her breast almost reverently. "You make me forget my objectives. I could contain myself before, but now? I'm not so sure."

"Because you're a wolf?"

"No, I had...encounters after the transformation. Enough for a quality check." His fingers caught her nipple, the reverence disappearing. Blurring into something else. Something darker. "It's because you're you."

Katie stared up at him and confessed a deep desire she'd never told anyone. Not even herself. "Has it occurred to you I don't want you to contain yourself?"

"If I lose my grip, I may not be able to get it back." But even as he said it, he bent toward her, scenting her again. It wasn't impersonal like before. His mouth opened on her skin. He pinched her nipple softly. Rolling it. Stretching it. Waking her. His lips brushed her pulse—which leaped for him, as if on command.

He tugged her nipple sharply enough to hurt. She gasped. She grabbed his wrist to drag it away, but he was far too strong.

"You can't hide what arouses you from a wolf." He did the same to her other nipple, his fingers a heady clamp of sensation. His mouth brushed her jaw. His tongue brushed the corner of her lips. "Your scent is delicious. Tell me again about your pain tolerance, Katie."

"I don't think I…"

He bit her neck. She squeaked, but an excited ache stirred between her legs. When his fingers pulled her nipple again, she squirmed.

"Is this dull now?"

She shook her head. "I'm not so sure about the pain."

"Pain and pleasure often have similar neural responses." He licked the place where he'd bitten her. It stung. Had he broken the skin? "But that might not be it. Perhaps your desire is more about submission."

While she liked the idea of a passionate, involved Marcus, one who wanted her for reasons beyond science, she wasn't so sure about yielding control. She'd imagined something more along the lines of sharing it.

"I'm sure it's not," she lied.

"That's unfortunate." Marcus's cock pressed her hip, large and hard. "Because I have a profound desire to dominate you."

Katie shivered and gulped.

"Maybe you're right about following procedure," she said, suddenly nervous. He could do anything he wished to her, and she had no magic or strength to stop him. This could fundamentally change the person she imagined herself to be. "Your charts. Your experiment."

She'd toyed with the wolf lust all her life. With the idea that a wolf, a man, might overpower her self-control and send her tumbling. She'd been forced to use her hunger as a weapon, never truly wanting to follow it to a conclusion.

Until Marcus.

He was different, and he made *her* different. But why?

Ignoring her hesitation, he shook off her fingers and pinned her wrist to the bed. "Don't interrupt me. I'm working."

He nibbled his way down her neck while continuing to tweak and pull her nipple. He kissed and bit her in a way that hadn't been in his charts. His mouth hadn't been involved at all, and she needed his mouth.

When he ran his tongue across her aching nipple for the first time, she moaned. He licked like a cat—licked and licked, wet and fast, until her tension mounted. A kiss on one, a pinch on the other. Alternating, but then at the same time.

He sucked her into the hot cave of his mouth, making her arch her back and gasp. He growled softly and reared over her. His fingers were hard around her wrist. His cock thrust toward her. He continued to work her breasts as he positioned himself between her thighs, shoving her wide when she didn't move fast enough.

Would this wreck her?

She'd gone from zero to two hundred in the space of three minutes. He dropped a hand between her legs and found her clit with the unerring accuracy of a scientist.

Claws scraped her pussy. She twitched with alarm—and something else. He chuckled at her breast, teasing her until she kicked his leg. "I'm not into piercings, Marcus. Please don't."

"Since you said please." The claws disappeared. He

flicked and rubbed her until her folds grew slick. His fingers spread her juices until she whimpered for him.

His teeth on her nipple, his hand between her legs. Yes. He had taken control of her body. No chart, nothing but desire. She'd never let a man top her before, not for long. His finger, two fingers, sank into her welcoming pussy.

He released her wrist and shoved his fingers into her hair. Unable and unwilling to hold still, Katie embraced him. She learned the curves of his shoulders, the texture of his hair, the lean strength of his arms. His skin was smooth and warm, his muscles bunching as he fucked her with his hand.

She was helpless beneath his masterful touch.

He kissed a path up her neck, his hand changing angles as well. His palm rode her sensitive clit as his fingers thrust inside her. She wound her legs around his hips, trying to get closer.

Closer to his body, closer to the orgasm she hoped she'd be enjoying—but closer to something else too. Because it was Marcus on top of her, because his movements were growing rough, harsh, because she could hear the wolf in his pant and his growl, Katie's whole being shuddered with the need to truly surrender. To be taken. By him and him only.

This was happening. A wolf—Marcus—was about to fuck her senseless. A lifetime of battle was over. Battling the wolves, battling herself and her urges.

Katie nearly climaxed as she considered what this meant.

She was being conquered. At last. Her power was nothing compared to his power over her. She couldn't hurt or kill right now even if she'd wanted to.

"Don't forget to stop me," he whispered against her neck. His lips caressed her jaw, her ear. She held on to him with a death-grip as a strange ferocity surged inside her. Like a turbulent ocean, like her magic fighting the lattice. She tingled with it, everywhere she and Marcus touched. Inside and out.

"Katie." He took his fingers out of her. His cock slid across her pussy, eliciting a groan from them both. She arched against him, begging. "Katie, you have to stop me in time."

"Uh-huh," she managed. The only thing that would make this better was if he wouldn't stop. If he told her there was nothing she could do to stop him. If he rubbed it in.

And rubbed and rubbed and rubbed. Goddess, it was happening.

He grabbed his cock and probed her folds. The fat, rounded head kindled pleasure between her legs. "Tell me what you're feeling," he demanded.

"Good."

He smiled against her neck, and then he bit her. Hard. She whimpered.

"How good, Katie?"

He teased her slit with his cock. Up and down. Close but not close enough. She ached so much, it was as if he'd struck her, and only his cock could make it better. "Please."

"How good?" he repeated, all growly and hot. "Describe."

"Crazy." She was not at her most analytical. All she could think of was his cock driving into her pussy, driving today out of her head. All she wanted was Marcus pounding into her, sending her over the edge. But if she didn't answer as he wished, he might deny her. "Swelling with...magic."

"Yes." He plied her clit with his fingers, pinching and rousing. "What else?"

"Marcus, please." She caught at his head, his hair soft, perspiration dampening his brow. "I need you."

He pushed into her an inch, the wide head stretching her, the pleasure raw and wonderful. He went no farther, but continued to stroke her clit. She squeezed him tight with her inner muscles, loving his hiss. Bliss spiraled, fast and overwhelming, like something…something…

She curved her hips, trying to bring more of him inside her. His cock was thick enough to hurt at first, and she didn't want it easy. She pulled him, digging into his back, his ass. She kissed his neck, his taste as wonderful as his smell.

His lips teased her ear as he laughed. He reveled in her disintegration. She didn't care. Goddess, she didn't care. She just wanted him. "Please. Please, Marcus."

He withdrew until she could barely feel him against her slit. "Get the kava."

"I'm not that close," she lied. Why did he have to remind her of that? He couldn't stop now. Fantastical sensations coursed through her, a hint something was coming. Orgasm, yes, but…

He nudged his cock against her clit. The head entered her. *Yes, yes.* She hummed and curled against him, her head twisting back and forth.

When she said his name again, when she said please, he caught her lips with his. His tongue pushed into her mouth as his cock swelled in her sheath. He sipped and licked her lips, her tongue, tasting her, enjoying her gasps, her responses. She met him eagerly, showing him without words that her body was one giant *yes*.

The kissing—changed everything.

Katie's last reservation melted as she gave in to her

feelings. His cock slid farther into her, then back out. She bit his lip. Kissing her hungrily, he fell into a series of tiny thrusts that incited an erotic craving in her. His cock parted her again and again, over and over, until she couldn't bear it.

She needed him deep. Deeper. All the way. She needed completion. She opened for him everywhere, his kisses, his caresses, so intimate she could weep. Her hands and lips grew desperate, and when he quit kissing her, she whined.

With a muffled curse, he raised up, grabbed the kava and upended it on her chest. She inhaled its sweet-spicy odor. Her senses seemed razor sharp.

"Link us."

She wouldn't deny him anything. He ruled her now. She released her magic, shot it through the kava and into his psyche. As soon as she located his lattice and linked him into the spell, he shoved his cock into her up to the hilt.

Katie cried out. Goddess, it hurt. Yet it felt almost too good. Waves of stress, stress and spectacle, crashed inside her, a madness she couldn't control. She couldn't stop it. She was taken.

That's when she realized what the feeling was. It was her wolf, zinging through every one of her veins like liquid pleasure.

FOURTEEN

MARCUS PLUNGED INTO her as though he were falling. Her sleek, wet pussy obsessed him. Her lips clung to his, no longer withholding her emotions. At last she'd grown soft, vulnerable and feverish with desire. Her heart raced for him. He tried his best to concentrate on her lattice, but her scent ripened as she neared her peak, the most delectable thing he'd ever smelled.

Frantic, hot alpha female. It stirred a primal need in him to conquer her, fuck her harder and longer, in every position imaginable.

He could lose himself in a woman like Katie.

Honeyed. Alluring. Challenging. Overwhelming. His ears buzzed with the magic she'd released, the spell seething around them. Her aura fluttered wildly, a light show around their bodies.

His wolf howled its excitement. It had what it wanted—the woman, her surrender. But she was the one who needed to understand the wolf, not him. He already knew its power.

It had changed him from a mild-mannered scientist into a dominant, demanding beast intent on making this woman his possession.

Gritting his teeth, amazed he had the resolve, Marcus hoisted himself to a ninety-degree angle so he could see her lattice. He slowed his thrusts, each one sliding deep to keep her high and focused on their goal. He caught her swollen, pink clit between his fingers and stroked.

Katie's spiky, black lashes swept down over her eyes as he pleasured her. Her legs around him tensed. Her heels dented his ass with urgency. When she rocked with him, her aura undulated. Brighter than his own chi had been near transformation, her colors glowed. He could see the purple, the mottling of the gray wolf spirit as it rose, the blending of everything into a beautiful kaleidoscope. Tides flowed through her unhindered as the barrier between witch and wolf dissolved.

She was like a starburst inside. And her lattice handled the flood without allowing the wolf to channel deep.

Damn, for a camera to capture it! He absolutely had to invent one. For now he reached for the digital recorder.

She knocked it out of his hand. "No."

"Katie, the spell only lasts three—"

Her pussy clamped down on his cock, sucking the breath out of him. "Harder."

She wasn't begging. She had been, and this wasn't a plea. Her demand pulled him into her like a fierce undertow. She stared into his eyes, reached for him, and he couldn't resist. He fell on her, their bodies twining.

He was supposed to be in charge. Katie smiled. She caught his head and dragged his lips to hers in a kiss that marked him as surely as her tattoo had. Except this was a mark he couldn't shift away.

Marcus drove into her again and again, forgetting the lattice, forgetting science, forgetting everything but their mutual need. His powerful thrusts inched them up the bed until she had to brace one hand against the wall to protect her head. He kissed her over and over, catching her encouraging moans on his tongue. The chi spell disappeared with an ear pop. Nothing interfered now with his view of her lovely, rapturous face.

All he wanted to do was fuck her. Take her. Be with her. Nothing else mattered.

Her eyes bright, almost avaricious, she stared at him as they came together. As his balls tightened, as her body tightened, the intimacy and trust of their embrace cut him deeply, and he couldn't handle it anymore.

"Come," she whispered.

He climaxed with a groan, the pulses in his cock as intense as thunder. His whole body shuddered as he poured himself into her. He was on top of her, pinning her, but she commanded him.

"Yes. Yes. I feel it." She held onto him with her arms, her legs. "Goddess, you're so…" She drew in a deep breath, exhaled. She hadn't reached her peak, so he kept up the pace. He buried his nose in her neck, letting her scent guide him. His erection remained as if she'd willed it, her slickness and heat wrapping him in perfection. "That's it."

He rolled into her, grinding her clit. She climaxed, crying out and holding him. Her inner muscles grasped his cock strongly, like a fist. He rocked her through the orgasm and aftermath, intending to push her over again, until she batted at him weakly.

"Stop. I can't." Her head lolled to the side, her eyes closed, her air peaceful. "I'm dead."

He relaxed too. Her entire body clasped him. She held him as though he meant something to her, and her fingers stroked his neck.

He tried to roll off her, since he was heavy. Her arms tightened. "Mmm, not yet. Stay inside me."

There it was again. Her will lured his into alignment and he couldn't rise.

"Something's happened." Was it lassitude? Was it a natural desire to please the woman in his bed? Was it something else?

"Something awesome," she agreed. She locked her ankles behind his hips to trap him against her.

He'd been around Harry Travis—though obviously not in bed. Harry had, at Marcus's request, exerted his alpha. Marcus had felt the magnetism of it, similar to this. "Your alpha is awake. I'm sure of it."

"My wolf did wake—I felt it." Her fingertips traced his hairline, around his ears, caressing him as if she liked touching him instead of merely fucking him. "First time since I was a teenager. You were right. That was insane. But it's faded now. I guess it wasn't like that for you?"

"The wolf stayed with me." After his wolf had put in its command appearance, it had inundated him. His awareness, his senses and his consciousness had guttered faster and faster until his essence…exploded. He'd quickly, and rudely, deserted his lover's bed so he could be alone when he underwent the physical transformation.

It had been torture that first time, excruciating pain and frustration that the wolf was stronger than he was.

"I'm back to normal now," she assured him. "I am sorry I doubted you. The wolf was—is—inside us. I agree it's worth pursuing, as long as we don't lose track of the big picture. Lars and my family. Not to harp or anything."

While it gladdened him to hear those magical words—"You were right"—she wasn't right about everything. "You're not back to normal. You've changed."

"Because I can say I'm sorry? Because I see your point? Because I let you stay on top?" She smiled. "I'm not a complete asshole, Marcus."

"No, because you aren't the same as you were before."

"I confess. I feel better than I did." She rotated her

hips, squeezing his half-hard cock playfully. "I feel better than I have in a long time."

If she kept doing that, if she kept toying with him and touching him, Goddess, if she kept agreeing with him, he was going to get excited and fuck her again. And he needed to...

She leaned toward him, touched her nose to his neck and inhaled. "You smell so good. Sex has made you... sexier." She laughed. "And your hair. All these tiny curls. I love them." She twirled fingertips in the short swirls. Her touch on his scalp was soothing, her possessiveness satisfying a different primal need in him—one to belong. "You're gorgeous, do you know that?"

"Thank you." What did he need to do again? Make love to her? Yes. His cock twitched.

No. His experiment. She hadn't let him record his notes and had distracted him from full observation of the cycle.

With dogged determination, Marcus extracted himself from her arms and legs, instantly bereft. He ignored that and ignored her complaints.

He couldn't ignore her alpha. She tugged his arm as her will tugged his spirit. He only made it to a sitting position.

"Don't get up yet," she coaxed.

"You're using your alpha on me," he told her with a growl.

She sat up, shocked. "I'm what?"

"You're mentally pressuring me. Stop it."

Witches had known alpha wolves could influence them since anyone could remember, but Katie wasn't a wolf. She was a witch. It hadn't occurred to him it might be possible. He was fairly certain, however, that alpha witches couldn't influence other witches because there would have been records of it by now.

The question was, had Katie changed? Or was she no

longer hiding her talents from him since they'd grown…
close? Was persuasion one of Chang Cai's secret weapons, a function of being convex?

"I'm not using magic on you, Marcus. I can't. I have
no components."

That the compulsion he felt might be a witch spell
hadn't occurred to him. "Do you have magic left?"

She stroked his arm while sprawled on the bed, an
open invitation to rejoin her. "Not a lot. Do you need another true eye? I wasn't conservative with that last round."

Marcus enjoyed the sensation of her petting him for
another second before he made himself stand. Pulling
away from her felt like ripping duct tape off himself. He
winced. "I don't think this requires herbs."

"You're not doing what I asked." Her eyes narrowed;
her lips tightened. "And I asked so nicely."

"Nor shall I do what you ask on a regular basis, I suspect." His wolf skulked inside him, trying to return to
her side. Where he belonged.

She was alpha, and he was not. This was a natural reaction, wasn't it?

"You really think I'm exerting mental coercion? Do
you mean…" Katie bit one corner of her lip, concentrating. "Is this the alpha?"

He felt her allure and put his hand on the wall to steady
himself. "Stop."

The sensation disappeared. "Well, that's new."

Was it? "Don't do that to me again."

"I'll try." She leaned on her elbows, unselfconscious in
her nudity, her beauty—and her power. "I've felt it used
against me enough times."

"You haven't let me record my notes," he said pee-
vishly. "I've got to enter the data before I forget." To-

tally naked—without showering—he sat at the laptop and booted it up.

"Do you realize what this means?" Katie rolled off the bed, wrapped herself in a towel, padded across the Airstream and peered over his shoulder. Her warmth heated his side; her hand caressed his neck. If theirs were a real relationship, he'd think she didn't want to be apart from him. "I don't recall being convincing before we had sex. I couldn't talk you into anything. For example, how many times have I asked if we can call Vern or go back to the tattoo shop?"

"A few."

"We didn't." He felt her alpha quest and fade, as if she wanted to see what he'd do. "Can we?"

"No."

"Please?" She bent, her cheek brushing his, soft as velvet. Not her alpha, but something just as potent—her skin. "I'll make it worth your while."

"No. I won't risk you getting caught." As enticing as she was, going back wasn't smart. It would endanger her. Him too, he supposed. He wasn't set on the rendezvous, either, on the off-chance it ended up being a trap. Not to mention the better chance it ended up ruining their arrangement.

He wanted Katie to himself. For science.

"Worth a shot." She straightened, her fingers still folded over his shoulders and neck. "I've been trying to get you to do what I wanted from the minute I walked downstairs yesterday, saw you and wished you would leave." She tweaked a strand of his hair. "If I had the power to influence you, trust me, I'd have used it. Repeatedly."

As he would have used it on her. "I see your point."

"You're the one who said I changed." She dragged the

second chair to his side. "After you pointed it out, I could tell what I was doing. I know how to do it again."

She didn't try it, though she left the threat there, lingering. She might want him to take control in bed, but outside of it? Never. And his urge to dominate her was likewise different outside of bed, more about protection than eroticism.

"What is the alpha like for you?"

She nibbled her lip a moment. The power quested, gently, and disappeared. "It's like pushing magic at someone instead of into a component, but it's not magic. It's... want."

"If it's true the ability is new—"

"It is." She sat, tucking her towel under her bottom, and met his gaze with complete candor.

"—your wolf seems to have left behind a calling card," he finished. Then it dawned on him what that confirmed.

They stared at each other in growing amazement. Or consternation. Or insight. Or all of the above.

She could use the wolf's power. And she was a witch.

KATIE SHUT THE Airstream door with a quiet snick and hustled to Tonya's station wagon. She hadn't lied to Marcus, exactly. She'd merely obfuscated the truth about how much magic she had left in order to preserve it for her purposes.

The sun rose, glaring through the windshield like an accusation. She deflected it with the brim of his stolen ball cap and the sunshade. Good thing there were never cops around here, because she was in a hurry. She lead-footed the gas and squealed onto the paved road like a stunt driver.

This recon would have been much, much easier at night, when any keepers and packers in the area would

have been hindered by darkness, but Dr. McHottie had
hunched over his computer for hours after they'd had sex.

Did he need no sleep? Damned competitive wolf.
Maybe he'd intended to outlast her.

He had—but the dried agrimony from her pants cuff
had served her eventually. The component wouldn't put
someone to sleep, but once they were already snoozing,
ensorcelled agrimony under the pillow would eliminate
sleep disturbances—such as your bed companion sneaking off with the car.

Fresh would have been better, but she'd had to make
do.

It wasn't as if she were betraying him. He was the only
person in the world willing to assist her, whether that
be rescuing her family, finding a better hiding place or,
apparently, indulging her unexplored kinky side. She'd
agreed to work with him, and she'd meant it. She planned
to be back, updated on Dad, Tonya and Vern's where-
abouts, in time to wake Marcus with sausage biscuits.

And she *had* left him a note…

The guilt she felt—she, a former keeper—was as new
as the wolf in her lattice. Had she partially transformed
during sex because she was, as Lars had always insisted,
weak? Too weak to resist? Except there was zero trace
of her wolf now. As she understood it, transformed and
born wolves could always sense their canine companion
if desired.

So no, she wasn't weak.

For all her adult years, once her sexuality had matured,
she had, quite frankly, wanted to sleep with a wolf. She
hadn't done it.

Until now.

Because he'd kind of blackmailed her.

After sausage biscuits, if he wasn't too mad, she was

going to suggest he blackmail her again—and again and again. That would be a highly intelligent use of their time.

Katie wriggled in her seat, the ache between her thighs a reminder of this very shallow reason to keep her bargain with Marcus. She had her freedom. She could disappear and never see him again. Beyond her conscience, beyond the fact she needed help, as did he, she could confess that she didn't hate him.

She respected him. She admired his drive. She wanted him in a way that frightened her. It meant she had to confront the part of her that longed to be dominated. She would let him cause her pain, because she trusted him to give her pleasure. She would say yes to anything he desired.

For someone who governed her environment and the people around her in order to stay alive, it was both horrifying and cathartic.

She turned west at a crossroads, hitting a state highway that would take her on a wide circumference around the tattoo parlor. Marcus believed anyone hunting them would assume they'd hightailed it out of the country. It was what she'd have done if given the option—and if her family had been with her.

The sticking point was whether Lars had caught Vern, Dad and Tonya. If he had, could he fathom Katie's familial attachment—an attachment other keepers didn't share? Their families had cast them out. Anathema. Unlike other shifters, no keeper would lift a finger to help a relative, least of all Hiram Lars. It was rumored he had numerous children, children *he'd* cast out when they'd emerged normal instead of convex.

Would Lars realize Katie had healed in her years away from the keepers? Would he realize her love would bind her until she could rescue her family?

Her actions in the near future hinged on whether or not they were safe. Katie couldn't go another day and a half without knowing.

When there was nothing at the Garner post office, she took the direct route to Marcus's Airstream. It just happened to run by the tattoo parlor.

Katie, unlike Marcus, was willing to risk that Lars wouldn't have conscripted any wolves who might detect the whisper of juvenile wolf. She'd muddy her physical appearance for keepers or elders who might be present. She'd be fleet, invisible. This used to be her life, and she'd been the best—at this and other things.

She might be able to examine the Dumpster and confirm whether Vern and the others had been forcibly extracted. That would tell her everything she needed to know.

Still anxious, but more settled than she'd been for days, Katie ducked into a fast food restaurant long enough to don a physical disguise before heading to the tattoo shop.

The fact her hands were sweaty on the wheel was only natural.

FIFTEEN

THE CAR WAS gone. Katie was gone. Marcus's patience was gone.

She'd left some shit note about sausage biscuits, a bluff to keep him off her trail. The dried agrimony under his pillow confirmed how she'd slipped out without him waking.

That sneaky witch.

He was done trying to treat Chang Cai as anything close to an equal partner. Not that he thought she was motivated by malevolence—more like foolhardy loyalty. She wasn't the merciless predator the keepers had described. But she'd agreed to stay with him and lay low.

She'd lied to him yet again.

She'd put a spell on him yet again.

And he was so worried about her, he almost forgot to activate a mask and buckle on his travel pill pack before he shifted into wolf form and headed toward the tattoo parlor at top speed.

After a hard run through mostly rural countryside, Marcus reached the perimeter of the tattoo shop area in approximately fifty minutes. He allowed himself a moment of grim satisfaction at his physical achievement before settling into a discovery pattern.

What were the chances Lars had wolves working for him? Katie thought none, but she'd left the keepers years ago. She hadn't been there after Lars had taken the helm, hadn't seen what he was happy to do to wolves.

She wasn't safe here. Lars could have her already. How could she be so stupid? A lone witch, a nearly drained and defenseless witch, going up against a psychopath like Lars and his minions was insane. Why couldn't she wait for the rendezvous? Marcus hadn't told her he didn't intend for them to go. As far as she'd known, they'd be verifying her family's status in twenty-four hours.

But as soon as he'd fallen asleep, she'd bolted.

This was the last time he turned his back on her without there being handcuffs involved.

Marcus had flown solo since Elisa had died. Their parents had been in their third pass-through before they'd managed to have him, and both had succumbed not long after to the cancers that plagued witches more frequently than they did humans. When Elisa had contracted cancer as well, he'd been prepared to challenge the Goddess to keep her and her unborn child with him.

He'd failed. Since then, he'd not allowed any relationships to deepen beyond the superficial. At first, he'd had to outwit the keepers, and then he'd had his quest.

Now he had…his quest. And some familiar fears for someone beside himself.

Marcus sorted through animal and human scents in the vicinity of the tattoo parlor. No wolves. No spell components—the best way to detect witches when you didn't know their DNA. The closer he got, the more troubled he grew. He wasn't worried about himself—his mask disguised him as a normal dog—but he was worried about Katie. His resource. His test subject.

His lying, cheating, car-jacking, distrustful, sexy, infuriating pain in the ass.

What if he couldn't find her in time?

Antsy as hell, Marcus emerged from the neighborhood he and Katie had escaped through yesterday. It was tempting to sprint to the shop, but he made himself check every approach. He behaved as doggishly as possible. While wolves, coven members and humans who spotted him would think nothing, keepers might be suspicious of random dogs poking around their base of action. The wolf sympathizers' use of animal masks to conceal their clients was known to keepers.

On the road that intersected the street to the tattoo parlor, he plopped down on the shoulder and scratched himself. Then he ducked his head between his legs and pretended to lick his balls, something true shifters rarely did, for obvious reasons.

Instead he checked for spoor on the ground.

Yes. There.

Faint whiffs of spell-grade monkshood, loosestrife and hops combined with guns. Coven witches wouldn't smell like monkshood. Cops would smell like guns but not herbs. That left keepers.

From his vantage point, the back of the store and Dumpster looked normal. All spoor was from yesterday. Marcus looped around the tattoo parlor and concealed himself behind a clump of bushes. The only vehicles were Katie's and her father's. His truck and the Smart car were gone. The front window glass was still busted out. No crime scene tape. No unusual sounds. Not much traffic.

He felt no urge to leave the vicinity, which meant no aversion wards had been set to chase off onlookers. From here, he could identify the herbal components from the berserker bomb on a shattered pneumatic gun. The mixture made his skin twitch with memories. Definitely his work. If Katie hadn't been with him when Lars had released the spell, he'd have gone as mad as the Birmingham packers. He analyzed the scent and committed it to memory for later study.

After a sneeze that cleared his sinuses, he caught vestiges of humans and wolves. Blood spatter marked the street in several places, but he didn't smell any fresh blood.

The wind blew gently toward him, and he did smell fresh Katie.

She'd been here. Recently.

The upstairs curtains fluffed in the breeze. Except the breeze was coming from the opposite direction.

She was still here.

Silent and swift, Marcus crossed the road. He slowed as he neared the window to leap gingerly into the building. Broken glass had been swept haphazardly to the side of the room.

The scents of people and wolves thronged in the small space. Many shifters, many components, a few humans, but no pressure in his ears to indicate a spell being cast. Behind the counter, books splayed on the floor, with papers flung everywhere. He had no doubt everyone who'd entered had tossed the place. The keepers in hopes of finding Katie, Vernon or him. The cops, packers or elders in hopes of discovering what had happened.

Was it possible no one had gotten what they'd wanted?

Marcus slipped between the beaded curtains. The second room bore similar evidence of a search. Tattoo ink splashed the walls, and an autoclave lay in pieces on the floor. Other paraphernalia had received similarly rough treatment. The bathroom door canted off its hinges and the door to the upstairs was cracked open.

He rushed up the stairs. In wolf form, he was dark gray, almost black, and rangy. He placed his paws lightly so his claws wouldn't tic. If Katie spotted him, she'd see a black dog, not a wolf, but he doubted that would fool her for an instant.

Logically he knew if she'd wanted to escape him, she wouldn't have come here. Escape wasn't her goal. He entered the apartment and spotted her on the couch. Just sitting there, unmoving. Her spine was curved, her head bowed. She held a leather bag he recognized as Zhang Li's tattoo kit in her lap.

Relief rushed through him, but it didn't displace his other emotions. He barked once, sharp and angry. He wasn't sure if he was pissed as hell at her for leaving or glad to see her alive.

She glanced up, her expression guarded. "Oh, look, a stray dog. Whoever could it be?"

She smelled of resignation and unhappiness. Because he'd recaptured her? Marcus focused his magic inward, shifting into his accustomed body. In under a minute, he stood before her, clothed, armed with supplies and highly annoyed.

Time to let her know in no uncertain terms that she'd regret conning him.

His first words came out rusty and fast—and weren't what he meant to say. "You could have been killed."

Even as he said it, the truth rang in his head like a fire alarm. Her safety was his primary concern—not the betrayal, the lies or their bargain. Feeling that way about her, though, wouldn't advance his cause, so he tamped it down.

She nodded. "I know."

"What if this is a trap?" He said it because it was logical, but didn't entirely believe it. In Lars's world, a keeper wouldn't risk herself for family. Keepers learned to be comfortable with collateral damage—and saw no need for self-sacrifice.

Katie shrugged. "We're alive. Hence my belief that this is, shockingly, not a trap."

She was so certain, so uncaring of her well-being. She hadn't worn a mask when she'd come here. She had no safeguards at all. Her recklessness was a danger to herself and others. "It was a poor choice to return to the shop."

Her jaw flexed; her dark eyes turned hard. "Are you not going to ask what I found? I realize you don't give a shit about my family, but it's sort of a big deal to me."

He wouldn't lose his temper. He'd caught her, and that was that. Marcus's objectives didn't involve sacrificing himself for quests that weren't his own. The fact that this made him more like the keepers than, say, Katie, with her willingness to do anything for her family, was uncomfortable but unavoidable. "Tell me about the others."

"He has them, of course," she said simply. "It's our fault. We shouldn't have deserted them."

"If we'd have stayed, he'd have captured us too. What good would that do?" Marcus considered sitting next to her but remained standing, in a position of authority. She needed to remember he was in charge and his actions had protected her. "How did you find out?"

"I found Ba's ink kit in the panic room and a coded note from Vern." She dug in the bag and extended a wad of paper, her movements listless. "I translated it. Read it and weep."

Apparently she had. Faint tear-trails shone on her cheeks, though her nose and eyelids were barely pink. She relaxed—slumped—on the couch, laid her head against the back and closed her eyes.

Marcus uncrumpled the paper. In bad handwriting was a detailed grocery list. In small, neat handwriting beside it was a translation: *Overheard "the whore" escaped.*

*Rampage. Cops spelled away. They're checking for safe
rooms. Will...*

Vernon's part of the note ended with a jagged scrawl.

"Do you believe they got away?"

She shook her head. "Ba couldn't have outrun the
keepers. He has magic-resistant arthritis." Heal-all wasn't
a cure-all, especially not for deeper human ailments.

"There are two vehicles missing. They could have
driven away."

"Vern would have left a sign. Finished the note. Lars
has them. I'm sure of it."

"You can't trade yourself." He wouldn't be surprised
if Lars had immediately murdered Vernon, considering
Lars's feelings about his predecessor and the ills he'd
claimed Vernon had continued to inflict on him. Tonya
and Zhang Li, however, he might keep around. "He'll
kill you all."

"He can try. I think he'd be willing to let them go in
order to get his hands on me."

"There's nothing you can do to ensure that."

She didn't open her eyes, just said in a flat voice, "That
remains to be seen."

"You have to quit working against me, Katie. It's more
important now than ever." It occurred to him she wasn't
taking his project seriously because she saw no function
in it. It provided her no aid, no resolution to her immediate problem. "If we break the barrier between witch and
wolf, it will be the answer you need."

"Sounds self-serving to me."

He'd explained this to her already. He'd keep trying
until she understood. "Think about it. A huge scientific
discovery like the ability to recover transformed wolves
or a cure for cancer would entrench us in the coven net-

work. Even you, a convex witch. It's the safest place to be if the keepers want to kill you."

Right now, Marcus and Katie had no respect, little safety and few advantages. His experiments must succeed for them to be free. Otherwise they'd be trapped in hiding for the rest of their lives.

Though Katie seemed to have accepted that sentence, it had never been Marcus's plan. He would never quit trying to disable Hiram Lars and the keepers so they couldn't torture and kill anyone else.

He frowned at the scribbled message, wishing Vernon had shared more details. He could only imagine the chaos as the keepers closed in on Vernon and the two amnesiacs. "The note doesn't mention whether Lars identified me."

Katie's outward appearance was peaceful. She rested her head on the back of the couch, features expressionless. Except for the tear tracks, she could have been meditating. "It's not always about you. If he did recognize you, Marcus Delgado is just some wolf now. Probably one that whore Chang Cai is fucking." She raised her head and laughed. "Oh, hell. I guess even psychos like Hiram Lars have to be right sometime."

It was true Lars didn't think of wolves as possessing higher intelligence, even transformed ones. Despite the fact IQs of wolves varied as widely as witches or humans, to Lars, many keepers and some subsets of the coven network, wolves were such primitive throwbacks that it invalidated their rights and their—for lack of a better word—humanity.

The threat of a scientist turned wolf, even one who used to work for him, would hardly worry Lars. He'd treat Marcus like any other animal, and his primary goal would be capturing Chang Cai.

He handed Katie the note. "You're not a whore."

Finally, she looked at him, bemusement replacing the bleakness in her expression. "That's your takeaway from all this?"

"Do you want another? You endangered us both, not for the first time. You're hotheaded, mistrustful and underhanded." He'd seen it in her chi and her actions.

"You've got my number, all right." She shrugged, her gaze dropping to the paper. "I won't apologize for leaving. I knew you wouldn't let me, and I had to know if they were okay. What's your excuse?"

He'd had to know if *she* was okay. He'd hurled himself into a situation that could have been stupid and dangerous, same as she had. However, he'd had a mask, defensive spells in his pouch and a four-legged disguise.

"I have to protect my interests. We have important work to do."

She huffed, without much energy. "I'm still here, aren't I?"

She wouldn't be if Lars had caught her. Marcus wouldn't have known whether she'd run off or been taken, and he'd never have recognized Vernon's grocery list as a code. "Am I supposed to believe you intended to come back to me?"

"Believe whatever you want." She folded the paper in half as if she couldn't bear to read the text again. "My family comes first, and you're not my family."

For some reason, that made him even angrier. "No shit."

Her expression changed yet again as she narrowed her eyes. "Considering what you did for your sister—what you're still doing—one would think you'd be understanding about my detour."

He hadn't thought of Elisa when he'd rushed out the door this morning. He'd thought only of Katie. "If you present a rescue plan with a measurable chance of success, I'll consider it," he conceded. "Until then, can we stick to our original agreement, the one that doesn't end up with both of us dead?"

For the briefest moment, he thought she might smile. Or cry again. Instead she said, voice raw, "Did you really think I wasn't coming back? Where else would I go? I'm not fool enough to think I can tackle Lars alone."

"It would instill more confidence in me if you didn't dupe me every chance you get."

"Fine." But her tone left no doubt in his mind it wasn't fine.

Marcus ran a hand over his close-cropped hair. This wasn't the morning-after conversation he'd envisioned in the wake of last night's revelation. He'd imagined shared excitement, like sunlight breaking through clouds. He'd imagined cohesion as they expanded their knowledge of how she was using wolf magic—and how he could access his witch.

He'd imagined a lot of sex.

Instead, they were completely at odds again and he wasn't sure, no matter how concerned he was about her welfare, that he could trust her. Ever.

Whenever he relaxed his guard, she cheated. She lied and tricked and conned. She felt remorse only when circumstances didn't work out to her liking, if then. She might not be evil, but her nature was fundamentally deceptive.

But still. What must it be like on the other side of her loyalty? To be part of her family? Would he consider her deceptive if everything she did was for him instead of against him?

It didn't matter. She was too hard and too angry and too broken. She'd never let him in.

And he didn't need her to. He only needed her magic.

"That's settled, then. Did you happen to find your own bag in the Dumpster?" He took the leather satchel of tattoo supplies from the couch. Now that he could maintain tats, one of Katie's permabrands might be advantageous… if he wanted to let her near him with a tattoo needle.

"I packed another one."

"I'm going to have to search it."

"I don't care."

"And I have to search you."

"I really don't care." She rose, walked stiffly into the kitchen and yanked a duffel off the counter. When he followed her, she pelted it at him. "Want to check for monkshood?"

Why did she look so offended? She'd mickeyed him several times already. Granted, she hadn't tried to kill him, but they both knew what she could do. "Later."

Next she threw the keys at him as if they were a grenade. "I assume you insist on driving?"

He did. As it happened, she didn't care.

SIXTEEN

"WHY DOES THIS feel so incredibly familiar? Seriously, Marcus, I'm not in the mood." Aggravated, Katie batted at the wolf when he came to unlock her handcuff. "Give it a rest tonight. I'm not going anywhere."

Probably.

As soon as they'd returned from the tattoo parlor, he'd searched her and her bag. There had been no monkshood, of course. She didn't know how she felt about Marcus, but his death wasn't part of the picture.

Next he'd run a battery of tests involving her alpha ability and her five senses that purportedly measured her access to wolf magic. After that, he'd secured her to the bed and proceeded to ignore her while he mucked around with his computer.

She didn't care. And she really, really wasn't in the mood for sex tests.

She thought about kicking him, but she wasn't ready to antagonize him that much yet. He unclasped the handcuffs—still not using the key, she noticed—and helped her unnecessarily off the bed. "Do you really think I want to screw around when I just found out my father, Tonya and Vern are probably dead?"

Putting it into words for the first time knotted her throat. She'd concentrated on revenge scenarios today, not wanting to blubber in front of Marcus. What would be the most satisfying way to kill Lars? Shooting, magicking, stabbing, poisoning, steamrolling, drowning, woodchoppering—she'd imagined enacting them all and it failed to comfort her.

Needless to say, she didn't think there was anything the wolf could do to make her want sex with him.

Possibly if he told her how he had a foolproof plan to kill Lars. She'd gladly hop into bed with the man who loved her enough to... No, the man who could give her that. It had nothing to do with love.

Marcus regarded her with a frown. "They're not dead. Or at least your father and Tonya aren't."

"You know this how? Did you contact Lars when I wasn't listening?" Death and suffering were constant companions for keepers. Taken from their families as soon as their magic emerged—or dumped on the council like trash—their ties to loved ones withered. Keepers never juggled this crippling attachment and grief.

Katie had grown back into love, inch by inch, as she and her father had come to know one another again. Now their bond was stronger than ever and included Tonya in the tight, devoted circle. As for Vern, he'd been instrumental enough in saving everyone's life that she felt a significant obligation to him as well.

"Of course I didn't contact Lars." He didn't blink, just watched her.

"Then how do you figure Ba and Tonya are alive?"

"Since you've been with them since your disappearance, Lars may assume you developed familial loyalty. He'll hold off killing Zhang Li and Tonya in case he gets to kill them in front of you."

"Now that is a lovely image." Despite her sarcasm, the knot in her throat eased enough for tears to quit threatening. He was right. There was a good chance they were alive. Marcus had promised to consider rescue schemes.

If he weren't a basically decent person, that wouldn't be the case. "You're so romantic. I'm ready for the sex now."

"Good. Undress." He checked the locks and wards on the front door, remaining between her and the exit as if he expected her to bolt. "Showers first."

"I was kidding." She slid her glasses up her nose so she could see his face better. Was he smirking? "I'm not ready and not going to be ready."

"Would you prefer I lie to you? Seduce you?"

"Do you have a diagram for that?"

"It doesn't matter." He crossed his arms. "Lying and seducing are your province, not mine. You asked me about your family, and I answered honestly. It would hardly inconvenience Lars to imprison two amnesiac witches. No one but you will be looking for them. In fact, I daresay he might order a few experiments and—"

"Shut up." Marcus had an uphill battle getting her into bed tonight. If he forced the issue, she didn't want to know how her turncoat body would respond.

But she did know how he would respond to certain types of questions. He might enjoy research, but there was another thing he enjoyed just as much.

Talking about research.

"After this afternoon's tests, do you still think I'm half wolf?"

He frowned at her, as if uncertain whether her interest was genuine. It was, but mostly she was stalling. "Your sensory input remains within non-wolf parameters. Your minor alpha ability is the only difference between you and another witch."

In his morning tests, he'd included several requests for her to "push" him to do things. She'd failed to budge him, though she could sense the aptitude lurking inside her like a half-cast spell—a whisper, not a roar.

"What's on tap for tonight theory-wise?" she asked, stalling more.

Still hovering between her and the door, he picked up his smartphone and swiped to access his notes. "Tonight we'll analyze whether your ability to access your wolf increases during intimacy. Sexual relations with a wolf shifter stimulate that side of a witch's psyche until the wolf overwhelms. This we've known for eons. I believe an alpha's increased strength helps them withstand the inundation of the lattice. The wolf simply becomes another tool in your arsenal. The more we kindle it, the stronger it will be."

They'd confirmed that the new thread she'd used to access her wolf magic, the alpha influence, was comparable to other threads in her lattice. Marcus said if he hadn't been a lattice researcher he might not have noticed. She sure as hell couldn't tell it apart.

"You're getting better, Professor. I understood most of that." If she exercised the speck of wolf inside her, could she do more, like Marcus believed? "Let's wait until I have more magic to spare. This time next week, I'll be flush. I can cast all the chi spells you want."

"We're not postponing sex for a week. We're having it tonight. Now." He raised an eyebrow. "I'm not sure I trust you at full power."

"You're keeping me drained on purpose?" Drained and chained. It would be humiliating if she didn't understand his motivations. As it was, it just reiterated his lack of trust. "You do realize I'll begin to refill faster, right? My combat bonus may already have been kickstarted."

"Take off your clothes," Marcus said, not answering her question. "We have work to do."

She removed her glasses, but instead of setting them on the table, as if preparing to undress, she rubbed them on her shirt. He should at least try to be seductive. "What about next time?"

Though his words had revealed his impatience, his tone remained even. "Since wolf magic is what overwhelms a non-alpha witch, next time we'll supersaturate me with witch magic. My hope is that it will return me to witch state or provoke an optimal dual state where the witch and wolf lattices combine."

She'd never passed her magic to a witch who wasn't a spell focal. She wasn't even sure it was possible. His theories, pretty on the screen, seemed like facts their ancestors would already have hammered out. Granted, it had stunned everyone five years ago that witches who were resistant to transformation existed beyond rumors. But a wolf turning into a witch?

Marcus was operating on a pipe dream. It wasn't bloody likely that miracles would occur, angels would sing and his magic would come orgasming back to him. Nothing that positive ever happened to her or anyone connected to her.

She merely had to remember where Dad and Tonya were right now to confirm that. She brought misery and destruction wherever she went. She didn't need scientific method to prove it.

"I know you're probably thinking about Harry Travis right now," Marcus said, as if it had any sort of logical connection to their conversation.

"Amazingly, I am not." She was thinking about Lars's methods of torture and how she'd like to return the favor. Which settled things, in her mind. There was no way she was going to be in the mood to have sex tonight.

"You're probably asking," Marcus continued, "why isn't Harry a witch? I can answer that. When we last spoke, he and his wife weren't attempting to convert him into a witch. I proposed it, but neither was receptive."

"The nerve. They didn't want to have a threesome with you?"

He huffed. "That's not what I suggested. Either way, I'm focusing on transformed wolves," he said with a glimmer of humor, "and I'm unaware if June has wolf magic. I can't assume she does simply because you do."

That hadn't occurred to her. "No?"

He inspected her from head to toe, leaving her wondering what he saw. Scruffy, depressed malcontent in desperate need of an army and open season on one Hiram Lars? Because that was how she felt. "I gather there's a theory you're just that perverse."

That startled a laugh out of her. "Thanks."

"Now, if you're finished delaying, could we continue?"

"What if I refuse?"

He stared at her, and she stared back. Tension filled the air and sang in her ears like the whine of the Airstream's generator.

"I'd rather not find out."

Hell. A sour feeling in her stomach, she stripped off her clothes and tossed them as messily as she could onto his office chair. He'd already turned away to tap on his phone.

"I'm having the first shower," she declared. He didn't answer. With a grimace, she stalked to the tiny cubicle and twisted on the pitiful spray of water.

When she tried to close the curtain behind her, he stopped her.

"What the hell are you doing?" she snapped.

"Surprising you." Curtain still open, he watched as the tepid trickle splattered on her head. "I'm turning off the water in thirty seconds."

Katie grimaced but decided it wasn't worth arguing. She angled herself under the weak spray, wetting her hair and skin.

The shower curtain rustled. She opened her eyes to see Marcus's beautiful bare ass as he set his neatly folded clothing on the toilet. He turned, and of course she checked out his package. Large even when flaccid, his cock and scrotum nestled in dark curls. He reached toward her. She froze, but he grabbed a bar of soap instead of her.

He stuck the soap and a washcloth under the dribble of water. "Five seconds left."

Halfheartedly, Katie tousled her hair to be sure it was wet. Marcus twisted the faucet off.

"Is this a shower or a peep show?" She held out her hand for the soap. Did he think she wouldn't wash behind her ears?

However, instead of handing it over, he rubbed the washcloth up her arm.

"Wait just a hairy minute." She backed against the thin interior wall, but there was nowhere to go. Her shoulder bonked the faucet handle. "I'm capable of a big-girl bath all by myself."

He caught her wrist and scrubbed up to her shoulder. "It's no trouble."

The stall was so small that when he stepped over the cubicle lip, his body almost touched hers. The soapy-rough washcloth crossed her chest and headed down her other arm. Rattled, Katie could do nothing but gape as Marcus lathered her forearm and then her hand, paying special attention to her fingers.

For no reason she could understand, his precision woke a flutter of arousal in her. He washed between her fingers.

Her palm. Her body piqued. He didn't miss an inch, and she suspected that attention would translate...elsewhere.

At that thought, she goose bumped all over, in spite of the heat of his body breathing down her neck. Literally.

"You're cold. I'll go fast." The washrag traveled along the underside of her arm and across her breasts. She glanced at his face, but he appeared to be deep in concentration. "Hands up."

Slowly, she raised her arms. Bubbles trickled down them, onto her ribs. He washed her stomach and then up, catching her other armpit. His skin wasn't touching her, only the cloth, but she could feel the firm pressure of his hand steering it.

"Turn," he said.

Steering her too. When she rotated, she deliberately pressed her bare hip to his lower half, where she hadn't dared look again.

He went from semi-hard to rock hard in the time it took her to obey him.

"Ah-ah." He nudged her away from him. "Don't distract me."

He didn't want to be distracted, did he? He shouldn't have admitted that. She wasn't going to strike up a conversation about science, either.

Katie rested against the wall, plotting, while Marcus circled the washrag on her shoulders and back. Her breasts pushed against the glossy fiberglass. Her toes curled against the plastic floor, where the cooling water drained.

"Don't use your alpha ability until I request it," he said as he washed her.

"Okay." She half meant it too.

His ministrations reached the small of her back before

the washrag disappeared. He twisted on the water and angled it at her head. "Thirty seconds."

He draped the washcloth over her shoulder. Katie rubbed her front, knowing he was watching, and lifted her breasts into the stream. Water trickled between them. She added a shimmy for good measure. "Can you get my back?"

He hesitated, but his bare hands, his fingers, stroked her curves through the suds. Katie bit back a sigh. The soapy water trailed between her buttocks, tickling and popping. When he reached around her to clean the suds off her front, she leaned against him.

Yes. Full contact. His slick, hot body towered over her, his cock rubbing suggestively. His big hands cupped her breasts and pulled her tighter against him. He closed his fingers on the tips as the water rained down her front.

Funny—that part of her was already rinsed.

He twisted her nipples. Pleasure shot from her breasts to her pussy. She wriggled her ass, and his cock jerked. He hissed through his teeth. Whatever reluctance she'd felt about sleeping with Marcus again—however he wanted her—disappeared.

"Grab the top of the stall." His voice had roughened, revealing his involvement.

She thought about disobeying. She didn't like him assuming he could boss her around, in bed or out of it. At the same time, it might be better to save the clash of wills for something major. Sex could take her mind off her cares temporarily.

He turned the water off, and his voice rumbled in her ear. "Katie, I gave you an order."

"Is it for science?"

"Of course." Which was not what she wanted to hear.

"Everything I require of you has a documented purpose. Grab the top of the stall or there will be consequences."

Like what? He'd make her memorize the quadratic formula? As short as she was, Katie had to reach high, above his head. Her fingers gripped the cold, metal edge of the cubicle.

He retrieved the soap from the narrow holder. Lathering his hands this time, he rubbed her hips. Could he stay scientific? She held her breath as he eased two broad palms down her thighs. When he curved between her legs and up, his fingertips discovered her pussy. The air gusted out of her in a hum.

"This part needs extra attention," he whispered. With one hand washing her, flirting with her clit, he held the soap behind her and slid it between her ass cheeks. Up and down he washed her, jiggling and rubbing. Toward her pussy and back again. Katie couldn't tell which hand was more talented as sensations trapped her in place. The smooth end of the soap paused at her anus. Wiggled. Explored. What did he...

He pinched her clit and pushed the soap. Katie's knees nearly quit working. "Marcus, let's go to bed."

The soap thunked to the floor. "Sixty seconds."

Despite a great reason to hurry, he rinsed her slowly. He cupped a hand between her legs, sluicing away suds. His thorough cleansing made her want to writhe. Madness whispered at her to jump him and force the issue, as he kept threatening to do. She was the alpha here, not him. When he finally unhooked her hands from the shower rim and let her face him, he flicked off the water and proceeded to nonchalantly soap himself—and his big, hard cock—as if his eyes weren't as pale as an opal.

As if he were in complete control of his scientific process.

As if he weren't thinking of pitching his stages and charts and fucking her right here against the flimsy shower wall.

How could he be so aroused and so calm at the same time? She watched his hands on his body, admiring his taut abs and the hollows of his hips. As she stood there, he took his cock in one soapy fist and pumped it. Four times. Five. He muttered something and exhaled.

His cock grew larger as he masturbated. *Oh, Goddess.* That was a show. She wanted him. Her pussy throbbed for him. He could help her forget everything. But as soon as she reached for him, he stopped.

"No." He turned the water on and rinsed.

"Don't you need to be stimulated too?"

"Stop asking questions." He splashed the now-cool water on them both, and she shivered. "It will ruin the surprise."

He twisted off the water one final time. Droplets had splashed all over the tiny bathroom. He stepped out backward, grabbed her arms and hoisted her out of the stall. After he set her on the Airstream's dry floor, he gazed down at her for a long moment.

She tried to eel out of his grasp, but he held her without effort. She swallowed nervously. "What are you staring at?"

"You." With a quick tug, he slung her over his shoulder as he had when he'd kidnapped her. The resemblance ended there. For one, they were naked. For another, his hand splayed across her ass possessively.

Blood rushed to her head. Warning bells sounded in her brain. "Is this necessary? The mattress is ten feet away."

"Yep." He stalked through the trailer. Pausing at the

bed, he ran a thumb between her ass cheeks all the way to her clit, twiddling her, testing.

"Come on, I'm getting dizzy." She pushed against his back, trying to squirm off his shoulder.

His hand trailed from cheek to cheek as he rubbed, massaged and probed her. Her squirming increased as she became more aroused. His cheek, his lips, brushed her hip.

As a subtle encouragement to put her the hell down, she kneed him in the ribs. He reciprocated with a smack on her ass, a swift, unexpected pain.

Katie squealed out a protest. "Cut it out! I told you, I'm not a masochist."

"I don't think I'm a sadist, but..." He did it again, his palm landing at the soft juncture of her legs. The sound of flesh against flesh was loud in the quiet room. She drew a breath to curse him. Another stinging blow sucked it out of her lungs. The third and fourth blows grew louder, harder, the pain lingering.

"I rather like this," he concluded, his voice a growl. "I think you do too."

His angle wasn't the greatest, with her over his shoulder. She couldn't tell how much of his enhanced strength was involved, but it definitely hurt. She chopped and punched him in the back every time he struck her, but her angle was ineffective too. His shoulder in her gut made thrashing and breathing a challenge.

Between gulps of pain, Katie regulated her airflow enough to share her horrible opinion of his actions. Since one of his arms trapped her at the knees like an iron band, she couldn't cause anywhere near as much damage as she wanted.

She couldn't free herself. She was completely at his mercy. No rescue, no escape.

She could fight all she wanted, and he'd still fuck her.

"I don't care if you like it," she said, trying to ignore the thrill that went through her. "You're a—"

Katie whooped, startled, as she sailed through the air. Her stinging ass hit the bed. When she lashed out at Marcus, she wasn't holding back anymore—and it didn't matter. He jumped her, trapping her arms. In another second, her wrists were handcuffed above her head.

Her backside twinged as it pressed the mattress. Her ego twinged the same way.

"These seem secure." He rattled the cuffs. His body loomed over hers, big and bossy. "Now, where were we?"

"Nowhere." She twisted and kicked to hide her titillation. "Let me go right this instant. I did not sign up for this." Though if she'd known what it was like, she might have.

"I appreciate you sharing your emotional response," he said smugly, fending off a foot. "I'll add it to the report."

She flexed both cuffed hands, displaying her middle fingers. "Put this in your report, asshole."

He laughed, reached down and cupped her pussy. She held her breath. One finger pressed between her folds to find her…wet. Wet and needy. "And this?"

Her face flamed. "Why are you torturing me?"

"Alphas like control." He plucked her clit, and she nearly jolted out of her skin. "I'm taking it from you as part of the experiment. I'm taking charge."

He rubbed her gently, long enough for her to hope he was done proving his point. His fingertips felt so good, so knowing.

"But mostly?" he said, pale eyes glittering. "I'm doing this because I want to. I liked dominating you, Katie. I liked it a lot."

"All right, I admit it. I'm turned on." She blushed harder. "I don't know why."

"You do know why."

"I can't believe you spanked me. Jesus." And that it excited her.

"I can't believe I waited this long." His gaze feasted on her. Every inch of him gloated. "Stay."

As if she had a choice. "If you crack out ball gags or nipple clamps, I swear I'll kill you."

From the side table, he grabbed the shaker for the chi spell. To her surprise, he shoved up her legs and spread her wide. His hot breath wafted across her stomach. Then he sprinkled the herbs onto her exposed flesh.

She yanked up, trying to see. "Hey! You can't just put…that's a delicate area. Is that safe?"

His tongue stroked her from end to end. Katie wheezed. Sensation exploded in her aching pussy. He swept around her clit, then over it, licking kava into his mouth.

"You taste incredible. Let me see your aura," he ordered, making it sound dirty.

Since he'd paused, she managed to say, "I need to touch the components with my hands."

Instead of freeing her, he lapped her pussy, all the nooks and crannies. Goddess, the man had a heavenly tongue. She tried to concentrate on opening herself to her magic, but the hot, wet suckle of his mouth on her clit was all she could handle.

Marcus growled softly, eating every inch of her. His fingers dented into her spread thighs. She'd never been devoured like this. When she moaned, he pushed her legs farther apart and higher. His tongue drove into her, faster and faster. She writhed as he fucked her with his mouth. His teeth scraped her clit, then his tongue, and she nearly lost it.

Katie felt the approach of an orgasm and her wolf, thrashing her with pleasure. The spell he wanted her to do—she cast it. Her aura burst into life between them like passion, and she brought him into it so he could see.

He rose up her body, his cock poised at her entrance. Intense pale eyes blazed at her with a wolfishness that aroused her even more. He looked…feral. As if he—he who had her restrained, helpless, fulfilling her dark fantasies—couldn't control himself.

What would he do to her?

"I see the new channel." His eyes glazed over as he stared at her aura. "Your wolf. Beautiful. What do you smell?"

"Wh…what?" She arched her hips, rubbing his cock.

"See how keen your senses are. Tell me anything that surprises you." He leaned down and sucked a nipple into his mouth, his teeth sharp.

She inhaled. Her body, her cream. Soap from the shower. Marcus's skin, a whiff of cinnamony kava. Laundry detergent. Sex. His tongue laved her breast. Her eyes practically rolled back in her head, it felt so good.

"Nothing." She rubbed herself on his cock, her ankles behind his hips. When Marcus exhaled, that was when she noticed it. "Wait." She breathed deep, letting the moment buoy her. "Peppermint."

"Good. Your wolf is stronger now." His eyes practically glowed with wildness.

"There's no peppermint in a chi spell."

He kissed her then, his tongue sliding as deep in her mouth as it had her body. She twined everything she could around him and wished he'd free her arms. She needed him closer. She needed to hold on when things got crazy. Their tongues danced. The kava and musk of her body flavored his kiss with the faint addition of peppermint.

"There's no peppermint in a chi spell," she repeated when he lifted his head.

He smiled. "I added some to test whether you'd sense it." As if rewarding her, he pressed his shaft against her slit, almost entering her but not quite.

She could get used to the wolf coursing through her, heightening her senses, her emotions, her needs. "Test me more."

He lowered an arm and caught his cock in his hand. He fit the broad, smooth head against her opening, coating himself in her wetness. When his fingers pleasured her clit, she groaned.

"Marcus," she pleaded.

"Use your alpha," he whispered. "Show me what you want."

She let her wolf magic nip him. "I am. Can you tell?"

"Yes." His cock inched into her. Goddess, it felt so right, to be under him, to be connected to him. More. She needed it all.

He bared his teeth, fighting her command. His cock seemed to swell. He promptly dragged it out. She pressured him, and he thrust into her, deeper. Harder. Her pulse leaped.

"That feels so good." Pleasure threatened to overwhelm her concentration. He'd made such a big deal about controlling her, as though it got him off.

It had almost gotten her off.

He had his confirmation. His experiment was a success. There was no reason to use her alpha to persuade him. He could have all the control. He could do what he wanted. Couldn't they just enjoy one another now?

The chi spell faded, and she didn't know if he'd seen enough. She blinked uncertainly. "Marcus?"

"Don't stop," he said hoarsely. He was motionless between her thighs, his arms trembling, veins standing out in his neck. "Force me."

"I don't want to force you." She wanted him—to want her. To just want her.

It was a horrible revelation.

"Do it anyway." He pinched her clit, and she squealed.

Instead she shoved her power at him with a command to loosen her wrists. He was fumbling at the handcuffs before he realized what she'd done.

"Dammit, Katie." He lurched away and glared down at her. "That's not part of the experiment."

She rubbed a foot up his muscular thigh.

"You already know what you need to know." Her toes located his hard, velvety cock, and she rubbed him with her instep. "Come kiss me."

Marcus grabbed her ankle, his fingers so tight they ground against the bones. "Use the wolf."

She licked her lips. "I tried."

"Not hard enough." His eyes narrowing, he slid both palms up her body until he grasped her hips. "I think you need motivation."

He flipped her to her stomach, the canvas strap that secured the handcuffs twisting with her. With a single hand, he held her down while he rummaged in the end table. Katie struggled to see what he was doing. The spanking and the cuffs had been educational, but she wasn't sure how deep into kink she wanted to go.

Marcus emerged with a swath of fabric. He positioned it around her eyes, knotting it tight. It pulled her hair.

"Ow." She rubbed her head against the mattress to try to dislodge the blindfold. "This isn't necessary."

"Take one sense away and the others will strengthen. I want you to feel every single thing I do to you." He hoisted her hips into the air, lifting her until she was on her knees, her cheek pressed to the mattress. He kicked her legs wide. Once she was presented to him, completely vulnerable, he uttered a noise halfway between a sigh and a groan. He gripped her ass and drew the cheeks apart.

She struggled into a sustainable position, with her elbows and forearms supporting her head. "You have my cooperation. I don't see why you have to…"

Smack!

The blow landed precisely between her legs, jolting through her pussy like electricity. Her thighs smarted like mad.

"What was that for?" Katie tried to hunker away but he trapped her in place. His hands caressed her ass, squeezing, before he struck again. Again. Again. His position behind her, their calves partly aligned, gave him significant leverage.

Spank her, would he? Arrogant wolf! She'd make him pay. She told him how much.

Marcus laughed and spanked her again. His hand stroked her ass between blows as she struggled and threatened. Every time she tried to dodge, he punished her for it.

"You're bright pink. There's a handprint on your ass. Mine." He traced it on her burning skin. "I like seeing you this way."

"Pervert." Her breath came fast and hard. In the darkness behind the blindfold, it was harsh in her ears.

"If I am, so are you." The next blow caught her pussy again. It didn't hurt, exactly, yet it did. "Surprise."

"Shut up." She bit her lip and refused to give him the satisfaction of a moan. "Are you adding this to the report?"

"Perhaps." He massaged gently, as if soothing the pain away.

"I should have known you were rotten. Damned wolf." She turned her head sideways, wishing she could see.

He popped her twice in quick succession, both sides of her ass flaring with pain. She yelled at him, and he wouldn't stop.

Tears threatened, more confusion than pain. "Are you mad at me?"

"If you want me to stop," he said, "you'll have to make me."

"I can't."

"Then I won't stop until I feel like stopping." He rubbed and spanked her, tempting her with his cock. His hands, when he caressed her, trembled. He fingered her pussy and anus. His breathing grew harsh. "Or I could fuck you now and then start all over again."

She ached. She needed him. "Yes. Please. Whatever you want."

"I want you to use your wolf. Do it, Katie."

"No."

He teased and paddled her until she did cry. Darkness closed in, helplessness, frustration.

Arousal.

When an intense glow began to soak her ass like a heat lamp, Katie realized Marcus's slaps were the cause. The pain and heat were alarmingly erotic. His cock nudged her folds, and she felt it twice as much. Twice the yearning. A finger gliding up and down her crack nearly set her on fire.

Humiliation. Stimulation. Desire.

Her nerve endings blossomed, and when he smacked her something inside her melted.

The shameless wetness on her thighs felt like surrender. Something she never, ever did. Ever. She wanted to spread her legs and feel more of this pain mixture where it hurt the most, where it scalded her, where she craved him.

She was throbbing, liquid and achy by the time Marcus thrust a long finger into her pussy. His touch against her swollen clit was an electric shock of pleasure. He flicked her and she gasped.

"You're soaked," he said, husky and growling. "You want more, don't you?"

Yes, please. "No."

He paddled her for the fib. "How's your wolf now? Is she ready for me?"

"She wants to rip your head off," Katie lied. "For that matter, so do I."

"Prove it." He rubbed her juices up and down her crack, and it catapulted her to some knife-edge of arousal she'd never before imagined. "Or are you going to let me win?"

She tried to answer and he spanked her. She moaned and squirmed when the hot burn followed. Everything felt so hypersensitive, from her clit to her toes. How much more could she take?

When he tickled her fiery thighs, his palm cupping her mound, she pushed her ass against his groin, begging him to take it to the next level.

Any way he wanted. "I don't want to fight you. I don't care about winning."

"You do outside the bedroom. You won't stop fighting me."

"That's different."

"Is it?" Slowly, he tucked two fingers into her, traveling deep. She tightened instinctively, knowing how wet she was, knowing nothing could hide the truth from either of them anymore. His other hand caught her clit, pinching and rubbing.

Katie arched her spine and ground against him.

"What do you want?" he asked. "Tell me."

"I want you."

"This?" He stroked in and out of her with his fingers, good but not enough.

She whimpered helplessly. "More."

Marcus leaned down, covering her with his body, intimate as hell, and whispered in her ear. "You tasted better than I dreamed, Katie. Did you like my tongue in your pussy?"

Oh, Goddess. "Yes."

His hips thrust against her ass, his cock finding her slick folds. "Do you want me?"

He had no idea how far beyond sex her wanting extended. "I do."

"I want to come inside you." He caressed her with his whole body, their skin sensual, sweaty. "I love to feel my cock in your pussy. I love to feel you beneath me. Do you know how hard it is to resist you right now?"

"Agree," she managed.

"But I'm stopping," he said, "unless you make me."

Tears threatened again. She was an emotional wreck, a miserable watering pot trying to soothe her fear and sorrow with sex. "I can't."

"Try harder."

"Please be with me, Marcus." A tear escaped the blindfold, and she tilted her head to hide it. "Make love to me."

He was silent for a long moment. In a quiet voice, he said, "That's what you want?"

"Yes," she admitted. "I do."

He kissed her shoulder and began to move. His cock slid through her folds, bumping her clit again and again. Katie started swirling higher, aching for him. All she could do was feel.

Then he stopped. "Use your alpha."

She squirmed with unrelieved sexual hunger. "I'm out of magic."

"No, you're not," he said, his voice scratchy. He started to pull away from her. "You're afraid, Katie. You're too broken to trust me."

"Like you trust me? I'm not the one who carries around a monkshood antidote."

"Does that bother you?"

"It hurts that you think I'd...after we..." She couldn't finish it. When he said nothing, something inside her snapped.

She wanted to be with him, really be with him, and he didn't care. It had nothing to do with trust. He was simply curious to know what her wolf could do.

Time to find out.

When she released her alpha this time, she didn't hold back. He stiffened, his hands confining her hips, before he drove into her with a groan. Katie groaned too, the connection so deep it hurt.

He slid along her back as he fucked her, gradually pressing her toward the mattress until she was prone. With one strong arm, he propped her hips, kept her angled toward him. Though she couldn't see him, it allowed their lovemaking to remain...personal. Snug.

And what she'd nearly admitted. Was he wondering what she'd left unsaid?

He pumped between her legs at a measured pace. Touching everywhere. They moved together, sighing, gasping, striving toward mutual satisfaction. His every thrust took her slowly, slowly, out of her head and into a dimension of pure sensuality.

Moisture slickened her inner thighs, her ass, his cock. The wet glide of their bodies and their heavy breathing filled the quiet trailer. Her stiff, sensitive nipples scraped the sheet as he pushed her. The sultry cream of her longing and the kava and peppermint on his breath tantalized her heightened senses.

He hadn't said a word about the fact her alpha was gone. All she'd forced was that first delicious entry. Now she simply held on. Not with her legs or arms—the arms were tied and the knees were jelly. She wrapped her magic around him to show him how she felt. She wouldn't, couldn't use words.

When her orgasm approached, he sensed it. He muttered something highly unscientific and adjusted his arm around her hips to find her clit.

Katie cried his name when he touched her, and surrendered, yet again, to his direction. He bit her shoulder. His pace increased. Like a lodestone, he drew her magic and her climax to the surface to bloom.

She convulsed beneath him, trembling and gasping. He was kissing her neck, her ear, encouraging her, staying deep inside her, rolling through her. Couldn't she please him too? Riding the blissful waves, Katie recklessly poured her magic into him. Her essence found his. They pooled until the boundaries disappeared. There was no slap of rejection, and she didn't take anything from him.

She gave him everything.

She filled him with magic until he howled.

SEVENTEEN

MARCUS'S BODY FELT like lightning had struck him. A massive orgasm squeezed his balls and spurted out his cock. He hadn't thought anything could feel better than emptying himself into Katie last night, and he'd been wrong.

His heart raced so fast it nearly choked him. His throat closed. When the orgasm finished, he came to rest against her, his cock lodged deep. He didn't want to move.

It had been so incredibly difficult to keep his mind on his experiment. His wolf turned his senses razor sharp as he reveled in Katie's smell, her taste, her satiny skin. The sound of her soft cries, the heat in her flesh after he spanked her. The emotion and urgency when she begged him, when she handed herself to him completely. He reveled in her surrender and rejoiced that she didn't want to force him to take her. She yearned for his mastery, and conquering this powerful, sensual woman satisfied everything he was as a wolf and a man.

He should feel relaxed after lovemaking that passionate, and his bones did resemble slurry. But his brain and nerve endings jangled, as if he'd had several espresso shots in a row.

Katie rested her face on her arm with a sigh, her profile to him. The black silk of the blindfold matched her shiny hair. "Mmm. Was the experiment as good for you as it was for me?"

"I met my goal." He nuzzled her neck, the fine hair at

her nape tickling his chin. His lips felt oddly numb. "I should write my report now."

"You should test me some more." Her inner muscles clenched him playfully. He twitched, oversensitive. He wasn't numb in his cock, that was for sure. She laughed at his reaction and did it again.

"Are you incomplete?" he asked, though he'd smelled her fieriness when she'd climaxed. He didn't smell it now, another oddness—last night it had lingered for an hour. It had made concentration on statistics difficult.

Right offhand, he could list fifty-three ways he wanted to consummate their relationship. If she wanted another orgasm, he could provide it.

Except he didn't feel like himself. His innards jostled at him to get up, get up, while his outsides felt blunted and dull.

"I'll tell you what would make my life complete." Her knees bent enough for her small bare feet to rub his legs. He could feel it, barely. "Healing powder. My head hurts. And then a nice long nap."

"I believe it's standard to complain of a headache prior to sex, not afterward." He untied her blindfold clumsily, his fingers like hot dogs. "Was this too tight?"

When the silk fell away, she blinked several times and wrinkled her nose. "Next time, you wear the blindfold."

"That's not going to happen." Increasingly concerned, he went through various spells she could have cast to slow his reflexes. Not only had she been deliciously clean and nude, but as a wolf, he'd have noticed. He'd have felt the magic pop in his ears.

Whatever was happening to him had nothing to do with a spell.

"Are you sure?" Her cheek dimpled as she smiled. "I hear it heightens certain senses."

The orgasm he'd experienced had been incredible. Too incredible? What if he was having a heart attack? He might require assistance. He reached up and tugged her wrists, intending to free her, but the metal clasp on the cuffs didn't release. "Huh."

"That wasn't a good huh." She yawned. "Can you hurry? I need to smack you around some before I pass out."

"You're not going to hit anyone." He rolled off her and inspected the handcuffs. His eyes refused to focus. With a growl, he pried the cuffs. It hadn't taken much effort before the shower, but now he found himself straining. One loop popped with a clink.

The other remained firmly around her wrist.

"I will too hit you. I'm a killer," she protested. "You said so yourself once."

"A killer who likes to be spanked."

"I, ah." Her gaze met his for one long moment that silenced the crazed pulse in his ears. Her embarrassment was palpable. "I would destroy anyone else who touched me the way you did."

"What does that mean?" The freckles across her nose and cheeks tempted him to kiss her, but the sex was over until tomorrow night. Kissing had no purpose.

But her lips looked so sweet as she blushed. "Are you going to undo my cuffs or not?"

"Sit up." Too many concerns nipped him simultaneously. Her blush, the cuffs and whatever was wrong with his sensory receptors. Heart attacks didn't cause fizziness inside and torpor outside. And if this were a heart attack, gazing deep into his—his test subject's espresso-hued eyes wouldn't pause it. "I need a different angle on your wrists."

With an ill-concealed mutter, she scuffled into a sitting position. Squinting at the handcuffs, she wriggled the metal. "Got a bobby pin?"

He rubbed his left arm. It didn't ache, which seemed to verify this wasn't a heart attack. Whatever was happening to his body, it was bothersome but not critical.

"Marcus?" Katie prompted. "Hairpin?"

He quit rubbing his arm before she asked him why he was doing that. "I barely even have hair."

"What about a paper clip?"

Tired of this, he seized the remaining cuff and pulled hard enough for the metal to hurt his fingers. The unexpected bite of pain made him wince. "Dammit. I don't understand."

"You probably warped it when you kept he-manning the lock instead of using a key. Brute strength isn't always the answer."

"Well, I can't he-man it now." He flipped his hand, shaking away the hurt.

"A likely excuse." She glared at him, an expression that matched the fact her hair was sticking up all over her head. "You don't trust me being loose."

"I wouldn't need an excuse." What would she do if he told her he might be sick? "I'd simply keep you handcuffed."

Katie squeezed her forehead with her free hand. "I don't want to argue. I'm too drained."

"There's no reason for you to be drained. You cast one chi spell." Hiding the fact his knees bobbled when he stood, Marcus went in search of a paperclip and healing capsules. "Perhaps you weren't economical with your reserves. You were distracted."

"It wasn't the chi spell." She pulled the sheet around her and groped for her glasses on the side table. "Are you telling me you didn't notice?"

"Notice that you were distracted?" He shuffled through his odds and ends drawer, discarding straws, plastic utensils, a compass, several screwdrivers, a USB cord, a slide ruler and a penlight before he found a paperclip. "I caused your distraction."

Marcus tried to remember when he'd started feeling unlike himself. Before the sex? No. He'd felt like his horny self. During the sex? No. He'd felt like his domineering self. At the end?

Possibly. When Katie had orgasmed, she'd sought the dittany link. He'd felt it. That connection would have made sense for a real couple during intercourse since mental openness expressed affection. But they were business partners at best, and she'd been frank about her dislike of him.

After he'd sensed the dittany link, he'd been busy with a monster climax, and everything else had faded to insignificance.

"You're the one who's distracted," Katie said, and he realized she'd been speaking to him for almost a minute. "Are you all right?"

What should he tell her? Marcus stared at the small, lovely woman in his bed, wishing she were trustworthy. Wishing she did feel enough affection for him that she'd bared her essence when he'd been inside her. "I'm fine. I was thinking of…something in the next experiment. What were you saying?"

"I was asking if you noticed that I gave you my magic." She rubbed her cheek on her bare shoulder as she yawned again. "That's why I'm drained."

Marcus froze in the act of handing her the paper clip. "You did what?"

He sank onto the bed, flabbergasted. She'd given him

magic? He had witch magic, Katie's magic, inside him, right now?

She poked him with the paperclip. "You're welcome."

"That wasn't part of the experiment!" He shouldn't feel like shit with witch magic inside him. He should feel powerful. She must have done something wrong.

She straightened, her eyebrows flying toward her hairline. "How does this change your experiment? You confirmed my wolf gets stronger. We were just...wrapping up."

He hadn't calculated the variables. He didn't know how she'd done it or how much power she'd given him. He hadn't *known*. "I need to see my lattice."

"I'm sorry. I didn't save any power to do that."

"What have you done?" He rubbed his temples. Taking magic from a wolf was one thing; transferring was another. She'd just barged into his psyche without any pretesting.

He hadn't authorized her to give him...anything.

She was watching him with big, worried eyes. "I thought you'd be pleased."

The fizzing anxiety shot him back to his feet while his bones and muscles protested his weight. He rested a hand on the cabinets above the pull-down bed. "I'm not pleased."

"You're never pleased. Not with me." Katie realigned the paper clip into the appropriate shape.

She manipulated the cuffs with expertise. She'd done this before. Marcus found himself irritated by the thought of her encountering handcuff issues with a prior lover, but lock picking was more likely due to keeper training than sex play. She'd seemed as surprised by her reaction to the light kink as he was by his.

Was it his wolf who'd enjoyed it—or him? He'd never

enjoyed anything kinky prior to the transformation, but he'd never tried anything kinky. Which didn't answer the question. Was it him or the wolf?

He hated when he couldn't control his primitive side. That too had been absent prior to the transformation and had plagued him ever since. However, he couldn't deny he took a keen pleasure in dominating Katie. Seeing her helplessly aroused and at his mercy. No other wolf could have done it, perhaps no other man.

He'd captured her, he'd outsmarted her and now he'd mastered her. He'd had the deadly Chang Cai bound and begging him to fuck her.

What's more, he'd had Katie Zhang, who'd been a pain in his ass since that first horrible dragon tattoo, begging him to do more than fuck her. She, not her wolf, had confessed his bay capsule hurt her feelings and asked him to make love to her.

Maybe he had.

The Katie who'd wanted him to love her had left part of herself inside his body. Part of him was inside her body.

He might be numb on the outside and ticked as hell that she'd screwed up the experiment, but it didn't stop his erection from returning.

Marcus put on sweats to hide it. After he was dressed, she tossed him the handcuffs. He caught them, glad his reflexes hadn't taken a complete hiatus.

"Do I get clothes?" she asked, saucy and belligerent at the same time. "Or are you planning on keeping me naked and chained up?"

"It's a thought." If he didn't allow clothes, no doubt he'd wake tomorrow and she'd be fully dressed anyway. "I suppose you might get cold."

"Let me see if I can find where I threw my..." She rolled over on the mattress, the sheet slipping to reveal the supple curve of her back. A mark high on her shoulder showed where he'd bitten her as they'd made…as they'd wrapped up the experiment.

The sheet dropped lower. Her ass was pink from what he'd done to her.

He'd like to bite her there instead of her shoulder. He'd like to hear her cry out his name, desperate for him. He'd like to make love to her again.

Right now. Because he wanted to.

He realized she wasn't looking for panties and walked to her side of the bed. Wordlessly, he held out his hand. She was in the process of secreting the bent paper clip beneath the mattress. She offered him a shameless grin and held it out. It was almost as if she'd done it to amuse him.

It wasn't particularly funny that she'd ditch him the first chance she got. She wouldn't be leaving him so much as undertaking a suicide mission to rescue her father and friends, but either way, he wasn't going to smile about it.

"Do what you need to do and get back into bed." He wasn't giving her that chance. They had a deal, and if she were dead, he'd—he'd not be able to complete his experiments. The experiments she'd torqued, leapfrogging weeks of planning because she'd had some half-baked impulse to please him.

Fucking hell.

"I'm tired," he added.

Her smile faded. "You're angry."

"Tired," he corrected. He disappeared into the facilities long enough to mop up the water and prepare for bed, knowing she wasn't handcuffed and could escape, or try to. He was a wolf. He'd be on her in two seconds. At least, that's what he told himself.

His body felt so worn and old by the time he fell into bed beside her, he couldn't hide a groan. Sore spots that shouldn't exist throbbed up and down his back, with a particularly large one in his rib cage.

He cuffed one of her wrists for sleep. If he couldn't get the lock open in the morning, he'd give her the damned paper clip. He squinted and couldn't see fingers wiggling, or Katie, or the windows, or anything. When had the trailer gotten so freaking dark?

Covers rustling, she patted his arm, then his chest. "Are you sure you're all right?"

He couldn't confide in her. If she knew he was ill, she'd take advantage.

"Good night, Katie." Marcus rolled onto his side, wincing when his sore hip found the bar beneath the foldout mattress. He couldn't hear the night birds outside or the wind in the trees, sounds he'd grown accustomed to in this section of the park. The fizzing inside him drowned out noises, mucked with his vision, clogged his nostrils. It was a long time before he could sleep.

EIGHTEEN

MARCUS DREAMED HE was on a cloud. Heavenly scents surrounded him. Sex and woman. The peppery taste on his tongue heated his body. Softness cradled him. His hips jabbed into it, filling him with lust. He thrust again, pleased when the friction ratcheted up.

Unfortunately, he was jolted out of this pleasant dream by a stout blow to the shoulder. "Get off me, sleeping beauty."

During sleep he'd tangled in the bed blankets and Katie's limbs. His leg was flung over her, his cock shoved against her warm hip. His hand cupped her breast.

The nipple was hard. So was he.

She kicked both her legs, knocking him aside. He raised his hands to show he meant no harm, but she bounced off the bed anyway, even more tousled than she'd been last night.

Hands on hips, she glared down at him. It wasn't terribly effective when her hair looked like a rooster's comb and she was wearing one of his old T-shirts.

She wasn't wearing the handcuffs.

He flew out of bed. When his feet hit the floor, he stumbled. Righted himself clumsily. She blinked those thick eyelashes at him, not offering a hand or an explanation.

"What did you do with the cuffs?" he barked.

Unperturbed, she pointed at the canvas strap, where the handcuffs dangled. "Relax. I didn't break your toy."

Marcus rubbed a hand over his chest, feeling every one of his hundred-plus years. Did he have the flu? Wolves didn't get the flu. "You aren't supposed to be at liberty."

She raised an eyebrow. "You're not a morning person, are you?"

Marcus growled. Today he needed to begin calculations for the next phase of testing. Analyze what she'd done to him. He was behind in recording last night's observations and felt like death.

Katie, in contrast, looked razor-sharp and completely rested. Her scruffiness didn't hide that. He'd have to bust ass to stay ahead of her today, and he had enough work to do.

"Coffee," he grumbled, though he hadn't required caffeine since his transformation.

"You don't have any. Let's go get coffee and sausage biscuits and check the rendezvous point." She pulled on a pair of jeans, wriggling to slide them over her ass. He glimpsed red panties and soft, kissable abdomen. "Look, Vern's note didn't say for sure Lars caught them. There's a chance they escaped. It's not like they have our number to leave messages or know where we are. Vern will be expecting us in Garner."

"How long have you been awake?" he asked, tearing his gaze from her hips.

"Around four this morning I puttered around before coming back to bed. I wanted to assess our options for the rescue." On his prep counter, she'd unpacked her tattoo supply kit and the remaining components they'd collected from the shop yesterday. "I thought you'd never wake up."

"You dosed me with agrimony again."

"Nope." She gestured toward a plastic baggie full of

a tan-and-green mixture. "If I wanted to knock you out, I wouldn't use anything as lame as agrimony."

She could have taken off. Again. Yet she hadn't.

Why had she stayed? Gotten back into bed with him, no less?

Because he was useful to her? Or because she wanted to?

He didn't care which one it was.

Something akin to relief built inside him. She had no idea how close he was to dragging her into bed right now to celebrate. He sniffed, checking to see if she might reciprocate, but smelled nothing out of the ordinary.

Nothing period.

Nose? Still malfunctioning.

Relief that she hadn't ditched him? The fizzy jumble from last night. He wasn't happy. Her magic had screwed him up inside.

Marcus advanced on her and gripped her shoulders. "Take it out," he said. "Take the magic back out of me."

She raised her chin to study him. "It's not that simple. It's been twelve hours. The dittany that lets us link has worn off."

"I have more." He let her go and yanked open a supply cabinet. "Your deposit wasn't timetabled properly. You didn't have my permission—"

A finger poked him in the ribs, and he hissed at the flash of pain. "That's a nasty-looking bruise."

"Bruise?" The narrow bathroom door had a mirror on the outside. Marcus, who'd slept shirtless, twisted to examine his torso. To his shock, reddish-purple bruises darkened his skin in various areas. "What the hell?"

She stroked his injuries, her touch gentle. "You didn't seem bothered at the time, but I beat the hell out of you last night before you took me to bed. Serves you right."

When he'd had her confined over his shoulder, spanking her shapely ass, she'd reciprocated. The knee in the ribs—Marcus gingerly probed the bones to see if anything was cracked—had stolen his breath. He should have shaken off the damage within the hour.

He slammed the bathroom door, unwilling to see more. He felt imbalanced—not like a witch and not like a wolf. "You didn't give me magic. You put some kind of curse on me. I feel like shit. I can't smell, I can't hear, I can barely stand. What the fuck did you do, Katie?"

"A certain scientist might say I reversed the direction of the focal current and fed my magic to your lattice. It was your idea, might I add—some techno-babble about supersaturating yourself." She leaned against a counter and crossed her arms. "We had the dittany link and nothing else. You can't make magic out of hair and spit."

"That's all you did?" He wanted to believe her, but he also wanted to believe he could convince her that his experiments would facilitate a rescue of her family. Was he a fool?

"That's all I did." She scrubbed the hair on top of her head. "You know, this reminds me of something. I was the focal for a lot of group workings with the council, and I—well, I may have used those opportunities to clean the hell out of everyone's reserves."

He raised an eyebrow at her. "You took more power than necessary?" To do so in the coven network was considered extremely bad craft. Other witches wouldn't team with a colleague who'd leave them needlessly drained, unable to defend themselves.

"Every chance I got," she said. "It rendered the others useless for up to a week and gave me a fucking break from the backstabbing. The council isn't exactly the Girl Scouts."

"That I know." The keepers had been competitive to the point of sabotaging rivals. Chang Cai had been near the top of the ladder most of her time with the council, the go-to witch for plum and difficult assignments alike. After Vernon had arrived, she'd been in his inner circle, and Lars had not.

Lars had spoken of her as depraved and weak, resorting to various ploys to conceal her failures. Other long-term keepers—the few Marcus had been allowed to meet—had described her ruthless competence. Out of Lars's hearing, of course. They were all thankful she was dead, because apparently she'd scared everyone. They'd worried someone with her power could actually kill them with magic if she tried. At the same time, envy of Chang Cai's abilities had lingered.

Marcus had no doubt the woman before him was competent. Potentially ruthless. Even scary. But depraved and weak?

Hardly.

"I have some experience with your situation," she told him. "There are ways to deal with it that don't leave you… vulnerable. Any kind of vulnerability got exploited by the council one way or another."

The more she revealed about her time with the keepers, the more he had to wonder why she'd remained with them for so long. Exploited was an understatement. She'd confessed they'd used her as bait. Her sexual curiosity disarmed male wolves, and her alpha would have compounded their fascination. He'd struggled against the combination himself. With wolves, hormonal responses like lust were seen as normal, but witches, like humans, preferred to think of themselves as above physicality.

"Go on," he encouraged.

"You have an excess, more magic than you're used to.

I used to be able to handle a lot because of how often I amped up, but everyone has limits. My guess is you've never overdrafted." She grinned. "Better add that to your charts."

He didn't appreciate her levity. "We need to fix it. At once. I feel like rubbish."

She considered him with what seemed like actual sympathy. "The easiest thing to do for an excess is burn it off. Waste not, want not. I used to use cayenne—it can store whatever you throw at it."

"Yes, if you want to create explosions." Cayenne was troublesome enough when filled with a standard amount of magic. It irritated the skin, requiring additional magic to relieve pain. The layered, supercharged cayenne some keepers created was harsher.

"You did say you needed a backhoe or some magical TNT to remove your constraints," she said. "I used to layer it with a whole coven's worth of power. Carried it around my waist in a hidden pouch so nobody would know what I was doing."

"How does one use it without significant damage?" he asked, distracted by curiosity. And where would they get a coven's worth of power? "Cayenne that strong blisters the skin down to the dermis or worse. That's not practical."

When Katie raised her eyebrows and started to answer, he lifted a hand. "Never mind. I can't prime cayenne anyway. I need you to remove the excess for me."

She gestured toward the front door. "I bet if you shift, it will take care of the overdraft *and* your bruises."

Why hadn't he thought of that?

Ah, yes. Because he hadn't had a chance to prepare for this phase of the experiment. Irritated and stiff, he undid the many latches on the front door and hurled it open. Once in the bright morning sunlight, he willed the wolf to take over.

Nothing happened.

Just as witches could run out of power, wolves could become form stuck if they shifted too many times in a row. Marcus hadn't shifted since yesterday, but this didn't feel like empty. Or overfull.

It felt like something was barricading his wolf.

Ignoring Katie in the doorway, watching him, he crouched on the ground, placed his knuckles in the mulch and closed his eyes. With all his might, he compelled his body to shift.

His extremities prickled as if they'd fallen asleep. Otherwise, nothing happened.

He sprang to his feet and nearly crumpled. Katie was there, bare feet sunk in the pine needles, to catch him. "Whoa. Take it easy."

"Can't shift." He was fairly certain he could walk on his own but let her support his weight as they shuffled to the trailer. Pinecones and bark pricked his soles. "Before you ask, I'm not form stuck."

He shook her off and climbed the stairs like an old witch at the end of a third pass-through. The weakness, the anesthetized senses and the bodily aches had started after Katie had given him her magic.

This was no mere excess. So what was it?

Yes, he hadn't prepared, but everything he'd calculated had indicated witch and wolf magic were the same. Transferrable. A witch could use magic from a wolf without issues; so should a wolf be able to use magic from a witch.

Magic was magic. It was a neutral force, created inside a shifter, neither good nor evil. Whether taken or given, it would change nothing about the power itself. A witch could take magic directly from a wolf and prime cayenne with it to use in any spells. He shouldn't have any issue using Katie's magic to shift into a wolf.

"That makes sense," she said, her chin on her hands as she perched on the other side of the small table. "Would a sausage biscuit help? Because it would help me. I'm starving."

He realized he'd been thinking aloud. And had seated himself at his computer, booted it up and begun several mathematical computations to assess the power transfer.

"We need to view my aura and lattice," he said, right before his stomach let out a loud grumble.

"Breakfast first. How can you concentrate when you're hungry?"

"I can't." He closed the laptop and considered nearby food sources. He didn't often eat at restaurants, but his weekly grocery run had been delayed.

Katie popped up. "I want to go to the rendezvous point. I'll use one of Tonya's masks from our go bag, and you can use one of yours."

"Food only," he corrected. "While Tonya and your father have amnesia, Vernon knows all about us." The more he thought about it, the more he realized Lars probably hadn't murdered Vernon yet. He would interrogate and torture the old witch first.

"Vern won't tell Lars a damn thing," Katie said.

"He may not have a choice." Had she forgotten how keepers employed calming mix? "It takes time, but they can extract information from people one way or another."

"Compulsion magic can take weeks to function as a truth serum. Vern's crafty. There's no way he would have broken yet."

Marcus rubbed his temples, wishing Katie were…easier. He had no idea which one of them was right, but he didn't plan to endanger her. Them. "I'm not driving you to Garner."

"We'll see," she said in a tone that left little doubt they'd have another argument about this.

She got dressed, washed up and found her backpack in the time it took him to put on a shirt.

His progress seemed unduly lopsided. Perhaps the disproportion wasn't all him. Katie was friskier than he'd ever seen her. Determined, even. Her depression yesterday had been a concern. He'd tried to keep her from activating the combat bonus, but it seemed probable that he'd failed.

"Precisely how much has your refill pace increased?" he asked. "Are you flush already?"

"I've a ways to go before I'm flush," she said, answering only his second question. "Keep in mind—my reserves are larger than most. I heard a rumor I'm alpha." She was at his side, already, car keys jangling impatiently. "Do you really need that?"

Marcus slipped the bay capsule into his pocket. "I hope not."

"Look, if you still think I..." Her lips tightened and she quit speaking.

"You're not the only convex witch, Katie." He could see it bothered her, but it wasn't a protection against her. Was it?

"I'm just the convex witch who's ready to go now," she said. "You don't even have on your shoes. Hurry up."

Partly because it was smart and partly because she was dancing with impatience, Marcus triple checked his utility kit before dosing himself with some primed heal-all. It helped. He offered it to her, and she waved it off.

"Heal-all? How bad do you feel?" she asked. "Shall I drive?"

"I can drive."

With a little smile he didn't trust—but which he still liked, for some reason—she handed him the keys and followed him to the car. Once they were on the road, he struck up a conversation. If he kept her mind busy, perhaps she'd relent on the matter of the rendezvous. The local pack, the coven and any number of elders might be combing the Birmingham territory by now, keepers or no keepers. Unnecessary risks weren't on his agenda.

"Tell me about your permabrands," he encouraged. Magical tattoo artists like Katie were extremely exclusive. Rare to begin with and crazy expensive, they worked through agents and concealed their identities, else they'd be constantly bombarded. "Could you create one that was a mask?"

"With some effort." As much as she was fidgeting in her seat, tapping her fingers and rearranging herself, he thought she might be closer to flush than she'd let on. "They're not simple spells. It wipes me so completely I get a dry socket in my brain, and the components aren't always easy to come by."

"And a witch can only sport one brand at a time?" He considered the possibilities. The mask he wore right now would wear off in approximately three hours. To be free of the daily need to mask would be a relief.

"That's right," she said. "I'd go for 20/20 vision, but I can't tattoo myself. And if you're thinking of asking for a brand—"

"I'd choose a mask." Heal-all wasn't necessary—or hadn't been before today. "Are your brands as attractive as your dragons?" he asked, trying to get another smile out of her.

The corner of her lip twitched. That was close enough.

"Unfair comparison. I don't want to get rid of my perm-abrand customers."

The conversation paused as they hit a drive-through. Katie indicated she wanted him to park with their food, and he did, assuming she needed to avail herself of the facilities. He unbuckled his seat belt. He'd have to stand guard so she didn't give him the slip.

Instead of getting out, she turned toward him. "I want to check the rendezvous point."

He leaned against the seat, slumping a little. This again. "Not safe."

"You have a mask already. I brought my mask. We'll drive by the post office, and you can use your wolf senses to see if there are any suspicious characters hanging around before I go in. I really doubt Vernon gave us up, but we can take precautions."

"My nose doesn't seem to be working," he reminded her. "For example, this smells delicious." He held up the bag of biscuits. "I know what goes in fast food. It shouldn't smell delicious."

"We have to do something. We can't pretend my family isn't in trouble."

"We are doing something. The experiments will give us a huge edge in bargaining for what we want." With the region elders, if not the keepers. "Patience."

"I just want to find out what's happening outside the Airstream. If we check the post office, I promise I'll—"

"No, you won't." Sighing, he tore open the biscuit bag and arranged it on the seat between them like a platter. "I know your priorities, Katie, and whatever you're about to tell me isn't your priority. You'll break that promise and any others that interfere with your goals."

Though their discussion was contentious, she didn't

raise her voice. "Like you're any different? What if there was a chance your sister would be waiting for you?"

"My sister's dead. Checking the rendezvous point is an unwarranted gamble, even with masks." He dumped extra sugar in his coffee, not looking at Katie. He understood why she kept misleading him. If there was anything she could do for her family, she meant to do it, at the cost of her own life—or his.

That didn't mean he was willing to make that choice.

"Well, my family isn't dead. We both know I'm never going to let this go. Stay in the car and I'll go in. My face would mean nothing to anyone but the keepers, and they—"

"We aren't separating again. I'm not saying this to be cruel, but I believe Lars caught your family. The likelihood of a message being at the post office that wasn't there yesterday isn't sufficient payoff."

"It is to me." She crumpled a biscuit wrapper, her expression mulish. "This question has to be answered."

"Not immediately, it doesn't." Her loyalty and tenaciousness were admirable. But barreling into a situation wasn't the best way to succeed. If they were going to mount a rescue, she had to heed him. He wasn't the one overwhelmed by loss. He had perspective.

If he'd had Katie's assistance when Elisa had turned, could her perspective have resulted in success? Could Elisa and the child have survived?

He'd had no one then and had placed his trust in the wrong people. The sympathizers and Tonya Applebaum had meant well but performed poorly.

So had he.

"I didn't go when I could have," Katie reminded him. Her discretion did evidence an improvement in her behavior. "I waited until we could discuss it. I want to agree."

"You want my assistance."

"I want your help." She bit angrily into another biscuit, chewed, swallowed. "And you want mine."

He wanted more than her help. He wanted her trust. He wanted to trust her. He wanted their facade of teamwork to be real teamwork. If he negotiated here, would that build a bridge between them?

"Yes, I do," he said. "I want to believe you won't trick me anymore."

"Twice now, I could have disappeared. But I've stuck with you." Unexpectedly, she scooted toward him, biscuit forgotten. She caught his shoulder. "Please, if you don't feel safe going to the rendezvous point, can I go alone? I'll come back to you, Marcus."

He needed more than that. "Will you?"

"Why wouldn't I? You're my best bet." She stared straight at him. "And I like the sex."

"The tests have been successful, except for the one," he acknowledged. They'd been so intent on their conversation, he'd forgotten the fact his wolf was on the fritz.

She clarified. "I don't like the tests. I don't like the charts. I don't like the science."

"Then what do you—"

"I like the sex. With you."

Her words seemed heavier than a factual statement. "Because I'm a wolf and you possessed a certain curiosity." Wolf lust. He'd smelled it on her from the first and known what the keepers had done to her because of it.

"That I did. But no." She touched his jaw, lightly, as if confirming the length of his stubble. He hadn't taken the time to shave in days. "I realized last night if you were someone else, I would not be okay with this. I would not help someone else, and I would not ask someone else to help me. I would not come back to someone else."

"Since you haven't done this with anyone else," he said, nonplussed by her intensity, "you can't be sure of that."

"No?" She regarded him with wide, bright eyes and that same faint smile that mystified him. Her lips had a tiny dimple in one corner, an indention he only noticed when she wasn't…angry. It was a precursor to the dimple in her cheek that appeared when she was amused. "Would you do this with anyone else, Marcus?"

For some reason, she was leaning into him, close enough to kiss. His gaze dropped to her lips. "My experiments? I approached a former colleague I suspected of being alpha, but she notified the elders, who notified the keepers, and I—"

"Yeah, I don't actually want to know that." She backed off and shoved both hands under her legs. A shutter closed over her expression, rendering it neutral. "I want to go to the rendezvous."

Marcus had never been great with women. People, actually. People's behavior, human or shifter, didn't abide by formulae. He suspected he'd just stomped on Katie's feelings, or her toes, or her plans to wheedle him. Something. He'd driven away her smile, the one that did funny things to his insides.

Would she really come back to him?

Did he really want her out there alone?

"All right," he said, going against logic. This wasn't safe. This wasn't smart. But confirming there was no message might help Katie settle. "Put your mask on. No other detours."

AFTER THEY CRUISED the post office, Marcus's confiscated ball cap tugged low over his eyes, Katie directed him to a lot several blocks from the rendezvous point. They would cut through a well-populated area—a public playground and a kitschy shopping district—to reach their destination.

They left the car in the large, crowded lot, taking a few essentials in case of emergency. His chattiness had disappeared. The farther they'd driven into Birmingham territory, the twitchier he'd gotten. At this point he practically jangled with nerves. Whatever her magic had done to his wolf senses, he wasn't adjusting to their loss well.

But that was a puzzle for later. Right now, Katie was just relieved he'd agreed to come. She was growing more and more reluctant to be at odds with him. They needed each other.

"Relax," she told him. Her scientist had only been living incognito for a year and hadn't perfected the art of nonchalance. Not only was he jumpy enough to attract attention, but she was responsible for making him this way. "The coven and the pack might be searching the Birmingham territory to figure out what the hell happened at the tattoo shop—"

"There's no 'might be.' They are." Marcus jammed his hands in his pockets. In one he had his beloved bay capsules, and in the other he had a few spell pods—formulated for throwing, in the event skin contact wasn't feasible. They'd do a wolf no good because they weren't primed, but he'd insisted on a weapon of some sort. They'd left the gun in the Airstream, and the tire iron would have been conspicuous. "We could be walking into a trap."

"I avoided capture for twenty years. Give me some credit. Covert is my middle name." She had spell capsules and packets stashed on her too—and enough power to use all of them. She'd forgotten how convenient the combat bonus was. The magic boosted her confidence and sharpened her determination.

Marcus muttered something.

"What's that?" she asked.

"I assumed your middle name was Chaos."

"Ha, ha." She took his arm, slowing his pace so they'd look like a typical couple out shopping. "Before you, there was no chaos. A couple relocations, the occasional biker gang or drunken fraternity group trying to talk us into giving them tattoos. You brought the chaos."

"I feel like shit."

"Because you brought the chaos?" They strolled past a bistro with several outdoor tables full of coffee drinkers. The scents floating past—pastry and coffee beans—were delicious despite the fact they'd had sausage biscuits an hour ago.

Marcus inhaled, his nostrils flaring. "Because of what you did. I could use more caffeine."

She gestured. "You want to—"

"No."

Grump. Not that she had anything to smile about in the grand scheme of things, but a grin tugged at her lips. "We're nearly there."

The busy postal building sat between a bank and a historic home converted into offices. Birds chirped, and the sun shone warmly. Nothing pinged Katie's radar. It looked exactly like yesterday. The parking lot had no cars she recognized, though Vern would have parked elsewhere.

Correction—Vern would have parked elsewhere if Dad wasn't with him. Dad would have demanded the handicapped spot, which was empty. Katie doubted the amnesia spell had erased that part of her father's character. She swallowed a touch of disappointment that he wasn't there, cane in hand, waiting on the bench. He wouldn't remember why she was important to him unless Vern had worked a miracle in the past couple of days, but it wouldn't matter.

He'd be safe.

"I don't see anybody suspicious," she told Marcus. "No rental cars. No keeper minivans."

She, Dad and Tonya had become familiar with the names and appearances of Birmingham's adult coven members, and wolves tended to stand out regardless. In her time, keepers had been trained to blend in, but the keepers who'd chased them out of the tattoo shop had made zero effort to look like civilians. She certainly didn't see any black-ops types lurking behind vehicles. An older model Cadillac and a red SUV were parallel parked in two street slots, while the side lot was full.

Marcus froze next to the Cadillac. His eyes narrowed. "That's out of place."

"A land barge? Why?"

"Out of state tags." A lady and two children exited the glass front doors of the post office. He growled quietly and it thrummed through his body into her.

California tags would have been noteworthy. West Virginia tags, not so much. Katie pinched the inside of his arm. "Hush. Alabama does get some tourists."

"At a post office?"

His tension was rubbing off on her. Her stomach tightened. Would Tonya, Dad or Vern be inside? Humans— she assumed they were humans—came and went on the sidewalk and street. Inside the glass frontage of the post office, a long line waited. All keeper, pack and coven protocol prohibited discernible use of powers in such a populated area. The crowd should be a buffer against overt actions against Katie and Marcus.

Despite that, he wouldn't budge any closer to the post office Nostrils flared, he stared at the Cadillac. "I don't like this. Vern drove from West Virginia. The keepers tracked him."

"Do you see any keepers?" He'd have a better chance at recognizing them than she would, since he'd been there six years ago. The ones with Lars had seemed young to her.

"No. But I didn't know everyone. I wasn't in the main stronghold."

"If that Caddy belongs to the keepers, they wouldn't have parked out front. Stand guard. I'll check the box." She released his arm and headed for the front door.

He pounced on her before she'd gone three steps.

"We stay together."

"There's no back door. I'm not going to sneak off." He was so openly paranoid, the lady with the children, a man on a cell phone and an older couple were all giving him the stink eye. Katie raised herself onto tiptoes and brushed her lips across his cheek en route to his ear, where she whispered. "Chill out. You're attracting attention."

He caught the back of her neck and kissed her. A hard, high-handed kiss that let her know he'd listened when she'd admitted she liked the sex. He grabbed her hip, possessive. She let him. Right there, in front of several children.

Foolishly, her knees weakened and her pleasure points tingled. His tongue stroked hers. She reciprocated gladly. He broke it off sooner than she liked but later than he should have, considering they had an audience.

Usually when he kissed her, his eyes turned silver. They were as brown as her own as he gazed intently down at her. "We stay together."

"Okay." If he kept kissing and touching her like a man who wanted her instead of a man who found her useful and worried she might kill him with monkshood, she'd agree to just about anything.

He studied her for a long moment, his thumb stroking her neck. "And for your information, the answer is no."

"The answer to what?"

"I wouldn't want to do this with anyone else."

While he might have heard her praise the sex, Katie had hoped he'd forgotten her near-confession of...whatever it was she felt for him. All he'd done was explain she wasn't his first choice, proving what a fool she was. Her emotions gave him more power than he needed over her. And it resulted in the emotion she had right now.

A crazy urge to tell him she was in love with him.

Stupid. Instead, she said, "I bet your former colleague would have been more cooperative."

"I bet I wouldn't be thinking about taking her back to the car and ripping off her clothes," he said in a growly voice.

Great, now she was thinking about it too. Flustered as hell, Katie cleared her throat. "I, um. Seriously?"

He raised an eyebrow. "I'll wait inside the door and watch the road. You get ninety seconds to check the box, and then we're leaving."

Leaving so they could have sex, like his grip and his expression promised? She could get into that. "Then what?"

"We drive far, far from this territory. I'm not going to risk losing... I want us to exercise more caution in the future."

"Us. Caution. Right."

But she didn't go into the post office. Her feet were rooted to the ground. That kiss hadn't had anything to do with science.

He was still riveted too, because his hand tightened

on her neck, trapping her in place. *Goddess.* She nearly melted on the spot. He bent toward her.

A man's voice called, "Luis Rodriguez?"

Marcus whirled instantly, placing himself between her and the unknown person. He snatched a spell pod out of his pocket.

Why had he done that? He couldn't use a spell that wasn't...

Magic rose around them in a rush. Confusion spell. She recognized it. He flicked it toward the person who'd said his old name with a gesture that could have been someone swatting at a fly.

It pinged the tall Caucasian man in the chest. He staggered into the blonde woman behind him, shaking his head.

"Holy smokes," the blonde exclaimed. The man was too heavy for her. He knocked her into the passenger's side of the Caddy, her pink skirt winding around her legs. "Harry, get off me."

The man rubbed his shaggy dark hair. "Hey, babe. What are we doing here?"

Katie jostled past Marcus to see what was going on. Harry. That sounded familiar. Harry rubbed his jaw and wandered toward the street. The woman untangled herself and headed him off. "Hold on there, cowboy."

"Shit." Marcus trembled and clutched her shoulder. "Something's happening."

"Darn tootin' something's happening." The small woman whipped open the back door of the Caddy and redirected her roving companion into it. He tried to open the opposite door. She flicked the locks. "Where are your manners, Luis? I swan. Is a confusion spell how you greet friends these days?"

NINETEEN

MARCUS GRABBED HIS head and cursed. He'd cast a spell, a witch spell, at Harry Travis. Suddenly his senses were bursting open. The wolf inside him exploded. From numb to razor's edge in the space of two seconds.

He couldn't hold on. He was going to shift.

"Get him in the backseat. Now." In a no-nonsense voice, June Travis directed Katie and opened the door wide.

Katie didn't argue. Perhaps she felt the tug of June's alpha like Marcus did. He didn't have time to reflect on the other witch's power. Katie shepherded him to the vehicle at a brisk walk, eyes darting in every direction. Harry was already in the back of the car, trying to climb into the driver's seat.

June grabbed the seat of his pants and yanked him down. "Sit with Luis."

"Oh, hey, Luis." Harry waved at him, his pupils dilated. "Long time, no see."

Claws pierced Marcus's fingertips. He dove into the backseat without further prodding. June hopped in front, as did Katie, and the Caddy pulled onto the street at a pace that was way too sedate.

"I thought he was a wolf now?" June said to Katie. "How'd he activate a confusion spell?"

"I have no fu—excuse me, freaking idea." Katie's

voice, echoing in his ears. "You're June Travis, aren't you? Let me guess. Vern contacted you."

Marcus couldn't follow the conversation. He poured himself into fighting the wolf. To shift against his will meant he was feral. A failure in every way. Though the wolf plagued him and he resented the primitive impulses, the only time he'd truly lost it had been the first transformation. He'd even endured the berserker spell upright.

He crouched on the floor and thought man-thoughts. Science. Computers. Driving cars.

The taste of Katie's lips. The way she'd surrendered to him. The way she would again.

His teeth sharpened, cutting his lip. His clothing grew insubstantial. His hair follicles zinged.

No. No. He was in control. He controlled this situation. He controlled himself. He had mastered this.

The shimmer of transformation swept his control away. In another minute, Marcus, as a wolf, let loose a frustrated howl.

Harry clapped a hand around Marcus's muzzle. "What's up with you? Is this really a good time to four-leg it?"

Marcus bit him. The fucker was a wolf. He'd heal.

"What the hell was that for?" Harry recoiled and began to shimmer too, aggression rippling all over him. "Lie down."

Harry's command, as powerful as a pack alpha because of his coven connection, crushed Marcus to the floor. And made him furious. He was nobody's subordinate. And he was, quite frankly, too damned big to be in this cramped space.

A floorboard? Really?

He gnashed at Harry's leg, and Harry scrambled out of reach. He wrapped his wounded hand in a towel.

"I said down," Harry repeated.

Marcus hunkered on the floor. To display his indignation, he started barking as loud as he could. Harry, whose senses would be wolf-acute, winced.

"Should we spell him?" Katie, anxious. "I've got lavender."

"You're the convex witch Vern told us about. Maybe you shouldn't do any spells." June's coolness was evident over Marcus's racket. Vern must have shared more than the rendezvous location with June and Harry.

"You're driving. I'm not. It's a reasonable solution." Katie's tone was level, no trace of the hostility she'd exhibited when Marcus had made assumptions about her.

It surprised him so much to realize he no longer held negative views of her that he almost quit barking.

The bay capsules weren't for her. They were so no keeper could stop him from protecting her if she needed him.

"Got any earplugs?" Harry glowered at him. Marcus yipped, coyote-shrill. "Jesus, lay off the noise. You're killing us."

Marcus thought about doing what Harry wanted so he could hear the women better—but then he'd be doing what Harry wanted. He released a full-throated howl.

"That's enough." Harry's boot caught him in the shoulder. Not hard, but hard enough.

Marcus snapped at him and focused on his opponent. The alpha's eyes lightened as they engaged in a power struggle. Marcus, his blood hot, his fury white, hated the fact he'd shifted when he didn't intend to. Hated the fact Harry was stronger than he was. Hated the fact he was crumbling, centimeter by centimeter, beneath the other wolf's dominion.

Hands grabbed his ears and yanked.

He smelled Katie.

He didn't hate Katie.

With a sudden *whumph,* Marcus quit barking and growling. He nipped at Katie's hand to keep up appearances and cast Harry an evil glare.

"He doesn't like you either?" Harry sprawled across half of the back seat in a deceptively casual posture. Marcus wasn't fooled. He could read the tension in the man like he could read the uneasiness in Katie.

"Not really," she said.

"That's understandable," June put in, snippy.

The June whom Marcus had interviewed had never been curt. What exactly had Vernon told the Travises about Katie? It pissed him off to think of that cocky bastard badmouthing her, a woman who'd done everything she could to put her keeper years behind her, who was doing everything she could to save her loved ones. Vernon had been director of the entire council. He had no grounds to criticize anyone.

But all Katie said was, "I take it Vern explained about the keeper council and its role in the North American coven network?"

"He has. I think it's terrible."

"I recall something about that." Harry frowned at Katie. "Who are you again? And where are we, anyway?"

"I'm Katie Zhang. This is Alabama. You're under a confusion spell."

"That explains it." He scratched his neck. "The coven has tested nearly everything on me once or twice. I just can't imagine why in the hell I'd want to come to Alabama. It's not safe for out-of-state wolves here."

"I'll fix you up at the hotel," June said. "The Birmingham pack's not going to bother us. We have protection wards on the car and room, remember?"

"Nope, but I'll take your ward for it. Get it?" Harry laughed.

June didn't. To Marcus, she smelled like cake and conflict.

Katie didn't laugh either. She scruffed the hair on Marcus's head, patting him like a dog. He'd never been touched by another person as a wolf. When her hand ruffled down his spine, he hopped halfway in the seat so she could reach him better. His wolf transformation had erased the bruising, and her caress enhanced how good he felt, physically.

"If you're calmer, would you like to rejoin the bipedal world so we can have an actual conversation?" she asked. "Such as, what the hell happened at the post office?"

Her gaze met his. With his wolf vision, he could see the minute adjustments of her pupils as they drove through sunlight and shadows on a tree-lined road. When she blinked, he heard the tiny click of her eyelashes and lids.

He could smell again, hear again, see again.

He was a wolf again. With attendant benefits. But for a moment, at the post office, he'd been a witch. He'd fucking done it.

He couldn't wait to tell Katie. He needed normal vocal cords.

Unfortunately, when he did shift back, his clothes hadn't remained with him.

"Don't look, Ethel," Harry said to June. "It's the streak."

Marcus hadn't been a wolf long enough to be completely comfortable with nudity. He accepted the jacket Katie offered him. She inspected his body as he placed it in his lap, and a slight blush tinged her cheeks.

"Excuse me," he told everyone, trying not to overappreciate her reaction. A hard-on in mixed company wasn't particularly civil.

And just like that, his mood transformed. Yes, he'd had five minutes where he couldn't govern his body. But had he been feral? Or was it akin to the original transformation when he'd shifted from witch to wolf after sex? The rush had been similar.

What he wouldn't give for his computer right now. And a chi spell. And a mirror. And pants. Was he in dual state or had he exchanged lattices? Would he sport a thread for the confusion spell he'd cast at the post office?

Oh, and dittany. He needed Katie to pour more magic into him. He wanted to try dittany on Harry and June too, and instruct them through a power transfer. After that, they'd guide Harry through a spell casting. His first ever.

Marcus might be days away from spinning the entire witch network on its foundation.

"You have that look," Katie said.

He emerged from his stream of consciousness. She was watching him in the mirrored sun visor. "Hmm?"

"Your scientist look." Katie flipped up the visor, cutting off his view of her face. "What's going on in that big head?"

He leaned back in the seat, his wolf warm and solid inside him. Like victory. "First, I'd like to finish our original discussion. June, can you run me through a step-by-step description of how you came to be here? It will aid in strategic planning."

He'd need to set a strict schedule of experimentation, and if June and Harry were being pursued by the keepers like Vern, it could interfere.

June nodded, handling the large car like a granny. A pickup truck passed them, the driver honking. She didn't bat an eyelash. "A couple days ago, Vern told us the truth about keepers and sympathizers and his connection to them. He said he needed to intervene in a situation involving a former coworker but didn't want to disappear without backup."

"That was probably when Tonya first called him." Marcus didn't elaborate on what he'd done to Katie to necessitate Vernon's involvement. His descent into kidnapping and blackmail was between him and Katie. "Why did he enlist you two?"

"He couldn't trust any region elders or sympathizers because of—" June glanced at Katie hastily, as if one peek could turn her into a salt pillar "—a need to conceal the truth."

Katie's jawline, the only part Marcus could see of her face, tightened. "I'm supposed to be dead. Vern's the reason I'm not."

"I remember him telling us that," Harry said. Confusion spells only affected recent events. "I wish we'd known about sympathizers when I was being hounded through Mill County. Maybe things wouldn't have blown up all to hell. Guess we should just be glad Vern didn't sic these keeper fellows on me."

"Two days ago, we got another call from him," June continued.

"Did he mention if my father and my friend Tonya were all right?" Katie interrupted.

June flicked on the blinker and spoke to Marcus instead. "Vern didn't say what you had to do with this mess, Luis, but if he didn't call again, we were supposed to find you."

"Please call me Marcus. Marcus Delgado," he said. "Luis Rodriguez has been retired."

June slowed the Caddy near a motel located in an outlying community. "Well, he didn't call again, so here we are. And these keepers—you think they kidnapped Vern and the other two? He didn't have time to explain."

"Yes," Marcus said. "As I'm sure you can guess, keepers aren't nice people. I suggest we relocate our base of operations as soon as possible." One of the places he'd vetted was in Ohio, an inactive factory that contained some immovable laboratory equipment.

June pulled around back and parked next to some motorcycles. "We didn't take Vern as seriously as it appears we should have. I thought he was exaggerating. He tends to do that. Conspiracy this, world domination that."

Harry got out of the car almost before it stopped moving and opened June's door. She allowed her husband to pull her to her feet, and they came to Marcus and Katie's side of the car. "Have they contacted you with ransom demands?"

"They wouldn't know how to contact us." Katie inhaled and blew out a breath. She opened the passenger's door. "Ba and Tonya wouldn't remember, and I doubt Vern will talk. I've gotten nothing on voice mail either. We can definitely use your help mounting a rescue."

June had been ignoring Katie since their initial exchange. Her round blue eyes regarded Katie with skepticism. "I need answers first. Vern came because of you. I get that. You're his former…he called you a protégée, which I wouldn't take as a compliment. Why did you drag Marcus into this if it's between you, Vern and the keepers? Isn't he in enough trouble?"

"Marcus dragged himself into it." Katie slammed the door while Marcus remained in the backseat with his window halfdown. Wrapping the jacket around his privates like the world's stupidest kilt would be awkward. "One could say he precipitated the entire situation."

"One could say you did, as well," Marcus said, though

he could appreciate her perspective. "The blame game is unproductive."

June inspected Katie as if she expected the former keeper to yank out a philter of monkshood and start assassinating people. "Are you Marcus's girlfriend? I saw you kissing. Wasn't it your job to kill cognizant wolves?"

"She's not my girlfriend, she's my research assistant," he corrected. Katie's lips thinned, though he didn't know why. His statement was accurate. "She's alpha, like you. Did you know you and Katie possess abilities we previously thought were limited to wolves? You both have wolf magic."

"The alpha influence," June said immediately. "She has it too? Mine wasn't there until…"

"You two are sleeping together?" Harry eyed Katie with new appreciation. Not a masculine appraisal by any means, but it raised Marcus's hackles. A silent growl vibrated in his chest. Harry was the only one who heard it, and redirected his gaze toward Marcus.

That meant the other man wasn't looking at Katie anymore. Good.

Harry smiled at him, but Marcus didn't smile back.

Katie crossed her arms and stared at a point somewhere to the east of June's head. "Yes, we confirmed that I'm alpha. I guess he didn't test you two the same way."

"I should think not." June regarded Marcus with disapproval. "Stay where you are. I'll send Harry out with clothing. Katie and I are going to have a chat, woman to woman."

Marcus was alone in the car for five minutes. He strained to hear inside the motel but couldn't, perhaps due to the protections June had set. His ears popped when an unknown spell was cast before Harry emerged. Marcus dressed in the proffered clothing without comment.

Once inside the room, he looked between Katie and June for signs of battle. All he could tell was that somebody had overindulged in disinfectant. The spiky odor invaded his sinuses.

He sneezed. Harry laughed at his expression and tilted his head at his wife. "She cleans everything, everywhere."

Harry's eyes had lost the bleariness caused by the confusion spell.

"All better?" he asked the other man.

"I am. Not sure about you." Harry invited him to sit at the small table while the women murmured near an array of herbs and simples on the bathroom countertop. "Do you need help with control issues? You transformed types don't grow up dealing with it."

"I don't have control issues," Marcus said gruffly. He caught Katie's gaze in the mirror over the sink. "Today was a new development. One I've been anticipating. It may be of great service in the near future."

The future of all witches. The thought of a protracted study wasn't as acceptable as it once had been, though. It would never have been soon enough for Elisa, but Marcus needed results sooner rather than later.

Disabling the keepers hadn't ceased to be about Elisa and revenge, but now it was also about helping Katie and her family.

Katie dusted something pale green off her hands. "You cast a confusion spell."

"I did as you suggested, used the excess magic. Once it was gone, I reverted to wolf."

"This I gotta hear." Harry sat beside his wife, slipping an arm around her. "When June told me about witches and wolves, that's the first thing I wanted to know. How long would I have to go without shifting before I could abracadabra?"

Marcus clasped his hands loosely between his knees. "You've both heard my theory that the magic witches and wolves use is the same—simply redirected." June and Harry nodded. "Now I can prove it, and more. You can even help me. Do you happen to have any dittany?"

TWENTY

KATIE HAD NEVER enjoyed killing. Not even feral wolves trying to kill her. But if she had to endure another day of Marcus's empirical detachment, June's polite suspicion and Harry's jovial balkiness, she would have to kill something.

Preferably Lars, but no one seemed interested in discussing strategies for his demise. Not only did Marcus keep them on a strict regimen of driving, sleep and experimentation that left little time for strategizing, but Katie's companions shut her down when she proposed action. Harry and June were as content as Marcus to believe his discovery would inspire the region elders to change the way things had been for millennia.

The rescue of her family becoming a secondary concern. An afterthought.

It was almost the only thing Katie could think about.

She certainly wasn't thinking about sex. Or, when she did think about it, she wasn't getting it. Marcus had abandoned the sex trials now that he had new guinea pigs. All the four of them did was relocate to avoid being tracked through conventional means, read lattices, pass deposits of magic back and forth like hot potatoes and try to teach Harry how to cast spells.

At least they'd been eating well. Harry and June refused to miss any meals and made Marcus eat too. Katie fed herself, though she suspected nobody would care if she didn't.

On the fifth day after they'd begun their indirect path to Ohio, they finally reached Marcus's abandoned factory cum safe house. Since Lars had traced Vern's phone, they'd taken all the extra precautions Katie and Marcus could think of, but nothing they did shook her sense of foreboding after confronting Lars again or the horror of her nightmares as she imagined what he was doing to her family. Her bullet wound hadn't left a scar, but if anything happened to her family, she'd never be whole again.

Katie kept these thoughts to herself since everyone else was engrossed in Marcus's experiments.

The lab was the one room that didn't seem in danger of falling down around their ears. Marcus was running a computer simulation while simultaneously readying a batch of dittany mix. It was the single component they seemed to have in unending supply. June napped on the cot with a pillow over her ears. Harry paced from one side of the large room to the other, eating a sandwich. Katie cross-referenced several topo maps of the area around the keeper stronghold, considering which approach would give her the best chance of not being immediately shot.

Again.

Though the aerial views one could obtain through the internet were helpful, she could really use the sympathizers' information about current security at the stronghold.

She refolded the maps into perfect rectangles. "June, have we heard back from Nathaniel Oman yet?"

June, a blanket crease on her cheek, emerged from her cocoon. "Someone say my name?"

Despite remaining leery of helping Katie, June had called select people, trying to locate anyone who could tell them what was going on at the keeper stronghold. They'd learned little.

"I asked about Oman," Katie repeated.

"No. There's nothing. I'm troubled by the lack of gossip. Covens love to gossip." June started to push herself into a sitting position, and Harry darted forward, solicitous, supporting her with a hand at her back. She cast him a glance Katie couldn't interpret. "How could Vern have gone missing after a public shoot-out and nobody realize something's afoot? When I called my friend in Birmingham, it was business as usual in pack and coven."

"The keepers covered everything up," Katie said. "They have experience at that." They'd poppy the local police, the Birmingham coven and pack, and any human witnesses, without regard for covenants or people's rights. She had had to do touch-ups on witches and humans in her time, but the only incident that had come close to the volatile nature of the shoot-out had been her final mission.

The fact Lars had been willing to battle the Birmingham patrol in the street before he'd known Chang Cai was involved frightened her. It should frighten everyone. Now that he knew she was alive, he'd stop at nothing.

The elders were fools to ignore what the keepers had become in her and Vern's absence. Vern's directorship had been their attempt to regulate the council, but it seemed they no longer kept tabs on the organization's activities, if Lars was to be believed.

"I'm sure they're very experienced at cover-ups," June said, her lips prim.

"Witches do it to humans and wolves. The keepers do it to everyone." Katie shrugged, aiming for nonchalance, but June's attitude grated her nerves. Marcus had quit harping about her past after a day or two, and he had more reason to resent keepers than June did.

Of course, he also insisted everyone carry bay capsules with them at all times. She didn't even have monkshood anymore. He'd flushed her tiny stockpile, and there were only a few vendors who dealt in spell-grade monkshood. The keepers, of course, had their own supplier.

"The keepers do more than poppy renegade wolves," June said, as if reading the direction of Katie's thoughts.

"Because sometimes, someone has to preserve the covenants and shifter secrecy. And it's not like convex witches are welcome in regular covens."

"I didn't mean to insult you." It was the first time June had acknowledged she might have overstepped, but it wasn't enough. Katie knew damn well why no one would discuss helping her family beyond the results of Marcus's experiments—they didn't consider her needs to be of equal consequence. "It's just disturbing to find out what's been going on behind our backs."

To give her hands something to do that didn't involve fists, she restacked her maps and paperwork. Normal witches assumed they were managing everything, but there was more to keeping shifters of all stripes concealed than they could guess. "The council isn't a recent invention. Did you never wonder what happens when a juvenile winds up convex?"

"I assumed you went independent," June said. Harry, his arm around his wife, was watching Katie mistrustfully. The wolf could sense her irritation with June—with all of them—in a way Marcus seemed oblivious to. Engrossed in his computer, he hadn't so much as glanced at June, Harry and Katie, though the conversation had become tense.

"I don't like the way you're talking to my wife," Harry said, his tone sharp. "You keep this up, I'll show you how much I don't give a flying fuck how badass you think you are."

Katie eased back in the folding chair, making no sudden moves. She'd never seen Harry's eyes go that silver, not even when Marcus bossed him around. He loved his wife so much, he was willing to die for her.

And Katie knew, if it were Harry versus her, she'd win.

Anyone could kill. With a gun. With a knife. With poison. But she was made for killing. It wasn't biology. It was magic. Her magic. It didn't matter that she'd never enjoyed what she was born to do.

Katie, on the opposite side of the room from the others, remained seated. Where she belonged—separate. She kept her hands flat on the card table. "I know you three ruled out spying on the stronghold, but—"

"No," said June and Harry at the same time.

She wasn't an ill-mannered child, to be disciplined by her betters. Katie bristled. She had the most at stake and the most experience in combat yet the least influential vote. How was that smart?

"Standard information gathering hasn't borne fruit. I'm considering other options instead of burying my head." If she decided to infiltrate the stronghold, she'd be doing it alone. "I need to contact some people Tonya knew. Gaia festival organizers, herb suppliers." She suspected most were sympathizers, though Tonya had never admitted it. "Eventually we'll find a link to somebody who can tell us what the keepers are doing."

Suddenly, Marcus's gloved hand caught the back of her neck. She'd been so intent on facing down Harry and June, she hadn't noticed him cross the concrete floor.

His touch was firm, imperious and far too pleasurable. "You're not going anywhere."

The other couple watched their interaction silently.

Katie forced her spine to remain unbowed. As if Marcus looming over her, his hand heavy on her neck, meant nothing. Whatever connection she and Marcus had had, that flicker when they'd kissed outside the post office, was gone.

At least from his perspective. She, stupidly, suspected she was in love with him. Since she'd never felt like this before, she couldn't be certain. It might not be love. It might be a demented combination of lust, guilt, despair and fury. She might be clinging to Marcus because she was afraid. Afraid of dying, and his plan was a safer path to rescue her family. Not even in her most wrathful daydreams did she imagine she could attack the keeper stronghold alone and do much besides get herself killed.

She was likely the most powerful convex witch on the planet. As it turned out, being the most powerful convex witch on the planet wasn't all that useful.

But being the person Hiram Lars hated most in the world? Might be her ticket, if she could bring herself to cash it in.

"If Katie wants to track down people she thinks can help her, let her," June said. "She's an adult. She can take care of herself."

"Absolutely not." Marcus stepped around Katie, into her line of sight. It was almost as if he was putting himself between the Travises and her, but that would be irrational of him. "We stay together."

Did he mean the two of them or the four of them? Likely the four. He wasn't looking at her. He was looking at Harry and June.

Harry raked a hand through his black hair, frustrated. "Staying together is getting us bupkis. We should try something different." He echoed Katie's sentiments, though if she'd pointed that out to him, he'd have denied it. "Are the experiments doing shit or not? Every time you load me up with magic, I feel like I've got the flu, not like I'm Gandalf."

"Wolves don't catch the flu. Or cancer." Marcus, apparently satisfied he'd squelched anyone's intentions of absconding, returned to his workstation. The lab was on the bottom level of the factory, accessible through a well-concealed iron door. Granted, the lab had protective wards on it, but even if it hadn't, Katie may never have found this bolt-hole. She supposed this was why Marcus could leave the building unguarded for years and keep his hidden lab secure.

"I haven't cast a single spell." Harry glared at Marcus's back. Since Marcus didn't flinch, Katie was relatively sure Harry wasn't exerting his alpha. "You're wasting your time."

"You're not focusing hard enough." Marcus, calm as ever, crushed herbs with a pestle. The *scritch-scritch-scritch* of porcelain against porcelain was a familiar sound. "The wolf lattice is more inflexible than I previously calculated. It requires more will than you're exerting to change it."

She couldn't be sure, but as Marcus said the last sentence, he might have been gritting his teeth. Harry hadn't been especially accommodating. Unlike the way Marcus shifted between witch state and wolf state, Harry had remained a standard wolf the entire time. That being said, Marcus had yet to combine his lattices and function as both witch and wolf. When one was ascendant, it was as if the other didn't exist. They remained as separate as—

As Marcus and Katie.

"I need to exert more willpower as well," Marcus said. "I plan to have Katie place me under a compulsion as part of the next experiment. It may increase my natu-

ral capacity." There was only so much excess Harry or
Marcus could contain. Past that, neither June nor Katie
could force more magic into them. It wasn't like being
the focal of a group spell—or cleaning the energy out of
your keeper chums—because that overflow was funneled
directly out again.

"Why would I need to compel you?" she asked.

He decanted powders into a test tube. He never stopped
moving, never stopped tinkering. Whoever said men
couldn't multitask had never met Marcus Delgado.

"It's possible I'm raising an involuntary barrier when
my lattice saturates. A compulsion should override that."

They'd dumped her power into him. They'd dumped
Katie's, June's and Harry's power into him. They'd
dumped it all at once. They'd tried layering. It bounced
back, wash after wash.

"I don't think it's your willpower, Marcus." If fortitude
were the deciding factor, he would have achieved world
domination months ago. "You don't have the reservoir
for it. June doesn't even have the reservoir to hold that
much power, and she has the largest capacity of anyone
I've ever known."

Katie had never met a witch who could swing more
magic than June. The small blonde woman was a power-
house. She wasn't nuts about Katie, though.

Despite her claim she hadn't intended any insult, June
was a regular witch. She'd never understand what life had
been like for someone cursed with the ability to kill and
expected to use that ability so that normal witches—who
wanted nothing to do with her—could stay safe.

"I refuse to accept conventional limits." Marcus, goggles reflecting the light from the bare overhead bulb,
strode to a side table and fired up a burner. After adjusting
the flame, he began heating the test tube. "Muscles can

be strengthened. Senses can be trained and sharpened. Reaction time can be improved. This is a biological—"

"Unless it's magical," Katie suggested. "When you dissect a witch, there's no unique area in our brains that's different from humans. Wolves too, in either form."

"I didn't know that." Harry paced the perimeter of the shadowy, windowless room. "Is that true, Marcus?"

Marcus briefly regarded Katie as if she were rattling the bars of her cage and throwing poop at his sparkly glass beakers.

"Yes, it's true." He raised the test tube when the contents began to burble a noxious yellow, cooling it. "Nevertheless, a compulsion is our next experiment. You did say you wanted to try something new. If the compulsion works on me, June can place you under—"

Harry interrupted rudely. "Fuck that. The last time my wife put me under a compulsion, she forced me to leave her at the mercy of a fucking psycho."

"It's been five years, potty mouth," June grumbled. "Let it gooooo."

Harry regarded his exhausted wife with concern and adoration, which Katie envied. Whenever Marcus looked at her, it was like the lab rat she was.

If Katie were tired from the work Marcus had asked of them, June was practically comatose. She pretended to be fine, but everyone knew better. June wasn't energized by rage and frustration, her heart and soul committed to her course of action.

That being said, Katie suspected June did sleep during their limited time off. Katie huddled alone in the Airstream and worried about her family, wishing Marcus would talk to her, wondering if the time had come to slip away.

Wondering if she could bear to leave him.

Knowing she was going to do it soon, whether she wanted to or not. Her conscience would allow nothing else. Vern, Dad and Tonya had risked their lives to save her twenty years ago. Dad and Tonya had lost their futures, their friends, their dreams. All for her. A keeper. Chang Cai. The woman she used to be and would need to be one final time.

She couldn't afford to wait for Marcus's miracle.

"Look," Harry said. "I respect what you're trying to prove, but enough is enough. I've made up my mind. June is done with these tests. You're not wearing her out anymore, and I don't like that these people are after us."

That snatched Marcus's attention away from his test tubes.

"Why would you quit?" he asked, genuinely puzzled. "We haven't achieved our goals. My ability to enter an abridged witch state is hardly going to sway the region elders to rethink their policy on transformed wolves."

"They've already rethought their policy." Harry pointed a finger at himself. "I'm the evidence."

"Do you know how many witches transformed and had to be poppied in the past five years?" Marcus racked the test tube and shoved his goggles onto his head. "Do you know how many witches died of cancer?"

"Uh, no."

"Your existence hasn't changed policy. As I said, we haven't achieved our goals." It was impossible to argue with Marcus when he was in scientist mode. Katie had quit trying.

"Maybe it would help if we weren't running with our tails between our legs while the keepers have been doing who knows what to my family," she interrupted, though it wasn't an argument, just a statement of fact. "The experiments could happen just as easily after my family is safe."

Marcus met her gaze evenly. "We're exercising caution," he said, "not cowardice. With any experiments, results are never immediate."

"That's the problem," Harry said. "It's taking too long. This is pointless."

Marcus blinked. "I disagree. I've overcome my urge to shift when I exit witch state. I've cast spells. Now I need a way to absorb and maintain more power. Cayenne has proven helpful but insufficient for permanent retention."

Harry pulled a face. His frustration with scientific method was no surprise. He was an act first, think later type of individual. However, he'd been much more easygoing than his wife about their relocations, double-backs and false trails.

June pulled her notebook and pencil from under the cot. "The cayenne worked, Marcus? What was your dry volume yesterday? You made it through five spells before you switched back to wolf state."

He checked his smartphone. "I used two ounces of supplemental cayenne. For the amount of power I'm talking, I'd need to carry several pounds of cayenne at all times."

"That doesn't sound practical." Her pencil flew across the page. "We don't have unlimited supplies. We're low on a number of components."

"Cayenne can be made stronger," Katie reminded them.

"What if you eat it?" Harry asked. "You are what you eat, right?"

June laughed. "You always think with your stomach."

Wolf logic indeed. Katie thought about her supercharged cayenne and a body's digestive tract. "If you eat it, I guestimate it would kill you in three minutes."

Harry whistled. "I don't think it would have time to cure cancer."

"What about heal-all?" June asked. "Would it be possible for Marcus to eat it while a witch was healing him?"

"That's hardly permanent," Marcus said, scratching his chin. "Though taken orally, the cayenne would be integrated."

Some spells were more effective as pills, but Katie didn't know anyone willing to touch, much less eat, primed cayenne longer than he had to. Even standard cayenne caused skin irritation. Layered cayenne like she created was much more damaging.

"Marcus is right," she said. "The healing would have to last as long as the cayenne was in contact with the digestive system. I don't know any witch who can cast nonstop for, what, twelve to eighteen hours? The only way to obtain nonstop healing is to have about twelve witch friends who take turns or get a—"

A wisp of possibility hovered in the outskirts of her mind. She placed a hand across her forehead like a visor, blocking out her companions, blocking out the factory, blocking out everything, and chased it down.

Swallowing primed cayenne wasn't the answer. The healing components needed to be applied with the cayenne, and oral healing mixes didn't last eighteen hours.

But there was an organ, an organ she knew well, that was integrated with the body and accessible to a witch's healing touch.

"Katie?" Marcus said, snapping her out of the spinning tops in her brain. "What are you thinking?"

"Your skin," she said. "We have to permabrand you with the cayenne."

TWENTY-ONE

THEY FINALLY HAMMERED out the permabrand procedure, and Katie wished the others had let her make the ingredient purchases solo. She had her reasons, and she didn't care to share them with people already inclined to be suspicious about her. However, when she'd suggested she make the trip alone, even June and Harry had agreed it was a bad idea.

The closest individual who dealt in the supplies needed for the tattoo ink was in Kentucky. With Lars and who knew who else after them, mail-order wasn't going to cut it.

After a several hour drive in Tonya's old station wagon, they arrived at the log cabin structure in Podunk, Kentucky. Katie had never been here personally, but Tonya had. The gardening shop, between a Dairy Dip and a used-car dealer, was in a shabby downtown area that had more closed storefronts than open ones. Witches tended to choose out of the way locations for their businesses. It cut down on drop-in traffic from humans, if not always wolves.

The parking lot had seen better days, almost as much bare dirt as it was gravel. Two trucks and three cars occupied the lot, plus two bicycles and a motorcycle. Numerous flower towers, potted trees and concrete sculptures lurked at the sides of the cabin, in the outdoor section.

Harry told them to wait and slid out from behind

the steering wheel. Katie, in back with Marcus, who'd pored over calculations on his smart phone almost the entire trip, could almost see Harry's nose twitching. He stretched casually but exuded tension.

He wasn't fooling anyone. Not even with the heavy-duty mask he wore. The magic could only shroud his appearance and DNA, not his posture or actions.

Harry, whose outward appearance now resembled a white-haired grandpa, trotted around the front and leaned through June's window. "This seem like a lot of customers to you?"

"There's not another shop this extensive in Kentucky or Ohio." June powdered her nose and dropped the compact into her purse. "It's not like Millington, where we can get most of what we need from our local shop. Don't forget you're supposed to be an old man."

June's mask disguised her as an elderly lady, and Harry kept calling her Sandie. Her acting was a lot more convincing.

"Wish we were in Millington now." He opened June's door, casting Katie a dark look. Though this trip satisfied Harry's definition of "trying something different," it hadn't eased the alpha wolf's wariness.

"If the keepers are as out of control as Marcus says, we're doing the right thing." June stood and straightened her skirts. She handed Harry the cane he was supposed to use and took his arm. Everyone who wasn't Katie had decided June should head up the components transaction. June wasn't persona non grata with the council, the elders, or anyone.

With June in charge, Katie hadn't quite decided how she was going to sneak in the other purchase she needed to make. Nobody would be happy to know she intended to buy monkshood.

Having it as available in the days to come could prove regrettably necessary. While she wouldn't be able to use it on convex witches, she didn't know who else might be in Lars's employ. She wouldn't put it past him to engage feral wolves as an offensive measure. Or human mercenaries. She'd hate to kill anyone, but faced with a choice between Lars's flunkies and herself, she'd pick herself. She had a family to rescue.

If the permabrand experiment didn't bear fruit, her life was going to be forfeit anyway. Executed for her crimes at last.

Katie bit back a bitter smile. Some of her companions wouldn't miss her. She wondered if one of them was Marcus.

Harry, who definitely wouldn't miss her, escorted June into the shop almost as slowly as a grandpa with a cane. He forgot to stoop, though. Or shuffle.

Katie and Marcus were supposed to remain in the car. Their masks camouflaged them as Caucasian teenagers. Marcus certainly fit the bill—the grouchy teen boy who sulked in the car with his tech rather than hang out with his grandparents. Of course, no witch worth half her kosher salt would assume another witch's outward appearance was faithful, but every smidgen of subterfuge helped.

As they waited, a muscle car pulled up at the shop, its motor a deep grumble. A tall, thin young man got out. He tugged on a ball cap to shade his eyes in the noonday sun and inspected the parking lot. His gaze paused on them before continuing.

Marcus, engrossed in his phone, didn't notice. Katie did.

"We got a lookie loo," she said in a low voice. The kid's countenance had no wrinkles, but if he was a witch, there was no telling how old he was. The trick to deciphering other witches was in the body language, the tonal quality of voices, the personality and the vocabulary.

Marcus, in wolf state today, glanced briefly at the newcomer. "He appears to be meeting someone. You're in a high state of alert. Possibly higher than necessary."

"Disagree." She'd racked up years on the council and years in hiding. Alertness was an old habit that didn't need to die, hard or otherwise.

The kid leaned against the driver's door of the low-slung car and lit up a cigarette. Then he checked his phone.

Marcus's nose curled. "I can't imagine a witch would voluntarily smoke tobacco."

"Let's go inside," she suggested. "Then you don't have to smell it."

"We're supposed to remain with the car."

"I might be needed in case June has to make substitutions." That was true, not merely an excuse to get her hands on some monkshood. The supplies for tattoos weren't intuitive. Permabrand artists guarded their recipes closely since the occupation was so lucrative. Luckily it ran in Katie's family.

"She'll send Harry after us."

"You can stay. I'm going in."

As she unlocked the door, Marcus laid a hand on her arm. "Is there a problem?"

"Why would there be?" His big hand restrained her with just the power of his touch. "I want to finish the supply run and get back to our project."

Not that she was enthusiastic about the idea of branding Marcus with multilayered cayenne that could blister a person down to the bone if you let it, but she'd also be branding him with heal-all. The hypothesis was that it would counteract the damage.

"You haven't spoken to me much the past several days."

"Funny thing for you to say." He'd been chillier than winter in Wisconsin.

"We have much to accomplish." His thumb rubbed her forearm. "Are you frustrated with the lack of progress?"

He wasn't as clueless as she liked to tell herself. "Yes."

Now he needed to ask if she was frustrated with the lack of sex.

His fingers tightened perceptibly. He wasn't hurting her, but the strength in his grip gave her shivers. She wished they'd continued the sex trials. Why didn't he want to? Was he done with them—with her? She should never have admitted she simply wanted to be with him. She'd probably disturbed the hell out of him with that bit of info.

Who would want a convex alpha witch obsessed with him? She might start boiling bunnies next.

"Are you planning anything rash?"

She shot him a cocky grin. "Always."

"My experiment will succeed." His brows drew together. His masked face was nothing like the handsome scientist she'd come to admire, but his expression was pure Marcus. "I'm not ignoring the importance of helping your family, Katie. Or the fact Lars could coerce the location spell out of Vernon. It's also possible he killed Vernon so the spell won't be a factor. Our time may not be that limited."

He seemed to be convincing himself as much as her. If he believed what he was saying, he wouldn't be scowling. She'd barely known him a week, but she could interpret his facial expressions—through the mask of a pimply teen—like a memorized code. Or a grocery list of bad omens.

"My family's time is limited," she said. "And it doesn't thrill me to assume Vern might already be dead."

"Bad memories can be wiped. Your father and Tonya won't necessarily suffer forever."

"It sucks that you realize they'll need their memories wiped." She raked a hand through her hair, wishing the discussion hadn't swerved this direction. She should have insisted she had to pee and bolted into the store. "Can you imagine what Lars is doing to them? After seeing me again, after we got away from him, he'll have so much rage it'll choke him."

Lars had been censured for unnecessary violence numerous times during her tenure with the keepers—especially while Vern was the director. It was no surprise Lars had intended, all along, to hijack the council however he could. Though not frequently enough to raise suspicion, moderate keepers, such as herself, had tended to die on missions. She'd wondered if there was any way Lars had stage-managed her final mission into such a disaster. That disaster had nearly resulted in her death, two times over.

Conspiracy theories hadn't done her any good then and wouldn't now.

"I do know what Lars is like, and I'm sorry," Marcus said gravely. He touched her cheek. The sweetness of the gesture nearly did her in. "I've had years to come to terms with my grief. I want revenge, but I can wait until it's certain. I know delaying is harder for you."

She freed her arm. If she didn't get away from his solicitous touch, she'd slump over in his lap and sob. "That's why I'm going into the store. To make it easier. I'll be doing something besides sitting here."

"I'll come with you."

"No need." Marcus hanging on her would make it difficult to snake some monkshood. "Guard the car."

"I'm not a dog, Katie."

She raised an eyebrow, Marcus-style. "Of course you're not. Don't you have some calculations to do?"

He watched her for a long moment. Unlike Harry, she was an excellent actress. "Five minutes."

Katie nodded, as if agreeing. "Be right back."

She slid out of the back seat and flounced like a kid into the store. The young man with the muscle car regarded her through the haze of tobacco and tar. He remained relaxed, or more convincingly relaxed than Harry, but something about him spoke of watchfulness. His eyes were a pale shade of gray, almost wolflike, and his high forehead curved above his eyebrows so far, it resembled a receding hairline.

He pinged her radar, and she couldn't put a finger on why. If he weren't smoking, she could have Marcus or Harry sniff him. But the chemicals and shit in human cigarettes clogged up wolf noses like seasonal allergies.

Katie flipped the guy a playful smile as if she really were a teenaged girl. He raised his chin at her in acknowledgement. She bit her lip and feigned a giggle before she trotted up the stairs to the veranda. She wondered if he'd follow. Inside the store he'd have to put out the cigarette, and Harry could smell him.

If the kid were a talented witch, his mask would be impenetrable and he'd read as human. That would be a clue in and of itself. Young human males in small Southern towns probably didn't patronize gardening shops with great frequency.

Chimes rang as she pushed open the front door. A frenzy of scents invaded her space the moment she entered. Because of her perpetual state of incognito, Katie hadn't often had the opportunity to patronize actual witch-run herb shops. The subtle evidence of components, paraphernalia and recipes momentarily filled her with giddiness, like a kid in a candy store. Or her dad in a candy store.

A pang lanced her, sharp and mournful. She missed her father and Tonya. What she was doing was all for them. It wouldn't do to forget that as her feelings for Marcus strengthened.

Shaking off the melancholy, she regarded her surroundings. The place was larger than it seemed from the outside, arranged to maximize shelf space. Flute music played softly over hidden speakers. Katie didn't spot June and Harry down the closest aisles, although a woman browsed a nearby selection of fertilizers.

Looked like regular gardening supplies, not witch items. Could be humans in here. She'd need to be inconspicuous.

She picked another aisle and went searching for an employee to sell her monkshood. Hopefully the witch wouldn't ask too many questions, but Katie and June had slipped poppy mix into their pockets in case they encountered a need for tiny memory wipes. She'd buy her monkshood, poppy the clerk and disappear like a bad dream, the only evidence whatever money the clerk had in hand.

The quiet murmur of voices snagged her attention, followed by clacks. She peeked around a corner and saw June talking to a woman in a red apron and Harry messing with a Zen rock display.

His head quirked to one side when Katie's tennis shoe brushed the hardwood floor. She ducked behind the display of gardening books before he noticed her.

"I saw you outside."

The tall young man appeared behind Katie as if out of thin air. She pasted on a smile. A quiet one, wasn't he?

"Well, I was outside. So, you know. You saw me." Katie propped a hand on her hip, sassy and youthful. All she needed was some bubble gum and a boy band T-shirt. "Hi."

"I don't recognize you." The kid stared at Katie as if he could pierce her disguise. Crap, could he? There were a few little-known ways to deactivate a mask with magic, but she didn't think he'd tossed herbs on her.

"That's because I'm from New Jersey. My grandparents are dragging me on this trip. I swear we're hitting every gardening store and quilting expo between here and the east coast." Oversharing information was a teenaged thing to do, right? She knew few teens, and only for the amount of time it took to ink them.

They had all overshared.

"How old are you?" the kid asked.

One didn't ask another witch's age. Did he know she was a witch? Was he one?

"Sixteen. What about you?"

"Old enough."

"You don't look old." There were certain oblique questions one could ask to confirm species, so to speak. But asking would confirm her species too.

"Do you have a boyfriend?"

"No." She plucked at a frayed belt loop on her jeans. "Do you?"

"I don't have a boyfriend or a girlfriend," he said, unruffled. Impressive—and a point in favor of him being a witch. This was still the Bible Belt. "How long are you in town?"

"Not very. What are you doing here? You into gardening?" She giggled inanely, while trying to think of a way to get Harry to smell this guy or to end this awkward conversation. When she was a teenager, it had been the 1950s. A contemporary teen might not appreciate discussions of Elvis's discography.

"I work here part time."

Interesting. If he was employed here, he had to be a witch. He'd be knowledgeable about the shop's inventory.

He stepped closer to her. He was at least six foot five. Katie hadn't masked her height or build—that was way too hard—and he towered over her in a different way than Marcus did. The kid, all gawky arms and legs, seemed more like he was going to trip over her.

She stared up at him through her lashes. He reminded her of somebody. The way he carried himself, the shape of his head. Based on her instinctive response, it was someone she hadn't liked.

Goddess, there was no telling. She had a terrible memory for the faces of people she'd encountered—especially wolves she'd dealt with. Tonya was the one who never forgot a chi.

This guy was just some witch kid who liked girls and fast cars. Neither was a crime. Marcus was right. Katie was suspicious of everything and everybody. Her trust-o-meter was completely busted.

Instead of looking for treachery behind every outdoor statuette, she should take advantage of the fact the young man was flirting with her. This might be her best shot at getting the monkshood discreetly.

"You work here?" she said. "Awesome. Can you show me where the bathroom is?"

His eyebrows wagged, and he smiled. He seemed thrilled to be asked. Maybe she'd made her mask too pretty. "Since you asked so nice. Come with me."

She followed him toward Harry and June. Since she'd

been talking, Harry would know she was inside the building anyway.

She smiled as she traipsed past the wolf. "Hi, Grandpa. Going to the potty."

"We're ready to leave." Harry glared at the young man, and his lip curled like Clint Eastwood. It was a refreshing change to have his ire focused on someone besides herself. "Can't you hold it until the next stop?"

"Nope." She hopped from foot to foot, like a child. "Supersized slushie."

The lady in the red apron rang June up at the register. Because of the specialized purchases, that lady would know Katie, June and Harry were witches. The boy's attention snagged on June's items.

Now the boy would know too. Did that matter? He shambled over to the counter.

"Hi, Adele. Busy day?"

"You're not scheduled to start your shift until five." The lady counted out June's change. They'd paid in cash, as many witches did. Witch businesses preferred that for their less public transactions. Tax officials might wonder why people bought cayenne and kava and such in bulk— and at such exorbitant prices.

Not to mention many witch transactions occurred as barters. Tonya had netted them a lifetime supply of ginseng for one permabrand.

"What are you buying?" the kid asked June. "Anything cool?"

The lady at the cash register tsked him. Her tag identified her as a store manager. "Frank, I've told you before, it's none of your business what our customers purchase."

He shrugged. "Just curious." He gestured for Katie. "Adele, I'm showing her where the bathroom is."

One didn't ask another witch's age. One didn't ask another witch's recipes or purchases. Was Frank a socially awkward witch teen? Or something else?

June and Harry watched Katie follow the kid toward the back of the store, concern written on their fake elderly faces.

"Since you're here, you can finish weeding the seasonal beds," the manager called after Frank.

He huffed in a very authentic fashion. "Whatever."

"My name's Sherrie," she told Frank. "Your manager seems like a hard-ass."

"She's all right." After he unlocked a set of heavy double doors, they passed into a well-organized back room where Katie recognized many of the simples and supplies. It was alphabetically arranged. A witch's dream.

No time to drool. She scanned for the *M* section. They appeared to be on the opposite side of the first row. There was a single door marked Restroom. Beside it was a rolling bucket with a mop. A quick inspection didn't reveal any cameras.

Frank jerked his thumb toward the door. "There you go. I'll wait out here for you."

She stalled for time. She was out of sight of Harry and June. Could she wrangle her supplies from Frank… or steal them?

"Your car is hot." She wandered through the room as if the bathroom had been an excuse to get him alone. Which it had. She approached the desired section and tried to act blasé. "How fast does it go?"

He leaned against a shelving unit and crossed his arms. "I've had it up to one-thirty."

Katie faked awe. "What about the cops?"

He laughed. "Come on. You know we can handle cops. And a lot of other problems too," he added with a smug grin.

"Um." She strolled along the shelf. Marjoram. Milk thistle. Moss, reindeer. Damn, where was monkshood? "I don't, um, have it yet."

Growing into one's magic occurred anywhere from the age of fourteen until early twenties. At sixteen, it wouldn't be unusual for a witch to be a juvenile.

"I do," he bragged, goggling at her tits. "I'm older than I look."

"I bet you are." Despite the missing bin on the *M* shelf, she knew for a fact this place had monkshood. It wasn't advertised, but she knew. "Why do you ask what people are buying?"

Frank cut his gaze to the floor. "I want to own my own store eventually. Of course I want to know what people buy."

"Do you have any—you know—contraband stuff?" she asked conspiratorially.

He fondled his chin. "Like pot?"

"Like high octane nutmeg." The herb, very different from the human seasoning, was used in a few spells for lust and intoxication. Tonya said all the witch kids these days tried to get high on it.

The kid swaggered down the row, toward her. "I could be convinced to find some nutmeg, I guess. For the right price."

When he had his back to her, Katie checked out the *W* herbs on a hunch. Shoved behind the witch hazel was a small, clear container labeled Wolfsbane, a colloquial name for monkshood.

It didn't have dust on it. It was graduated to the ounce and appeared to be nearly empty.

"What about something harsh, like monkshood?"

Frank froze.

She froze too.

He turned slowly, his posture wary. It was a definite shift—not her imagination and not her broken, untrusting nature. "Monkshood? That shit can kill you." He glowered at her, looking much older and harder than his—was it a facade? "What do you want it for?"

Katie's thumb brushed her poppy sachet in her front pocket. "I don't know. Because it's cool?"

He marched toward her, his lanky limbs like a walking scarecrow. A scarecrow from a horror movie. "Are you going to use it?"

She wrinkled her nose, but at the same time broke open the poppy with her thumbnail. "Duh. I don't want to die. Suspicious much?"

He pulled out a packet, and Katie's heart plummeted to her shoes.

It wasn't just a packet. It was a spell pod, like the keepers used.

"What's your real name?" he demanded, ditching the teenage-boy act. This was no child.

Neither was she. "I told you already. Sherrie. Are you some kind of old man? Pervert. I'm sixteen."

In lieu of a response, he hurled the pod. She was ready. She collapsed onto the floor. The pod flew overhead, and she had the guy by the knees, toppling him backward, before he knew what had whammied him.

Nobody ever expected the short, cute female with glasses to fight like a cornered honey badger. Katie kneed the guy in the groin, disabled him of another pod and pressed her knife to his jugular before he could scrabble in his pocket for more.

Whoever he was, he was no match for her. For Chang Cai. "Who do you work for?"

He grinned. He had crazy eyes. No mask could hide those. "I work here."

When he tried to squirm his hand into his pocket, she sliced him enough that he started bleeding. "Hands above your head, Frank. I can stick my knife in a lot of places if I use heal-all, you know. You won't die fast."

He blinked, taken aback by her matter-of-fact menace. He also raised his arms. "You're lying about your age."

"Yeah. I also think your car's a piece of shit." His blood would need to be mopped off the floor to hide what had happened. Better not cut him too deep. "What did you throw at me?"

"Maybe it was monkshood. It's so cool, right?" He laughed. His large front teeth reminded her of a rabbit, but his crazy eyes reminded her of...

Who? Dammit, who?

"What the hell is going on?" hissed an angry voice.

Harry and June, laden by their purchases, had entered the storeroom—luckily without Adele the manager. Perhaps she was helping other customers?

"First shelf. Under the ginkgo" Katie ordered. "What kind of spell pod is it?"

Keepers weren't the only witches to grasp the usefulness of projectile spell components, but they utilized them more aggressively than the covens. The pod alone wasn't enough to condemn this guy.

Harry growled at her command. June huffed. Katie had added alpha to her not-so-polite request, and she hadn't done it on purpose. It came naturally.

She didn't have time for other alphas, dammit. "Shut up and do it. Be quick."

Muttering imprecations, Harry poked under the stock shelving until he freed a small, bullet-shaped packet of herbs.

"Be careful with it. Breaks on impact. Might be primed." She didn't care that her knowledge was giving

Frank clues about her, because she was going to memory wipe his scrawny ass in about three minutes. "Sniff it and tell me what it is."

Frank tried to twist out of her grasp, and she pushed the blade deeper into his neck. He cursed. The blood flow from the wound increased from a dribble to a stream.

"I don't know what the hell it is," Harry said. "It's green stuff. Doesn't smell like it goes in pie. Uh, honey?"

At least he had the sense not to use June's name. Packages rustled as June accepted the spell pod gingerly. "Hops and valerian. But there's more."

"Is it thyme?"

"I think so, yes."

Katie grunted. That confirmed it. Only keepers added thyme to their sleep spells. This guy, somehow, was a keeper.

She had to wipe him. Or kill him. Before Adele got curious about how long her customers were in the bathroom. Before he reported to Lars. Then they had to get the hell out of here.

"Are you…is he bleeding?" June asked. "Why are you hurting him?"

"He likely threatened her in some way," said a new voice.

Goddess be damned. Marcus. Well, it had been nine whole minutes. He'd given her five. Generous.

With two wolves prowling through the stock room and Katie riled up, Frank stood zero chance of getting away as long as she could keep him from any spell casting. She jumped up and took the pod from June, who handed it over with a judgmental sniff.

"Make sure nobody comes in here," Katie told the others. "Tell them the bathroom's in use. This shouldn't take long."

Frank sat up resentfully and palmed his neck. Blood escaped, spattering his shirt and jeans. "Daft bitch," he cursed. "I'm going to bleed to death."

He was beginning to look pasty. She refused to let herself care. If he reported them, if the keepers figured out who, exactly, had been in Kentucky hunting down monkshood, it could ruin everything.

It could ruin everything…again.

"Don't be a crybaby." She kicked his leg, hard, wishing she had her steel-toed work boots instead of tennis shoes. "You can't afford that car on a part-time clerk's salary. Who else do you work for?"

"I'm not telling you anything." He tugged up his shirt and squashed it to his neck.

"Is Lars in town?" She flicked the knife so the guy's own blood dripped on his pants. "Is he on his way here? Does he have an old Chinese man with him?"

"I don't know anybody named Lars, and I don't know anybody Chinese. Who do *you* work for, sneaking around, trying to get your hands on wolfsbane?"

"Why do you need that?" Marcus asked.

To hell with this. Katie grabbed the monkshood off the shelf before anybody could stop her.

"You've got two choices, Frank." She flipped up the hinged lid of the small container. "Tell me where Lars is and I'll use your spell pod on you and maybe a little heal-all so you won't actually bleed to death. You're starting to look peaky."

His eyes shifted to the right and the left, as if seeking other choices. Answers. A way to escape. "And if I don't?"

"If you don't, I use the monkshood."

June gasped.

Frank's eyes widened. "You can't use that. It would kill you too."

Odd. If he used keeper pods but thought monkshood would kill her...was he not a keeper himself?

"You sure about that?"

"Shit," he moaned. "You're one of them?"

"I'm one of them," she agreed, though she hadn't been in a long, long time.

"Look, lady, it's not easy to make ends meet in this economy. I'm supposed to tell him if anyone buys specific supplies. Wolfsbane. He issued a code red recently, so I'm putting in extra hours. I thought I...I thought if I could knock you out and keep you for him, he'd be proud of me."

"Company's coming," Harry said, his head cocked to the side. "I know you're enjoying yourself, but can you wrap up torture time?"

Katie narrowed her eyes. The others would never let her kidnap Frank to get answers, despite Marcus's propensity for it. She had about fifteen seconds before they had to split. "Is your boss named Lars or not? Does he look..."

Does he look like you, except two lifetimes older?

That's why she hated this kid, this man, for no reason. He looked like Lars. He looked eerily and terribly like Lars. Did the old psycho force his spies to wear his face?

"I don't know, okay? I've never heard of Lars. He makes us call him Sire. I don't know what he looks like."

"What else can you tell me? Come on, Frank." She shook the monkshood. "Don't make me use this. It gives me indigestion."

"He's got a network. People in herb shops and witch establishments. I only know my immediate supervisor."

Her blood ran cold. While the elders had been assuming the keepers had lost their proficiency, Hiram Lars had been infiltrating the entire coven network. Was the council the only organization he intended to take over?

"Is Adele your immediate supervisor?" she asked the trembling man.

"She doesn't know anything. I get phone calls."

"Scent him," she told Marcus. She didn't have time to put together a mask dissolver, but the guy was bleeding. That beat nearly all masks.

"Scent me? What do you mean?" When Marcus, his dark gaze on Katie promising retribution, did as she asked, the guy scuttled away from the wolf. Marcus took his shoulders, avoiding blood spatters, and sniffed. Sniffed again.

"Oh, fuck. That's a wolf, isn't it? A feral."

"Do I look feral?" Marcus released the witch, who backed against the shelves. More than blood loss drained the guy's countenance now. "He has Lars's scent. There's a definite association."

"Shit," Harry commented. "Didn't see that coming." June remained silent.

"I swear, I don't know a Lars," the guy begged. In Katie's experience, men this frightened of her lied poorly. It didn't seem like a lie. "Oh, God. Don't kill me, okay? I won't tell anybody."

"You're right. You won't." She was out of time. Who knew when another customer would need the restroom? Unceremoniously, she flung the spell pod at Frank.

He screamed—until the pod hit him and burst. He passed out in a sprawl on the bloody concrete floor. She dragged the poppy mix out of her pocket and activated that next. She pressed her hand to his forehead. Quick erase. One day.

Her body, her magic, fell quickly into old patterns.

They didn't have time to clean up the mess. Her mess.

Granted, the only thing Adele would know is that two senior citizens and two teenagers purchased an assortment of supplies and then assaulted her employee in the back room, but that was odd enough in coven culture that the news would spread.

Without glancing at her companions, she sprayed the guy's throat with her travel can of heal-all. "Let's go."

No one spoke much on the way home. What little conversation they shared related to the upcoming permabrand experiment, which Marcus wanted to begin ASAP. Katie's savagery, her apparent willingness to kill and their narrow escape weren't discussed. They didn't even debate what Frank had revealed about a network of witches who reported on monkshood purchases.

So no one spoke much. But no one tried to take her monkshood away from her either.

Katie had never felt so alone.

TWENTY-TWO

THE RED BULL'S-EYE on Marcus's biceps blazed like a hot poker, drilling into his humerus. He clenched his teeth and didn't utter a sound as Katie etched the cayenne permabrand into his arm.

Over the months, he'd had a number of tattoos. This was not the same. Adding the cayenne was like adding molten anguish.

"Easy." Katie wrapped gloved fingers around his arm, but he could barely appreciate her touch. His heart monitor beeped rapidly, recording his stats for risk assessment. "Harry, the belts aren't enough. Hold him still. June, if you could remove the blood. I can't see my outline."

Marcus realized he might not have been complaining, but he had been inching away from Katie and her father's gunlike tattoo machine she wielded to such painful effect. The makeshift straps that bound his torso to the heavy chair hadn't prevented his involuntary twitches.

"It's a one-inch circle. The outline doesn't matter," Marcus told her. Pain ebbed and flowed like his pulse, diving beneath his skin and resurfacing. The healing components in the brand would offset blisters and burns but not all the hurt. "Go faster."

"It matters to me," she said. The tattoo machine whirred off. Marcus blinked rapidly, surprised to find his vision sheened by tears.

He ducked his head. *Christ.*

They hadn't discussed the incident at the gardening store as a group, but Harry had told Marcus privately that he didn't like his wife being around a killer. He made June carry extra bay capsules and wanted the monkshood destroyed. Marcus had refused. Yes, he or Harry could sniff the monkshood out, but he didn't believe Katie would kill them.

Desert them if she thought it would help her family? Absolutely. Kill them? No.

Nevertheless, the aftereffect of the incident was undeniable. Lars's probable infiltration of the coven network had added a layer of urgency to the experiments. To everything.

Marcus had never intended to dawdle, but now that he knew Lars had secret connections, he wouldn't wait between tests. No more resting or running. They had to have answers now.

Gently, June dabbed the raw mark on his arm with clean cotton. "Does a permabrand normally get so inflamed?"

"It's the cayenne," Katie said.

"Finish it," he ordered. A permabrand was the answer to his reservoir limitation. He could feel it. Goddess knew he didn't like the sensation—but he could definitely feel it.

"You want me to finish this, quit wiggling. It's lopsided."

"I honestly don't care what it looks like." A good thing, considering Katie's dubious art skills. While she promised she'd do a better job than his dragon, he wasn't sure he trusted that. She seemed cool and cooperative, but this woman was the definition of still waters running deep.

He needed this to work. Though she hadn't disappeared yet, Marcus wasn't sure how many more days that would be the case. If he wanted her to stay, he'd have to produce results—in his work or in a rescue plan.

She was disappointed. In him. She drew further away from him every day, and soon she'd be gone. He couldn't let that happen.

The needle whizzed on. Harry's grip on his shoulders hardened, and Marcus braced for the pinch. Instead, Katie rubbed him beside the tattoo. Her knees touched his thigh. "Aren't wolves supposed to have a high pain tolerance?"

"That's immaterial." He looked at her, hoping for eye contact, but she was intent on his arm. She was wearing his goggles, bulky on her smaller head. "Completion is necessary in this phase. Please continue."

Had it been a deliberate callback on her part? It was on his. He stared at her lips and reviewed his and Katie's original discussion of pain tolerance—and what it had led to. Spanking her. Fucking her. Rousing her alpha. If he drifted away on a cloud of lust and fantasizing, perhaps he could learn to appreciate the pain.

The tattoo machine jabbed like a bullet striking his flesh. Marcus flinched. The belts cut into his arms.

Harry pressed him in the chair with a steely grip. "Come on, man. Is it that bad?"

"Harry, you're the biggest baby in the world," June said. "When we dotted the cayenne on your arm with Q-tip, you howled."

"It blistered."

"I healed it."

"Well, I don't want to be a witch," Harry said. Marcus's ears buzzed with the effort to hold...still. His heart rate increased, the beep of the monitor becoming a drone. "If a tattoo turned me into a witch, I think you'd miss a few things about your old wolf."

Marcus regulated his breathing as the Travises ban-

tered. Katie, hands steady, continued the torture he'd
asked for—the torture he'd insisted on. The agony spread
from the bull's-eye to his entire upper arm as the cayenne
took hold. Burning. Burrowing. Blistering.

He refused to look. He'd looked in the beginning. The
raw hamburger flesh created by the cayenne had offended
his stomach.

More heal-all. The agony eased. Then it started again.
"We're almost done."

Marcus closed his eyes again and tried to ignore the
pain, but it seemed to intensify. He remembered another thing he'd told Katie, about how losing one of her
senses would sharpen the others. He'd blindfolded her
to heighten her responses. She'd begged him to take her.

Goddess, to relive that night! Either night they'd
shared. He didn't care. It seemed like years ago. He'd
wanted her every moment since, but he couldn't have her.
Sleeping with her and calling it science seemed dishonest
now. If she realized how he felt about her, if she knew he
just wanted to taste her and love her and wake up beside
her, what would she do?

Hands slapped his face lightly.

Numbness faded enough for him to sense Katie hovering in front of him. He lolled upright in the chair, courtesy of the belts. He opened his eyes. She'd removed the
goggles, the gloves—the impartiality. Worry lines creased
her forehead. Her fingers stroked his cheek.

He licked his lips. His voice came out rusty. "That
feels good."

As soon as she realized he was aware of her, the Chang
Cai mask slid over her features. She whipped her hands
behind her back and straightened.

"He's alert," she told the others. "Pulse back to normal."

At some point, he must have hazed out. Imagining sex with her had succeeded, after a fashion. He didn't think he'd tell everyone that the secret to enduring a cayenne permabrand had been picturing Katie naked on his bed, begging him to make love to her.

A little shakily, he unbuckled the belts holding him to the chair. They'd been placed to help him stay motionless, not restrain him.

She handed him a bottled water. "Drink."

He raised the bottle to his lips and gulped. The bull's-eye was a low, annoying throb. When he was done with the water, he pivoted his arm so he could see it.

She'd not added much ink to the brand, and June had healed it as if it had been there for months. The center dot of the bull's-eye was blackish green. The heal-all. The rust of the cayenne dominated the ring around it, somewhat indistinct against his medium brown skin. He rubbed it with a finger. Smooth but sore.

His senses weren't as dull as they usually were in witch state. He could smell the antibacterial soap from the Airstream, where he and Katie had been taking turns sleeping. Never together. She hadn't asked; he hadn't insisted. It wasn't right to insist anymore.

The wind had picked up outside, and rain poured down. A crack of lightning. Glancing at the sky she couldn't see, she crossed her arms.

"Did June add more magic to the cayenne?" he asked. The necessity of regular deposits into a permabrand's cayenne was something the region elders could accept if it meant recovering a transformed wolf or stopping cancer. Not the pain, though. After they calculated the square inches required to boost him to true dual state, they'd test anesthetization and pain management options.

"She doubled it." Katie helped him unhook the heart

monitor, hands impersonal. "You aren't going to like your readings."

A little stiff, he shrugged into his dress shirt but left it hanging open. If he was too fumbly to manage the buttons, he didn't want her to see. "That high?"

She nodded. Her short, messy hair pronged everywhere, as if she'd been rubbing her head. Her gaze dropped down his torso and then back to the ceiling when thunder boomed.

"Next time, we'll create the initial brand with weaker cayenne and layer the magic afterward." They couldn't enlarge the current brand. A person could only host one at a time.

"Next time," she said slowly, "you might have a heart attack."

"I'll run the math," he promised, but he had no intention of letting high readings intimidate him. A difficult permabrand would be preferable to human cancer treatments.

Once he broke through the wolf-witch barrier and possessed both magics, they could go straight to the region elders with their demands. In exchange for the cure for cancer, the elders would ferret out all of Lars's spies, protect them from the keepers and rescue Katie's family. The keepers might be combat veterans, but coven members outnumbered them.

The keepers would no longer be allowed to torture and murder innocents like Elisa and her unborn child. For all Marcus knew there was already a contingency plan for keepers gone rogue. Too bad Zhang Li and Vern weren't here to ask.

Too bad they had no idea if the elders would consider the keepers' attempt to capture him or nullify Chang Cai—convex witch, assassin and security threat—as

going rogue. Could they prove the keepers had been torturing and violating the covenants? Could they prove the
keepers had overstepped in Alabama, if nobody remembered it? Could they prove Frank was part of an unap-
proved monitoring network, or was that something the
elders had allowed Lars to create?

Would it matter, if he was handing the elders the cure
for untreatable cancers on a silver platter?

"June?" he said. "Let's record my lattice."

He preferred Katie, of course, but she was drained
after a brand. June, already armed with the shaker of
kava mix, sprinkled some on his hand and activated the
true eye through a dittany link. Harry ambled over with
the full-length mirror.

Marcus squinted at the glass. His aura coalesced
around him, less gray than usual with his exit from wolf
state—and more purple. June, a novice aura reader,
wouldn't know what purple meant. He glanced quickly
at Katie, but she was weighing her ink caps on the digital scale and recording it on the chart.

June, as instructed, focused the chi spell, passing
through his aura to the core. The dimness of the lab sharpened the witch lattice that shimmered into view. Was it
stronger? He'd been a wolf when the tattoo had begun;
now he was most definitely a witch.

"I see the witch thread you used to create the healing
gel. Looks unbroken." She patted his hand, as if he were
a young witch being taught spells for the first time.

"Hmm." He'd expected a stronger lattice response. "I
need to upload my stats and test how many spells I can
cast."

Harry sniffed him. "Juvenile."

He wasn't calling Marcus immature; he was confirming Marcus's scent was how an unmasked witch would register to a wolf.

"As I suspected," Marcus agreed.

June's burner phone trilled. He paused. Everyone paused. Even the storm seemed to pause.

Few people had that phone number. Vern, the four of them, Rachel from Cardholder Services and select individuals June had contacted while looking for information about the keepers.

For that phone to ring...

She flicked it on. "Hello? Annette? Slow down."

A tense hush descended over the room. As she spoke to her friend from the Millington coven, Marcus wished he had his wolf hearing so he could tell what was being said on the other end of the phone.

June, who was fair-skinned to start with, paled and sank onto the cot. "Witches in military gear are looking for you? I assume, since you're talking to me, they didn't find you. Is Pete all right? He's a policeman in the human world. He can't just vanish."

Katie and Marcus exchanged a glance. Whatever this was, it sounded big.

June didn't pause long before continuing. "No, we haven't seen anybody like that. Why?" She leaned against Harry. "They're looking for us too?"

Even Marcus with his witch-dead ears could hear Harry growl.

"The white-haired man specifically asked for someone genetically related to me?" June laid a trembling hand over her eyes. "I have to call my mother."

Marcus didn't like the information adding up, even though he was only hearing half. Witches in military gear questioning coven members, searching for biological family members, abandoning subtlety—and a white-haired male witch in charge.

Hiram Lars.

But keepers didn't, weren't supposed to, interfere with covens and witches. Their job was to perform the tasks requested by the elders. With Lars declaring the covenants no longer applied to him, nobody would be safe from the keepers if they weren't stopped.

Harry ejected himself off the cot. Without saying a word, he sped through the lab's only door. He made as much noise as a cat. When Marcus glanced at Katie again, she'd retrieved her gun. Her expression had gone cold.

Had Harry heard something outside? Had Katie? Marcus, right now, had limited magic—the contents of the untested brand. Because Katie had just inked it, she was drained. She'd require human weaponry or primed spell pods for defense. June's reservoir of magic hadn't been flush since they'd begun the lattice tests.

If Annette's news precipitated some sort of keeper-led takeover of the coven network, they were in a poor position to counter it. It might be time to direct-dial region elders. How could Lars imagine he and his team could blatantly hunt down witches like June or Annette without alerting his erstwhile superiors?

Of course, no one seemed to have found out about Alabama. Decimating an entire Birmingham border patrol had to have been a larger cover-up than wiping a few observers. Then again, perhaps Lars had employees like Frank in all sorts of places. Perhaps he had more support than they realized.

After another comforting murmur to her friend, June hung the phone up with a snap.

"The keepers and Hiram Lars are in Millington." She pressed a hand to her lower stomach, as if holding back nausea or protecting herself from harm. "Why would they want to find me and Harry? How would they realize we helped you?"

"No good deed goes unpunished," Katie said.

"Could this have anything to do with Frank?" June asked. "Maybe the memory wipe didn't take."

"It took." Katie checked the clip in the gun. "The problem is, even if Lars heard chatter about four witches who jumped one of his lackeys yesterday and concluded you and Harry were the other two, it doesn't explain why he's hunting your friend Annette."

"I'm afraid I can answer that," Marcus said. "Annette is Vernon's sister. That's her connection." Since Lars already had Vernon, the only reason Marcus could conclude Lars needed Annette would be to use her to convince Vernon to cooperate.

Or to murder the poor woman in front of him to watch him grieve.

However, it did mean Vernon was probably alive.

Harry, oozing menace and rain, reentered the room. Marcus didn't need his wolf abilities to sense the ferocity steaming off the other man.

"Nobody's out there right now." He glanced at Katie. "But I don't like this."

Marcus reassured the Travises, who'd never expected a life or death situation when they'd agreed to help their friend Vernon. "Katie and I have experience living under the radar. There's no reason to believe Lars can find us despite the supply run to Kentucky yesterday. We owe you, and we'll help you."

This factory had been one of his first investments when he'd begun planning his revenge. In all this time, it had been undisturbed by humans, witches, wolves—practically even animals. It wasn't likely Lars would be suddenly inspired to look for them in a moldering Ohio factory.

"You expect us to hide while our friends are being hassled by those bastards?" Harry asked, bristling. "Millington is my home, and those are my friends. I will deal with this."

His classic alpha reaction to territorial invasion was noteworthy, considering a coven wasn't a pack, but right now it was more a hindrance than a help.

"What could one wolf do," Katie asked, "against trained convex witches? If they can handle a pack, they can handle you. You don't want to be anywhere near them."

"Don't underestimate me," Harry growled.

"I could handle you." Her voice held little inflection. "I could handle you right now."

It was her first reference to the monkshood she'd stolen. Even though Marcus trusted her not to hurt them, the comment prickled his skin like a cold breeze. He appreciated her competence and experience, but that didn't mean the glimpse of her deadly side wasn't daunting.

Harry's eyes flashed silver. "Don't fuck with me, Zhang. I've got Marcus's bay pill on me, and I know you're drained."

Katie shrugged and placed her gun on the table. Her hands remained near it. "Lars isn't drained. He's never drained."

Though Marcus's wolf was subsumed by his witch lattice, at the threat toward Katie he grew instantly provoked. "She's providing tactical information." He rounded the heavy armchair and calculated the distance between himself and Harry.

If this escalated, he could get to Harry before Harry

got to Katie. Her threats were empty ones, and he refused to allow the other man to touch her.

Harry's head whipped toward him. His eyes narrowed and his alpha flared. Marcus's skin crawled. It wasn't his wolf answering Harry's but something angry and innate. Something protective. Something that didn't care what or who Harry was. "I'm sorry to inform you, but any convex witch with the right components is more than a match for an alpha wolf."

"Maybe keepers can handle alpha wolves, but they aren't trained to take down alpha witches," June said fiercely. "I can help him in Millington."

Katie, who seemed surprised by Marcus's defense of her, began to speak.

Harry interrupted. "Not you, June. You're staying here where it's safe. I'll go and—"

"You aren't an acceptable sacrifice." Marcus might be ticked at Harry for snarling at Katie, but that didn't mean he wanted the man dead. "You'd get yourself captured or killed, and then what would your wife do? If Lars covers Millington up like Alabama, it's all the more important for us to offer the region elders a solid motivation to attenuate the keeper council. Once transformed wolves are no longer so hazardous, the keepers are no longer that necessary. They'll be curtailed and their spy network ferreted out."

And he, Katie and her family would be safe.

"How long will that take?" Harry said.

Marcus hated rushing experiments. He hated rushing science. He hated this whole situation.

He didn't hate Katie.

"We'll go to the region elders in three days no matter what," he decided. "Until then, the factory is warded and has no traceable connections to any of us. We'll be safe here."

"You're wrong." Katie's voice was level but foreboding. "If they're gathering biological family members, they deciphered Vern's location spell. They have my father. That gives them a direct link to me."

"Don't jump to conclusions." Since Lars hadn't laid a trap for them yet, Marcus had changed his opinion on how much knowledge the keepers had. "I presume Lars wants family members for blackmail purposes."

"How would someone in June's family be used to blackmail her when he can't contact her to negotiate?"

"He could be planning ahead. Collecting leverage." If Marcus reached his goal tomorrow, the region elders could extricate the captives from Lars. Did Katie not see this—or did she have other reasons for wanting to leave him?

It wasn't as if she'd remained with him voluntarily. Her focus had been helping her family the whole time.

"I don't want to take the chance." She set a full backpack on the table. "If Lars has Vern's location spell, none of you are safe around me anymore. I'm the one he wants. I have to go. Now."

"You've been planning this." He'd sensed it in his bones, in the space between them that had grown chillier and chillier. He'd hoped to appease her when his experiments succeeded.

He hadn't been fast enough.

"It's too soon. What about the permabrand?" he demanded, grasping for straws. "My experiments can't progress if you leave."

"Your experiments can't progress if you're dead."

Marcus crossed the floor, hands fisted. Not because he intended violence—because he didn't want to snatch her.

"We should leave you two alone," June said tentatively.

Katie yanked the straps on the backpack. The one she carried with her everywhere. Marcus had known it was a go bag but hadn't realized she meant to use it to go away from him. If he were hooked to the heart monitor right now, it would register him at dangerous levels.

"The three of you relocate," she said. "After what happened in Kentucky, you ought to realize you can't fuck around with the keepers. Apparently they have eyes everywhere. None of you can handle their firepower."

Harry scoffed. Katie raised a hand, and her expression silenced him. "Shut up, Harry. You can't. Ditch the macho and get your pregnant wife out of here."

Pregnant? June was... Marcus turned to her, piecing together impressions and facts.

The blonde slumped against the wall behind the cot and sighed. "How did you guess?"

"It's not because you look fat," Harry said instantly.

Katie stared at them over the top of her glasses. "Your husband is not a subtle man."

"You shouldn't be here," Marcus said. Not that they'd have been safer if they'd have ignored Vernon's request and remained in Millington.

June straightened, glaring. "I'm pregnant, not an invalid. I've still got more magic than any of you."

"But you have twice as many reasons to avoid the keepers now," Katie said. "If the keepers get their hands on you, you don't want to know what they'd do to an alpha witch pregnant with the child of an alpha wolf. I'd advise leaving the country."

June blanched. Harry's manner lost all cockiness.

"All right," he said gruffly. "We'll relocate, but you should come with us. Keep helping Marcus. They can't track us as well in another country."

"They still have my family." Katie twitched the last pocket on the backpack closed. "Do you have passports? Your crossing will show up in the humans' systems, but if you're quick, you can disappear before the keepers realize what happened."

Marcus caught her hand. It was a trapped bird in his grasp, frantic to escape, while the rest of her was pure steel. What was she actually feeling? "No."

She finally looked at him. Her eyes glistened like winter ice on an overpass—black and deadly. "I'll give you a list of the other witches who do brands. Save up a couple years and you can hire one to finish what we started."

"That's not my primary concern."

She raised an eyebrow. "That's funny, because it's the only concern you've mentioned the entire time we've known each other. What I can do for your research."

He stared at her, trying to find the right words. When he couldn't find them—when he couldn't find any words—she sighed. "Marcus, it's time for me to go."

A clank distracted him—June and Harry sneaking out the metal door.

"We're, ah, going to the hotel," Harry said. Their room was protected with stronger wards than the standard ones Vernon's location spell had pierced when Tonya and Zhang Li had found Katie in Marcus's trailer. "We'll call you early in the morning to see if...to see what you plan to do."

Echoing the metallic thunk of the door, the storm outside kicked up again. Thunder rolled overhead. Katie tried to tug away from him and follow Harry and June, but Marcus didn't need to be at full strength to hold on to her.

"Three more days," he bargained. "Two."

She shook her head slowly, side to side. "I'm death. I've brought misfortune to everyone I've ever lo—everyone I've ever known. You have a future, Marcus. You're going to help people. Maybe not tomorrow, but eventually. Go make good things happen."

She slid free of him and backed toward the door. Her gaze never left his. If she was using alpha to persuade him, he couldn't feel it with his witch lattice. Hell, right now he couldn't even feel the permabrand.

But he could feel pain. Ripping. Something inside him breaking.

Katie reached the door.

Laid her hand on it.

Throat completely dry, he said, "Wait, Katie. Wait."

She nudged her glasses up her nose, that familiar gesture almost more than he could handle. His panic crested, a desperate, edgy sensation that bore little resemblance to the oddness he usually felt in witch state.

"Why would I wait? My being here puts everyone in danger."

"One more day." He needed time to find the words, to find the right persuasion. "Do the brand tomorrow and…"

Her eyelashes lowered and she twisted the handle on the heavy door. Wrong answer. "Goodbye, Marcus. Be safe."

He was on her before the door opened all the way. It slammed as his body hit hers, as she hit the door. He didn't know where he'd dug up the speed to move like that and didn't care.

Marcus shoved the backpack off her shoulder and kicked it sideways. Katie raised a hand to punch him in the throat, and he deflected it, pinning her wrist to the door. She cursed him. He trapped her other hand behind her back. Their bodies touched all the way down.

Who was he? Was this the wolf taking over?

When he looked at Katie, nearly any time he thought

of Katie, it was a struggle not to ravish her. He had crude impulses. Base desires. Raging hormones. He wanted to tie her up and never let her go. Desire simmered inside him no matter which lattice was ascendant. His preoccupation had worsened by the day.

Now it had exploded.

He wanted to be inside her.

He wanted to fuck her until she agreed to stay with him.

He wanted to imprint himself on her until she could never leave him.

He wanted her to want him back.

"I don't…" How could he express what he didn't understand? "I can't…"

"Control yourself?" she suggested. "I thought you were in witch state."

"I am."

She struggled a little, and he pushed his thigh between hers. He had no wolf senses to tell him if she was aroused, furious or frightened. He had to rely on his experience with people to read her. It was giving him nothing.

He was completely adrift. All he knew was… "I want you to stay."

"I'm aware of that." As the storm raged, the power flickered. The lights popped off and back on. "Let go."

"Never." Lightning struck again, followed by a hissing bang. The electricity gave up the ghost and dropped them into complete blackness except for the pallid light of his battery-powered laptop.

Even after his weak witch's eyesight adjusted, he couldn't see her. But he could hear her soft breathing and feel her heat through their clothes. He could smell her soap and the spicy relics of cayenne and kava.

When he bent his head and found her lips, he could taste the reason he wanted her to stay.

Because he was crazy in love with her.

TWENTY-THREE

KATIE FROZE IN astonishment when Marcus kissed her. When she didn't yell at him, he let go of her wrists and caught her head.

His hands were trembling.

"Katie." He stroked her hair, placing butterfly kisses beside her mouth, on her mouth. His tongue brushed the seam of her lips as if he'd never done this before. Though it was pitch black, she closed her eyes, bewildered by his tenderness. "Don't go. Please don't go."

Couldn't he understand? It wasn't just her family in trouble, or Harry and June. Marcus was in danger. "I have to."

"We got away from Lars. You poppied Frank. We'll think of something." He trailed kisses along her jaw. His teeth scraped her pulse. He returned to her lips and teased until she let him inside. His tongue quested for hers, tasting her until her knees weakened and her stomach quivered. Tentative, not sure where this was going or how stupid she was for hoping it meant something, she placed her hands on his warm chest.

His heart raced.

She tilted her face toward him and kissed him back. When her fingertips brushed his neck, he pulled away from her with a gasp. The faint blue light from his computer screen revealed little, no matter how wide she opened her eyes.

His voice rasped over words she thought she'd never hear. "I love you."

"You can't." It was impossible. He couldn't love her. This was lust. This was possessiveness, the wolf in him. She felt the same way—reckless, needy. Willing to sacrifice everyone for another day with him.

Leaving him felt like stabbing herself in the chest, but it had to be done.

"I do." He shoved his fingers in her hair, and his mouth found hers again. Whiskers abraded her lips. "I love you. I can't help it. I would have told you but I didn't know. Until you said you were leaving."

"I'm still leaving," she insisted, but he had her snared against the metal, his big body a cage with no door.

One hand dropped to her ass and hoisted her more firmly against his growing erection. "Let me have this. I need you so much I can't think straight."

His breath sizzled against her skin. His need kindled hers, a profound longing that was so much more than lust and had nothing to do with him being a wolf.

He wasn't a wolf right now. He was Marcus, and she loved him too. Enough to do anything she could to save him.

The next time his lips found hers, she opened for him in helpless invitation. She pushed the unbuttoned shirt off his shoulders. Muscles bunched under the smooth skin she admired with her fingers. She found his nipples and he groaned.

Katie melted between him and the door. His kisses became savage. His tongue curled into her, demanding she surrender. Ardent hands massaged her ass, between her legs. He stole her breath. He stole her heart.

She could never tire of touching him. She ran her hands

all over his torso, down past his belt. She groped for his cock and noticed a tiny lump in his pocket.

Fucking antidote. Katie ripped the capsule out and hurled it toward the corner. It pinged off the extra glassware on the shelves. "I hate that you carry that around. Like you don't trust me." She took his face and kissed him. "I would never hurt you."

"Lars would kill me. Then I couldn't protect you."

"Protect me? I—"

He lifted her, suddenly, so he could nuzzle her breasts. "Stop arguing."

Katie leaned her head against the cool surface of the door as his teeth locked on her nipple. She stifled a cry. It hurt her and thrilled her at the same time. Her pussy began to ache for him, for his attention, his cock. He bit her other breast. The heat of his mouth bled through her shirt to her skin.

Need rushed over her like the thunderstorm pouring outside. Lightning crackled. Marcus lowered her feet to the floor, pinioning her against the door when she would have crumpled. Eager hands fumbled at her waistband. He shoved down her pants, her panties, before dropping to his knees to yank off her shoes.

She groped through the blackness and brushed his close-cropped hair. Chilly air whooshed up her bare legs under the bottom of the door as gusts of wind tore around the factory. His teeth scraped her thigh. She grabbed his hair and tried to pull him up, but he tossed one of her legs over his shoulder and buried his mouth in her pussy.

When his tongue searched out her clit, she cried out. He ate her as if he was famished. His teeth snapped, his lips sucked. He licked every inch. Two fingers thrust into her so powerfully she nearly swallowed her tongue. He brought her to the brink of ecstasy.

"Lonely up here." She wanted to come while he was hard and high inside her, not like this.

He rose, nearly thumping her chin. Her turn to fumble with his pants. Her hands shook as much as his. He growled against her neck, sucking the skin, raising her blood. Finally she freed the part of him she wanted. He wasted no time, lifting her with impatient hands, parting her thighs, seeking her wet, slick heat.

The angle wasn't right. His cock slid up, between their stomachs. He drew back, thrust forward. Another miss glided past her clit in a way that made her moan out loud. He gripped her ass, adjusting her position. She tightened her thighs around his hips.

"Katie, I need…" He braced her firmly against the door when she started to slip. "Help me."

She wriggled her hand between their bodies. When she latched on to his cock, he groaned. Guiding it down, she fit the hot knob against her entrance.

She expected him to jam himself deep and take her violently, but his lips found hers. As he kissed her, he mated their bodies. Inch by inch, his cock pushed inside until they were as close as two people could be.

When she was completely impaled, he rested his cheek against hers. Air wheezed in and out of him. "I love you."

She wished what he said was true. "That's not what this is."

He rocked her. Their pelvises tilted and swayed. The angle of his thrusts chafed her clit. Good. So good.

His lips moved against her jaw. "I know what I feel."

Her pussy clenched around him. Every movement of his body drove her wilder. She clung to him with all her might. He kept the rhythm, stroke for stroke, like a conductor. Steady. Steady.

Faster.

Rising tempo.

He kissed her again. His tongue twisted with hers, his lungs breathed with hers. "I love you."

"No."

He added more speed. The push and pull of his cock weakened her resolve even as it strengthened her feelings. "I love you."

"Why?"

"I don't know. I don't care." Two hard thrusts. She was going to come. Another. Katie gulped. Gasped. Held onto him. As her climax spiraled closer, she grew wetter. Her nails bit into him. "Because I do."

Goddess, she needed this man. "Don't stop."

He obliged her, thrust after thrust. Three. Two. One.

She burst like the clouds and rained down on him. He groaned. Could he tell? Could he tell she was coming so hard she could see stars against the utter blackness of the room? His cock rammed inside her, hard and high, exactly where she wanted him. Where she always wanted him.

His breath harsh, he drove her through her climax. He didn't rest. Her juices spread all over them. Now his beast emerged. He fucked her until she was over the crest and rising again.

"Katie." All he said was her name.

"Yes. Do it." He thrust deeper, somehow, or grew larger, his cock swollen with desire. She dragged him close. Her heels dug into his ass. She found his face in the darkness and kissed him instead of telling him how she felt.

One of his hands dropped down. He had her so tight against the door, she didn't fall. He withdrew almost all the way from her pussy and smacked her ass with the flat of his hand.

Katie moaned. She wouldn't hide from it and didn't

question it. She loved the pain he gave her. She loved Marcus being so crazy for her that he let himself go. He let his wolf do what it would to them both. And his wolf would have her submission.

He spanked her. Thrust in and out, catching her clit on the stroke. Spanked her again. It wasn't like the first spanking; his angle was shit. But it was hot. Goddess, she wanted it harder, wanted it all harder. She wanted him to whip the truth out of her and make her admit it.

He thrust his tongue into her mouth and his cock into her pussy. The next time he paddled her, it was particularly keen, like a tightrope of rapture. She whimpered into his mouth.

Her cry shivered through him as if he could feel the same thing. She realized her cheeks were wet with tears. Marcus cupped her ass again with both hands, his fingers slick with her juices. "Tell me you love me."

She opened her mouth to obey, and he thrust into her cruelly, thumping her against the door. She lost her ability to speak. His cock deep, her legs wide, he found her anus with his fingers.

"Tell me, Katie."

Again she tried to obey. This time he pushed fingertips into her, past the tight muscle. The intensity of that sensation arrested her words in her throat.

He had two fingers in her. Not deep, but her heart raced like a hummingbird. He began rocking her with his hips and his fingers. In and out. Both entrances pleasured. His cock deep, his fingers shallow.

His lips moved against hers, barely making sound. "I love you. Believe me. I love you."

A tear slipped past her jaw. She gave him what he demanded. "I love you too."

"Don't leave me."

"I couldn't bear it if they hurt you because of me."

"It will hurt worse if you go."

She rested her forehead against his. Her body trembled with passion and a spinning rush of relief now that she'd said it. She'd said the words. She'd never been more vulnerable to anyone in her entire life.

"Make love to me," she said. "I want you to come inside me."

He didn't say anything else. He didn't have to. She could feel him release the last of his restraint. He rolled into her, slow and deep, then faster. Wilder. His cadence ensnared her and she started begging. *Please, Marcus. Please. Harder. Fuck me.*

His fingers slid deep into her anus.

She gasped. He whispered things to her. The nonstop strokes of his cock, the way he was filling her. His fingers, she couldn't believe his fingers. The strange wonder of it pushed her over the edge into a ferocious orgasm.

Marcus drove relentlessly until he clenched and came. He spurted inside her, cock throbbing. He quivered like a spear that had struck the ground. They held each other for several minutes until they caught their breath.

He loved her. She loved him. As impossible as it seemed.

It was going to be so much harder to leave him now.

MARCUS SHRUGGED OUT of his shirt as Katie watched. His hands were steadier than hers, and he was the one about to experience hours of excruciating pain.

June cinched protections around the hotel room, which she claimed would block Vern's tracking spell. Katie, a full snoot of power after the best night of sleep she'd had since before Marcus, could sense the brick-solid magic settle around them. An expensive spell with rare components, it wouldn't do for everyday use. It deadened input from the outside by half. But they'd all decided—after June obsessed about impurities—that these protections had a high percentage of success.

Well, the three witches had decided. Harry's vote had been to drive straight for the Mexican border and disappear.

They hadn't heard from anyone since last night. June obtained another burner phone and dialed several numbers, including Millington, but nobody knew anything.

Annette didn't answer at the last number she'd used. They downloaded a contact list for region elders but hadn't escalated to it yet. How could they prove anything was amiss in Millington if the keepers cleaned up after themselves like in Alabama?

Because of who they were, they'd never sway the region elders without substantial backing. Marcus and Katie were renegades, and June and Harry weren't universally acclaimed themselves. Frank's existence might be approved instead of an illicit infiltration. Soon, they'd call the region elders regardless. They had to act one way or another.

Katie recalled, with a pang, her father's claim that he'd hacked the region elder forums. That would be really useful right about now.

So would a fast forward button. For the next several hours, she had agreed to cause her lover the worst pain in his life. If Lars had Vern's tracking spell and began his search in Kentucky, the brand had to be inked as soon as possible, no matter how strong June's ward was. They'd run out of time. They'd run out of options.

They'd almost run out of cayenne and heal-all. It was going to deplete their stores to set Marcus's brand.

"I'd rather be doing this in my laboratory." Marcus inspected the flawless expanse of his back in the mirror. He hadn't wanted Katie to draw designs on him before the tattoo, as she usually did, since it would take extra time.

"The power's out and it's isolated," she said. Not to mention large, spooky and decrepit. "This is the better choice."

The electricity in the factory had been whacked by the lightning storm. They'd transported the essentials here, a busy hotel, rather than the Airstream in a nearby RV park. Not that it was optimal to place humans in the crossfire, but the throng of people would serve as camouflage and deterrent.

They hoped.

Nobody had mentioned June's pregnancy—but nobody had mentioned the love bites on Katie's neck, either. Or the fact she was still here.

Harry prowled the room nonstop. Though he was in two-leg form, Katie could practically see the prick of his ears and his hackles.

"How long is this going to take?" he asked again. Did he think Marcus's estimate would have changed in the past hour? "I want to be on the road before dark."

Once Katie set the brand, Harry and June were headed out of the country until this blew over. June wanted to stay and help, but the others had outvoted her.

All of them were getting outvoted on something.

Katie had been outvoted on this fucking permabrand.

She didn't want to cause Marcus this pain. He theorized the massive power would flood both lattices and raise him to dual state. Theories and extrapolation. It wasn't enough to go on.

She wasn't a scientist. She had no idea how a wolf could become a witch or why most witches became wolves after having sex with one. She was just a former keeper, a soldier, as torn between her lover and her family as Harry was between his wife and his coven.

How could you save everyone who deserved it when there was only one of you?

Marcus read from his smartphone in response to Harry's question—again. "Eight hours and sixteen minutes. If you want to leave today, we should begin."

He climbed onto the bed and the white coverlet like a sacrifice. "Don't stop as frequently to sterilize and apply pain relief. The heal-all and my constitution will prevent bacterial infection."

"I'd rather you be anesthetized and unconscious for this," Katie said. The tattoo machine gleamed on the bedside table like a weapon. The two types of ink had been simmered and strained. The people not getting tattoos wore protective clothing. Everything was ready—except for her nerves.

"We don't have time to determine an inert anesthetic," he said with a slight smile. "As for unconscious, I suspect I will be."

"Shit." Katie's stomach lurched. One tiny, inch-wide brand had been so unpleasant he'd hazed out. How could she do this to him?

"I was thinking a striped pattern on my front and back." Marcus settled himself on the bed. His jeans—had she ever seen him in jeans?—rode low on his hips. Harry, face grim, strapped him down with cloth bindings that should restrain Marcus as long as his wolf didn't gain ascendancy.

June restacked the sterile gauze for the fourth time. She wore a set of long-sleeved coveralls, as did Katie and Harry. They expected today to be messier than yesterday, and Marcus's blood would be tainted by high-powered cayenne. "What about the heart monitor?"

"I don't want you intimidated by my readings," he said. "If I seem…anemic, I have faith in you to revive me. You're very powerful witches."

"Revive." Katie slumped onto the opposite bed. How could he be so nonchalant? So detached from the fact that this could kill him? And he knew it. He'd just admitted it. Revive.

"Front first." Marcus, on his back, tested his bonds. He caught her eye. "I'll be fine."

She clenched her hands. Her whole body shivered like leaves in last night's storm. It was a good thing he didn't want an attractive tattoo design, because she was going to have the manual dexterity of a drunk.

He smiled at her. It was eerie, knowing she brought happiness to someone, instead of just death. "I trust you completely, Katie. Check my pocket if you don't believe me. There's no capsule."

"All I'm saying is…" Her breath caught in a sob. She wasn't sure if it was dread or love or happiness or a muddle of all three. "This had better be worth it."

Her words lacked romance, but she didn't know how to be sweet.

He chuckled. He actually laughed. The man was insane. "You're telling me."

Harry and June were watching, but Katie leaned down and kissed him anyway. "See you on the other side."

Marcus closed his eyes and gripped the stress balls she'd given him, one in each hand. Humans liked them for large tattoos, and she'd had them in the kit they'd recovered from the tattoo shop. "If you require additional square inches, let's skip the genital area, shall we?"

BY THE TIME they finished his back, Katie was weeping openly. She could barely see Marcus's bloody, enflamed skin, the tattoo gun needling in and out of him, leaving red agony in its wake. The designs she'd fashioned were covered by blood and blisters. June had taken a turn since all that was needed during the inking was a willingness to point and shoot the tattoo machine, but she'd ended up going to the bathroom to vomit.

Even Harry was pale when Katie unplugged the machine and laid it, hands shaking, on the table.

Marcus's blood splattered the white sheets. Her coveralls. Her gloves. It was done. Now that she'd fused it into a permabrand, he'd have to live with pain for—she didn't even know. Ten years? Twenty? Forever?

These weren't scars he'd be able to shift away. Doing this to him would haunt her forever too.

Her whole head pounded like the world's worst sinus infection from the magical draining. Sweat beaded Marcus's forehead. Pain etched his unconscious face like the cayenne etched his torso. The only complaint he'd uttered was when they'd turned him over midway through the procedure.

He'd muttered curses when his tortured front side hit the sheets but had lapsed quickly into semi-consciousness.

At least she could temporarily relieve the burn. Or try. Her hands shook so much when she tried to uncap the last spray bottle of heal-all that she couldn't get it open.

A big hand touched her shoulder. "I got this part."

Harry rotated her away from the devastation she'd wrought. Surprising Katie even more, June caught her in a hug. "He chose this. You told him what it would be like, and he still chose it."

"I love him," Katie said brokenly. Her vision filmed with tears and fatigue. "How could I do this to him?"

Behind her, the spray can emitted a continuous hiss. The heal-all in the brand would offset the damage from the cayenne—they assumed—but the burns and blisters from the application process needed a booster.

"What if it works?" June asked. "What if he can be a witch and a wolf at the same time? This has the potential to be huge. Bigger than me and Harry."

"It also has the potential to be nothing." Katie's headache crept down her neck to her shoulders and arms. This might be the worst draining she'd ever experienced, and the procedure couldn't be easily replicated. If her combat bonus weren't active, she'd be unconscious. She'd had to take magic from June and Harry to set Marcus's giant permabrand. The largest brand she'd done prior to today had been a quarter the size.

She didn't even know if she'd gotten the lines straight. She couldn't see her handiwork through the blood and blisters.

Fresh tears trickled free. She'd mutilated the man she loved.

June patted her back. "He's already managed something nobody else has ever accomplished. Progress isn't painless."

Katie kind of laughed.

"He had to try. I think…I think he'd do anything for you."

"This isn't about me." Katie extricated herself from June's comforting arms and found tissues. She kept her back, carefully, to the bed where Harry fizzed through the last of the primed heal-all.

"That's where you're wrong. He knew if he couldn't make something happen that you were going to leave him to rescue your family. We all knew."

Katie's eyes were swollen, her nose sealed shut. She'd developed a talent for emotional subterfuge with the council—and a short time with Marcus had destroyed it. "I suppose it doesn't take a genius to figure me out."

"You have so much loyalty and devotion inside you," June said. "You aren't what I expected. You wouldn't have killed Frank, would you?"

"If it was between him and one of us? Yes."

"There was a man in my past I would have killed too, but someone else did first. You wouldn't kill if you had other options. I get that now."

"Just don't assume the other keepers are like me." Joining the council shattered nearly everyone who'd experienced it. It would have shattered Katie, but Vern's arrival had pulled her from the brink, and Dad and Tonya had mended her the rest of the way. That was why, no matter how much she wanted to be with Marcus, she had to help them.

If the permabrand didn't work, she'd leave him and do what she had to do. Trade herself. Lars couldn't possibly hurt her worse than knowing she'd let her family die or gotten Marcus killed.

June and Harry's luggage waited by the door. They would head for Mexico as soon as they confirmed Marcus was as healed as he was going to get. The keepers weren't their battle, and they weren't equipped to fight it. Marcus had his science and Katie had—herself.

June added her giant pocketbook to the pile and inspected the screen of her phone. Her brows pinched together—she must not have gotten any calls. She looked up at Katie. "I'm supposed to add a layer to the cayenne before I leave."

"Don't." Her tears dry, Katie began preparations for the battle ahead. She'd give Marcus one more night before they parted ways—for his safety. "He needs to heal. I'll layer him tomorrow."

WITCH INTERRUPTED

"The protections will last on this room until morning. Get some rest." June was out of the ingredients needed to reset the particular ward she'd put on the hotel room. She'd left Katie the recipe and others, including one for apple pie.

As if Katie knew how to bake. Tonya was the baker in her family.

"Can't sleep yet. He'll want to run tests." She risked a glance at the bed. Harry had cleaned the blood off Marcus with the last of the cotton and gauze. The small bedside trash bin overflowed. She'd need to burn it before leaving, else the maid might raise an alarm.

Marcus's flesh, still angry, was crisscrossed by jagged black-and-red lines. As clinically as possible, she inspected her handiwork. From a center of rings, the cayenne and heal-all zigzagged like starbursts or a witch lattice, which was what she'd been going for. On the front, she'd tattooed his wolf lattice. Two designs to represent the two halves Marcus claimed were inside them all.

It would never win an artistry award, but the tattoo had a certain stark beauty. Or perhaps it was Marcus who was beautiful and the brands were part of him now.

He shifted restlessly on the bed.

Goddess, she hoped this had worked the way Marcus intended. It would mean he'd done it. He'd be so happy. Not to mention, sharing these results with the elders in exchange for help with the keepers would be imminently preferable to her demise at the hands of Hiram Lars.

For the first time in days, Katie allowed herself a sliver of hope. Marcus had survived the procedure, which had been the first hurdle. Now they just needed to wake him.

June peeled off her gloves and tossed them into the trash. "Do you need help getting him to the car?"

"Just cast eyebright on him, if you don't mind." Katie

wasn't up to simple spells. She'd squeezed her brain into a pulp to extract every last dribble of power. "He'll want to see you off."

"No problem." June dug in her purse and came up with a bottle. She cast the wakefulness spell on Marcus, her hand on his forehead and her full lips murmuring words Katie couldn't hear. Katie stood behind her and laced her fingers together. They felt as arthritic as her dad's hands. How he managed to keep tattooing like a champ, she didn't know.

"I'm going to load the car." Harry shouldered nearly all the items, including a large cooler, in one go.

"Stay alert," Katie warned him unnecessarily. If the keepers found a person with the right DNA for Vern's spell, it could lead them to the hotel lobby, if not the warded room.

June and Marcus would avoid any keepers downstairs some other way. Once the protections on this room vanished, though, Katie and Marcus would be exposed. Her normal wards couldn't fend off Vern's spell. They weren't too different from the ones on Marcus's Airstream when Tonya and Dad had found her…in the nick of time.

Now she wished they hadn't found her. She wished she'd succumbed to her out-of-character urge to be with Marcus from the beginning. Love had breached her defenses and turned her into a better person—turned her from Chang Cai into Katie Zhang. First she'd loved her family. Now she loved Marcus. She loved wholly. She loved them all so much. The question was, would love give her strength? Or would having a reason to look forward to tomorrow dull her edge?

After a peek down the empty hallway, she locked the door behind Harry. June hadn't managed to rouse Marcus.

Katie returned to his bedside and cast a worried glance over the grayish tint of his skin. "Why won't he wake?"

"I don't know. I don't specialize in healing. Let's roll him over." Carefully balling up the bloody sheets, Katie and June eased Marcus onto his back. His limbs flopped. His head lolled. "What's his pulse?"

Katie placed two fingers against his neck. His artery throbbed rapidly, and his skin was moist with sweat. "Faster than normal."

"I don't mean to scare you, but I don't like how Marcus is responding. We should have ignored him when he told us to skip the heart monitor."

At June's calm but firm words, a chill swept through Katie. Keepers weren't taught a great deal about first aid. They didn't need to know how to save lives—only how to neutralize them. "Okay. What do you want me to do?"

"Keep monitoring his pulse."

Katie knelt on the bed beside Marcus and rested her fingers on his jugular. The longer she timed his pulse, the less normal it seemed. His breaths puffed in and out in uneven pants.

Increasingly concerned, she lifted his eyelids. His pupils were pinpricks. "June, there's something wrong with him."

"Irregular pulse...we need better blood flow. Holy mother of grass, I know I've got ginkgo and hawthorn in here somewhere." June upended her handbag, spilling the contents on the bed and floor in her haste. She dropped to her knees and scrambled through the clutter.

Marcus's huffs turned to gasps.

His body twitched.

Katie's sore fingers trembled. He was definitely not okay. He'd survived the branding. The worst should be over. Why would he be reacting this way to eyebright?

And there was nothing she could do. "Should we—is there anyone we can call? Anywhere?"

Marcus's pulse throbbed to a stop beneath Katie's anxious touch. His chest, his lungs, went silent.

Goddess, no. She could barely choke out the words. "He's not breathing."

"Breathe for him." June hopped to her feet, expression stern and herbs in her hands.

That, Katie could do. She tilted his head back, held his nose and filled him with air.

His chest rose and fell. Shivering, she waited five seconds and did it again. "Marcus, wake up. Please wake up."

June tore open the herb packets. "I think he's having a heart attack."

Terror raked Katie like a mountain lion's claws. This was her fault. She'd hurt him. Killed him. She loved him so much. How could this be happening?

"Try something. Anything." Her hand hovered over the telephone. "We could call 9-1-1." A heart attack was a heart attack. Human medicine was effective sometimes.

"Not yet. Give me space." June rubbed herbs between her palms, littering his motionless chest with green and brown. Tears slid down Katie's cheeks. She brought death to everyone she loved.

She should have disappeared last night. She should have gone. She was a self-indulgent, weak person who'd made this happen.

"Goddess, give me strength and steady hands," June prayed. She leaned over Marcus and pressed her hands over his heart, as if she were going to start compressions. She drew in a deep breath. "Here goes."

Magic exploded from the small woman so forcefully a wave of heat blasted Katie. Marcus's body stiffened, arching off the bed. Choking sounds issued from his mouth.

Light flared around June's fingers on his chest. Her body curled into a painful twist, and she shrieked.

Katie leaped between them, breaking the contact between the witch and her patient. Marcus flopped onto the mattress with a grunt.

A grunt meant he was alive—right?

June nearly crumpled. Katie caught her by the arms. "June, are you okay?"

"I'll be fine. Check him."

She set June on the other bed and quickly pressed an unsteady hand to Marcus's pulse.

Nothing.

Nothing.

There! His heart thumped. Blood flowed.

After several beats, Marcus inhaled as if he'd simply been holding his breath this whole time. His body shuddered.

June coughed. "Is he…"

"He's alive." Both women fell silent as the miraculous intake and exhale of his lungs echoed through the room. Katie felt like throwing up but continued to assess his pulse.

Steady. Strong. "I think it worked."

On the other bed, June squeezed her temples. "Holy moly, it was like he was sucking the magic right out of me. Once the spell started, I couldn't cap it off. We'd better add some calming mix. I think he's…"

Marcus woke with a cough and sat straight up in bed.

Then he screamed.

TWENTY-FOUR

PAIN.

Redness, blood, torture, brutal agony.

A thesaurus of suffering.

Marcus had gone through all the entries and run out of language.

He tried to swim through the scarlet ocean of hurt, but he had no strength left. He'd struggled for hours to stay afloat. He'd thought about sex. Thought about Katie. Thought about the periodic table. Thought about all the people he could save.

Thought about dying.

When a new pain lanced through him like a chainsaw cutting him in two, he knew he was finished. He'd failed. He couldn't—nobody could survive this.

At last the blackness of death descended and he knew no m—

Wait.

That fucking hurt.

Marcus's throat fucking hurt.

He jolted awake and realized he was screaming at the top of his lungs. Hands patted him, pushed him down, grappled with his flailing arms and legs. Someone was—holding him.

"Marcus. Marcus, baby, wake up. Oh Goddess, Marcus, please be okay."

He quit yelling.

"Katie?"

He opened his eyes. Everything in the hotel room was unnaturally sharp and glaring. Katie held him, her arms like firebrands. She was crying. Behind her, June's shaking hands clenched an assortment of herbs.

"I love you." Katie rained kisses on his face. Her lips, like her arms, were fiery hot. Her tears were made of cayenne. He'd been burned to a crisp and was so damned sore he didn't want to move. "I thought you were dying. I love you so much. Jesus, I did this to you. Your heart stopped. We had to… This was a bad idea. We should never have done this. What can I do? I have to make this go away. You can't suffer like this."

He loved her too. Hearing her confirm his affections was a great pleasure.

Not for long, though, because he tried to answer.

"I love…" Knives jabbed his throat when he spoke. "Water."

June produced a bottle, and Katie held it to his mouth. He gulped.

The water hurt his throat.

When he coughed, it hurt him…everywhere. "Fuck."

This was, quite frankly, the worst suffering of his life. He'd thought losing his sister had hurt. He'd thought the five years with the council had been torturous. He'd thought his initial transformation to a wolf had been the depths of possible pain.

He'd been wrong.

He hazed back out of consciousness. The agony sloshed over his head and he lost the ability to feel Katie. Then the wave ebbed again, and she was still holding him.

"Do we have more heal-all?" Katie begged June. "We can't let him suffer like this."

Marcus couldn't see much. The world looked red and

blurry. June responded in a sorrowful voice. "We have the gel, but I don't think it will help. He has no external injuries."

"What about willow bark? We have to do something."

Herbs that could heal weren't rare, but like June had said, the pain Marcus felt wasn't due to overt injury. It was the cayenne. It had infiltrated his nervous system, and he burned. Everything burned. His eyes boiled so hot he was afraid they'd pop out of the sockets, so he had to close them.

The next time he opened his eyes, Harry was sniffing him.

"He doesn't smell coppery. I don't think he's bleeding inside."

"We should use valerian and hops," Katie said. "Maybe he can sleep through the worst of it."

"No," Marcus croaked. She adjusted her hold on him, wriggling so her back was to the headboard.

He groaned. The shaking bed was like apes jumping on his sore body. Hands jounced him. Katie held the water to his lips again.

He managed to get the rest down. Or was it another bottle? It tasted funny. Bitter. He closed his eyes.

When he opened them for the seventy-eighth time, he remembered that he'd been thirsty after both permabrands. They'd need to note that on the charts.

After a moment—since he was able to think about charts—he concluded his pain levels had receded. The hotel room no longer looked like an active volcano, and his companions no longer looked like they were attending a funeral.

"How long?" he asked.

Harry checked his watch. "Eighteen hours, man. Nine for the tattoo, nine to do something about your screaming. Luckily there aren't many other people on this floor to hear."

"Sorry," Marcus said, though he knew Harry was ribbing him. The man looked worried. They'd begun the brand at six in the morning, as soon as Katie had been able. No one had wanted to wait—one of the few decisions that hadn't been a compromise of some sort.

Eighteen hours. That meant it was 3:00 a.m. Where was the clock? His gaze fell on the tattoo machine on the bedside table, and he flinched.

Never.

Again.

Katie helped him sit up but kept a firm grip on one of his hands. The air felt clammy and cold against his fevered skin.

"What happened?" With some reluctance, since it was extremely sensitive, Marcus tapped the tattooed skin of his bare chest. From his perspective, the giant brand was a snarl of reddish and dark ink that resembled a spastic molecular model.

"You died." Her hand tightened on his, as if by her doggedness she could keep him in the land of the living. "Probably just once."

"I see." Slowly, his arms hating him, he covered her hand with his free one. "And when you say died…"

"Your heart quit beating and you weren't breathing." June's purse appeared to have vomited its contents on the opposite bed. She quit repacking it to answer his questions. "I used gingko and hawthorn to restart blood flow."

"Use of that combination is dodgy at best." Did she say his heart had stopped? Surely not. He wouldn't have lost enough blood to cause heart failure, and it wasn't as if they'd shoved the tattoo gun into his internal organs. "Was that necessary?"

Katie caught his chin. "Look at me. Your. Heart. Stopped. Do you think we're too inept to diagnose when somebody isn't breathing? June saved your life." Her lips thinned, and her eyes glistened. "After I nearly took it."

Marcus's companions radiated tension, fatigue, fear. He could smell it on them, just as he could smell cayenne, heal-all, peppermint, lavender, ginkgo, hawthorn—such a cornucopia of scents it gave him a twinge in his sinuses.

The impact struck him like a bowling ball to the gut. He'd always known if the keepers got their hands on him again, he could wind up dead—or enslaved and wishing he were dead. He hadn't expected his own experiments to send him there. "You did what I asked you to. The procedure appears to have some bumps, but it's not your fault."

June and Harry exchanged a tired glance. Not merely tired—even Harry looked exhausted. As an alpha wolf, he should have three times the energy as the witches in the room.

Katie sighed. Some of the strain left her expression. "Don't mind him, June. I'm sure Doctor Frankenstein appreciates the fact you saved his life with your dodgy spellwork."

"Thank you, June," Marcus said, realizing his oversight. "Apparently I'd be dead without you."

"You would at that," June agreed with a twinkle of humor. "All your systems appear to be normal now. You're out of the woods. Is the pain manageable?"

"I'm not sure yet. It comes and goes."

"You've got calming mix taking the edge off right now," Katie said. "We made a chart."

June handed him a stack of papers with notes, responses, chronology, amounts and herbs scribbled all over it. They told the tale of his procedure from start to what had almost been his finish. As the horror of his near-death experience crept over him, he realized his friends would also not have enjoyed the prior eighteen hours.

"Thank you," he said again. He needed to analyze and input this data as well as get an updated lattice reading. Except for his sensitized skin and rollers of pain, he felt normal. His senses seemed wolf-keen—with none of the numbness that had characterized previous witch states— yet he could detect magic inside him.

This might be it.

This might have raised him to dual state.

Marcus knew it to be true but didn't experience a surge of triumph. He was literally death warmed over. He stood to lose so much more now, and rescuing Katie's family, making her happy, had superseded beating the cancer and taking down the keepers who had killed Elisa.

Katie had become more important to him than anything in his entire life. His sister's memory, which had driven him for years, was second place. The experiment wasn't a success if it didn't sway the region elders to their cause. The permabrand had certain drawbacks.

That much unrelenting torture wasn't something he'd recommend. To anyone. For any reason. Especially considering it might kill you.

"This procedure might not be repeatable," he announced.

"No fu— Excuse me, June. No freaking kidding," Katie said.

"If I had known…" Would he have done it? June had restarted his heart. The pain might be manageable. He didn't feel like screaming at the moment. It had only been eighteen hours. Of torture. Which might not be over.

And he'd died.

If this wasn't enough to convert the region elders, he was devoid of other ideas to rescue Katie's family. Their agreement had been that they were going to the elders after this, no matter what. Why did success taste like failure?

"If I had known, I would have refused," Katie said.

Harry paced to the other side of the room. Marcus was pleased to note he could see that far—in natural colors. "I wanted to get June out of here before dark, Delgado, not dawn the next day. Could you speed up the recovery, buddy?"

"Why are you still in Ohio?" Marcus asked. Harry had been—rightly—anxious to get his pregnant wife to safety, yet here he was. "After the hawthorn, I'm sure Katie could have—"

"Don't be silly." June rested a chilly hand against his forehead. "We couldn't leave you and Katie in...in dire straits."

"Thank you," Marcus said for the third time. Dire straits indeed.

"But you two need to go." Katie stood and awkwardly adjusted her T-shirt. "The keepers are gunning for us."

"The wards on the room will last three more hours," June said. "They can't find you here. I wouldn't even be able to find you if I didn't know the room number."

She gave Katie a huge hug, which surprised Marcus. They must have bonded over his deathbed. Surprising him even more, Harry hugged her too—and Marcus didn't feel the tiniest bit jealous.

Katie loved him. Marcus sure as hell hadn't earned it, hadn't treated her respectfully, hadn't been a good friend to her. But she loved him.

It was time to get serious about saving her family.

INTENSE MORNING SUNLIGHT reflected off the rearview mirror and into Marcus's eyes. Because he felt like shit, his body scalded and achy, he'd let Katie drive. His clothing bothered him. His bones felt swollen, pushing the wrong way. His muscles protested everything he did. His face hurt when he squinted. He couldn't remain under the influence of calming mix, since it dulled him mentally, but his increase in soreness now that it had worn off was undeniable.

If this was what dual state felt like, it further convinced him his experiment had flopped. He'd never persuade other witches the risks and pain were preferable to radiation and chemotherapy, much less permanent wolf transformation.

There were joys to being a wolf. The chance you might die and be in the worst pain imaginable was the opposite of joy.

Despite feeling like death, he was increasingly confident the brand had worked. The science behind the theory was sound. Magic was a science of sorts. It wasn't fickle or lacking in consistency. Though there were unknowns, it could be plotted and calculated and behaved according to certain laws, like chemical reactions. Magical surprises were generally wrought by the person casting.

Not precisely human error, but close enough.

Once Katie cast true eye—or he cast it on himself for the first time in over a year—confirmation he'd reached a dual state would decide his next course of action. The first matter of business would be convincing Katie not to leave. He didn't doubt she loved him but had no illusions about her intentions. If she thought she could protect him by leaving him and also have a shot at helping her family, she'd jump out of the car into traffic and take off.

He loved her for that. He loved her for everything. But he didn't want to be protected if it meant losing her. If she left, he'd follow.

He didn't know what he could do against Lars without the region elders as reinforcements, but he'd follow.

Ignoring the scream of a thousand internal bruises, he lifted his arm and shaded his eyes from the sun's glare. Katie glanced nervously into the rearview mirror.

"Do we have a tail?" she asked. Not for the first time.

"I don't believe so." They were in the thick of morning rush hour and headed through suburbs. Cars behind them hardly indicated pursuers. And Katie's driving, he had to admit, wasn't as unskilled in Tonya's vehicle as it had been in the stolen truck. "How long before you anticipate having enough magic for a chi spell?"

"I probably have enough." Katie's combat bonus didn't trickle magic at a steady rate. The larger portion of the refill occurred during sleep, and she'd only napped for two hours.

The factory didn't have June's wards. They'd have to work fast and then dash.

Today everything would change, one way or another.

Would it be for the better? When all this was over, Marcus hoped to make proper love to Katie. Their first time outside blackmail or a dark, dirty factory would be miraculous.

He looked forward to sex without heart monitors, true eye spells, biometric measurements and his godforsaken charts.

He looked forward to sex without arguments.

He looked forward to sex.

In order to have the sex, he had to convince her not to leave. But he wouldn't lie about the probability that the region elders wouldn't be swayed by his ill-advised solution to wolf transformation and cancer. Could he convince her Lars wouldn't release her family unless they both offered themselves?

Was there any way, any way at all, to outsmart the man?

They both knew Lars, albeit from different perspectives. It was questionable whether Lars truly knew them, and he would have no way of guessing what Marcus had been testing. Yet Marcus knew a great deal about Lars's weapons, seeing as many were based on Marcus's research.

Did that give them an advantage?

Katie swerved the car from the direct route to the factory, jolting him from his thoughts. He braced himself with a hand against the door. "What are you doing?"

"Just checking." She peered into the rearview mirror suspiciously. The car that had been closest to them didn't turn, nor several cars behind it. Finally, one did.

However, it pulled into a driveway. The side street led through several neighborhoods, similarly constructed houses with minimal yard space. People walking dogs along sidewalks. Joggers with reflective shoes. For Sale signs. Katie rerouted to the main road, but her tension didn't ease.

He knew what she feared, and it wasn't sex or experiments. Not anymore.

"I'd like to discuss the fact you're thinking about how to ditch me."

"I, ah…" She sighed. "I didn't realize you could read me so easily."

"I know how I'd feel in your position," he said. "If I could protect you by deserting you, would I want to do it? Yes."

"Isn't it hypocritical of you to expect me to respond differently? If this is because you're a man and I'm a woman—"

"It's not," he assured her. "I want a chance to outsmart Lars. We've outsmarted him before. What can we accomplish together if we focus on Lars instead of my experiments?"

"I don't know."

"You don't have to leave today," he said. When she sighed again, he knew that was exactly what she'd been planning. "Lars isn't currently torturing your family. He activated his informant network with a red alert. He invaded Millington. It's obvious we are his focus, and he's pulling out all the stops. Finding out Chang Cai was alive may have triggered a—a mental break."

"He was already fucking nuts. You're saying he's crazier now?"

"Unless you believe he's been attacking covens and packs for years and nobody suspected," Marcus said. "Open defiance of the covenants correlates to a change in his perspective or goals. It correlates to recklessness. That's something we can use against him. He'll be less cautious if he thinks he can catch you."

"I definitely know how to be bait."

"That isn't automatically our plan." He reached across the seat and cupped her neck. Her hair tickled his hand. "But it's worth considering. One hint of your presence, and we could lure him anywhere."

Dammit, they needed the cooperation of the region elders on this. Perhaps they should place the calls before Marcus finalized his tests. What if the elders possessed a failsafe for keepers gone bad?

"Do you have your wolf senses?" she asked. "We could use your nose and eyes when we get to the factory. You know, in case the hint of me has already lured him there."

"Some." Right now he couldn't smell much beyond the yarrow in the heal-all Harry had sprayed all over his tattoos. He leaned closer to Katie and breathed deeper.

There she was. On the edge of the yarrow, her scent. Something harsher too. "Are you carrying monkshood?"

"For you to notice that, you must have access to your wolf. That's good, right? You're dual?"

What Katie could do—it was simply part of who she was, part of her magic. He could kill as well. He would kill anyone who threatened her. He'd just use a different tool than magic. "Are they contact capsules or pods?"

"Pods." She decelerated at a stop sign, turned right and picked up speed on a state highway. This put the sun beside the car instead of behind it, and it no longer blinded Marcus via the mirror.

"Good. That's safer for you." She'd been prudent to steal the monkshood. He never should have destroyed her original supply or criticized her for having it. For being what she was. A warrior. A fighter. A protector. "Do you have enough?"

"Enough for what?" she asked, eyebrows arching.

"To defend us. And, should the occasion arise, to kill Lars." He wanted her to know he was secure about her abilities and was grateful she was convex. He loved her with complete acceptance.

She cast him a questioning glance. "You're comfortable with this discussion?"

"Spare no detail. It might spark ideas." To properly evaluate the situation, he needed to tabulate their advantages. Katie's training and abilities would be needed. He might not believe Vernon had given up the location spell yet, but it would happen. Soon.

So they'd prepare. Now.

If that meant discussing the best way to ambush keepers and commit murder, they'd prepare.

"All right." She nodded slowly. The car cruised down the empty highway until they neared the factory. His warehouse was one of several buildings in a vacant, half-constructed industrial park, signs of a depressed local economy. His factory was the most dilapidated.

"I can't kill Lars with monkshood. It'll refract and go who knows where. Keepers die, of course, in the line of duty. Not usually old age or by one another's hands...not publicly, anyway. I'll carry the pistol and a knife, and we should get you a gun."

"I'm not a great shot." As a witch, he'd never seen much need for guns. "I could shift to wolf form and attack Lars if the occasion arises. We'd need to deplete his components or magic reserves first, else a standard wolf attack wouldn't be that effective."

"I like this conversation. It's romantic." Her lips quirked.

It wasn't. It was honest and open and realistic. He liked it as well, because of what it meant about the two of them. She was willing to plot with him instead of desert him for his own good.

"I've never killed anyone," he said. "Lars didn't worry about the health of the wolves they captured, but I did. If we're forced into a fight, how will killing impact me mentally?"

"When you kill, you feel like the worst person on earth. Even when you're doing it because you have to."

That was how she'd lived—how she'd been forced by the council and witch culture to live—for thirty years. She'd considered herself the worst person on earth. It was a miracle she'd healed into the woman she was today. The fascinating, beautiful, intelligent, loyal woman he loved.

"I'll take that into consideration. I'm not conditioned to respond with lethal force, and I don't want my lack of training to put us in jeopardy. I don't want to hesitate."

She scrunched her face as if trying to scoot her glasses

up without using her hand. "I have faith you'll do what's needed when the time comes."

As a precaution, Katie traveled around the industrial park's access road before directing the station wagon to a spot concealed by large, rusted equipment. There appeared to be no other vehicles on the premises. Marcus rolled down the window and sniffed.

Rust, oil, dirt. Puddles dappled the muddy ground after last night's thunderstorm. The station wagon splashed through a rut. He smelled autumn decay in the foliage, drowned earthworms and concrete.

"Smells normal." They retrieved their baggage. His muscles and skin complained, but the discomfort was nowhere near as intense as it had been. Perhaps the brand had toughened him—or fried his pain receptors. It was also possible his wolf was erasing some of the pain, but he didn't want to get his hopes up.

Though he did feel like a wolf. A wolf who'd been pummeled, but a wolf. A wolf with endless witch magic inside him, simmering like a secret.

They conducted a perimeter sweep of the factory, which revealed nothing. Back at the entryway, the aromas of ozone and burned plastic struck the first note of discord. "Something nearby must have been struck by lightning last night."

If it was the transformer, he hoped the utility crews had repaired the damage. When they unlocked the factory door, the burned plastic smell increased. Marcus's nose wrinkled. Which hurt, but so did walking.

Katie appeared to be oblivious. She latched the door behind them. "Interior sweep. Check all the exits."

"Can we visit the laboratory first and check if there's electricity?"

She pursed her lips and didn't meet his gaze. It wasn't

because she was being shifty—she was checking everything. Assessing their surroundings. This was Katie on alert.

He didn't see anything out of place, but her tension increased along with the burned plastic smell.

"That's a terrible odor. Can you identify the source?"

"No." When he was a wolf, he relied on his senses, and they were telling him nobody had been here but his group. The scorched plastic could be anything from a lightning-splattered electrical system to a chemical spill.

It invaded his sinuses until he couldn't rely on his nose. Murky sunlight poured in through the vented windows three stories up in the main room of the factory. The bowels of the factory grew darker and narrower as they wove through assembly areas and the huge storage tanks. Pausing, they unlocked and raised a wide lift gate before entering the first floor storage section.

The *clack-clack* of the rolling gate echoed painfully in his ears. If anyone was here—and he doubted it—they'd know someone had arrived. He always left the gate down and secured, to dissuade vandals. The gate out of the way, Marcus retrieved his flashlight. He hadn't installed electricity anywhere besides the lab since there was no need. He shone the beam ahead of them into the dark, low-ceilinged room.

Stacked pipes rose on pallets in no particular order, creating corridors. A maze. He'd organized things to his liking when he'd bought the factory and used industrial remnants to both construct and conceal his hideaway.

"Something's wrong." Katie had been holding her gun in an easy, practiced grasp. She aimed it down the last corridor between them and the laboratory's secret door.

He shone the flashlight ahead. It looked normal to him.

"How can you tell?" Marcus couldn't discern anything

beyond that horrible scent. The sharp odor stabbed his sinuses, and from there stabbed his whole head.

She glanced at him as if he was nuts. "The ward's gone."

He'd installed permanent boundary markers around his lab that—when he'd been a witch—he could activate with few additional components. Like the aversion spells on Katie's safe room, they deterred curious visitors. The ward, though they'd set it upon arriving at the factory, didn't appear to be operational.

Had the lightning negated his wards? Was that the smell?

Not possible.

Something *was* wrong.

He wiped his face, rubbing his nose and cheeks where the piercing odor hurt the most. "Let's get out of here. We'll take a closer look at— "

The laboratory door opened, and Katie's father. Zhang Li, stepped through. Behind him was Hiram Lars, holding a gun to the smaller man's head.

TWENTY-FIVE

"Look who it is." Lars's gloating voice sliced through Katie's dismay. "My old friend Chang Cai."

She could react many ways to the current situation, and all of them would accomplish the same thing.

She was dead. Marcus was dead. Zhang Li was dead.

Unless she could neutralize Lars and however many keepers he'd brought with him in the next couple of minutes. She assumed they were surrounded. The plastic scent would have been applied throughout the factory to baffle Marcus's nose.

Shit. She'd done that herself on missions…usually *with* herself, though, not chemical spills.

Her chances of saving the day weren't looking good.

"Lights, please," Lars said.

A giant spotlight clunked on, flooding the area with enough intensity that Katie squinted. Beside her, Marcus growled. She waited to see if Lars would greet the scientist he'd once held prisoner, but Lars smiled at her, his unnaturally straight teeth gleaming. "Put the gun down or I kill your precious papa before your very eyes."

She knew he'd do it, so she lowered the pistol to the dirty concrete. Hands out to the side, she rose. "How are you, Ba? They treating you well?"

"What the hell are you still doing in this country?" Zhang Li asked. "Idiot girl."

She didn't see bruises on him, and he was wearing

different clothes than when she'd last seen him. His hair looked washed, so he'd been allowed to bathe. Did he still have amnesia? He'd called her girl, not Katie. She wished she could hug him. "Love you too."

"Shove the gun toward me." Lars tapped his gun against her father's temple. Dad flinched.

Katie considered whether she could miraculously kick the gun in such a way that it would discharge into Lars's high forehead. If possible, he looked even sicker than he had last week.

Good.

Sick or no, his brains would look fantastic splattered all over her father and the door behind them. She suspected Dad would agree.

If she hooked the gun just so with her toe and it flew into her hands... Would cinematic shit like that actually work?

"Are you too ill to cast a better mask spell?" she asked Lars instead of kicking the gun. *Drag it out. Find options.* "Unless you enjoy looking like a withered lemon."

"I've no need of such ridiculous ploys anymore. The gun. Now." Lars cocked his weapon, and Zhang Li closed his eyes.

Katie kicked the pistol toward Lars.

"That's better," he said. "The best anyone could expect of a depraved harlot, I suppose. Look at you. Standing there like you have a right to breathe our air after committing bestiality with that...disgusting animal. I suppose you think you're superior now that you're a so-called alpha witch."

Marcus kind of laughed. What was funny about this situation?

"I see you're still a judgmental prick," she said to Lars, hoping he'd ease off on Dad.

He did, but only to gesture toward her with his gun. "Take her."

Shadowy figures moved into the corridor around her and Marcus. Younger, fitter keepers—zero gray hairs or wrinkles—divested her and Marcus of their possessions without touching skin. They were gloved and armed to the teeth. She recognized a few from Alabama and nobody from her time with the council.

None of them would make eye contact with her.

Was her reputation that extreme? Did they think she could inflict magic with her eyeballs? They hadn't been so leery in Alabama. Lars had probably taken his frustration out on them in the past week.

Marcus was not so silent. "Hello, Yasmine. Bill. Anthony."

None of the men reacted, but a female keeper with black eyes and hair glanced briefly at him. "Don't speak to me, mongrel."

"Now that we have that nasty gun business out of the way," Lars gloated, "I have some questions about how you averted the wipe twenty years ago." Despite his physical changes, his voice bore the same patronizing, vaguely European accent, his country of origin lost in his personal history. "I'll give you a chance to explain yourself before I kill you."

"You're so gracious," Katie said.

"We've wiped keepers for centuries, but of course Chang Cai was the special one." His mouth soured as he said the words. "The unwipeable one. We haven't been able to replicate what you did. So tell me. Was it intentional? A defensive spell? Or was it an accident?"

"If you release my family and Marcus, I'll tell you." What keepers had been sacrificed for Lars's experiments—anyone who disagreed with him and his philosophies? That would explain why his current team was composed of young witches. Though keepers were conscripted from all over the world, gathering an entire team in twenty years was a stretch. Convex witches weren't born every day.

Nor were witches who looked like Lars. Toward the back of the group, Katie spotted several tall men who could have been Frank's brothers. She noticed Marcus eyeballing them too.

"Why would I release anyone?" Lars said. "I believe I'll keep you all, and you'll tell me what I want to know when I start cutting off fingers."

"Psycho," Zhang Li muttered. "I'm the only one he's still got."

Lars's calculating gray eyes narrowed and his mouth tightened so much his lips vanished. "Shut up, old man, or I'll shoot you. You're of no use to me now that I've found her."

What did Dad mean? Had Lars killed Vern and Tonya? Katie's anger, already hot, began to fume. It boiled into her brain, which clicked furiously through scenarios that involved fighting, blood, gore and death.

Unfortunately, logic insisted most of the blood would be hers.

"This discussion is going nowhere. Search them," Lars directed his team. "Be thorough. She's treacherous."

"Whoever hurts her dies," Marcus informed the room at large. Everyone ignored him. She hoped they continued to do so, because that would give him a chance to come up with…something. Anything. She was drawing a blood-soaked blank. The only thing she could think of was to pretend she'd bounced the poppy intentionally instead of it being the luck of the alpha draw.

The keepers began patting them down. With a vicious

grin—the closest he'd come to acknowledging Marcus was more than a statue, Lars added, "Don't forget her genitals. They're probably diseased."

"Oh, good fucking grief." Katie refused to hide her contempt. Did Lars think she'd quail because he ordered a cavity search? A rape? Torture? She would never break for him. His insults meant nothing. "Ba, don't watch."

Her father already had his eyes closed. His posture had deflated, as if he expected to be killed at any moment. He might know something she didn't, but she refused to speculate.

He wasn't dead yet. Marcus wasn't dead yet. She wasn't dead yet.

When the keepers began stripping her as Lars commanded, she smiled her widest smile. "Do what he says, children. He's the boss and you're the peons."

One or two paused, but not for long. More professionally than she expected, they undressed her and Marcus to their underwear and searched for weapons and spell components. Marcus, needless to say, received a desultory inspection, since wolves couldn't do magic—but he did receive several shoves and cuffs.

He didn't fight much. He, like her, seemed poised for a different action. His brands appeared tribal in the harsh spotlight, primitive and striking. No one commented on them, despite it being unusual for a wolf to wear ink.

Marcus could do magic. Katie's magic had accrued too. How could she get her hands on some herbs? How could she convince Lars she had information he wanted so he'd postpone whatever murderous fantasies he'd concocted?

Her bra and panties provided no warmth in the cold, dank factory. She shivered but didn't cower as the female keeper called Yasmine inspected her privates.

"She's clean," the woman said. Marcus watched them with death in his pale blue eyes.

Pale eyes. He had the wolf in him, rising up, reaching out.

And how much witch did he have?

The keepers sure as hell wouldn't be expecting that.

"Almost disappointing," Lars commented. The nature of the witch and wolf relationship meant keepers with brutality on the brain didn't rape their target wolves for fear they'd transform themselves. Katie—not a wolf—wasn't sure what to expect. "The great Chang Cai trapped so easily, without so much as a trick up her sleeve. I'd hoped for a better show. I'll give you one more chance to tell me the truth, Chang Cai. Is there a recipe to prevent wipes?"

"Maybe," she said. "Vernon Harrower cast it on me. Too bad you killed him or he could have shared it."

Lars grimaced. "He's not dead."

Not dead? Then how was her father the only prisoner Lars had left? "Where is he?"

His grimace deepened. Wherever Vern was, it pissed Lars off. "Do you have the recipe or not?"

She could fake one. They'd test it before killing her. Possibly. She glanced at Marcus, and he shook his head.

He'd taught her about defenses for many spells, including monkshood, magic drain, calming mix and pack bonds, but had admitted there was no defense against a wipe. Did he have a plan—hopefully a better one than hers?

She trusted Marcus.

Taking a deep, shaky breath, Katie said, "No. I don't have the recipe."

Lars rolled his eyes. "Of course you don't, because there isn't one. Now you're of no use to me either. You, you, you—" he pointed at members of his team

"—throw them in the holding tank and bring me the berserker bomb. I'd like to see her ripped apart by the same animal she's been consorting with. Right before she dies, we'll shoot him in the head, so she can enjoy it."

"No!" When Marcus started struggling, one of the keepers restraining him brandished a spell pod. Black as tar. The only black pods she knew were monkshood.

"Marcus, stop." He couldn't fight monkshood.

He growled—but he stopped. The keepers didn't kill him.

The keepers wrestled her and Marcus through the storage areas. Lars handed her father off and followed them, chuckling to himself.

Like a crazy person.

Time was running out.

The berserker spell, no matter how much Marcus loved her, would take him if cast specifically on him. He would try to slaughter her.

She was pretty much naked and defenseless.

They reached the huge holding tanks, twenty-foot-high metal silos with tall rims. She didn't have to see the inside to realize there was no way a witch could hop out of one, else Lars wouldn't be laughing himself sick over the thought of trapping her with a feral. Goddess, to force Marcus to do this to her! He'd never forgive himself.

A ladder had been propped against the first tank. They pushed her toward it. Another spotlight clanked on, throwing the tank into stark relief. Center stage. Two men climbed to the tank's access hole, waiting for her so she couldn't hurl herself off the other side and run.

"A little poetic justice, dying at the hands of a monster, considering how I almost killed you the first time." Lars's rheumy eyes gleamed with excitement. He clutched a giant wad of herbs in his hands—an unnecessarily large dose of berserker mix considering his target was a single person.

"How you almost killed me the first time?" Lars had always loved the sound of his own voice. Time to rile him up so he'd shout and make mistakes. "Your guy shot me in the arm. Barely. You didn't even come close to killing me."

"Not in Alabama, you dumb whore."

"Do you mean when your son Frank attempted to capture me in Kentucky?" She took a stab in the dark. Perhaps her hunch about Lars's one-man breeding program was true. "He was simple to outwit. Just like you will be."

"Frank?" His laughter was phlegmy. Somewhat strained. "He's not convex. That makes him a failure. I don't care what happens to failures, as long as they serve me."

None of the flunkies uttered a word—perhaps they weren't allowed to speak. She did, however, notice a few glances. Did Lars make them call him Sire too?

"But no, this has nothing to do with Frank. Did you think the wolves you'd been sent to neutralize twenty years ago lusted after you so much they fell into that much of a frenzy? You were arrogant. Convinced all you had to do was flash your cunt and everyone would fall at your feet."

Ah, Lars was talking about her final assignment for the keepers—the one where she'd nearly died because the ferals she'd been sent after had gone crazy. Crazier. And her team hadn't arrived as scheduled.

When they'd finally shown up, Katie had been in huge trouble—bruised, naked, defenseless, ferals ripping into each other over who got to fuck her to death and then, apparently, devour her internal organs. She'd remained alive as long as she had by pitting them against one another.

Lars had been with her team. At the time she'd been too intent on survival to notice whether he'd seemed disappointed to find her in one piece. But since then, she'd wondered.

Yasmine, her back to Lars, scowled. She was close to Katie but not one of the keepers gripping her arms. When the man to Katie's left began to speak, Yasmine gave a tiny, but decisive, headshake.

Had the other keepers not realized Lars had tried to kill Katie—Chang Cai? Or how? Was this about Frank?

It could be anything. They maintained blank expressions, but Katie could read posture. Nuance. The four burly keepers on Marcus were starting to have trouble keeping him in one place. They seemed distracted. And her guards were definitely showing signs of disquiet.

Lars's team was uncomfortable right now, whether due to Lars's confessions or his intent to have Marcus butcher her under the influence of berserker herbs.

"What are you saying?" she asked, to make him clarify aloud. "I don't understand."

"I set you up, of course. You were supposed to die. The wolves were supposed to take care of you since our incompetent director frowned on culling unworthy keeper whores from the ranks. Spell components are easy to dissolve in alcoholic beverages, and wolves will drink and eat anything. Even humans."

"Wolves don't eat people," Katie said, though the ferals had certainly discussed it. If Lars had given them tainted food...

"That shows how stupid you are," he declared. "Precious little Chang Cai, groomed to bring the keepers into a new era. A modern era. No one...no one...is a worthier keeper than I am. No one is more devoted. No one is bet-

ter suited to issue in a golden age for witches, one where
the stench of animals no longer taints our bloodlines."

She'd heard it before—Lars was the most fanatical
purist she'd ever met. In the larger coven network, it was
considered backward to maintain such a belief, and on the
council, many keepers had simply wished to do their jobs.

At least some of Lars's ranting seemed to be news to
his team. Their increasing unease, evidenced by shifting
weight, downcast eyes, hunched shoulders and frowns,
was obvious to her.

How could they not have known about his extremism?
She knew. Marcus knew. Or was the team's discomfort
more about his other disclosures?

Lars seemed to sense his team's reaction too, because
he addressed them next, the herbal bomb held aloft like
a sorcerer's crystal ball. "Look at her. I told you how
impure she was, and now you can see. She fucked her
way into Harrower's inner circle and nearly destroyed the
council. Everything we stand for. Everything we stand
against. She is a traitor. A mongrel abettor. It's our duty
to make sure she gets what she deserves. Such treachery
cannot be tolerated."

Lars's motives shouldn't matter to her. If he hadn't
tried to assassinate her, she might never have fled the
council. Why be upset about the act that had inspired her
to escape her despised existence? Especially not if she
could use it to confuse his team.

"Still ranting that purist claptrap?" she said to him.
"You're stuck in the Dark Ages. A keeper's purpose is to
protect the existence of all shifters, not just witches. Or
did you forget our creed as well as our honor?"

He scoffed. "Get in the tank or I'll shoot off your
papa's fingers one by one."

The men restraining her father brought him to Lars

and pressed him to his knees. One yanked up his arm. Lars stuck the herbs under his arm, took his gun out of the holster and made a show of cocking it and holding it to Zhang Li's hand.

Shit. Fuck. Damn. Katie reluctantly approached the ladder, keepers shoving and jostling her. Marcus growled and snarled like a chainsaw in the background. There were too many keepers, and they were too obedient… or too afraid. Lars's fuming hadn't fazed them enough.

She, Marcus and Dad had nothing. No weapons. No ideas.

No goddamn clothes.

"I will never hurt you, Katie," Marcus said suddenly. "Don't be frightened."

Considering he had to realize she was furious, not frightened, it seemed like unusual advice.

"Shut the animal up," Lars said.

One of Marcus's guards punched him in the mouth. His dark head rocked back and straightened. Blood trickled down his chin. With his strength, if he wanted loose, he could get loose, but the keepers had monkshood.

He licked blood off his lip and smiled. "Lars is the one who's terrified."

Lars's jaw worked. "Drop her into the tank before I get angry. We have other business to attend."

The keepers prodded Katie up a few more rungs. This gave her leverage. She kicked the one closest to her, and he muttered, grabbing her leg. Yasmine took out a knife. She offered it to the man Katie had kicked.

He promptly jabbed her calf. Blood poured down her ankle.

Dammit! Before he could cut her again, Katie climbed. The metal ladder was uncomfortably cold. Her father's head bowed. He'd given up.

"Hiram is terrified," Marcus declared. "I can smell him. His fear is like piss. And he's dying. If the rest of you are hoping he'll succumb to his illness soon, you haven't long to wait."

"Liar. I am not weak."

"Most of all, Lars is terrified of me."

"I'm not frightened of a degenerate wolf," Lars raged instantly.

Instantly and…predictably?

"Do you know how many animals I've eviscerated?" He stormed toward Marcus, jerking the gun forward. "I'll kill you now. We'll find another beast to kill her. It will give me time to poke knives into her. Say good-bye, mongrel."

"No," Katie shouted. "He cured cancer."

All eyes turned to her. She'd nearly reached the top of the ladder. The men above her, extending their arms to drag her up, froze.

"You have cancer, don't you?" she said to Lars. He was third pass-through…but he shouldn't have gone downhill so much he was jaundiced and gaunt. Her father looked better than Lars did. "Marcus cured it. If you kill him, the cure dies with him."

"Katie, no," Marcus exclaimed. "Why would you tell him? Let it die with me. He doesn't deserve treatment."

Lars shoved Marcus, and he allowed it. He slammed into a storage tank with a dull boom. The keepers closed on him. Several unsheathed weapons—assorted guns and blades.

She couldn't let this happen. Goddess, what could she do?

Jump?

And then what?

"How did you do this thing?" Lars yelled into Marcus's

face. He slammed the butt of the gun across Marcus's cheek. "You were incompetent. A puling coward. A soft, lazy fool. There is no conceivable way you cured cancer. Just like there's no way she has a recipe to block poppy."

Before Lars had become sick, he would have been taller than Marcus, but now, his body had broken down. It was pathetically obvious. The contrast between his scrawny, jaundiced form and Marcus's vitality was almost painful to behold.

She hoped it pained Lars.

"Is it a spell? What is the recipe? How did you do it?" He gestured wildly with the gun. "Tell me the truth. I can make you tell me the truth."

Marcus sighed. "I cured cancer. After I left the keepers, I constructed this lab. It was what I wanted to study all along. Not weapons. Not the berserker spell you cobbled together from my research. Healing was my goal. You know my sister had cancer when you—"

"I don't care about your bleeding heart or some stupid mongrel whore. There is no cure. You're lying like she lies. Trying to buy time." Lars raised the gun.

But he'd gotten very close to Marcus while shouting and threatening.

Katie's vision blurred. No, Marcus blurred. He blurred into motion and struck Lars.

Chaos erupted. Lars skidded across the ground, shrieking with rage. Guns fired. Bullets pinged off metal deep in the factory. Keepers ducked. She hugged the ladder while the keepers above her plastered themselves to the top of the tank.

Where was Marcus? Keepers pivoted, guns pointed. Several raised spell guns but hesitated to fire. Zhang Li crawled behind a piece of machinery.

Where was Marcus?

When she saw him, magnificent, triumphant, atop the other storage tank, she nearly cheered.

Until she noticed he didn't have a gun. He had the stringy wad of berserker herbs.

What the hell?

TWENTY-SIX

WITCH MAGIC THUNDERED through Marcus's veins. A gun stopped one person at a time. If he could pull this off...

Desperate, he focused the cayenne magic, his magic, through the berserker bomb. He hadn't had much time to study the components in the past week, but he knew how to activate them.

Power shattered through the herbs and into the surrounding area. The blast caught everyone present.

Every...single...soul.

He continued to pour magic into the spell. A wolf who was a witch. A witch who was a wolf. If the spell sucked up everything he had, if it evaporated the cayenne and ejected him from dual state forever, he didn't care. He dredged up every smidgen of strength to drive the spell beyond what anyone could have imagined for it.

Anyone except him. Its creator.

Let this work. Let this work. Let this work.

When he heard the first agonized howl, he knew it had.

The howl resonated profoundly inside him. Rage, rage and need, gushed through him like it was gushing through the keepers.

Panting, he dropped to all fours. The rusted metal of the storage tank creaked under his weight. He should leap down...but not yet. Not until he could verify.

The spell was scattershot. Directionless. All-consuming. It was taking everyone. His vision misted with red.

He stared through the haze at the people below as they convulsed and twisted, limbs contorting. Faces lengthened into muzzles with sharp, white teeth. Skin sprouted coarse gray fur. Hands fisted, pads and claws emerged.

Before Marcus lost himself, he spotted two people unlike the others. Two people who weren't transforming into their other halves, perhaps their better halves.

One was a woman on the ladder. A woman he loved so much he'd give everything he had to save her.

Alpha witch. Katie.

One was an old, sick man on the ground, screaming obscenities, fumbling in the bright, white spotlight for a gun, a spell pod, anything.

The old, sick man wasn't Katie's father. Zhang Li hunched over, enduring the wrath of the berserker magic.

Fucking Hiram Lars was alpha. That was Marcus's last thought before his consciousness was overwhelmed by the magic.

It took Katie a stunned moment to absorb the scene. Marcus, amazing, incredible, inventive man, had funneled so much power into the berserker mix it broke the witch and wolf barrier. No one else could have done it—only him, with the cayenne burning up his lattices.

Wildness captured the other shifters and called forth the wolf inside them. Inside her too—but she experienced the magic as fury. Which might not be magic, because she was pretty fucking furious already. Her wolf stirred, as it did during sex with Marcus.

Her witch was stronger.

What would happen now? Was this a frying pan/fire situation or was this the miracle that would save them?

She had to act. Up the ladder or down? Two keepers

above her whined and howled. Twenty below her writhed
and tore at their clothing—including her poor father.

Would the berserker turn them all feral? Would they
all try to kill her?

Movement of a different nature snagged Katie's attention, and she spotted Lars. He was unchanged.

She'd once bemoaned that being the only convex alpha
in existence meant nothing—but it would have meant a
great deal right now. Too bad she'd been wrong. Lars, the
other convex alpha in existence, pulled himself to his feet
using a pipe bolted to the wall.

He saw her.

Shit. Time to evade.

Katie scaled the ladder and tumbled over the edge onto
the tank. The shifters on top were preoccupied by their
transformation. Should she…

One lifted his head to glare at her with a beady, blood-
shot eye. He shook off his clothing and started to rise. His
patchy fur bubbled with the rapid shift. She'd never seen
the change take someone so grotesquely. Wolf shifters
were part of the natural world, and their magical abilities were no more deviant than what witches could do.

What she could do.

Hard to believe this magic wasn't destructive when
it appeared to be excruciating. But the convexity of the
keepers hadn't protected them. They were powerless
against the berserker spell. All these witches had just
become the creatures they despised—and they would
vent their frustrations on any two-legger left standing.

The wolf who'd noticed her steadied himself on shaky
legs. Froth decorated his wrinkled, snarling muzzle.
Death gleamed in his eyes.

Praying she could move fast enough, she kicked. He
gnashed his teeth, barely missing her leg, which was al-

ready bloody. Her second kick caught him in the hind-quarters. He tumbled over the lip and off the tank. The other wolf, who hadn't finished transforming, was easier to punt.

He yelped as he struck the ground.

Okay. Okay. Channel Chang Cai. Strategize. Fight. She had a minute to plan. Wolves couldn't climb ladders.

Except...

Gunfire. A bullet pinged off the access hole railing. Flakes of metal struck and cut her bare skin. Katie dropped to her stomach, protected from Lars's gun by the angle. Chilly, deteriorating metal and rust scratched her stomach and legs. Her flesh goose bumped—fear, adrenaline, temperature. Across from her, on the second tank, Marcus crouched, snarling.

Was he...lost? Feral? Could she trust him yet?

Would he ever hurt her?

He saw her looking at him and barked, deep and throaty. Was that meant to be reassuring or a threat?

Not her primary concern. No wolf was as much of a threat as a lunatic with a gun.

"What have you done?" Lars screamed. "What is this perversion? I'll tear you apart, you fucking animal. I'll shoot you ten thousand times!"

Bullets peppered Marcus's perch. He nimbly vaulted off the backside. Katie belly-crawled to the lip of her tank, where gaps had rusted through the rim, and peeked down.

Lars hobbled across the floor, kicking wolves. They whined. Cringed before him instead of attacking him. She scooched sideways to peer through the corroded holes. The closer Lars came to the tank, the worse his angle was for shooting her.

Unless, of course, the bullet blazed through the old

metal. Or he hurled a spell bomb atop the tank. Calming mix. Sleep. Did he have anything besides monkshood?

Lars seethed. Yelled. Katie sensed the pressure of something urging her to hurl herself off the tank to her death. She started to submit but stopped herself before she was exposed to Lars's sight.

His alpha had a wide-area impact like a spell bomb.

Although…if he could do it, could she?

Kill him, she thought at the wolves.

Some growled. Hackles spiked. Lars lambasted them in earnest and cowed their rebellion quickly.

They were his pack. Slowly, emerging from their convulsions, squirming out of their clothes, they crept to their master. Their Sire. His influence curbed their reaction to the berserker. Heads low, they crouched around him. The wolf she thought was her father, who'd had white fur splashed across his muzzle, was nowhere in sight.

Insanity, rage, obsession—Katie had no idea which—consumed Lars. Spittle frothed on his chin as if he were rabid. His body shivered and trembled. He shot her tank a few more times before the hammer landed on an empty chamber.

Swearing, he hurled the gun at a small, dark wolf, who barked and ran. Three other wolves chased after it. Lars had no shortage of weaponry in his team's discarded clothes. She wouldn't be safe up here much longer.

She wouldn't be safe down there at all.

The last time she'd been in this situation, she'd pitted the ferals against one another. That wouldn't work. Lars was mostly in control of them, and the wolf lust she'd manipulated as a keeper was no longer generalized. She was in love with Marcus and wanted no other bed partner.

Her world crystallized into right here, right now. *Live through the next two minutes.* She needed weapons. The obvious ones were on the floor. Guns, spell pods, pipes, knives.

Wait. Her foot encountered cloth. The first man's pants. She rolled quickly to the garment, grabbed it and rolled back to the shielding lip of the tank. Patting the material, she pulled out spell pods, a knife and a cell phone.

"I'll shoot you down like a fox in a spruce. You're trapped, Chang Cai. You can't whore your way out of this." Lars monologued his intentions, probably hoping to intimidate her. Gunshots—two at a time—flicked the corroded metal around her. He had two pistols now, and he knew how to use them.

Lars was right. She was treed. Where were the eagles when you needed them?

Katie thrust her legs into the pants. Some covering was better than none. She cinched the belt tight. Knowing Lars couldn't see her from the ground, she crawled to the far side.

Twenty feet. She could land that if she were careful. She slithered over the side and let herself dangle. The overlong pants draped past her toes. Three, two…

A chorus of growls stopped her. She glanced down. A heavy body smashed against the tank beneath her. Wolves barked, tails wagging, leaping for her legs. Metal groaned on impact. Lars might not have heard her scuffles, but the wolves could.

She curled herself out of their reach. Good damn thing she'd maintained a semblance of an exercise regimen. Otherwise she'd never have had the arm strength to manage this. She swung a leg up and over, wincing when jagged metal shredded her baggy jeans and the skin beneath.

"Is she trying to fly away?" Lars's voice rounded the base of the storage tank. Katie clutched the knife and silently, silently, eased to the opposite side of the container.

Why couldn't the dudes on the tank have had guns? Grenades? She clutched the knife and inspected the pods.

One orange-red. Four white. Five green, five dark green, two yellow. Not much that could stop a convex keeper.

She sniffed the orange-red carefully, and her nose tingled from the cayenne-laced pepper bomb, a pod version of her cayenne spray.

What could she do with it? Not immobilize Lars, that was for sure. Would it work on wolves who'd been convex witches? Or would it refract off them and into the closest non-convex victims—her father and Marcus?

Where *was* Marcus?

The ladder poked past the rim of the tank. Aside from removing it to prevent Lars's ascent, could she use it? Somehow? She shoved the pods into her pockets, the cayenne separate, and slithered toward the ladder. Bullets ricocheted through the storage area.

She flinched but kept inching along. Was Lars not bothering to aim? A wolf howled. Several yelped. Lars railed at her but had remained stationary. Why wasn't he patrolling the bottom of the tank, looking for ways to hurt her? Perhaps he'd been injured when Marcus had shoved him.

Katie raised a cautious hand and placed it on the ladder. When Lars didn't shoot her fingers, she grabbed the other side and eased it into the air. The cheap, aluminum weight of the ladder wasn't unmanageable, but it clanked. Loudly. *Crap, crap, crap.* Growls and claw tics spread out on all sides of the tank. Surrounded.

Throwing caution to the wind, she rose to her haunches and hauled the hell out of the ladder until she had it atop the tank. Before she ducked, she turned.

Lars stood in the middle of the aisle, aiming at her with a hunting rifle.

She hit the deck.

Buckshot screeched through metal around her, ripping and tearing. A ball cracked off the aluminum ladder and then her scalp. Katie bit her lip, silent and motionless. The glancing blow—thank Goddess it was a glancing blow—stung like fire.

Lars would get lucky eventually….if she continued to wait here like a nice little target.

Maneuvering onto her back, she eyeballed the ceiling where the round spotlight shone on the turmoil. She hefted the keeper's knife—it was weighted well, better than she'd hoped—held her breath and stood up really, really fast.

She needed clearance. As soon as she got it, she flung the knife at the light. Hard. Lars fired at her. Missed. The recoil pounded him back a step. She wasn't sad that Lars, in his old age, seemed to have become a terrible shot.

She wasn't old. Or a terrible shot. Her knife struck the spotlight dead on, smashed the glass and plunged the storage area into darkness.

Buckshot, too close. She launched herself to the other side of the tank. When she hit the surface, the metal beneath her crumpled. Her lower half burst through it.

Katie scrabbled for a hold as the weight of her legs dragged her into the holding tank—and whatever the hell was inside. Chemicals? Bugs? She'd hoped the darkness would help her dodge Lars, but right now she couldn't see to stop her fall. Her flailing hand found purchase on the ladder. The whole thing trailed behind her several inches, screeching on rust and metal, before it snagged on something like a grappling iron.

She panted, heart racing, eyes adjusting. Diffuse light snaked into the storage area from the main section of the factory. The silver ladder was braced awkwardly between the lip of the tank and the access railing.

Luckily she didn't weigh much. Before the rusted metal cut her in half, she tugged herself to safety. Painful scuffs decorated her bare upper half; she didn't have to see it to feel the raw scrapes. Her leg wounds throbbed. *Hello, tetanus.*

Lars had gotten his hands on pistols and shot blindly through the dark. As far as she could tell, no shots were coming close to her. Another wolf yelped. And another. Lars bellowed with rage.

Was he shooting the keeper wolves? She could only hope. He hated wolves with all-consuming passion. Which would win—his hatred of wolves or his hatred of her?

"Find me her father," he ordered the wolves. That answered her question. "I'll dismember him. That will bring her to me."

Would the wolves do it? He'd been kicking, cursing, shooting and mistreating them, probably when they'd been two-leggers as well. How many were his offspring? That didn't seem to matter to him.

Claws skittered on the concrete in several directions as they scampered to do Lars's bidding.

Stupid wolves. She hoped her father was long gone. She could do nothing to help him if she couldn't save herself first.

Katie gauged the distance between her tank and the one Marcus had been on. She could just make out the shadowy bulk of it. Ten feet?

Another quick check in Lars's direction. No activity at

floor level, but a constant stream of demands and threats, pinpointing his position. The metallic *shick* of a clip locking into a pistol interrupted his rant. *Ugh.* Well, if *she* could barely see shit, he'd be able to see less than shit.

She chucked the ladder across the empty space. The other end hit the second storage tank and bounced.

Stayed.

"What do you think you're doing?" Lars, his face ghostly in the darkness, limped down the aisle between the tanks and pipes. Her ears told her he was wheezing. "I'm going to kill your father, you stupid girl, if you don't come down here and trade yourself. That's right. You wanted a trade. Come and get it."

Katie eyed the ladder. Eyed Lars. Maybe, instead of plan A, she should…

"You've found the old man. Good." Something—Lars's foot—thunked against flesh. A wolf whined and paws scrabbled against the concrete. "Chang Cai, I'm going to kill your papa. Don't you want to say goodbye?"

Was it really her father or was this a fake-out? She could make out dark, prowling wolves, the taller form of Lars. At least she could see better than he could. The factory, windowless here, was pitch black near the ceiling, which wasn't that many yards higher than the top of the holding tanks.

"You can't get away from me." Lars started blasting away at her tank again. When he reached the end of the clip, he scrapped the gun and disappeared.

The moment the bullets ceased, Katie slithered across the ladder to the other tank as quietly as possible. The ladder clanked and jiggled but she made it. She dragged the ladder after her just as fast. She'd need it for phase two.

Had he seen? Surely he'd seen. The ladder was pale, almost shiny, and she'd made a lot of noise.

Lars began shooting again.

At the first holding tank.

This was her chance.

TWENTY-SEVEN

THIS WAS HIS chance.

The old man fumbled in his pocket and pulled out a penlight to flicker around the dark factory. He was trying to locate the woman. Marcus's woman. The man was trying to kill her, which meant she was still alive.

Marcus crab-crawled under the tank, closer and closer to the two-legger and his guardians. He'd taken several wolves out already. Their blood tasted horrible on his tongue, salty and bitter.

He was pretty sure the man would taste worse.

That wouldn't stop him from tearing open that bony white throat.

Marcus had never felt such anger, or such single-minded purpose, in his entire life. He had one thing to accomplish. One.

Kill the man.

His sharp eyes narrowed when a small guardian spotted him under the tank. The wolves' vision wasn't hindered by the low lighting. Marcus growled threateningly. The man couldn't distinguish his voice from the others. The others would smell the blood of their companions on his fur and breath, letting them know what he was capable of.

He was better at being a wolf than they were. He was, after a brief period of confusion, the master of his body and actions. He doubted they'd challenge him.

When he inched from under the tank, the small wolf tucked her tail between her legs and bolted away from the man.

"Come back here!" The man aimed the flashlight and the gun in the direction of the fleeing wolf. Marcus could smell the rot of dying flesh from here. The two-legger's arm dipped, and the shot missed. The wolf disappeared.

While the man's attention was on the escapee, Marcus slunk into the group that encircled their alpha. Several were bumping and menacing an older wolf with a white muzzle sprawled on the ground behind the two-legger. Marcus could feel the pull of the two-legger's persuasion but overcame it.

Another alpha had his loyalty.

Suddenly, from the top of a tank, a ladder hurtled through the darkness straight at the man. It smacked him in the head, knocking him to the ground amidst his wolves. Bone cracked—frail, two-legger bone.

The man gargled and moaned. The scent of blood enriched the air.

Wolves teemed around their ruler, tails frantic, noses snuffling. The flashlight beam bounced off tanks, pipes, wolves, as the penlight rolled freely across the ground. In the chaos, Marcus became conscious of a new voice.

Alpha. Good alpha. His alpha.

Kill him. Kill him now. Kill him while he's down. You hate him. He hurts you. Kill him.

Her demand urged Marcus forward. She was right. He did hate the man. His jaws gaped wide. His muscles bunched. The other wolves, scrambled by the directive from the powerful woman, growled and snapped at each other.

In the confusion, the old four-legger with the white muzzle dashed forward and bit the man in the thigh. The man screamed in agony, and his scrawny limbs thrashed every direction.

"Stupid fucking wolves. How dare you? Obey me!"

The wolves milled, emanating fear scent. They were in Marcus's way. Waves of sickness, pain and rage enveloped the man. Caustic herbal smells marked him too, items Marcus would need to avoid biting. He shouldered another wolf aside, almost within reach.

This was going to taste very, very disgusting. He crouched, ready to jump over the last couple wolves.

The penlight's beam steadied on the holding tanks. Movement up high, slithering down.

"You bitch," the man howled. "She's trying to get away. Kill her!"

Scrapes, clanks and complaining metal interrupted Marcus's deadly intent. Rust particles rained on the concrete. All the wolves except him and the old one were pushed by their alpha toward the corroded tank, where Marcus's woman dangled off the side. The flashlight's narrow beam revealed her path.

She was trying to get down. Trying to fight or run. She'd been too slow.

"Shit," she exclaimed.

Wolves began leaping for her. Teeth snapped near her legs. She kicked, catching a wolf in the head.

The man dragged himself toward her, but something inside him was broken. Marcus waffled between the man and the woman. He wanted, most of all, to kill the man— but what about helping the woman?

What did he want more?

A wolf latched on to the woman's pants. They tore off her limber, two-leg body. Blood decorated one of her legs. The wolves harassing her yelped with excitement as they smelled it. With a shriek, the metal pipe she clutched gave way, bending out and down with the woman still holding on.

She fumed and kicked. Blood droplets spattered the wolves below. The thin tube of metal, her lifeline, twisted and swayed—back and forth, as if in a high wind. She was barely out of the wolves' reach.

Several gathered to spring. They'd have her.

The man Marcus wanted to kill had found a gun. He wouldn't have to stand up to use it.

Marcus charged.

KATIE BRACED FOR the pain of wolves ripping into her flesh as she dangled like a fishing lure on the broken metal pipe. A fitting end for Chang Cai—torn apart by transformed wolves.

The flashlight had revealed her getaway. Her knife was gone. The spell pods in her pants pockets were on the ground beneath the slavering wolves. The ferals hadn't been driven mad by lust or violence this time. Oh, no. They'd been sicced on her by Lars.

She heard him cackling his approval right before the pipe broke.

Katie landed on a squirming wolf body. Bounced off, hit concrete. Someone howled. She folded herself into a tight ball and let her alpha side loose. If it bought her a few seconds, perhaps something new and amazing could go wrong.

Do not hurt me. Do not hurt me. Do not hurt me.

The wolves erupted into a giant free-for-all, as if her command had spurred them to kill instead of show mercy. The strange thing was they seemed to be killing each other.

Vicious snarls, howls, barks, whumps. Every moment she expected to feel teeth sink into her. She didn't even

412   WITCH INTERRUPTED

have on any damn clothes! When her only wolf contact
was to be repeatedly walloped by large, hairy bodies who
then scrabbled away from her, she peered through cautious fingers.

Lars's penlight wasn't directed at her, so she couldn't
see much. Flashes of wolves struggling, jumping. Blood
on the floor. The thin, bright beam paused ten feet past
her, where a large black wolf, rangy and strong, leaped
onto another wolf and savaged its throat.

"What are you crazy fuckers doing?" Lars screamed.
"Quit fighting."

Katie gulped. Several wolves trailed the black one. She
could be the next victim if they noticed her. Should she
run or would that draw attention? Make herself a target?
Was one of these brawling wolves her father?

Where was Marcus?

Searching desperately for a solution, in the wavering
light she spied a few spell pods that had rolled free of the
pants. Green ones. Yellow ones.

A red one.

What could she do with the red one?

"Stop this nonsense," Lars commanded. He'd probably
broken a hip when she'd beaned him with the ladder, but
that wouldn't stop him from shooting guns—or directing his pack. He, like she, would use any tool he could
to accomplish his goal.

It was what keepers did.

"Kill Chang Cai," he insisted. "I am the director of
the council. I rule you. I know you understand me, you
damned, dirty mongrels. Do your job and perhaps I'll
let you live."

Katie concentrated harder on the alpha persuasion
Marcus had woken in her—she poured her strength and,
what the hell, some magic into her effort.

Do not hurt me. Do not hurt me. Do not hurt me.

She imagined it flowing out of her like the waves of a spell. If only she had some lavender in her bra.

"Kill her, kill her," Lars chanted. "If you don't kill her, I'll kill you all. Hey, what are you doing?"

Apparently "you" was barking and growling. Lars yelled. The light blinked out. Gunfire erupted close by. Wolves yelped. The asshole didn't seem to care who or what he shot.

Katie inched toward the place she'd seen pods. Her knees and hands squished in liquid, syrupy blood, warm on the cold floor. As she crept, she simultaneously commanded the wolves not to hurt her—and tried to keep the tussling beasts between her and Lars.

She had no idea why her influence was making them fight each other when all she wanted was for them to leave her alone. Well, it would be *nice* if they'd take out Lars, but that wasn't going to happen.

"Kill the woman," he shrieked.

The flashlight guttered back on. Katie, staying low, bumped into a crouching, hairy body. A wolf. It growled fiercely. One of its fellow wolves had bitten it in the leg. Blood trickled onto the concrete.

That didn't stop it from attacking her. Jaws gaped.

Katie smashed the cayenne pod into the wolf's muzzle. Magic popped through her and the spell components. The wolf yelped once and collapsed.

"Who's using magic?" Lars asked.

The bright beam fell on Katie. Beside her twitching victim, she froze and glanced toward Lars.

There were no wolves between them. Half seemed to be sprawled on the concrete, whining and bleeding. Others tussled. All of them ignored her and Lars. Lars displayed several bite marks but had gotten himself into a standing position, one leg hanging limp.

"Now we end this." Lars raised the gun. His hand trembled. A wolf—a wolf whose white muzzle she could see even in the dark—huddled behind him.

Dad?

"I called the region elders with your flunkie's cell phone," Katie lied. Though it wasn't a bad idea, if she could find it. "They know everything. The keeper council is being disbanded."

"They can't defend against my power. They will fall in line or die," Lars snarled. He hopped sideways, keeping her in the light. "Like you."

The black wolf jumped in front of Katie, growling. Its muzzle dripped with blood, but its hate was only for Lars.

Marcus.

"Come to defend your whore?" Lars, aiming at the wolf now, eased something out of his pocket with the other hand. Marcus crouched to spring. "Ignorant animal. No matter what parlor tricks you pull, your kind will always be inferior."

Marcus rushed him. Instead of shooting, Lars flung the spell pod. It splashed against Marcus with an audible pop.

He stumbled. Took several more uncertain steps. And collapsed at Lars's feet.

Katie smelled the draft of monkshood and cried out, the pain of loss so intense she thought she might be the one dying.

No, no, no.

Not caring that Lars had a gun, she charged across the space separating her from the director. He fired.

Something kicked her shoulder like a mule.

She didn't let it stop her. Fucker was dead. She slammed into Lars and they tumbled back. She angled herself so he took the impact of the fall. She landed on him knees first. His gun clattered free across the concrete.

She didn't need weapons, magic or even clothes to get her revenge for what he'd done to her—then and now.

Despite the jab in her shoulder, she closed hands around his throat and squeezed. Rage eased her pain and fuelled her with strength. Her own version of feral. He gagged and scrabbled, sick and feeble. Like her he had no gun, no magical weapons. His spells were all for wolves. Witches. Nothing he could do against another convex alpha.

Between the two of them, just the two of them, she was better. Stronger. Smarter.

Which is what he'd always feared, she realized. He would die knowing he'd been right.

"I win," she whispered. Not because she was glad of it, but because it would damage him. She might be better and stronger than Lars—but that didn't make her a good person.

His eyes bulged. His pulse beat against her fingers like a struggling animal. His fist caught her jaw, painful but not painful enough. One of his legs kicked while the other lay flat, broken. Tiny, muffled screams garbled out of his mouth as fear replaced his obsessive desire to kill her.

Good. He *should* wallow in fear. Fear and horror and regret.

His struggles flagged. His eyes fluttered shut. She squeezed harder. His body lurched with convulsive desperation. Her shoulder screamed with pain.

Time for this nightmare to be over. She felt no triumph in defeating an old, sick man, only exhaustion and heaviness and a soul-wrenching grief that he'd killed Marcus before she could kill Lars.

Monkshood. The ultimate weapon. Fast-acting, paralyzing, fatal. Goddess, why? Was she being punished? Could she at least say goodbye to him? There was no defense against...

Marcus's herbal cocktail. His defenses. *His antidotes.* The bay capsules. The damned bay capsules.

New energy, something so much cleaner than rage and grief, zinged through her. She leaped to her feet. Who the hell cared if Lars survived? As long as she had a chance to save Marcus...

She grabbed the gun with her undamaged arm. Lars remained motionless. She could shoot the unconscious keeper, the man she'd wanted dead for fifty years, or she could...

Deal with it later.

Blood dripped down her torso, front and back. The bullet had gone through, and soon the blood loss would affect her. *Tick tock.*

"Zhang Li," she called to the wolf cowering in the shadows along the wall. Goddess, she hoped that was actually her father. And that none of the keeper wolves interfered. And that Marcus wasn't wrong about his bay mix. "Guard him. Bite his throat if he moves. Kill him if you want. I'm getting medicine."

The wolf scampered forward, into the radius of light from the flashlight. His fur was dappled gray and white, his tail a lush plume.

His eyes were her father's. With what seemed like pleasure, he lowered his head to Lars's neck and bared his teeth.

Katie checked the prostrate Marcus. He struggled to sit up and failed. When she touched him, he whined and licked her hand. His tail thumped once.

"I love you." Her lips trembled. The monkshood had

felled him so fast. It usually took longer—but Lars was extremely powerful. "Hold on."

She took off through the darkness, woozy from the bullet wound. The lab. Marcus had supplies in the lab, his cocktail, his pills. Luckily she'd traversed this path before. She couldn't do it blindfolded, but she'd memorized all routes in and out of the factory, a habit developed during the previous twenty years.

Claws skittered alongside as several keeper wolves gave chase. Some were mobile. Why hadn't they defended Lars? If they wanted him dead—why chase her? She could almost feel their hot breath on her heels. Using her ears instead of her eyes, she took aim with her good arm and fired.

A wolf squealed and tumbled paws-over-head. She kept running. Her feet against the concrete shot jolts of pain through her wounded shoulder. She could feel her head swimming and blinked to clear her vision. As soon as another wolf grew close, she shot it too.

Bang. You're dead.

The rest kept back, leery of her marksmanship. They'd been evolved into wolves by the berserker spell, but they weren't fools. Their memories drove them now that the initial effect of the spell had passed.

Katie hit the storage area and nearly skidded into a stack of pipes. She caught her balance. Barely. The first spotlight blazed. The wolves wouldn't have a sight advantage anymore. The door to the lab stood open, its concealing machinery thrust aside. Staggering, she picked up her pace and hoped the wolves wouldn't notice her weakness. Tiny debris on the floor cut her feet. Two wolves crouched in front of the lab with hackles raised.

She shot one. The other fled. She wouldn't have stood a chance against born wolves or experienced transformed wolves, but the keepers were unfamiliar with their new bodies, senses and internal changes. Their entire lives had just entered the hell dimension, as far as they were concerned.

Too bad for them. She stumbled over the dead wolf and into the lab.

The place was absolutely tossed. What the hell?

Katie ran to the supply cabinet, which had been vandalized. Why would the keepers waste perfectly good components and lab equipment? Smash the cot to pieces? Shred the books? Blood dribbled down her arm. Her vision began tunneling, and lightheadedness dogged her.

Five more minutes and she'd pass out.

She had to be quicker. Smarter. She flung items every direction, trashing Marcus's lab the rest of the way. She sniffed here and there, but so many herbs and bases had been spilled, she couldn't suss out any bay. When she came across their last can of heal-all, she sprayed herself quickly, half-ass, enough to stop the blood loss. Ten more minutes, then. Maybe. Her head felt like an echo chamber. She rotated her shoulder—usable, as long as she favored it.

That handled, she searched frantically on the floor, in piles of rubbish, in boxes, for Marcus's spells. She finally located the remnants of his defensive cocktail. The greenish-brown mix had been dumped into a deep sink along with various liquids and herbs. If the cocktail was here, some bay capsules…the antidote…might be near.

She pawed through trash until herbs coated her hands and arms, getting in her scrapes, burning her skin. The keepers had been thorough. Everything in the lab was smashed and contaminated.

Dammit, dammit. A miracle existed, and she couldn't find it. She'd run out of time.

Despairing, starting to shiver so hard from the cold and gunshot and tension that her fingers wouldn't work, she fumbled on a pair of coveralls. Marcus's. She smelled him in the fabric. Tears blocked her windpipe. Like her hands had blocked Lars's windpipe.

Seven more minutes? Enough to finish that job. She'd go back and kill Lars. She swiveled to leave and her gaze fell on the items she and Marcus had brought to the factory today, including their clothing. The keepers had piled them haphazardly next to the door. Marcus's kit had been trashed, but his clothing, his pants pocket, where he'd carried a bay capsule since the day he'd met her?

Nothing there. Another fail. Tears trickled down her cheeks, and she remembered. He'd told her he trusted her yesterday. Teased her to check his pants pocket. He'd meant it. No antidote pill. No defense against monkshood. That meant he'd been without one since…

Since the night they'd made love. She'd flung his capsule into the glassware.

Stumbling, running, Katie ran for corner shelf. With a wad of paper to protect her hand, she pawed through shards. Dark green capsule. Dark green capsule.

Goddess, please.

There.

Small and green, sitting innocently inside a half-broken beaker. Shaking, she reached for it, but she was filthy.

She wiped her hands, thrust them into the ever-present rubber gloves and grabbed the bay pill, a smidgen of primed cayenne from the kit, more gloves and the oven cleaner canister. Pocketing everything, she checked the gun clip.

Three bullets. Half a factory to navigate. Unconsciousness loomed despite the heal-all.

No one interrupted her race—really, her stagger—back

to Marcus. When she reached him, the only living creatures were her father, hovering over Lars like the spirit of vengeance, and Lars himself. Maybe. Dad hadn't ripped open his throat, but Lars wasn't moving.

Except for a few bodies, the keeper wolves had disappeared. She had no idea where or why. As long as they weren't attacking her, she didn't care.

Katie knelt beside Marcus and dug into his thick ruff, trying to find a pulse. Nothing. He was dead—again. Was this a record? He'd gotten the tattoo so they could approach the elders and rescue her family. He'd intercepted monkshood to defend her, thinking it would be a bullet. Sometimes wolves could survive bullets.

Not monkshood.

How sensitive would the bay pill be? It was a mixture, which meant it'd be tetchy. If she only had one, she couldn't afford contaminants.

Katie snapped off the first pair of rubber gloves and donned a fresh one. Careful to hold her hands away from her grubby, bloody body, she dug out the bay capsule. It would be primed, since Marcus had assumed he wouldn't possess magic when he needed it.

She smashed the pill into his mouth and held his jaws closed. Magic bloomed.

Thirty seconds. Sixty. Her head felt like a balloon, disconnected and floating. Marcus's chest didn't rise. His tail didn't wag. The spell had done something, but it hadn't reversed the monkshood.

Frantic now, she yanked off a glove, probed his tongue with the herbs on it, and shot power through the components into him. She added all the power in the smidgen of cayenne to boot.

Inelegant, unpracticed, hopefully effective.

The spell responded explosively, sucking at her reserves like a vacuum. Katie coughed and held on to his furry body. Her vision blackened. She let the last of her magic flow into the components and Marcus.

Get up, Marcus. She ran out of magic and used her alpha on him. *Get up. Get up. Get up.*

She fell across him, praying. His fur smelled like him. His body was still warm. She couldn't see anymore so she closed her eyes.

Get up. You have to get up.

His skin shivered, as if he were shaking off flies. There on the cold factory floor, he shimmered and shook and shifted back into his human body. Her face rested against his smooth chest and his arms encircled her.

"I was dead again, wasn't I?" he said in a creaky voice.

Katie sighed with relief and passed out.

TWENTY-EIGHT

KATIE'S CELL PHONE buzzed, flashing a West Virginia area code. Hoping it was June or Harry with news about Vern, she quickly stripped off a glove and her goggles and answered.

"Katherine," said a voice she'd come to be all too familiar with—a voice that did not belong to either Travis. "I'm glad I caught you. You're so rarely home."

In truth, she was almost always home, working with contractors, fixing the new house to her liking and letting her father in and out the damn door eighteen times a day. She simply didn't answer Shirl's calls if she knew they were from Shirl.

"Glad you caught me too," Katie lied. "How have you been?"

Since the battle a month ago with Hiram Lars, the region elders had been setting the table nonstop, trying to sort order from chaos. While they'd suspected Lars of overreaching for twenty years, they hadn't been walloped with the proof until now. It would take years to untangle everything Lars had wrought, and his spy network—which had not been approved—had gone to ground.

Thank Goddess the elders had taken Lars into custody, saving Katie from the moral dilemma of a straight-up execution.

"I'm good." Shirl had been her main contact with the region elders. "I wanted to let you know that we've voted

to increase the salary and benefits package for the directorship position."

"How nice for the future director." Katie eyed her
workspace critically, components laid in neat dishes and
the Bunsen burner flickering. Two hours left to restock
their heal-all stash. Give or take interruptions like phone
calls and aggravating wolves. "I'm not changing my mind.
It's not about the money, Shirl. I don't want that life."

"It doesn't have to be like it was before," Shirl said. "It
can be what you and the region elders, working together,
feel is best for all shifters. We need someone we can trust
to manage the keepers, and we believe that person is you."

Vern, thirty years ago, had been sent to clean up the
council. Unfortunately, he'd underestimated Lars, and
the elders' plan had blown up in their faces. The elders,
wary of open warfare, had begun guiding covens to handle more wolf issues themselves to reduce the council's
clout—at the same time Lars had pretended his teams
could no longer locate renegade wolves. The overall work-
load reduction for the keepers had enabled Lars to pursue his purist interests and experiments aggressively. The
egregious covenant-breaking he'd committed in pursuit
of Katie and Marcus had given the region elders the kick
in the ass, and the proof, they needed to lower the boom.

Katie didn't want the boom lowered on her. The region elders had been at her for the entire month to take
over the council.

"If you agree to alter your policy regarding transformed wolves, I may be willing to negotiate." Her recent
experiences, and everything Marcus had discovered, had
changed her perspective. Perhaps Tonya—whom Katie
missed desperately—had been right all along. She was a
sympathizer at heart.

And perhaps she simply wished she could send her

father on a very long vacation with anyone who wasn't her, but she'd agreed to be personally responsible for him if the elders allowed him to remain cognizant now that he was a wolf.

Shirl sighed. "That isn't possible. We have to consider the good of everyone, not what a few of us might prefer. Dr. Delgado can't replicate his achievement at this time, and we aren't in a position to introduce ourselves to the packs. Transformed wolves are a security risk."

"Marcus is working on it," Katie said. He'd expended all the energy in his cayenne permabrand during the battle with the keepers. There were no traces left beyond silvery markings on his front and back in a lattice design. When he wasn't making love to her, he was in his lab testing benign ways to evolve a witch or wolf to dual state. "Don't rule him out."

"We haven't ruled out Dr. Delgado," Shirl assured her. "He has our support as long as he keeps us apprised and accepts a few commissions and, possibly, interns in the future."

"He's still looking over the proposals." They were stacked somewhere in the office. He'd scheduled time to read them once he completed a side project, which he'd hinted he might resolve tonight. "Anyone who wants to intern with him has to be comfortable with exceptions to the transformed wolf policy. He doesn't need to deal with prejudices."

"Of course. Speaking of wolves, how is your father?"

The registered exceptions to the elders' transformed wolf policy, which had been updated in the latest coven newsletters, were Harry Travis, Marcus Delgado and Zhang Li. Wolves aided by the freedom program weren't publicly acknowledged, and the sympathizers had gone deeper undercover, deactivating their hotline after the elders had tried to contact them for help with the keepers.

Katie just prayed Tonya and Vern were with the sympathizers instead of dead. Their continued absence was one of her biggest concerns.

Her other concern was her father. She was beginning to think he was never going to regain two-legger form. He'd been a wolf since the incident.

"He's hairy. Would you like to talk to him? I can put you on speaker phone."

"I shouldn't," Shirl said. "This is a business call." Katie and Marcus had taken Zhang Li to see Shirl two weeks ago in hopes it would inspire him to shift. While he'd been happy to see his old girlfriend, lounge on her couch and eat her pot roast, he'd stayed four legged.

"Our business is concluded," Katie said. "I'm not going to rejoin the council."

"We did vote to establish a reeducation program regarding public opinion of convex witches," Shirl said encouragingly. "You shouldn't be segregated from the rest of the coven network, and convex witches shouldn't be coerced in any way to enlist in the council."

"It sure feels like you're coercing me." Katie heard the *tic-tic* of her father's claws in the hallway outside her stillroom. He must be done with the movie she'd put on for him.

"Not because you're convex. Because you're the right person for the job. We want to work with you."

"I'm truly not interested," Katie insisted. "Once you locate Vern and Tonya Applebaum, you can get him to fill the position again." Her friends had definitely been at the council stronghold when all the shit had gone down. The keepers willing to speak to the council reported seeing them.

"I wish your father would communicate with us about what happened," Shirl said. "He still won't use the alphabet rug?"

Katie and Marcus, after Dad had entered his third day with no return to upright position, had purchased a preschool ABC rug so her father could spell words if he wanted.

He didn't.

"No, he won't use it. Surely the region elders can find out what happened at the stronghold? You have access to the council's files and the remaining keepers. Are you not allowed to tell me about any leads on Vern and Tonya or do you not have any?"

"You have pretty high security clearance," Shirl said. "The files weren't informative, and none of the keepers know what happened. We finished the interviews last weekend. Lars isn't giving us any lucid information, but there's evidence to suggest he repeatedly poppied keepers who weren't in his elite group. We also know he maintained a wing of the stronghold where only he and his team went—where the experiments took place."

Both during Katie's time and after, Lars hadn't involved the whole council in his purist endeavors. Marcus's stint there and the experiments had been off the books. The young keepers Lars had employed for his less covenant-friendly goals were nowhere to be found.

"Lars broke covenant and poppied fellow witches for selfish purposes? Color me shocked."

"There are probably caches of files elsewhere," Shirl said. "Most keepers only vaguely remember anyone on Lars's elite team. Since the deceased members died as wolves, no one recognized them. DNA has proven inconclusive. The analysis of that DNA is one of the commissions Dr. Delgado may receive in the future. Do you think he'll take it?"

Shirl was trying to sucker Katie into more conversation. Not going to happen. The elder would continue to badger her, guilt her, flatter her, bribe her and level with her in hopes something, anything, would change her mind. But Katie wanted to be left alone to tend to her wounds and her two wolves in peace. "I really need to go, Shirl. Got herbs to pick and cayenne to prime."

"I understand. Give my best to your father." They exchanged a few actual pleasantries before Katie hung up the phone.

Finally, she could get back to brewing. She wanted to be done when Marcus got back. They hadn't vocalized many affections or intentions since their near-death experiences had prompted all the confessionals. Marcus wasn't chatty, and she wasn't particularly emotive herself.

But they'd certainly restarted their bedroom activities—minus any experimental regimen. Marcus had somehow wound up living with Katie and her father in the new house. She helped whenever he needed a boost from a witch, and hoped the sex and magic weren't the only reasons he'd stuck with her.

It sure as hell wasn't her cooking. Though she knew damn well taste buds in wolf form weren't equivalent to taste buds in human form, even her father didn't like Katie's cooking. June's care packages of baked goods improved the cuisine in the Zhang-Delgado household exponentially.

Katie slid a fresh latex glove on her bare hand, popped goggles over her glasses and returned to the components. It was hard to quit living as if everyone wanted her dead. If she continued to stockpile components, maintain go bags and use June's expensive wards on her house, that was her business.

If she continued to track down Tonya's acquaintances with the information she'd scrounged from the tattoo parlor, doing anything she could to find Tonya and Vern, that was her business too.

And it would help everyone, including the region elders, if her father would shift back.

What had happened to him while he'd been with Hiram Lars? Did he still have the amnesia? Did he know what had happened to Tonya and Vern?

And would he ever let her work uninterrupted for more than twenty minutes? If she had to quit what she was doing to open the back door for him one more time today, she was going to—

From the den—the room with the back door—she heard him scratch and bark.

Katie thought about ignoring him, but if she did, he'd come into her stillroom and bite her. Because he was an asshole.

"Old man," Katie said, stripping off both gloves and her lab coat, "don't you want to have opposable thumbs again? And shit in toilets and use the TV remote and eat off plates?"

She tossed her gloves into the waste bin and laid her coat across the back of a chair. Growling like a wolf, she stomped down the hall to the den.

Her father, tail wagging, lifted a paw and scratched the painted wooden doorjamb, leaving long claw marks.

"What do you need out for?" Their house was in the country, near Marcus's lab, but they did have neighbors. And those neighbors had cats and chickens. "If you'd co-operate with the letter rug, we could communicate like people. We need to know what happened while you were with the keepers."

Zhang Li didn't want to communicate. But he did want in and out the door. A lot.

As she lectured, he wagged his tail and panted.

Katie stormed to the back door, jerked it open and booted his ass out. "If I hear one more thing from the neighbors about our dog chasing chickens, I'm going to put you in a coop. Don't think I won't."

All she saw was the saucy wag of his tail as he disappeared into the woods behind the house.

She sighed and checked the clock. Marcus would be home soon. Good. He'd said he was close to a breakthrough. Maybe he'd had a miraculous brainstorm for how to motivate Dad to shift. The hell. Back.

Marcus had run some tests on Zhang Li, who was as cooperative as a wolf as he had been as a witch. He couldn't determine anything magical or physical blocking Zhang Li's shift. It was possible to prevent a wolf from changing forms with certain spells, but there were no traces of those components on her father.

And who'd have put that spell on him? Not her.

Katie had barely finished her afternoon work when she heard the crunch of Marcus's truck in the gravel drive. She tossed her last gloves for the day into the trash and brushed off her oversized T-shirt and jeggings. Before she reached the door to greet her scientist, she heard Marcus talking. He fumbled with the door latch as if he only had one free hand.

"I think you'll like it here." His deep, calm voice resonated inside her, as always. She loved how he could be so calm and so passionate simultaneously. His control and intensity thrilled her—in and out of the bedroom. "You may not be allowed out for a time, but we can grant you the permission of the yard after your prove yourself."

Who in the world was he talking to? He rummaged with the many locks on their door. Katie got tired of waiting and opened it for him.

Marcus, poised on the porch with his keys out, had wedged a grocery bag under one arm and carried a large plastic case in his hand. Closer inspection revealed the case was an animal carrier, the size used for small dogs, rabbits and cats.

Katie squatted in front of the blue plastic case. "You got a cat?"

"I did." In the grocery bag, he had several cat-care items. "There's a pan and litter in the truck. Could you fetch them? I need to introduce the animal to her new home, and she's used to me."

"Sure." Marcus had never displayed any interest whatsoever in pets. Witches often kept them, but wolves rarely did—especially not cats. It wasn't that they disliked cats or cats disliked them, but many wolves seemed to feel cats were the antithesis of wolfhood. Though Marcus wasn't a born wolf, he didn't seem the cat type.

But he did surprise her sometimes…like the other night in the shower when he'd joined her for a lengthy cleansing session.

They hadn't used antibacterial soap, but she'd definitely felt refreshed afterward.

Katie retrieved the desired items and set them up in the washroom. A cat. She'd never had a cat. Pets didn't lend themselves to a clandestine, drop-everything-and-run lifestyle. But if Marcus wanted a cat, she was agreeable. A pet was a domestic, settled kind of decision. If domestic and settled was how he was starting to feel about her, she'd happily become the crazy cat lady. She didn't want a drop-everything-and-run lifestyle anymore, and it wasn't as if he was asking her to brand him with cayenne.

When she went looking for Marcus and his new friend, she found them in Zhang Li's room. Her father liked to sleep on a double bed in a pile of ratty comforters. Marcus sat on the edge of the mattress, watching the cat.

She—Marcus had said the cat was a she—sniffed the blankets and twitched her tail. She was...

She was scroungy as hell. Dirty white with gray spots, the half-grown kitten, while not emaciated, had not lived her days with a silver spoon serving her tuna.

"That cat's mangy."

The kitten sniffed a spot on Dad's favorite blanket before rubbing her whiskers on the fuzzy cloth. Then she rolled onto her back and wiggled as if whatever she smelled had transported her to a happier place.

"Actually, no." Marcus loosened his tie, one she'd bought for him as a joke, which had wolves all over it. After she'd given it to him, he'd worn it two days out of five. "But she does have fleas and common ear mites called Otodectes cynotis. I got her all her shots."

"She was a stray?"

"Yes, near my laboratory. I've been feeding her. I suspect some human dumped her in the woods near the building. She's quite friendly." He reached out and scratched the kitten under the chin, and she began to purr loud enough for Katie to hear from several yards away. "She enjoys this, but don't touch her stomach."

"Does she have a name?"

"If she does, she hasn't told me yet."

Katie opened her mouth to remind him cats weren't shifters, but when she looked at him his eyes were twinkling. "Gotcha."

"Smart ass. You do realize Ba has been chasing the

neighbor's cats, right? Are you going to bring home chickens tomorrow?" Maybe it would keep Dad from harassing the neighbors, though she wasn't sure how she'd feel about him tormenting animals that lived with them.

Marcus rubbed the cat affectionately several more times before he rose. "I think she's going to solve our problem for us."

"With Ba? How is a cat going to convince him to turn back into a person?"

"I don't know if it will work, so I don't want to get your hopes up." He shut the cat in Zhang Li's room and slid his tie out of his shirt collar.

Katie pressed a hand to her mouth in mock-surprise. "You have doubts? I am so disappointed in you."

Marcus eyed her as if considering whether she was being serious. "Where is Zhang Li?"

"Out. Probably until well after dark." She suspected, in addition to chasing cats and chickens, he'd been making rounds. Marking their territory and memorizing all the people in it. They cast a masking spell on him daily, so there was no fear the closest pack would take objection to an indie wolf poking around, but old habits probably died as hard with her father as they did with her.

Always know everyone around you and every escape route. Always be ready to run.

"Dusk falls in an hour," Marcus said. "That's enough time."

"For what?"

Without a change of expression, he unbuttoned his shirt, and she recognized the lightening blue shade of his eyes. His wolf was rising. And other things. "For me to repair your disappointment in me, of course."

"Is that a bay leaf in your pocket or are you just happy to see me?" she asked, before helping him undress.

LATER THAT NIGHT, after she and Marcus had made love, eaten dinner, discussed some of his proposals from the council, fed the cat, brushed the cat on Zhang Li's bed, which Katie found a bit odd but didn't question, let Dad into the house, let Dad out of the house, let Dad into the house, threatened Dad with the coop if he wouldn't quit growling at the cat, fed Dad, fed the cat again, made love more quietly since Dad was in the house and gone to sleep, Katie became aware of an odd noise emanating from her stillroom downstairs.

Glass clinked. Drawers open and slammed. The sink gushed.

Nobody was supposed to mess around in her stillroom. Marcus had his lab, she had her stillroom and Dad had his entertainment center. She shouldn't have to drag all her shit to another location in order to keep people out of it. Of course, that wasn't why Marcus had a lab—some of his decontamination and electrical needs weren't suited for this house—but Katie had no desire to leave her space every day just to work.

She sat up quietly and groped for her glasses. Cold air tightened her nipples. It was too late in the year to sleep nude, but she liked the opportunities it provided for more sex with Marcus. She checked the other side of the bed, expecting to see him missing, but he was there.

The whites of his eyes glinted at her in the moonlight shining through the curtains.

"Someone's downstairs," he said.

"Are you not bothered by that?" she whispered.

"It's probably the cat. She's curious about her new home."

"Cats don't turn on sinks." Katie slipped out of bed, put on pajamas and shoes, and grabbed a gun and a pouch of spell pods, which she buckled around her hips in a practiced motion. Protectiveness and anger at the home invasion woke inside her. Adrenaline surged. The wards hadn't woken her. That meant the intruder was a witch. "Stay here. I'll see who—"

"Katie." Marcus was beside her before she finished her sentence. "Whatever it is, we'll handle it together."

"If it's one of the escaped keepers, you're defenseless. Mostly." She slid out the door into their darkened home. The grandfather clock downstairs ticked. Another drawer slammed. Shit, she thought they'd hidden their location better. How had they been discovered? "Stay here. I don't want you caught in the cross fire."

She reached the top of the stairs, avoiding the creaky boards she'd already mapped. Marcus joined her, dressed now, carrying a weapon of his own. A cell phone.

"You're the brains. I'm the brawn. Get your ass back in the room and lock the door," she ordered in a low voice.

Ignoring her, he flowed down the stairs like a shadow— also avoiding the creaky steps, she noticed—and disappeared around the corner.

Goddess save her from wolves with hero complexes. She chased after him, slowing when she saw that the lights in the stillroom blazed. Whoever was inside had zero discretion.

Then she heard a voice she hadn't heard in over a month.

"Where the hell is the pennyroyal?"

It was her father.

Katie holstered the gun and raced through the den and down the hallway to the stillroom. "Ba!"

Her father, wearing a pair of pajama bottoms and a grimace, stood in the middle of the substantial devastation he'd wrought on her carefully ordered space. She ran to him and hugged him anyway.

Zhang Li hugged her back for a moment, which was as much as she'd ever gotten, and took her by the shoulders. "I'm all right, girl. I'm all right."

His grip was firm and his posture was straight. His face had lost none of its familiar wrinkles, but his whole body exuded—not vigor, but not infirmity. His hair was thick and extremely overgrown. His fingernails and toenails—well, the less said the better.

"What the fuck, Ba?"

"I need you to use some pennyroyal on me." He shot Marcus an irritable glare. "Wolf boy's damn cat gave me fleas. And my ear itches. It's driving me crazy."

"It worked," Marcus told her. "Now you definitely don't need to be disappointed in me. I'd like to keep the cat, though. I like her."

"Fleas?" He'd gotten the cat in order to give her father parasites? Parasites Zhang Li could more easily shed in human form. It was...

Genius. Marcus was a genius.

"Have you ever had fleas?" Zhang Li crossed his arms around his scrawny chest, thrusting his fingers in his armpits. "It's hell. Stupid cat. Why'd she want to sleep with me anyway? It's not like I'm a dog."

Katie opened her mouth to respond that *hell* was not knowing if her father was going to be a person again. *Hell* was not being able to discover if Tonya and Vern were alive. *Hell* was killing the man she loved with her tattoos and her magic. *Hell* was thinking Hiram Lars was going to murder them all.

Hell was not fleas.

Marcus slid an arm around her chilled shoulders, annulling the rant. She leaned into his warmth. The new house had many advantages, but she—in an effort to keep their bills down, because somebody had to be practical—decreased the heat to fifty-eight at night.

"Why have you waited so long to change back?" Marcus asked her father. "Your intractability hindered several ongoing investigations."

Zhang Li put on one of Katie's lab coats. "It's freezing. You don't have to be so cheap, Katie. Get back in the permabrand business."

"Can you please answer Marcus's question?"

Zhang Li swung his arms like a man warming up before his turn at bat. "I felt better in that wolf body than I have in thirty years. I was afraid when I started walking around upright, the arthritis would come back. So I just…stayed on four legs."

"The wolf cures ailments of that nature," Marcus said. "All you had to do was ask and I'd have reassured you."

"Well, I know now. Are you going to get me some pennyroyal or not?"

"Not," Katie said, suddenly irritated beyond belief at her father. He'd been able to shift this whole time but hadn't? He could have given them the answers they needed but hadn't? "You could have communicated with us about the keeper stronghold. It sounds like you've regained all your memories."

"Hiram realized Tonya and I couldn't tell him shit, so he and his punks reversed the life wipes." Zhang Li laughed. "We still didn't tell him shit. Took Hiram threatening to kill Tonya to get Vern to run his mouth."

"Vern protected Tonya?" Now Katie had heard everything. But if adversity had fused her and Marcus into lovers, it could have made Vern and Tonya civil. "Where are they now?"

"No idea." Zhang Li rubbed a hand over his hair, seemingly enjoying the feel of it. "After Hiram forced the location spell out of Vern, they disappeared."

Her stomach bottomed out. "Disappearing can mean a lot of things."

"It wasn't that kind of disappearing. Hiram was pissed as a wet cat. We went to Millington to get Vern's sister for that location spell even before Hiram used me to come after you. Talk about a nutcase. You should have killed him."

"You could have killed him yourself." Zhang Li, in wolf form, had had his teeth on Lars's throat. "I don't want to hear it."

Her father shrugged. "I didn't want it on my conscience."

"But it was okay if it was on mine?"

"You're tougher than any of us, Katie," her father said with an unaccountably serious mien. "When you turned out convex, I... Well, I thought I was doing the right thing, but you—you learned to do the hard thing. The thing nobody else would do. If you can't find an agent for your permabrand business, you should take the council job."

"Hell, no. I'm finished doing the hard thing." She crossed her arms, and her throat knotted. Her father had, a few times, apologized for handing her over to the council. For not fighting to keep her. She'd forgiven him—and he'd learned to appreciate her being convex—but it choked her up every time they discussed it.

"Then you at least need to get married. The way you two have been carrying on is a scandal," he said grumpily. "I'm too old for babies in the house."

"Babies? Come on." Katie glared at her father. This past month, she'd been happier than—well, she'd been happy. But she and Marcus hadn't exchanged declarations of love or permanence since they'd assumed it might be their last words ever. If he had been swept away by the gravity of the Hiram Lars situation, she wouldn't force him to own his confession.

She loved him, and she knew it. It was enough.

"We're not going to get pregnant." She couldn't hide anything from her father the wolf, but he didn't have to be so...meddling.

"Not anytime soon," Marcus added.

Katie's eyebrows raised of their own accord. They'd definitely never discussed children, though they'd paid enough attention to birth control to make sure they were covered. Magically speaking.

"You got a pet. That's the beginning of the end," Dad said. "Right before Katie's mother and I got pregnant, she came home with a cat too. I may not be able to do magic, but I mix a damn fine libido dampener. Ask Katie."

"The cat was for you, Zhang Li." Marcus opened a cabinet at eye level, extracted Katie's pennyroyal and handed it to her. "I would suggest holding this over your father's head until he cleans up the mess he made in here."

"I have something for you too," Zhang Li said. "Tonya gave me a message before she disappeared. It's about your sister."

It was Katie's turn to slip an arm around Marcus when he seemed likely to rant at her father. Not that Marcus was inclined to rant, but her father had spent an entire month feeling his wolfish oats. That probably wouldn't change anytime soon.

"And what might that be?"

"Elisa's not dead." Zhang Li took the pennyroyal out of Katie's limp grasp as they stared at him. "Lars lied about the accident. The wolf kissers got her to safety.

Tonya couldn't tell you because you'd thrown your lot in with the keepers."

Marcus eased himself onto Katie's tall stool, closed his eyes and pinched the bridge of his nose. He remained like that, silent and yet somehow volatile, long enough that she exchanged a worried glance with her father.

Was Marcus going to flip? Accuse Zhang Li of lying? Rage about Tonya's duplicities?

Was he going to find out where his sister was and leave?

She had no hold over Marcus. She helped him with his research when he needed magic. They had sex. They lived together. They'd lived through hell together. She loved him. But she had no hold over him and didn't want one. If he stayed with her, it had to be because he wanted to.

Marcus dropped his hand and turned his attention to Zhang Li. His eyes were completely brown—whatever emotions he was feeling, he was handling them.

"Where is she?"

"Australia. The baby was a girl." Zhang Li ambled toward the doorway, with none of the limp he'd had before he'd transformed. "I'll let you two cogitate that. Me and the cat are going to have a snack."

As soon as Zhang Li left, Katie took Marcus's hand. "Are you okay? That's great news."

He glanced down at her, his expression relatively calm. On the stool, he was still taller than she was. "When can we go to Australia?"

"We?"

He frowned. "You won't come?"

"I… I mean, I…" Her glasses had inched down her nose and she wanted to see Marcus's face, not a blur. She tilted her head back. "What about Ba?"

"We'll leave him primed wards and masks. I managed for a year without a witch at my side. So can he."

"Really?" She wasn't sure if she was asking whether Marcus really wanted her to come with him to meet his born family…or if he really thought it was a good idea to leave her father without a warden.

"Perhaps not," Marcus said. "We'll need to hire a sitter."

"You just found out your sister isn't dead and you're an uncle." Katie's throat, which hadn't quite lost the lump from her father expressing his feelings about their history, closed more. She coughed to clear it. "I'm so happy for you. I am. It's going to be—I imagine it's going to be—emotional when you see Elisa again. I'm so happy for you."

"You mentioned that."

"Don't you want a chance to be with your family? Just your family?"

"That's why I assumed we'd go together," he said. "If you insist on taking your father, I suppose he's family too, but I confess, I don't look forward to a transpacific flight with Zhang Li."

"Are you saying you consider us family?"

Marcus blinked. "Is that, ah, well…" He fumbled for words. "I thought we understood one another on this matter."

"I may have misunderstood a few things." Giving up, she wedged her stupid glasses tight against her face. "We never discussed the particulars."

"I recall mentioning to you in no uncertain terms how I felt about you leaving me. As in, I'd prefer that you didn't."

"That was when you were convincing me not to run off after Lars," she said awkwardly.

"That and more." Marcus dragged her against him,

parting his legs so their torsos would line up. "Did I not specify a timeframe? Ever. I'd prefer you didn't, ever, leave me."

Ever. It had a solidity that comforted her. It promised she could live without constantly watching her back and wishing for something different. Like Marcus, it was something she could depend on. She slipped her arms around him and sighed.

"I'm not leaving you," she said gently. If Mr. Rational couldn't state plainly and factually why he wanted her to go with him, she wouldn't feel right encroaching on his reunion. He'd come back to her, wouldn't he? "I love you, Marcus. I just don't want to intrude. You don' t have to—"

"But I do," he said. "Elisa is my sister. I'm overjoyed to know she's alive and well and living her life. I hope she's happy. I assume she'll be happy to see me. But you're the woman I love. The woman I choose. The woman who has killed me and saved me. The woman who means everything to me. Of course I want you to come to Australia. I'll likely be gone for weeks. That's too long for us to be apart."

"Well, okay," she said, trying not to let delight turn her soppy. He'd be confused by tears of joy. "I don't know Australian, though. Should we try to learn some of the language before we go?"

Marcus lowered his chin, as if about to explain that Australians spoke English. She smiled. "Gotcha."

"I disagree." His hands glided from her back to her ass, sliding under her pajama pants. His long fingers cupped her possessively, and she shivered. "I would say, more, that I have you, Katie. Now what should I do with you?"

She had a few ideas involving once-per-second thrusts, but she decided to let him surprise her.

* * * * *

ABOUT THE AUTHOR

Jody Wallace grew up in the very rural South. Always eager to learn something new, Jody earned a master's degree in creative writing. Aside from published author, her résumé includes college English instructor, technical documents editor, market analyst, web designer and general all-around pain in the butt.

Jody currently lives in Tennessee with her family: one husband, two kids, two cats. One of her many alter egos is "The Grammar Wench," which should give you an indication of her character. She is a terrible pack rat and likes to amass vintage clothing, yarn, books, Asian-inspired kitchenware, gnomes and other items that threaten to force her family out of the house. She also likes cats. A lot.